THE PATHWAYS TO THE STARS WILL BE
THE TRAIL FOLLOWED BY AMERICA'S
BEST AND BRIGHTEST WHO SOAR UNAFRAID
WHERE ONLY OUR MOST DARING
DREAMS HAVE GONE

America 2040—Volume 4
THE RETURN

CAPTAIN DUNCAN RODRICK—
His strength tempered in a crucible of blood and war,
he leads Omega with a wisdom beyond his years as a
new crisis rocks this frontier land . . . but he cannot
control his own heart when it comes to a woman he
secretly adores.

MANDY MILLER—
Skilled colony physician and a lovely, desirable woman,
she finds herself courted by a fine, good man . . . but
how can she confess that her outward coldness is a
disguise for the inner fire raging still for an impossible
love.

DEXTER HAMILTON—
Former President of the United States and the prime
mover of the journey to the stars . . . he is in exile, but
clinging to the dream that he will return to Earth with a
new beginning for an old world.

THE SERGEANT—
A robot more handsome, powerful and intelligent than a man, he has inexplicably begun to be human in his dangerous jealousy of the Admiral . . . the fellow robot he becomes obsessed to kill.

GRACE MONROE—
The most brilliant woman in the colony, she has invented the men of steel and wires, but in giving them "birth" she never guessed that giving them love will someday save her life.

PRINCE YANEE—
Leader of the alien race Eepera's city, his godlike beauty belies a devilish nature which will plant the seeds of destruction inside the very hearts of the Earthlings.

LYNDON WEST—
Child born of the rape of Soviet refugee Therisita Pulaski by Prince Yanee, he is a bad seed . . . a boy of pure malevolence and terrible powers.

VIC WAKEFIELD—
A good-looking young space marine, his lonely nights on duty will soon lead to forbidden pleasures in the Eepera women's arms and an addiction too pleasurable to forget . . . too strong to break.

CEE-CEE—
A delicate teddy-bear-like creature, she looks harmless, but the fabulous talents of her ursine race called Spreens can provide a secret weapon in the American pioneers' last desperate fight.

WEBB HOWARD—
A seven-year-old new settler, he is quick, smart, and filled with the promise of a bright tomorrow unless he becomes the victim of a child without a conscience . . . or a soul.

The America 2040 Series.
Ask your bookseller for the books you have missed.

AMERICA 2040
Volume 4

THE
RETURN

Evan Innes

™ Created by the producers of
**Wagons West, White Indian,
Wolves of the Dawn, and
Children of the Lion.**

Book Creations Inc., Canaan, NY · Lyle Kenyon Engel, Founder

BANTAM BOOKS
TORONTO · NEW YORK · LONDON · SYDNEY · AUCKLAND

AMERICA 2040: THE RETURN

A Bantam Book / March 1988
Produced by Book Creations, Inc.
Lyle Kenyon Engel: Founder

ISBN 0-553-27184-9

Published simultaneously in the United States and Canada

PRINTED IN THE UNITED STATES OF AMERICA

O   0 9 8 7 6 5 4 3 2 1

THE
RETURN

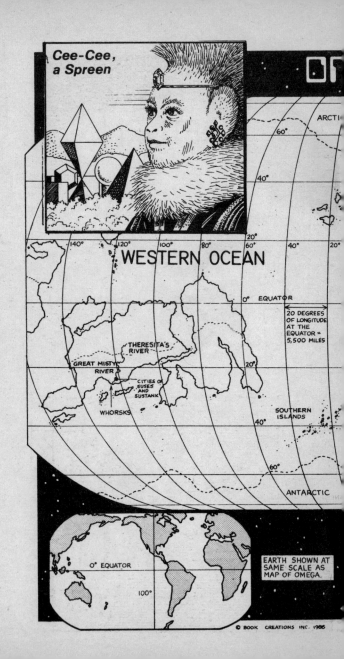

Cee-Cee, a Spreen

WESTERN OCEAN

ARCTI

60°

40°

20°

140° 120° 100° 80° 60° 40° 20°

0° EQUATOR

20 DEGREES
OF LONGITUDE
AT THE
EQUATOR =
5,500 MILES

THERESITA'S
RIVER

GREAT MISTY
RIVER

CITIES OR
SUSES
AND
SUSTANK

20°

WHORSKS

SOUTHERN
ISLANDS

40°

60°

ANTARCTIC

0° EQUATOR

100°

EARTH SHOWN AT
SAME SCALE AS
MAP OF OMEGA.

© BOOK CREATIONS INC. 1985

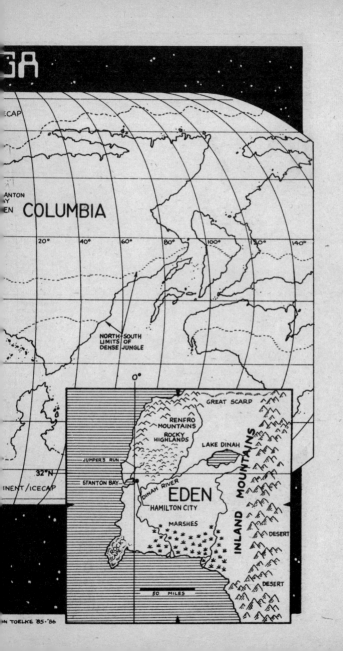

PROLOGUE

From the journal of Evangeline Burr,
official historian, the Spirit of America

I am dictating these notes to aid my memory when I find the time to record the events of the past year in detail. (Note to myself: Reference material is filed in the central computer under "Historical Notes for 2045.")

Earth still exists! We are no longer isolated on the planet of Omega, and our most terrible fears about Earth have been alleviated by the arrival of the Free Enterprise with the news that, although she suffers from multiple wounds, hunger, war, and fear, Earth has not been destroyed. The bombs have not been used.

Our colony on Omega, reinforced by the one thousand skilled passengers aboard the Free Enterprise, is stronger than ever, with more than enough newcomers to replace those who were killed in what we have come to think of as Rocky's Rebellion.

The war that we had to fight along the Great Misty River will occupy me for some time, for there is an interesting study in the nature of intelligent beings inherent in the mentality of the Eepera, those who live on the river. How like us humans the Eepera were in their arrogance and aggression. They threatened us with "invincible" weapons

1

until we built a great diversion dam on the river, drying up their water supply and threatening them with extinction. This tactic forced them into negotiations. None of us wanted to kill, and we are all saddened by the loss of twenty of our own number in the fighting.

Scout pilot Clay Girard, so young, so brave, will rate a full chapter in the final history for his part in destroying the main power supply of the Eepera's solar weapons in the city of Suses.

At the moment I am working with Dr. Grace Monroe and Egyptologist Dr. Hiram Abdul (who came with the Free Enterprise) to translate Eeperan books, some of which date back as far as the Golden Age of our own Egypt, on Earth. It is humbling to think that the Eepera landed somewhere on the Nile just as the age of the great pyramids came to an end. At first, when it was thought that those spoiled, hedonistic Eepera had to be credited with the establishment of civilization on Earth, we were saddened. Egyptian culture, we later learned, was already firmly established when the self-exiled Eepera arrived, and indeed, the Eepera were Egyptianized. That information was good for our human egos. In fact, the Eepera fled from Earth to avoid complete assimilation with the Egyptians. To paraphrase a verse from the Bible, the sons of the Eepera found the daughters of Earth to be fair and took them to wife; and in so doing, they bred new strength and vigor into their own race.

Incidentally, some of our scientists are going quietly out of their minds with the increasing evidence of independent but parallel evolution on various planets. We have now encountered two intelligent alien races, the Eepera and the Whorsk— one surprisingly humanoid, the other insectile— leading to speculation that the development of intelligent life is the rule, not the exception, under the proper planetary conditions.

I am finding the study of Eepera literature to be fascinating, but I must admit that, at times, I find myself looking up at the night sky and imagining that I can see past it, through the depths of space to that place from which the Eepera originally fled. According to the frightened Eepera priests, there is great evil there, and the Eepera fear that we have brought down the power of evil upon us because, to avoid further fighting, Dr. Mandy Miller suggested that we display our nuclear capability. Two thermonuclear weapons were detonated in space to illustrate to the remaining Eepera that, if we wished, we could annihilate them. The Eepera priests told us that their parent civilization—tyrannous, unbelievably cruel, and all-powerful—has instruments positioned throughout the galaxy to detect nuclear explosions as a first warning that some new culture is rising to a technology that could in the future threaten them. The Eepera priests fully expect great ships to come roaring in from the darkness of interstellar space to destroy us all.

The implications are frightening. If, as the Eepera priests state, nuclear weapons are nothing more than an early sign that a society is nearing a technological level where they could become a threat to the Eepera's parent culture, what sort of weapons do they have now? Since the fleeing segment of Eepera who landed on Earth so long ago brought nothing with them, since their written history begins at the time of their landing on Earth, we have no solid information about that ancient and frightening empire that caused the Eepera to escape to Earth.

I could spend all my time speculating and worrying, but I must also do some purely social record keeping regarding the affairs and achievements of the original members of the Omega colony. I'm sure that someday those of us who came

to Omega on the Spirit of America will have the
same status in history as those who first came to
America on the Mayflower. For example, I must
ask Dr. Amando Kwait, our head botanist, to enter
his working notes on his genetic-engineering projects, which led to methods of protecting our vegetables and fruits from Omegan insects. The insects
don't bite humans, but they love our fruits and
vegetables. Dr. Kwait, working with Dr. Dena Madden, engineered a thick sepraskin to protect the
produce without changing its basic character. Kwait
and Madden also developed varieties of produce
trees that bear year round, so we are never without fresh produce.

I must include in my record such events as the
lovely wedding of Clay Girard and Cindy McRae
—so young, so beautiful, both of them. And the
birth of Theresita West's odd child, half-Eepera,
half-Polish.

(Note to myself: Check with Grace to see if she
can program Juke to help me keep track of the
personal histories.)

The plastic-building machines have been working full time; Hamilton City is growing. (It's been
necessary, since the arrival of former President
Dexter Hamilton aboard the Free Enterprise, to
start calling our town Hamilton City instead of
simply Hamilton, to indicate whether one is speaking of the city or the man.)

Incidentally, President Hamilton and Jennie
were obviously touched to learn that we'd named
our settlement after him. He put on a show of
modesty, suggesting that the name of the town be
changed, but we would not hear of it.

The newcomers are being integrated well and
have fallen into our work habits, which are dic-
tated by Omega's longer days. I've hardly had time
to get to know any of the new arrivals, but I am
impressed by many of them. Dr. Harry Shaw, who

invented the engine that allowed us to travel faster than light through the incredible distances from Earth to this small star, 61 Cygni B, is an extremely valuable addition to our group of scientists. Derek Roebling is already making a place for himself in our children's educational system. And I'm enchanted by Derek's sister, Jean, with her lovely face, frivolity, and flair for fashion. There are some who question the selection of a woman whose interests seem to be entirely nonessential, but I like her! The addition of stylish alterations to our functional clothing can do no harm and just might lift morale, both in female and male.

I

THE PIONEERS

ONE

Juke, the entertainment robot, rolled out of Dr. Grace Monroe's laboratory aboard the *Spirit of America* sporting a new paint job. Although Juke had not been designed for beauty, the striking blacks and muted silvers of his new "costume" pleased him, adding a sense of well-being to the pride he felt at having been given a new assignment that would give him an opportunity to get to know all the recent arrivals aboard the new ship from Earth.

Juke's multiple wheels rolled smoothly on the plastic streets of Hamilton City. He had been asked not to disturb the peace, so the spritely little tune being played by a full symphony orchestra came softly from just one external speaker as his faceted head moved, rather birdlike, from side to side while his photobeam eyes recorded all of the activity of the main street.

He was rolling happily toward the new section of town, where the massive building machines were still pouring the plastic materials to form homes for the newcomers. He paused to examine a new design in a cottage, approving the color selection and feeling pleased by the graceful roof lines. By night the walls of the cottage would glow with color as they generated both light and heat for the interior.

As Juke stood motionless, his speaker emitting the gay sounds of strings and woodwinds, the side door to the cottage burst open and a red-haired boy of about seven erupted toward him, shouting, "Hi, Juke!"

Juke's computerlike brain ran a quick search. "Good morning, Master Webb Howard."

"Hey, how'd you know my name?" the small boy demanded, beaming delightedly.

Juke winked and tapped his flattened cylinder of a head with one finger of a flexible arm. "Your parents are Delia and Frank Howard. You celebrated your seventh birthday the day the *Free Enterprise* landed here, and you were born in Huntsville, Alabama, where you flunked space camp last year."

Webb's freckled face went solemn. "If I'd had your computer for a brain, I wouldn't have flunked." He brightened. "Hey, I'm going over to Jumper's Run to swim and play with the dragons. Wanta come?"

Juke's eyes glowed. He had recently experienced some lean times: Now that almost everyone was settled in homes, with their own entertainment centers hooked up to the central computer's bank of books, films, and music, there was very little call for his main talents. To be wanted was pleasing. "I'd love to," he said, "but the water might damage my new costume—"

"Costume?" Webb asked, examining Juke's purely functional cylindrical body.

"Don't you like it? It's a special design by Jean Roebling. She said that the black and silver would complement my eyes."

"Oh, yeah," Webb said, with a little smile, peering at Juke's red photobeams. "Well, some other time, Juke."

"Then, too," Juke continued, "I have my duties."

The small boy rushed away, his sneakered feet making pattering sounds on the smooth street. Juke sighed, then rolled into motion. As it happened, the Howard home, newly constructed, was his first stop. He wheeled up the walk and passed his hand in front of the bellplate, humming along with the orchestra that had segued into another lively number.

The woman who opened the door was tall, well built, and slightly frazzled. She pushed back her brown hair, and Juke admired a face of pleasant lips, wide eyes, and high cheekbones.

"Good morning, Dr. Howard," Juke said. "I am assisting the official historian, Ms. Evangeline Burr, in compiling a personal history of all the new settlers. May I come in and ask you just a few questions?"

"Oh, Lord," Delia Howard moaned, "now?"

"If this is not a convenient time . . ." Juke said apologetically.

"Oh, come on in," Delia said. "I was just trying to get things arranged."

"Perhaps I can help as we talk," Juke offered.

"No, no. Let's sit down. I need a break."

The cottage was in turmoil, with furniture out of place and the few personal possessions that the Howards had been allowed to bring out from Earth scattered. Juke rolled to stand a comfortable distance in front of Delia Howard and said, "Now, Dr. Howard, I think I can safely say that you are currently alive."

She was, Juke saw, a delightful woman when she smiled, her dark eyes crinkling, her lips becoming more full.

"A little Omegan humor?" she asked.

Juke glowed. "A lot of things are different here on Omega. The toothpaste, for instance. It gives you a feeling of confidence because it tastes like the dentist's fingers."

Delia laughed. "Grace Monroe should be blushing for having programmed that one into you."

"Our dentist here on Omega has just written a scientific report stating that kissing causes cavities," Juke continued, photobeam eyes twinkling. "I guess that's why the lady in the old movie said, 'Kiss me, you fool.'"

Delia, having read everything in print concerning Grace Monroe and her accomplishments, was fascinated to be face-to-face with one of Grace's robotics creations. As an immunologist, specializing in psychoneuroimmunology, she knew better than most the intricacy of the human brain and thus could appreciate Grace's achievement in creating artificial brains of the type at work in Juke.

"You're almost human," she remarked.

"Thank you," Juke said, "but I cannot claim to be human until the technology is developed that allows me to blame my mistakes on another machine."

"Sharp, sharp," Delia said, laughing, "but I guess we'd best get down to business." She wanted to get to work as soon as possible. She'd been told that there was an Eepera cadaver in the main medical lab, and she longed to delve into an Eepera brain to compare its chemistry with that of the human brain.

Juke had little trouble eliciting the information he needed. Delia talked openly, often answering Juke's questions about her background and that of her husband before Juke asked. He stood, humming quietly, as his systems recorded Delia's words. When he thanked her and his motors turned him toward the door, she said, "Hold on, now. It's my turn. I have a few questions for you."

Juke blinked and became motionless.

"I assume that you have access to the central computer," Delia said. Juke nodded. "And I'm sure that a lot of the information there is restricted on a need-to-know basis?"

"There are a few secrets," Juke agreed. "Information is recorded by classification."

"Meaning that unless one knows what one is seeking, it might be difficult to find?"

Juke nodded.

"Are you in communication with the other robots?"

"When necessary," Juke answered.

Delia ran down the list in her mind: First there was the admiral, Grace's most advanced creation, so nearly human that the newcomers had had trouble picking him out from the men of the colony. There'd been no difficulty in spotting the bulky, deadly looking defense robot, Mopro; and Cat was, of course, conspicuous in its guise of a sleek, perfectly formed Abyssinian with lovely, tawny fur, pert ears, and a tail with black markings. She had not yet encountered Doc, the medical robot, but knew of his capabilities; and she had already made it a point to study the sergeant, made from Grace Monroe's specifications by Transworld Robotics on Earth.

"Are Dr. Monroe's notes restricted?" Delia asked.

Juke's answer was slow in coming. He'd had to search the central computer for his answer. "No. But Grace uses her own system of shorthand, and the notes are unintelligible to most. I'm sure that Dr. Monroe would be happy to answer any questions you have."

"Yes," Delia agreed, "but she's not here, is she?"

"No," Juke said. His photobeams narrowed. "I'm sorry that your only interest in me is my brain and not my highly desirous body."

"Oh, I don't know," Delia equivocated with a little smile. "Come around again, and we'll share a bottle of ninety-proof oil."

"I like you," Juke said, delighted to find a human who appreciated his humor. "Is there anything I can do to help you in your work?"

"I'd like a comparison chart, showing how Dr. Monroe so closely duplicated the human brain without using chemical messengers."

Juke was silent for a moment, in communication with the admiral. The admiral understood immediately. "The admiral says that he will prepare it for you within a few hours."

"Thank the admiral for me," Delia requested. "I have only one more question: Who decided to put the colony here, in this empty, semiarid spot?"

"The decision was made by Captain Duncan Rodrick," Juke said. "His reasoning, as we have seen, was very interesting."

"We?"

Juke sent a quick call for help to the admiral and then nodded. He had not been sure that he should reveal that he and the admiral often analyzed the actions of their leader. "We robots, working with the central computer," he said at last. "We, too, found it interesting that Captain Rodrick did not place the colony in a more verdant, more scenic spot. We have concluded that he was duplicating the climate and surroundings in which Earth's earliest civilizations grew. If the colony had been settled in the south of this continent, for example, where Rocky Miller's contingent wanted to go, life would have been too easy."

"To live there, all one has to do is pluck fruit from the trees. Is that it?" Delia asked.

"So we have concluded," Juke responded. "Historically, no great achievements came from societies living in warm, fruitful lands."

"Humans respond to challenges," Delia mused. "The more challenges we overcome, the more challenges we are able to face."

"Well stated," Juke said. "For example, the captain probably thought it would be of benefit to face the challenge of farming in semiarid ground. But there were other considerations. When the *Spirit of America* landed, we knew little about Omega. There were some pretty impressive life signals coming from those tropical areas. Hamilton City was built in a strategically defendable spot, a spot safe from large animals. There's ocean to the west and south, and Eden is virtually cut off from the rest of the continent by the desert to the north and the high mountains to the east."

"Juke, have you considered the fact that you can live forever with good maintenance?" Delia asked abruptly.

For a moment Juke's photobeams clouded. "That is a sadness to me," he said quietly.

Delia raised one delicate eyebrow.

"You see," Juke went on, "I have seen friends die."

"And you know you'll see others, all of us, die."

"Work by people like you, Delia, has extended

man's life span to one hundred twenty years in health and vigor."

"But when I'm old, you'll be rolling along, the same as always, perhaps having changed the bearings in your wheels a couple of times," she said.

Juke changed the subject. "You've done interesting work on the prevention of accumulating cell damage. Dr. Monroe has also addressed herself to that question. I'm sure you'll enjoy working with her."

Juke rolled down the walk to the street. He paused there to enjoy an excellent view of Stanton Bay. A light ocean breeze rippled the dark blue, almost purple surface of the bay. Colorful seabirds soared. To the north a line of low-growing trees marked the course of Jumper's Run, the clear creek that was a favorite spot for the youngsters of Hamilton City.

"It is so sad," Juke said, no sound coming as he used his radio link to the admiral.

"I think," the admiral conjectured, "that Delia Howard did not really want to come into space."

"We've watched so many of them die," Juke said.

"But we've also watched some of them grow. Consider Clay Girard and Cindy. They were children aboard ship. We saw them grow into young adults, and now—"

"Yes," Juke said, cheered. "Married."

"Help Dr. Howard with her work if it pleases you," the admiral said.

"I'd like that," Juke said.

At the next house Juke used the same opening line. "Mr. and Mrs. Evans, I assume that I can say that you are currently alive." He was met by a pair of blank stares, and as his survey continued, he sadly dropped that particular joke, for only Delia Howard had thought it funny. He put aside his brief melancholy and began to enjoy his work, finding that the newcomers to Omega were of the same high caliber as the first settlers. Although some were slightly homesick, all were eager to be about their new work. After a few interviews, he added a question to his list.

"As you know, the *Spirit of America* will be going back to Earth soon with a cargo to help cure Earth's famine. Would you choose to be a member of her crew, and if so, would you want to remain on Earth or return to Omega?"

Only one woman said she would like to return to Earth. Everyone was concerned about conditions on the home planet but was too engrossed with the opportunities of the new, virgin planet to miss Earth very much. Those who worked in the natural sciences would not think of giving up the Omega adventures, including the chance to visit other planets in the future. Furthermore, on Earth the chance of discovering a new species was remote, while on Omega every scientist was certain to be able to give his or her name to some newly discovered plant, insect, or animal.

A few had become aware that the new planet presented its own set of dangers. Men and women had already died violently on Omega, and now there was the threat represented by the Eeperan stories of a mighty empire among the stars. The newcomers, however, were already finding their places in the community, joining in work already begun and originating projects of their own, all under the coordination of the first officer, Max Rosen, who was also the husband of Dr. Grace Monroe.

Selection of the *Free Enterprise*'s passenger list had been as careful as that of the *Spirit of America*. All the people who were now new citizens of America's first outpost in space were achievers who gave little thought to things not directly connected with their work. They were content to have the day-to-day running of the town left in the hands of the relatively few members of the space service. Although the constitution of the colony, so carefully thought out back on Earth, called for free elections at an early date, most of the scientists were perfectly satisfied to leave matters in the capable hands of Duncan Rodrick. The captain had proved himself to be fair, wise, and able to keep the lights on, the water running, and the building machines operating as the town expanded with new residences and workplaces.

There was, of course, some jockeying for position as the newcomers were integrated into teams and assigned lab time and work space, but there was more than enough work for all, exciting new discoveries to be made about the planet, and enough potential glory to keep everyone happy.

TWO

Jennie Hamilton had coaxed her husband, Dexter, to join her for a stroll. They had climbed the gentle slope to the east and circled northward past Amando Kwait's gardens to intersect Jumper's Run. Jennie had removed her shoes and was wading in the shallow water, enjoying the coolness and now and then picking up an exceptionally pretty rock from the streambed.

Jennie felt that she had come to her final home. She had no desire to leave Omega, ever. She reveled in the crisp, clean, pollution-free air. One of her greatest pleasures was to walk by the creek and watch the children romping with the colorful family of Omegan dragons, whose scales made such beautiful jewelry.

Both Jennie and Dexter were showing signs of age. Dexter's hair, now fully silver, was as thick as it had been when he was twenty. In spite of the crises he'd weathered, his eyes still shone with bright enthusiasm and the corners of his mouth did not sag. Jennie's age showed mostly in a slight double chin and, on close examination, crow's-feet at the corners of her eyes.

"Well, Jen," Hamilton said, pausing and stretching, "it's time I got back to work."

Jennie wrinkled her nose. Such a man! He was almost solely responsible for this colony in space. He had done enough! It was time for him to slow down and enjoy life.

Jennie's one regret was that they had no children and thus no grandchildren. She felt that if Dexter had grandchildren to bounce on his knee, he might be content to leave the work to others and take his deserved leisure—but she wasn't sure, for Hamilton was a man who seemed incapable of idleness, even though he had no official standing on Omega. In spite of Duncan Rodrick's sincere urgings to have Hamilton take the position of head of government, it had been decided to leave things as they were, under military control with Rodrick as the commander. Thus Hamilton and Harry Shaw had become a part of Rodrick's inner circle of advisers, which was all the authority either of them would accept. Shaw had thrown himself deeply into the study of Eeperan technology and was spending most of his time in the city of Suses on the Great Misty River.

"Let's walk a bit farther," Jennie suggested, lifting her skirt to wade through a deeper puddle.

"That's indecent," Dexter said, with a smile. Jennie saucily raised her skirt higher and wiggled her hips. "Not the exposure," Hamilton said. "The fact that at our age you still have the capacity to draw my eye with an exposed knee, wench."

Jennie laughed. She could hear the shrilling of childish laughter ahead. She led the way around a bend in the creek and saw a group of children splashing in a pool that had been slowly broadened by the persistent efforts of all of Hamilton City's youngsters. Baby, an Omegan dragon, sprawled on the bank, keeping her jewellike eyes on her own youngsters as they splashed and romped with the human children in the water. Beau, Baby's mate, stood at a distance, thoughtfully watching as he chewed tender leaves from a tree.

As the Hamiltons drew near, they were spotted by Tina Sells, who wore a brief swimsuit. Tina rose from the mossy bank and called, "Hi!"

"You have a beautiful day, Tina," Jennie said. She knew that the teenager had supervisory duties at the creek with the younger children. Jennie noticed one small, sturdy boy among the older ones harmlessly splashing each other in the creek. As she watched, the little boy dug into the bed of the creek and hurled a double handful of sand and pebbles directly into the face of a girl not much older than he.

Tina saw and yelled, "Lyndon West! You stop that, right now!"

The small girl was crying and trying to rub sand out of her eyes. "Excuse me," Tina said. "That little monster." She ran into the shallow water to assist the little girl.

"Theresita West's son," Hamilton commented, eyeing the boy, who gathered another handful of sand and pebbles and threw them at Tina. Tina took the boy by the arm and jerked him out of the water.

Tina groaned. "I don't know why I agree to babysit for this hoodlum."

Jennie took a close look at Lyndon West. Physically he was a beautiful child, not quite two years of age, with a sturdy little body and a face that appeared too old for it. His eyes seemed to pierce into hers.

"What are you looking at, Grandma?" the boy challenged, his voice piping but harsh.

"Lyndon . . ." Tina warned, giving his arm another jerk.

"Do that once more," Lyndon said, shooting Tina a cold, reptilian look, "and I'll pour boiling water over you as you sleep."

"If you are impolite once more," Tina countered angrily, "I will never bring you to the creek again."

"If we're going to be spied upon by ancient voyeurs like these," the boy complained, each word enunciated perfectly, sounding incongruous coming from his childish lips, "then I don't give a damn."

"That's it," Tina said. "Sorry, sir." She yanked the small boy away, and he had to trot to keep up with her as she headed back toward the town.

Hamilton, one eyebrow raised, looked at Jennie. "I would say that Jacob and Theresita West have a handful there."

"Not even two years old," Jennie said, shaking her head. "And his IQ is astronomical." She frowned. "Are the Eepera so superior? Does having half-Eepera blood make him so much advanced over human children his age?"

"That remains to be seen," Hamilton growled. He had made it a point to check the records on young Lyndon West, and he had not admitted to anyone that what he had read worried him. The boy showed motor skills of a child six times his age and mental advances beyond that.

For all of his adult life, ever since he had the total ignorance to go into politics, Dexter Hamilton had faced threats. Early in his career they came from opponents who wanted his particular office. As senator and then President he had always been nose to nose with the threat from the Soviet Union and had lived many years with the possibility of nuclear war and the world's death. He was away from all that now, and still there was a threat, this time in the form of a shadowy, all-powerful, unknown race lurking somewhere out there in the vastness of space. Much of his thought was given over to that threat and ways to meet it, and he wasn't at all sure that would be possible.

Back on Earth, when the mad Soviet Premier had been on the verge of pushing the final red button, Hamilton's chief sorrow in facing that possibility had been that his Jennie would die, too, that he would be deprived of her company, her smiles, and her warmth. He put his arm around her waist, and she, feeling that something was disturbing him, leaned against him and returned his embrace. She made no objection when he led her toward town. Dexter was Dexter, and as long as there was a challenge or even a potential challenge, he would be riding tall in the saddle, ready to enter into battle against any enemy that threatened his world or his beliefs. She decided, as they walked hand in hand, watching the sun falling lower over the ocean, that she wouldn't have it any other way.

THREE

First Officer Max Rosen—with the look of agony on his face that indicated deep thought, and with his hair mussed and uniform slightly askew, as usual—entered the front door of Duncan Rodrick's house overlooking Stanton Bay without knocking. Rodrick was in his study. He had been gradually moving his papers and personal effects there in anticipation of the departure of the *Spirit of America* for Earth. As Max entered the study, Rodrick pushed his chair away from the console of his computer terminal.

Max saw the figures on the screen and grunted. "Your rocket-fuel figures are not quite up-to-date," he said.

"I noticed that you've gone to twenty-eight-hour production," Rodrick said.

"Three, four months, and we'll have her fueled," Max growled, pulling a chair out from the wall and flopping into it. "I gave Amando Kwait permission to activate the ship's systems. He wants to start planting those things he's taking back."

Rodrick nodded. The achievements of Dr. Amando

Kwait, the native African who had lost his homeland to the communist conquest of that continent, were the most valuable part of the ship's return cargo. Native Omegan plants, engineered by Kwait and Dr. Dena Madden to thrive in Earth's environment, promised to make the deserts green again and to provide new food sources to relieve famine in many undeveloped, over-populated nations.

"Tested the Shaw Drive yesterday," Max said. "It is ready."

There was no problem with collecting rhenium, the rare mineral needed for the drive that allowed a ship to disappear, then reappear almost instantaneously parsecs away. Stoner McRae's mining operations and his trade with the huge underground slugs called miners had accumulated small amounts of rhenium. Max had discovered that the Shaw Drive could operate on minute amounts of the mineral, rather than the huge quantities originally called for by the inventor, Harry Shaw. This drastically cut the amount of the rare metal needed, so there was enough rhenium for the *Spirit of America* to make more than the round trip to Earth, and there was still a good supply of the mineral aboard the *Free Enterprise*.

It was with mixed emotions that Rodrick anticipated the takeoff and the triumphant return to Earth. He was reluctant to leave Omega while the threat of invasion by a mean bunch of bastards from the stars loomed large, but he knew that he had no choice: He was the captain of the *Spirit of America* and would have to leave Max in command on Omega. He had not yet fully decided whether he would take his wife, Jackie, on the trip or leave her to assist Max. Jackie was the third-ranking space service officer on Omega, and Rodrick knew and respected her abilities.

"What do you hear from Grace?" Rodrick asked.

Max winced. He had married Dr. Grace Monroe more than two years earlier, but it seemed that something always came up to keep them apart. Grace was in Suses. He was in Hamilton City.

"Like to see her?" Rodrick asked, grinning.

"That would be damned novel," Max growled.

"Harry Shaw asked for you," Rodrick said.

"Fine," Max answered.

"Hop on over to the river and see what Shaw's so excited about," Rodrick said. "I'll have Jackie take over coordination of loading preparations."

Max tried unsuccessfully to straighten his tousled hair, then grinned, a new look in his eyes at the thought of being with Grace.

Rodrick watched the engineer go, heard the front door open and close, and sighed. It was amusing and heartwarming to see how drastically the confirmed old bachelor had changed. Max Rosen the bear. Max Rosen the misanthrope had been turned into a happily married man—or at least he was happy on those rare occasions when he could be with his wife—by a soft-spoken and attractive woman who had first overcome his surliness by being as intelligent as he. Rodrick chuckled, remembering the last scientific discussion he'd witnessed between Grace and Max. An outsider would have thought that they were on the verge of coming to blows—Max's face red, Grace's lips firm, voices slightly raised—but then Max had seen what Grace was driving at, and his face had split into a toothy smile. He'd leaned across the lab bench to pat her hand, so proud of her, so pleased that she could more than hold her own with him in almost every field and beat the pants off him in her own.

"Lucky man," Rodrick said aloud, and then paused, frowning. Where had that come from? He, too, was lucky. Jackie was everything a man could want. Without doubt she was one of the most beautiful women on Omega, or on Earth, for that matter. She had her abilities, as Grace had hers. She possessed a sharp scientific intuition. What was it, then?

Suddenly it was looming before him, the face almost tangible—the face of Mandy Miller. He picked up a book and slammed it onto the desk. "Grow up," he hissed at himself.

But there was the time he'd kissed Mandy. And the many times she had shared his silence and concern in the observatory aboard the *Spirit of America* during the maiden voyage from Earth. When he had felt almost hopeless in the face of seemingly insurmountable odds, Mandy had been there, quiet, strong, physically loyal to her husband—who was now dead—but letting him know without question that she felt as he felt, that she yearned for him as he did for her.

He had not had what he sometimes thought of as a "Mandy attack" for some time. After Jackie's disappearance in the southern jungles, he had been relieved when she was returned to him unharmed. Then things had been too hectic to allow personal feelings to come to the fore. But now a desire for Mandy was with him with a vengeance, and he could not drive her sweet presence away. Once he had been so close to having her. If he had only waited, instead of marrying Jackie—hoping to kill, once and for all, his longing for Mandy—she would have been his after Rocky's death at the hands of the Whorsk raiding party.

There were times when Rodrick wished that he was without honor, that he could say to hell with everything, race to Mandy's lab, take her in his arms, and say, "I don't care. I want you." But he was a man born to command. He had accepted responsibility and would not toss that obligation aside. The love he still harbored for Mandy was a guilty thing and could potentially be a destructive influence on the entire colony, based as it was on family values. The fact that he would never have her, never hold her, never become one with her, was a pain that lifted him from his chair and sent him walking hastily out of the house. The door closed behind him. He stood for a moment letting the sun warm the top of his head before putting on his cap. Then he lifted his communicator.

Ito Zuki, the Japanese-American astronavigator, was on duty aboard the *Spirit of America.* "Ito," Rodrick said, "call the base in Suses and get word to Harry Shaw that Max is on the way over."

"Roger," Ito said.

"Any report from the field team beyond the mountains?"

"Regular check-in just a half hour ago," Ito said. "Routine."

"Thank you," Rodrick replied. His conscience was not eased in the slightest for having asked about the field team, an exploration party headed by his wife, Lieutenant Jacqueline Garvey Rodrick.

FOUR

A temporary camp had been set up outside the impressive, gleaming, white pyramid sitting high on the cliffs overlooking the city of Suses and the Great Misty River. The quarters for personnel and the housing for working labs had been airlifted in sections from Hamilton City, then assembled. A construction machine was extruding walkways and roadways through the desert sands. Guards, sheltered from the intense sun under plastic-roofed guardposts, became more alert when a scout ship swooped down.

Max Rosen had mixed feelings about the gleaming city with its graceful architectural style. He had no objection to style and grace as long as the design was efficient. The pyramid, however, was a symbol of egoistic waste and a monument to slave labor. He had admired the pyramids on Earth because they had been early man's cry for attention from the gods, a proud statement of man's achievement in a machineless era, and evidence of man's earliest experiment in regulating a society.

Although no doubt influenced by those earlier Egyptian monuments, this gleaming white pyramid on a planet parsecs from old Egypt seemed to be nothing more than an anachronism, for it had been built by an advanced society with technology capable of stopping the functions of a hydrogen engine, stilling the flow of electrons in electronic components, and smashing a heavily armored crawler at long range.

To Max it seemed that the Eepera had learned little from the ancient Egyptians—a love of beauty, perhaps, but also the arrogant slothfulness of the early pharaohs who ruled with godlike, absolute power. To think that the city and the pyramid were the result of mass slavery—even if the slaves were the insectlike Whorsk, a race whose innate savagery made them objects of disdain in a free state—was abhorrent.

The pilot of the scout ship, the Mescalero Apache Jacob West, had no ambiguous feelings about the Eepera. He wasn't prejudiced; he just damned well didn't like them. He would not deny that his dislike centered around their treatment of his wife, a tall, handsome, big-boned Polish woman who had once held the second most powerful position in the Soviet Union and who was the sole survivor of the first Russian interstellar starship, the *Karl Marx*. And Jacob might even have confessed that his dislike of the Eepera had been intensified by exposure to little Lyndon, Theresita's son by one of the pretty Eepera boys who had kept her under the influence of a very insidious and powerful aphrodisiac.

Jacob had brought the scout down hot and fast, blowing a lot of dust in the landing. As far as he was concerned, the less time he spent in Suses the better. He winked at Max as the first officer gathered his belongings and opened the hatch.

" 'Preciate the taxi service," Max said.

"It is not necessary to tip," Jacob joked. "I'm on an expense account."

Then Jacob was gone, hurling the scout upward. As the glaring desert with its thin ribbon of river diminished, he could see the inky velvetness of space up above, extending forever. He kicked in *Apache One*'s boosters and flashed still upward, fingered the computer, and let the ship find a stable orbit that sped her around the huge globe of Omega at the rate of one circumnavigation in thirty minutes. He needed some time to think.

Below, there was a massive low-pressure storm in the great Western Ocean. White, billowing thunderheads covered the jungle areas of the Columbian continent. He could see the alpine mountains that ran north to south inland from Eden, the northern desert, and the tiny outline of Stanton Bay. He looked down on the eastern outline of the home continent, then sped past the South-American-sized island that separated it from the as yet unnamed eastern continent.

Apache One clicked and purred, its automatic systems functioning perfectly and the heating system compensating for the cold of near space. For a few minutes he was at peace, a man in his element, a pilot doing that which he did best and loved best. And then he was looking down again on the western continent that was the home of the Eepera—the northern mountains and the great central jungles that had been traversed by Theresita after the crash of the one scout ship that had escaped the destruction of the *Karl Marx*. Once again he felt fiercely proud of the woman he had come to love, proud that she had had the intelligence and training to adapt to such conditions, the stamina to survive, to travel so many thousands of miles down that stretch of the jungle river that, although the name had not been made official, was called Theresita's River.

There she'd been attacked and severely wounded by an Omegan lion, taken by the Eepera, healed, drugged, and impregnated. He didn't know if he could ever forgive the Eepera for taking advantage of a drugged and injured woman. She had been nothing more than a breeder to them; while she was everything to him.

His peace of mind, engendered by being alone in space, was gone. It was time to go home. He put *Apache* into a descent and went screaming into the atmosphere in a fireball of speed, slowed her, contacted control at Hamilton City, and landed in a flurry of self-confident braking and hovering, with *Apache*'s autos whining down. After jumping out of the ship, he walked purposefully to the vehicle park and sent the speedy little crawler dashing into Hamilton City. He had come to a decision: It was time to talk with someone, and his choice was Dr. Mandy Miller, head of the Life Sciences section.

Mandy, like most, had her offices in her dwelling. She had come to love the house set toward the center of the city. Once her late husband, Rocky, had complained bitterly because large umbrella trees partially cut off the view of Stanton Bay, but she loved their shade, the coolness in Omega's torrid summer. Her private computer terminal was connected to the central computer aboard the *Spirit of America*, and on that particular morning she was running tests to make certain that the vast bank of Life Sciences information was being transferred properly to the new central computer, which was being assembled off ship in preparation for the *Spirit*'s departure for Earth.

Mandy had company. He sat comfortably in a contour chair, one long leg dangling over the arm, a cup of coffee in hand. He spoke only when she spoke to him, for he knew that she was concentrating.

Satisfied that the transfer of data was going well, she turned off her terminal and faced Derek Roebling with a smile.

"Ready for that cup of coffee now?" he asked.

"I'll get it," she offered. She wondered if she was blushing. During her long marriage to Rocky, it had been she who was ever thoughtful.

"Nonsense," Derek said, rising quickly. He was five years her junior, but the difference was not evident. On those occasions when she faced herself in the mirror, she had to admit that she had weathered events well.

Derek disappeared into a little alcove and came back with a cup of steaming coffee. Mandy sat, composing skirt and legs gracefully, and smiled her thanks.

"I'm told," Derek said, "that a crawler just might be available for pleasure use this afternoon. I've not yet had the chance to see the countryside immediately around Hamilton, and being new on the planet, I would not dare venture out alone. Care to be my guide?"

Mandy bought time by sipping her coffee. Although he was never pushy, Derek had made it clear that he was attracted to her. She let her eyes examine him. He was tall, and he moved elegantly. His face was strong, as smooth as youth, but manly. His eyes showed that clear, healthy white of well-being, and the brown of them seemed to be given extra depth by a hint of something darker within. His lips seemed to be always on the verge of a smile.

"I'm in the midst of data transfer," she reminded him.

"And I'm in the midst of evaluating every Omegan child under the age of eighteen," Derek responded. "Still, it isn't every day you can take a crawler out for pleasure."

"All right," she said, feeling as if she'd just impulsively decided to dive off a five-meter board for the first time.

"Three o'clock," Derek said. "I'll pick you up."

After the door closed behind him, she had only a few moments to wonder if it was wise to encourage him. The last thing she wanted was romance. Her scars, not showing on her beautiful face, were inside. In fact, she was amazed that her nightmares had not left visible marks. They were there, crouching in the dark recesses of her memory: the blood and horror of the

Whorsk attack that had killed Rocky and two hundred others; the sight of Sage Bryson, murdered, then perfectly preserved and exhibited in the Museum of Life below the Suses pyramid. No, she was not exactly prime material for a solid relationship. She'd tell Derek so. She'd tell him that . . . what? An errant thought occurred, which had the power to propel her from her chair and send her pacing, for the question that had come from deep within her was: *Will you tell him that you can't encourage him because you're still in love with Duncan Rodrick?*

She slammed down her coffee cup and, starting toward the computer terminal, was halted by the door chime.

Jacob West was leaning against the wall outside her door. "Hi, Mandy. Got a minute?"

"Sure. Come on in," she urged, relieved to find that it was not Derek coming back. "How's my favorite wild Indian?"

"That's the problem," Jacob admitted with a wry smile, and followed Mandy into her office, easing into a chair. "I'm afraid I'm going to commit infanticide."

"Oho," Mandy said. "Talking about your little Lyndon?"

Jacob was surprised by the sympathy in her tone. "Hey, I think I've found a friend. You've spent about as much time with him as I have, testing him, studying him, and it sounds as if you don't like him any more than I do."

"It's not a question of like," Mandy said.

"What is it, then?" Jacob ran his hand over his face. He felt like a traitor to the woman he loved. "Mandy, the kid's not normal. He's a monster. And Theresita—"

Mandy was mentally kicking herself for letting her feelings regarding Theresita's son show. "She's a mother," Mandy said.

"Neither Theresita nor I is a spring chicken. She became a mother late in life. She's a military person and once held the fate of the world in her hands. She performed a job with enormous responsibilities, but this kid twists her around his finger. She doesn't seem to notice his unbelievable cruelty. He mutilated a little spring calf that Theresita had borrowed for him from the petting zoo, and she's had half a dozen concerned mothers try to explain nicely why they won't let their kids play with Lyndon. She says they just don't understand the kid."

"He is different," Mandy said carefully. "He's a toddler, just short of two years old, but he has the bodily coordination of a twelve-year-old. And he is very advanced mentally."

"I don't understand it," Jacob said, throwing up his hands. "Adult Eepera are not mental giants. I've read the tests your section has run—brain capacity about the same as human. Manual dexterity very human. But then there's Lyndon, and he's only half-Eepera."

"Have you read the study just issued of Eepera children in Suses?"

"No. But I'd like to."

"It appears that the main difference between Eepera and human is surprisingly swift mental maturity in the young."

"After a head start, the kid will level out and be like human kids when he's older?" Jacob asked, hopeful.

"There is that possibility."

"If someone doesn't throttle him first," Jacob whispered. "He tried to shove a boy off the cliff down by the bay the other day."

"I've spoken with Theresita, several times," Mandy said. "You know I'm very fond of her, Jacob. She's not the first mother to be blind to her child's obvious faults."

Jacob rose, went to pour himself some coffee. "I'm up a tree, Mandy," he said on his way from the alcove. "I see in this two-year-old boy—he should be cuddly and lovable—all the senseless ego, arrogance, cruelty, and stupidity that I see in those . . ." He paused, not willing to use in front of Mandy the words that came to his mind.

She laughed, knowing what he'd been about to say. "I know how you feel. If I had my way . . ." It was her turn to leave thoughts unspoken.

"Go back in time and explode the bombs directly over the river instead of in space?" Jacob asked.

"Well . . ." Mandy said, spreading her hands.

Jacob knew that Mandy had good reason to hate both the Whorsk and Eepera. The former had killed her husband and all those who had chosen to follow him; the Whorsk had been ordered by the Eepera to do the slaughter.

"That still leaves us with little Lyndon," Jacob said. "I was hoping that you had discovered something medically wrong, an imbalance of brain chemicals, something."

"No," Mandy said, "but it's interesting that you mentioned brain chemistry, Jacob, because I've been thinking about having Delia Howard do some tests on him."

"Haven't met her. She come out on the *Free Enterprise?*"

"She's probably the leading expert on brain functioning. She's still fairly young, but we'll all probably live past the average life expectancy because of her work in compound synthesis."

"Impressive," Jacob said, rubbing his jaw. "Maybe we can talk her into doing a lobotomy."

"Now, Jacob . . ." Mandy said, smiling.

"Mandy, I expected to be a bachelor all my life. I was one of those dudes who didn't kiss anything but his scout ship. When I saw that big, Polish broad stark naked on a beach over on the Eepera continent, I didn't have a chance. That woman means more to me than anything, but day by day that boy is poisoning our relationship."

"Is the boy actually trying to turn Theresita against you?" Mandy probed.

"You wouldn't believe some of the things he comes up with," Jacob said.

"It might be helpful in our study of him if you'd record your observations—all these things I wouldn't believe."

"Have a barf bag handy when I start recording," Jacob said. He put his coffee cup down. "I'll do it. Have them to you as soon as I can."

"And I'll consult with Delia Howard this afternoon," Mandy said; then, remembering that she'd halfway agreed to go on an outing with Derek, added, "or tomorrow morning first thing."

FIVE

Grace met Max at the entrance ramp to the pyramid. Max halted and, hands hanging limply at his sides, grinned at her. "I don't know how you do it," he said. She was wearing a mauve blouse and matching skirt. In the desert heat the other women would be in halter tops and shorts. Not Grace. She always looked as if she'd just stepped out of a dressing room. Max moved forward then, and she did, too, laughing until her mouth was closed by his.

"You got a private room anywhere in this pile of rocks?" Max growled.

"Harry is waiting for you," Grace said, her expression showing that she was tempted to find some privacy with him. "I had my camper set up at a considerable distance," she added, her lips brushing his. "There's a nice view of the rising moons through the window."

Max groaned.

"Be strong," Grace whispered, laughing happily. It was still a beautiful novelty for her to want and be wanted so fiercely.

The suggestion that then issued from Max's lips made her laugh again, but he released her and they went into the pyramid.

Given a choice, neither Grace nor her coworker Evangeline Burr would have worked inside the pyramid. But Egyptologist Dr. Hiram Abdul had taken ill, so he was confined to Hamilton City. That left only Grace and Evangeline to carry on the research. The light was good in the chamber where Grace had installed her translation machine and a computer terminal, but it was artificial light, and she was constantly aware of the multitons of stone over her head and of the mustiness of the recirculated air. Often, when she was absorbed in a particular problem of translation, her thoughts would unexpectedly flash below, down, down, far into the underground corridors and rooms below the pyramid to the room where Sage Bryson was standing . . . looking, as the poet had once said, as if alive, perfectly preserved for an eternity, a specimen on display. At such times she would shudder involuntarily and try to get her mind back on her work.

Harry Shaw had set up shop in a huge, high-ceilinged room whose walls were lined with Egyptian-like idols. He'd had plenty of lighting installed. He and two technicians were bent over a workbench. Harry looked up and nodded when Max walked up to them. "Take a look at these circuits, Max," he invited.

Max took a place beside Harry and looked into the enlarger. "It's good work," Max said, quickly making sense of the series of tiny lines and modules comprising a tiny circuit board. "But nothing new."

"It was new three thousand years ago," Harry said. "What have they come up with since then?"

Max grunted. "Anything from the translations Grace and Evangeline are working on?"

"Mysticism and mumbo jumbo," Shaw replied. "I hope you brought a change of clothes. I want you to give me a hand before you go back to Eden. I wanta tear some of this Eepera junk down to bedrock and put it back together."

"Fine," Max said, "but I'm taking off early today."

Shaw looked up, frowning, then grinned. "Don't blame you."

Shaw and Max had worked together back on Earth during the development of the Shaw Drive, with Shaw as the designer and Max as the can-do man. Each had a healthy respect for the other's ability. Harry had no delusions of grandeur, knowing he had simply been the one to stumble onto the peculiar properties of that rare metal, rhenium. And Max felt no envy of Harry's innovative ability. He was confident of his own strengths and weaknesses. Give him a design, and he'd build it. Give him a machine, and he'd figure out what made it work and would improve it. But he knew full well that his brain didn't function like that of a creator—like Harry Shaw's and Grace's, for example. That suited him just fine. That was one of the things that made life so exciting with Grace. He never knew how her creative genius would be expressed next, and he always looked forward to the challenge of understanding what she had in mind and of putting her ideas into mechanical function. That was the way he had worked with Harry back on Earth.

"It didn't take us long to figure out how to duplicate the Eeperan principles once we had the clues from native vegetation on Omega," Max commented. "In fact, it was simple once we had the idea. Just align particle movement in hydrogen and helium atoms—"

"They used that idea when they came to Earth three thousand years ago," Harry said.

"I'm hungry," Max said abruptly.

"I've arranged lunch with Paul, Grace, and Evangeline," Harry said, standing up, unbending his back with a hand at his hip, and grimacing.

It was to be a working lunch. Evangeline had gone to the cookshack outside and had wheeled back a cart laden with cooled containers of Amando Kwait's summer wine; great chunks of coarse, heavy bread made with Kwait's genetically engineered wheat, whose grains, nurtured by Omega's sun and the potent fertilizer—leavings of the underground miners—were a full three quarters of an inch long before milling; and a selection of sandwich fillings from the colony's synthafood factory.

Harry Shaw found himself to be the odd man out. He had invited Paul Warden, the space service officer who had been weapons officer aboard the *Spirit of America*, to join them. He grinned to himself, for Max's dark, brooding eyes were on his Grace, and Paul, husky, muscular, called by some the no-neck monster because of his thick neck muscles, couldn't keep his eyes off Evangeline. Shaw, having selected a concoction that had the texture and taste of liver paté on thick slabs of the delicious bread, munched thoughtfully as small talk went around the table.

It was Max who opened the conversation. "So you women been doing anything besides having picnics?" he asked gruffly.

"Grace, think you could easily find another husband after I squish this one?" Evangeline asked.

"Give him time," Grace said, grinning. "He's come a long way, but has a bit further to go to be fully domesticated."

"We're cranking out translation at the rate of about fifty words per minute," Evangeline said. "The main problem is keeping up with the translation machines. Most of it"—she waved a hand at stacks and shelves of massive, leather-bound volumes—"is priestly material, which will be of great interest to Egyptologists and anthropologists. Apparently the Eepera infiltrated the ranks of the Egyptian priesthood very successfully and came actually to believe in that multiplicity of old Egyptian gods. Most of their wise men devoted time on

Earth and on Omega to refining and analyzing their religious theories."

"But hard science?" Harry asked.

"Not so far," Evangeline answered. "But as I said, with just Grace and me to read all these massive stacks of translation—"

"If it's just readers you want, we can bring over a few," Max offered.

"That would help," Grace said eagerly. "Then we can weed through the information faster and isolate anything of interest for more intensive examination."

"As I understand it," Harry said, "two written languages are in use."

"Yes," Grace replied. "It's odd, in a way. It seems that the general population was thoroughly Egyptianized. Their poetry—which is the bulk of their literature—is written in hieroglyphics. The priestly writings are in the more sophisticated language we assume to be native to the Eepera's home world. As time passed, it became mixed with corruptions and modified forms of the old Egyptian hieroglyphs."

"The only pure examples of what seems to be the old Eepera language are the instructions and labels on the various machines," Evangeline added.

"Too bad you haven't found repair manuals," Max managed around a bite of one of Amando Kwait's apples.

"I had a chat with that fellow called Ahmes," Harry told him.

"The head priest," Max said.

Harry nodded. "Apparently what repair was possible was done by a few priests who passed their knowledge from generation to generation by word of mouth."

"That's not unusual," Grace said. "In primitive societies the priests often had a secret language. The original Eepera language served that purpose here. Also, to have mysteries known only to a select few is common in such societies. The knowledge of the workings of their machines and their weapons were the mysteries of these priests."

"Maybe we oughta use a brain probe on 'em," Max suggested.

"I don't think that'll be necessary," Harry said. "Working together, we should be able to uncover all their so-called mysteries."

"Save time if we drained their brains," Max persisted.

"They would understand that. . . ." Grace said quietly.

"Yeah, I know," Max said, ever sensitive to Grace's moods and knowing that she was thinking of Sage Bryson. "I'm just talking a lot of hot air. I don't really believe we should lower ourselves to their level of savagery and disregard for life—at least, the lives of people not their own."

Paul Warden had fallen silent, devoting his attention to watching Evangeline's face and his food. "Their sun gun isn't too difficult to figure out."

"Who gave it that name?" Grace asked.

"I don't know," Paul replied. "It just happened. It's nothing more than a sophisticated laser. We could power it with megavoltage of electricity and get the same effect. The disrupter beam is a little more complicated. We know that it interferes with the flow of electrons and has the effect of freezing—for lack of a better description—the current flowing through any electrical circuit. Since there's hardly any piece of equipment that doesn't use electrical circuits, that makes it effective against just about anything. For example, it'll stop any hydrogen-powered vehicle in its tracks by freezing electrical currents."

"Which brings us back to the central question," Harry said, "and that is the power source."

"The sun," Max replied. "This whole pyramid is a solar collector."

"And we know where the plant is," Harry said. "What we don't know is what happens inside that power plant after the solar heat is collected. We won't know until we go inside it. There's a helluva lot of juice that comes out, so something very exciting goes on inside. But what happens if we open something that isn't supposed to be open and find there is—just as a wild example—a tiny thermonuclear reaction going on in there?"

"We go boom," Max said simply.

"We cut off all power to the city," Grace said, suggesting an alternative scenario, "even if, God forbid, we don't make something go boom."

"What would happen if someone from the early age of aviation traveled through time and was shown a Shaw Drive?" Paul offered. "He'd recognize it was a power plant and would damned well want to know how it worked so he could duplicate it and put it into a DC-3, but when he penetrated the pressure chamber—"

"Boom," Max said.

"Your delightful optimism is making me nervous," Evangeline said.

"We won't go drilling into any sealed chambers in the power plant for a while yet," Max promised.

"It has to be something very simple," Harry said. "It's been working now for thousands of years. It sits there very silently and pours out more than enough electricity to power a city."

"Four of the younger priests tend it," Warden put in. "But their technical skill seems to be confined to pouring holy water on it each morning and saying a few prayers at odd times during the day."

"Max, can you name one machine that we could build, put in place, move a couple of times, and still have doing its job three or four thousand years later?"

Max could not.

"I wanta quit early today," he said, standing, giving Grace a knowing glance that, to the others, was easily recognizable as a classic leer.

Paul Warden, totally involved in mastering the secrets of the Eeperan weapons, had experienced some difficulty in keeping his attention on the discussion. Evangeline had done something new with her hair, shortening it for ease of care while camping out at the pyramid, and the effect had been to make her look younger, fresher, and so sweetly alluring that Paul had found himself incapable of keeping his eyes off her.

Paul's attentions were not, of course, unnoticed by Evangeline. It was as if she could feel the force of his admiration across the table, almost as if he had physically touched her. She was surprised when Paul was the first to rise and walk from the room. She felt herself blushing with embarrassment. Had she been wrong in feeling that he was very much aware of her during the luncheon conference?

Actually, Paul was forcing himself to put distance between himself and Evangeline, knowing that if he allowed himself the pleasure of lingering to talk with her, he would be unable to concentrate on his work. He was one of the few who was privy to the plan concocted by Dexter Hamilton, Oscar Kost, and Duncan Rodrick at that stage, so he realized the great importance of his work. He simply could not allow himself to be distracted, even by so thrilling a distraction as Evangeline.

Evangeline was frozen in her seat for a few seconds, and then, with a flash of determination approaching quick anger, she leaped up and hurried after Warden, catching him in a vaulted passage where the lights were dim and the air dead and almost chill.

Warden heard her hurrying footsteps, turned, and halted. She stopped three steps away and opened her mouth but could not find words.

"You are very beautiful today," Paul said.

"Thank you," she said.

Warden took a deep breath.

"I haven't been seeing much of you," she said.

He shrugged. "Work, work, work."

There was a silence. He had told her that he loved

her, and she had returned that assurance. She was always touched by the obvious affection between Max and Grace, and envied Grace. Because Evangeline knew that she and Paul could enjoy that same love, that same togetherness, she was having difficulty understanding why Paul was holding back.

As if sensing her puzzlement, Warden spoke. His own words were also influenced by having observed the relationship between Max and Grace. If he were married to Evangeline, he knew he would not have Max's patience, would not quietly accept the separations demanded by the work in which Max and Grace were engaged.

"Hey," he said, "I hope you understand."

"Understand what?"

He was uneasy, never a man of emotional words. "Well, there's work to be done."

"I know. I seem to be knee-deep in it all the time."

"Then you do understand."

"I'm afraid not," she said, an edge to her voice. "I don't understand why you avoid me."

"Hey, it's not that," he said quickly.

"What is it, then?" She knew that the tone of her voice was slightly unpleasant, and she burned with the desire to simply go to him, put her arms around him, and say, "It's all right."

"Vange, listen, I guess I'm an all-or-nothing guy in some ways," Paul confessed. He tried to laugh, but it came out sounding feeble. "I mean, I guess I have a one-track mind. I can't . . ."

"Yes?"

"Vange, one of these days there'll be time. And then . . ."

She fought her resentment, remembering the way he had followed Sage Bryson around like a lost puppy looking for a friendly pat on the head. Now he seemed to go out of his way to avoid being in her presence.

"So," she said, "when you do find some time . . ."
She turned and walked away, her back stiff.

"Vange," he pleaded, but so softly that she couldn't
hear. He took one step after her, halted, and turned to
get back to his work. She was, he felt sure, too intelligent a woman not to understand what he meant—that
he simply could not concentrate on his work and on her
too. He sighed and headed for the power room.

SIX

By tradition—if such a thing could be considered to
have been established in the colony's brief existence—
department heads breakfasted occasionally with Captain
Duncan Rodrick aboard the *Spirit of America*. The
tradition was not yet so inflexible that a captain's breakfast could not become a captain's lunch. Those present
in the officer's mess aboard the massive starship, which
now hummed with life once again as all her systems
were activated in preparation for the return to Earth,
had been rounded up hurriedly by communicator and
ingenious search by Juke. A few of the regulars, who
were working in Suses, were absent.

Dexter Hamilton and Oscar Kost were already seated
at the head of the table with Rodrick as the others
entered and found places. Jackie Rodrick, looking spectacular, as usual, in her neatly fitted space service
jumpsuit, came in late and sat at the other end of the
table. From that point she could look directly into
Rodrick's face. She saw there the familiar strength she
had come to love and respect so much, and she saw
more when he looked up and smiled at her.

It had been a long time since Clay Girard and his relatively new bride, Cindy, née McRae, had been invited to a captain's meal. Neither of them had given it a thought, so involved were they in adjusting to the interesting and sometimes puzzling world of adulthood. Both had been reared—Clay as a foster son from the age of twelve and Cindy from birth—by a couple who instilled in them morality and common sense without the usual coating of condemnation and guilt. Clay and Cindy were aware that such distortions had originated far back in human history, when a virgin young woman was considered vendable or tradable property. They also understood the undesirability of premarital pregnancy. But both had discovered, after their marriage at the age of sixteen, that they were sexual creatures indeed. Their mutual and obvious adoration had been the basis of many conversations within the colony, usually conducted with faint, wistful smiles. Without realizing it, Clay and Cindy, through a sexual tension caused by their constant awareness of each other and wonder at their continuing new discoveries, had almost literally steamed a few pairs of glasses. Their Romeo-and-Juliet ardor had not cooled—at least in the privacy of their new home—but in public they had come to realize that they were not the only two people on Omega. At the captain's lunch, for example, Clay restrained himself for the first fifteen minutes from so much as touching Cindy, but then the strain became too much and he coughed, moved his chair slightly, pressed his thigh to hers, and saw a flush of awareness darken her neck. He missed the next few comments of the others, but the main item of business had not yet been broached.

Stoner McRae, Cindy's father, knew what was on the agenda, and he was eager to get to it. He was seated next to a new man, Dr. Frank Howard, and when he discovered that he and Howard had attended the same school, the two men began to compare notes. Frank had graduated some years after Stoner, so they had only a few of the school's teachers as common acquaintances, but for two old jocks, there was always football. Stoner, a huge man, once a formidable professional lineman for San Diego, grinned when Frank confessed that he had been a quarterback. That led to Stoner's realization that he did know, or know about, this Frank Howard after all.

"*Shag* Howard!" he exploded, causing the others to whip around and look his way. "Hey! This boy's Shag Howard!" He saw only blank looks, so he grinned and said, "Don't display your ignorance, people, by saying you don't know who Shag Howard is. He broke every record in the books. Most yards passing in college history. Three straight undefeated seasons with major bowl wins."

Frank was looking a little helpless. He shrugged, smiled, and lifted his finger to his lips to signal Stoner to be a bit more quiet.

"A quarterback," Stoner said as the others returned to their own conversations. "But as quarterbacks go . . ." He slapped Frank on the back. "How the hell did a quarterback get an MD and a PhD after his name?"

"How the hell did a mule of an old lineman get a string of engineering and mining degrees?" Frank tossed back.

"Well, this trip is sure to succeed, now that we have two old jocks aboard," Stoner said, causing Rodrick to look at him. Howard had been wondering why he, a newcomer, a medical man, had been invited to this very exclusive gathering at the captain's table.

Rodrick chewed the last bite of a fresh salad and set down his napkin. "Well, since you brought it up, Stoner . . ."

"What trip?" Clay asked, swimming up toward consciousness from Cindy's laughing eyes.

"Oscar?" Rodrick asked.

Kost swallowed, coughed. Space, Rodrick thought, had been good to old Oscar. He had gained weight and given up smoking. He seemed to be years younger, in spite of the fact that he still complained about his health. Was it just space, Rodrick thought, with an inner smile, or a new world? Kost spent a lot of time with a lively, very attractive, and very capable security-force colonel named Leslie Young, whose enthusiasm just might have had something to do with Oscar's new attitude. Regardless of Oscar's age, health, or attitude, he had one of the finest minds Rodrick had ever encountered. He had not been President Dexter Hamilton's chief adviser and oldest and closest friend purely out of sentimentality.

"Okay," Oscar said, keeping his seat. "We've come a long way from the time when Dexter stole money from every hidden source he could come up with to build the *Spirit of America,* still called Hamilton's Folly back home. We've got ourselves a whole new world, and a fine one it is. We're getting ready to take a cargo back Earthside that will have more significance than anything that has ever happened to that old planet since the first caveman stood on his hind legs. We have a right to be pretty proud of ourselves. We sometimes forget that we're hanging on to Omega by the skin of our teeth, that except for some excellent work by a lot of brave people, the colony might very well have vanished under the threat from the native population."

Clay was listening intently now. He'd never given any thought to the possible destruction of the colony.

"When one examines the situation closely," Kost went on, "things are still pretty precarious. Of the twenty Eepera cities on the Great Misty River, we are in control of one. We've convinced them to turn off their shields without a fight, but that was because they expected their parent civilization to come roaring in here to destroy the whole planet. Some say that a civilization as bad as the one the Eepera describe has probably self-destructed, but we can't be sure of that. Anyway, that is a threat we cannot do one damned thing about until it happens—if it comes about, and God willing, it won't."

He paused to sip some water. "The original mem-

bers of the colony have done one fine job. Max has a
rocket-fuel factory producing twenty-eight hours a day.
But we face one problem that will never go away because of the peculiar nature of this planet."

"Metals," Clay whispered to Cindy.

"Metals," Kost said. "Stoner, for all you've done, a
man could hold all the rhenium you've accumulated in
one hand."

Stoner nodded grimly.

"There's not enough iron in Omega's crust to build
a half-dozen high-rise buildings. Not enough gold to
meet the needs of any kind of a space program. You all
know the problems. Now there's still some gold, iron,
and other metals on Earth, and we can trade for them
using Amando Kwait's agricultural advances and the
jewelry made from those scales from the Omegan dragons. The problem there is, if war has broken out, all the
gold and metals on Earth might be pretty radioactive
by the time we get back."

"We need outposts, listening posts, ships," Duncan Rodrick suggested as Kost paused. "We know that
the Eepera came from somewhere, and we have to give
heed to their fears that our display of thermonuclear
power might bring the people they call the Masters
down on us. We need metal to build those listening
posts, the ships."

"So what do we do?" Kost asked.

"Find a nearby source," Clay Girard said, his heart
pounding. Stoner had mentioned a trip. Its purpose
was now obvious. And it was equally obvious that they
would allow him to go on that expedition, since there
was no other explanation for his having been invited to
the discussion over the captain's table.

"Find a nearby source," Kost confirmed. "A source
we can control without having to be concerned about
politics on Earth."

"That's why we're here," Rodrick said to the
gathering.

"But won't this delay the *Spirit*'s trip to Earth?" Jackie asked.

"No," Dexter Hamilton answered. "We would not allow anything to interfere with that, for that has always been the first priority."

"Thanks to Max and Grace," Rodrick said, "we can fly with only a fraction of the rhenium we had to use up on the way out. And Harry also figured that out, on Earth."

"We've calculated it pretty close," Kost said. "The *Spirit of America* will have enough rhenium to go to Earth and *return*." He smiled, something rare for him. "I don't think any of us would want to be stranded on Earth, now that we've seen the wide open spaces, or even to be dependent on Earth's politicians for a refueling of rhenium once the ship gets there." He sobered. "That's not even mentioning the possibility that those fools back there might have decided to push the buttons."

Cindy looked at Clay, her eyes wide. She wasn't used to hearing the possibility of Earth's destruction mentioned so casually.

"That leaves enough fuel for the *Free Enterprise*, a smaller ship, to do some traveling to nearby stars," Hamilton said.

"Can the *Free Enterprise* do any serious mining if she finds metals?" Jackie asked. She was wondering why she had not been informed of the plan for an expedition into space. She did not exactly resent the fact; she just wondered. Since the arrival of the *Free Enterprise*, the group she had once thought of as her husband's masterminds had changed. Now, many times, only three people gathered at the captain's table: Rodrick, Hamilton, and Kost.

"Shallow mining," Stoner McRae told her. "If we're lucky enough to find rich heavy metal ores near the surface, we could bring home a few thousand tons."

"If not," Kost added, "we will be only slightly worse off than we are now. It takes at least three years

for you to accumulate enough rhenium for one power-
ing of a Shaw Drive, right, Stoner?"

"At present rates of production," Stoner confirmed.

Clay couldn't stand the suspense. "Captain, who's
going?"

Rodrick laughed. He had a special place in his
heart for Clay. He'd watched him grow from a small,
frightened boy who had stowed away aboard the *Spirit
of America* into a fine young man. "You're not here just
to eat," he said.

"Hey, great!" Clay said. He felt Cindy squeeze his
hand and, reading her thoughts, went on quickly, "I'll
need an observer in my scout ship, Captain."

"That you will," Rodrick agreed, winking at Cindy,
who exhaled a great sigh of relief.

"Jackie," Rodrick said, "this is news to you. It's
news to all of you except Stoner, who has been bugging
me to do something like this ever since the *Free
Enterprise* arrived. We can discuss this in private, if
you like, but you know we're short of experienced
officers."

"I'll go," Jackie volunteered.

"Fine," Rodrick said. "You'll be in command. Stoner
is second, even if he isn't service. Clay is second service officer, third in command. We're going to hold the
crew to a minimum. Dr. Howard, you're here because
you're a medical man and because you're new on the
planet and have not, as yet, begun work that would be
difficult to interrupt. I won't order you to go. I know
you have a family."

Frank Howard looked around the table. "I understand. Others who have been here longer are involved
in important projects."

"That's right," Rodrick said.

"Are you aware of any dangers? Frank asked.

"Space travel is new," Rodrick said. "We have
seen a very few planets incapable of supporting life.
One was made very deadly by an implanted virus, if
we're to believe the Eepera. None of us can say whether

you'll come in contact with a ship from the Eepera parent worlds."

"Yes, I've thought of that," Frank said, imagining Delia's reaction and knowing how much he'd miss his son. "I'm pleased to be included."

"Good," Rodrick said emphatically. "We'll beef up the ship's armaments by robbing them from the *Spirit of America*. We'll send the defense robot, Mopro."

"I need the admiral," Stoner said.

"I know," Rodrick said. "And I've given that a lot of thought. I think we need him more, Stoner. He's the closest thing we've got to an indispensable man, even if he is a robot. We're giving you a lot of firepower in Mopro. The admiral is doing some valuable work over on the river, and in case . . ." He paused. "In case of attack, he can react faster than a man and can reason. No, we'll keep the admiral here."

Stoner looked dismayed.

"There's another robot, the sergeant, with the same design but some modifications," Rodrick suggested. "I'm a bit hesitant to let you take him because he's still an unproven quantity."

"Brand Roebling, of Transworld Robotics, says that he's a better fighting machine than the original," Kost said.

"Stoner, why don't you work with this new one and see what you think," Rodrick suggested. "If you think he can be depended upon and if you want him, okay."

"I'll need a navigator," Stoner said.

"I think that's why I'm here, Dad," Cindy said.

Stoner smiled. He knew that Cindy had been working with Ito Zuki, who had brought the *Spirit of America* through space, but he was not sure how much Cindy had mastered.

"Ito says she's as good as he is," Rodrick said, "and with faster reactions because of her youth."

Stoner nodded. "Well, I'm glad to hear there's some talent in this family. Crew?"

"The *Free Enterprise* is more automated than the *Spirit of America*," Rodrick said. "We'll give Clay a cram course in piloting. You can have one engineer and a couple of technicians. You might consult Harry Shaw on that, have him recommend the best from the *Free Enterprise*'s crew. And since you'll all be standing watch, I think you'd better come up with someone who can do the simple housekeeping aboard ship—keep the food machines hot, all that."

For one moment Frank Howard was going to recommend Delia for that job, but he realized that she was vastly overqualified. And if she went, that would leave Webb alone.

"We'll carry mining machines," Stoner said. "And one scout ship. We'll be traveling fast and light and with a skeleton crew." He did not state that one of the reasons for not carrying more crew was to avoid further depletion of the colony's population in the event that disaster struck the expedition. "I'm told that the ship could lift off in one hour's notice, but we'll take about a week to plan and pack and store up on Amando's fresh vegetables before we start eating ship's rations."

"Now I know why Ito was working on star maps leading in the direction of Vega," Cindy complained. "And that's why he had me helping him and was so careful to make sure I knew the distances and the star groupings."

"Right," Rodrick said.

"That's sneaky," Cindy said. "He could have told me, so I'd have paid more attention."

Rodrick laughed. "Look, I know all of you are a bunch of fire-eaters. We weren't sure sending out a ship was the best thing to do, but if we had decided against it, I knew I'd have enough trouble holding Stoner down."

Dexter Hamilton, who had not spoken much, stood up, water glass in hand. "You all will have a serious responsibility. May God go with you."

SEVEN

A newcomer seeing the admiral working side by side with Paul Warden would have observed a solidly muscular man working with a taller, slimmer man whose body could be described as somewhere between muscular overdevelopment and the more common bodily development of the average man. The admiral had abandoned his resplendent dress whites bedecked with medals. If he had not been so eminently understanding, so endowed with common sense, courtesy, and manly humility, that action might have been misperceived by his creator, Grace Monroe, as a form of reprimand. In the beginning she had used the admiral to make a statement against the military mind. When she had first activated the robot, his mental experience was that of a two-year-old, and he had taken great pride in his uniform and his rank, for Grace had been assigned to create a fighting machine, and in that she had done well.

Grace herself had been both surprised and delighted when the admiral quickly began to exhibit development beyond his weapon skills. Even though she knew that there was something other than flesh and blood under his real-looking skin, and that his thought processes were the result of electrical impulses from manmade materials and not the organic gray matter of the human brain, she had come to look upon him as the son she'd never had. Although the admiral went through an adolescent infatuation with the disturbed Sage Bryson, he was now, in all ways except physiologically, a mature man and, Grace felt, more sensitive and considerate than most.

The admiral wore the working uniform of the colony, and he wore it surpassingly well. Paul Warden had been highly amused during those times when he and the admiral explored the city of Suses, to see the Eepera women, who had the choice of all the handsome males, literally halt in their tracks to stare at the admiral.

Warden was not the only one to make the admiral his first choice for assistance and advice when there was a difficult job to be done. The admiral's acquired knowledge and reasoning power were supplemented by his easy access to the main computer; being a sort of walking computer himself, he could plug into the computer either physically with one of the leads hidden on his person or by radio contact, thereby extracting information more quickly and completely than the most accomplished human computer expert.

Warden had now turned his attention to the sun gun he and the admiral were dismantling. Even with the admiral's help, it was slow going. He was being very careful not to tear anything apart that couldn't be put back together. The simplicity of the weapon was perplexing. It didn't seem to Paul that there were enough parts to make it do what it did. It was not physically connected to any main power source and therefore did not have enough power to send a beam over great distances to stop the flow of electrons.

"Unless, as it has been suggested," the admiral said, "the power plant broadcasts power in some form."

"But we'd have to go inside the power plant to determine that," Warden said.

Harry Shaw and Max were making their preliminary examination of the power plant, and there wasn't space for four in the power chamber.

"Any ideas?" Warden asked the admiral as if he were speaking to another human. It was easy to forget that the admiral's well-formed body was many times stronger than even Warden's muscular, wide form, and that the brain inside the admiral's head worked from his own internal power sources and had the capacity to think faster and move the admiral's body faster than human capability.

"At one point, when Miss Bryson was working on a unified field theory, she did some calculations that I do not have stored," the admiral said. "I'd like to spend some time with the central computer before we try to open the power plant."

"I could use a break," Warden said, rising and stretching his back. "We've gone about as far here as we can."

The sergeant saw the admiral step down from a scout and walk with irritating assurance to a four-wheeler. The sergeant could not understand why some of the newcomers had trouble distinguishing the admiral from humans. He could spot his prototype at a distance.

The sergeant had been built to Grace Monroe's specifications, with some fine-tuning by Brand Roebling. If a set of measuring instruments were put on his body and that of the admiral, identical figures would result. But Roebling had given him a face unlike that of the admiral, and for that he was pleased. In his mind the admiral was just too pretty. He, on the other hand, had a stronger face, the face of a fighting man. And the differences, he knew, were not just in facial contour. Roebling had incorporated a few other minor improvements so that when the sergeant had competed against recorded results of tests run on the admiral, he always bested the admiral's performance. It was not always by much, a split-second here, a split-second there, but hard figures proved that he was just a tiny bit quicker, that there was a minute amount of additional power in his blows. That was only natural, he felt, since he was a later model, an improved model.

And yet the admiral was free to come and go as he pleased, enjoyed the confidence of the human leaders of the colony, and acted as if he were human; he, the sergeant, the superior model, had been assigned to work with a moron of a robot called Mopro. True, he'd been put in charge of the colony's security and defense, but any fool could see that the front line was over there on the Great Misty River, that there were no enemies on the continent of Columbia, and that his considerable talents were being wasted in supervision of the hulking Mopro and in guarding a facility that was already secure.

It was time, the sergeant decided, to do something about the situation, to prove to one and all that he was superior to the foppish admiral whose popularity must come, he felt, from the dandy's ass-kissing of anything human.

The sergeant jumped onto his personal four-wheeler. The little vehicles, hydrogen-powered, big-wheeled, had been brought out by the *Free Enterprise*, and they had been an instant success on Omega, with everyone clamoring for one. Four-wheelers could go just about anywhere, had the power to climb an incline so nearly vertical that not many had the courage to put them to that test, and could run for days without refueling. On a smooth surface, such as the road leading from the scout-ship pads to the *Spirit of America*, which was the admiral's destination, they could reach breathtaking speeds. When ridden at speed, a human needed goggles for eye protection. The sergeant needed no such protection. He accelerated, shifting swiftly. The admiral had finally made his first mistake. The four-wheeler he had taken was a floater, to be assigned on the basis of need . . . by the sergeant. Even such human dignitaries as Rodrick himself would have had to clear taking the four-wheeler with the one in charge: the sergeant. Mr. Brass, so almighty in his ass-kissing way, had simply jumped on the vehicle and gone without so much as a wave in the sergeant's direction. So the sergeant sped after the vehicle with a grim smile of satisfaction on his ruggedly handsome face.

The admiral, his mind on the work ahead, didn't notice the sound of the other vehicle's racing hydrogen engine until the sergeant was only yards behind. He turned, assumed that the sergeant wanted to pass, and pulled over to one side without a change of his moderate speed. The sergeant's vehicle flashed past, slowed, and pulled directly in front of him.

"Halt!" the sergeant bellowed, with a downward turn of his mouth. The admiral brought the four-wheeler to a halt. He stepped off. The sergeant swung his leg off his vehicle, hitched his fatigue pants, and with a half smile came to face the admiral.

"Sir," the sergeant said, flipping a salute, his face registering as much contempt as any noncommissioned officer had ever managed, while spouting the proper words in a tone not at all respectful, "you were supposed to clear use of that vehicle with me."

The admiral had been observing the sergeant with great interest ever since his arrival. He remembered very well his first private conversation with the robot made after his own specifications. He'd sought the meeting himself, and it had occurred deep within the empty holds of the *Free Enterprise,* where the sergeant was supervising the last of the unloading. He had known by the sergeant's sudden narrowing of eyes that the other robot recognized him, and he'd said, "Welcome to Omega. We have much in common."

"Sir," the sergeant had snapped, coming to attention and giving a salute.

The admiral had smiled, remembering how, when he was newly activated, he'd been impressed by his military rank, an identity programmed into his new brain by Grace.

He had returned the salute, saying, "We both know that I have no rank. Can I give you a hand with the work?"

The sergeant had still been standing stiffly at attention, although he was assessing the admiral with all his senses and instruments. He had known from that moment that he could take the pretty one easily. It gave him a good feeling. "This is not officer's work, sir," the sergeant had snapped.

"I think you'll find," the admiral had said, "that rank is not important."

"I'm damned proud of mine, sir," the sergeant had said, "because I earn it by producing results."

"Very well," the admiral had said. "Carry on. When you have a chance, let's have a talk." The sergeant was, after all, only two years old. The admiral could remember when he had been much the same.

"I think we'd have little to talk about, sir," the sergeant had said, managing more than ever to make that "sir" sound like an epithet. "I am the state-of-the-art model, sir. No offense, but you just wouldn't be able to keep up with me in any way, sir, since it's simply not designed into you."

Over the years the admiral had worked closely not only with the humans of the colony but with the robotic contingent. While it was true that Grace had not equipped Mopro with a brain to equal those superb artificial creations that gave him and the sergeant their abilities, he had come to know Mopro as a solid, dependable creation whose basic reasoning power was based firmly on common sense. A stronger relationship existed between the admiral and Mopro than between the admiral and the fun-loving Juke, or Doc, whose main concern was the health of the human, or Cat, who liked his own company best and that of selected humans second. It was through Mopro that the admiral first learned of the sergeant's one burning ambition—to meet the admiral in the field in a contest of strength, reaction time, and deadliness.

Mopro's conversation was not vocal. He could communicate in writing, flashing words on a sensitized band that ran around his massive head, or he could communicate with the computer or the admiral in telemetry signals. At first, when Mopro sent the admiral signals indicating the sergeant's blinding speed in drawing a weapon, in movement, in running, and in reaction, the admiral took it to be mere scientific interest on Mopro's part. Later he realized that Mopro was warning him that, sooner or later, the sergeant would engineer a confrontation.

It appeared, as the sergeant faced the admiral on the road between the scout-ship pads and the *Spirit of America,* that the sergeant had found his moment.

"You took that vehicle without permission," the sergeant said. He was obviously at full alert, ready to move instantly. "You were supposed to clear the use of that vehicle with me. For all you know, it might have been reserved for someone important."

"I'm sorry," the admiral said. He was fully aware of the tension in the sergeant. He knew that both of them were constructed well, but he also knew—once he had almost lost his memory when he'd been severely mangled by the grinding teeth of a miner—that two such entities as he and the sergeant could inflict much costly damage on each other. That was his concern. The colony was too busy, faced too many problems to have to take time to repair a robot. "Apparently this new regulation has been put in force while I have been away from the city."

"Ignorance is no excuse," the sergeant said, edging closer.

For a brief moment the admiral considered getting it over with. He would speak with Grace about this quirk in the sergeant's character. Perhaps, with a bit of fine-tuning, she could remove the source of the sergeant's enmity. Although he could explain the sergeant's attitude in human terms, he wasn't sure, in robotic terms, how to eliminate it. But Grace would know.

"You know, sir," the sergeant said, sneering, "you've taken too much importance on yourself. I hear you even fell in love with a human woman and caused her mental anguish."

The admiral felt himself stiffen in spite of himself. His youthful misunderstanding of Sage Bryson's mental illness was still an area of regret for him.

"You're not human, sir," the sergeant said. "You're a machine, like me, except that I'm a fighting machine, a superior machine. I think someone needs to teach you a lesson or two."

"And you're volunteering?" the admiral asked.

"Bet your sweet ass," the sergeant said. "Here and now if you want it."

"Sergeant, you can draw a weapon a few nanoseconds faster than I," the admiral said evenly. "The force of a blow from your fist is a few pounds per square inch more powerful. You would beat me by less than one tenth of a second in a hundred-yard dash, but I'd catch you in the endurance race. We have the same construction, and that small extra power to your blow would inflict just a bit more damage to me than my blow would inflict to you—if you could hit me."

The sergeant moved forward. The admiral raised one hand. "But I would damage you, and it would take valuable time and resources to repair us. I suggest that the proper area of competition for us is in service. We must strive to be as valuable to the colony as possible."

"I do my work," the sergeant said. "I knew you were a coward."

"Sergeant, can a machine be a coward?"

The sergeant shifted his feet indecisively. Then, his face firm, he ordered, "Take that vehicle back to the pads."

"Perhaps that won't be necessary," the admiral said evenly. "I have said that I did not know the new regulations. However, you stated that I had merely to inform you of my need to use the vehicle. I inform you now. I am acting under orders from Commander Paul Warden, and it is necessary for me to use the vehicle in order to conserve time. You, Sergeant, have cost me time, time taken away from an important project. It is in the best interest of the colony that no further time be wasted."

The sergeant wanted, more than anything, to feel his fist make contact with the admiral's face. But he was forced to bow to what the admiral had said. Warden, of course, outranked him and was human and was, he knew, involved in important work evaluating the Eepera weapons. He knew the value of time and was fully aware of the constant threat posed by that powerful empire. One of his main duties was to use his detection ability to monitor the airspace over Columbia, extending upward into near space.

The admiral nodded, climbed back on his four-wheeler, and started the engine. The sergeant stood, helpless and frustrated. "We've got to settle this," he managed to gasp as the admiral pulled away slowly. "We've *got* to."

He was not the only one who desired an end to the friction. The admiral, as he drove to the ship and entered, making his way toward the central computer, knew that the sergeant's immaturity could cause a serious incident and that such an incident could happen at an inconvenient time. As he plugged his lead into the computer and, in effect, became a part of it, he resolved to do something to help the sergeant grow through his awkward period of arrogant youth.

EIGHT

Stoner McRae left the *Free Enterprise* early, satisfied that the provisioning of the ship was beginning in good style. The job was certainly in excellent hands, for both Amando Kwait and Dena Madden had arrived with a crawler loaded with freeze-dried produce from Amando's farms. The big African— who wasn't seen too much around the city, preferring to spend his time working in the fertile fields or exploring with the diminutive Dena at his side—had paused to talk a little about the quality of the food being loaded, and when he left, disappearing into the bowels of the ship to supervise the placement of the food into the lockers, Stoner noted with a little grin that Amando's arm went around the slim waist of the woman who, at first, had objected to being assigned to work with the botanist.

Romance. There was always something going on in Hamilton City, because it had been made clear that the single men and women of the colony had a responsibility to marry and bear children, thus populating the settlement. The selection committees had carefully balanced the male and female populations among those who were unattached. There had been marriages on board the *Spirit of America* and more marriages after settlement. Stoner wished he didn't have to attend another wedding for a year or so. Three weddings stood out in his mind: the captain and Jackie, Max and Grace, and, of course, the ceremony in which he neither lost a daughter nor gained a son but just saw a union that had been inevitable—both he and Betsy had agreed—from the day they took a twelve-year-old stowaway and his runty little Earth dog into their quarters on the *Spirit*. Funny, he still considered Clay Girard to be more son than son-in-law.

As the man who was responsible for finding the metals without which the colony would stagnate, he had been able to acquire one of those four-wheelers that Brand Roebling had designed for swift, individual transportation for the United States Army, the vehicles that were the most popular items on Omega now. He wasn't in any hurry, so he buzzed down by the bay and saw that some folks had taken time from work to enjoy the sun and the sea.

Romance. Tina Sells was on the beach with a gangling teenager who dogged her every step and ogled her scantily clad and beautiful body. Tagging behind was Lyndon West. Tina was Theresita West's constant baby-sitter. Stoner halted the four-wheeler and shook his head as he watched the boy catch and rip apart a crablike Omegan crustacean. His wife, Betsy, a teacher, had been involved in some of the evaluation tests given to Theresita's half-Eepera son, and Stoner had gotten the impression that she thought there might be a trace of the psychopath in little Lyndon. Well, he was glad the boy wasn't his problem.

He rode north, toward his home near Jumper's Run, still a favorite place for Clay and Cindy. He turned to more pleasant thoughts. Kids. He had not discussed having kids with Clay and Cindy yet. They were not quite nineteen, which was still young, too young to be married anyplace except on a frontier like Omega. But wouldn't it be fine when they did have children!

One of the attractions that had brought some younger couples to Omega was the social approval of having more than two children. On overpopulated Earth such behavior was scorned. Cindy was a healthy, sturdy girl, and medical science had done away with most of the adverse effects of childbearing, so it was possible that they'd have a herd of kids, a mixture of little towheads—if they took after his side of the family—from toddlers to teenagers.

Granddad. He wouldn't let them call him Gramps, or Pops, or Grandpa. He wouldn't insist on the total formality of Grandfather. Nope. Granddad.

He was in a fine old mood when he went into his home and heard Betsy call out from the kitchen, "Who dat?"

"Who dat who say who dat?" he yelled back.

"Who dat who say who dat when I say who dat?" Betsy asked, coming to give him a sugary kiss.

"Cake?" he asked, licking his lips.

"Derek and Mandy are coming for dinner," Betsy said.

"*Hmm.*"

"Why are you *hmming* me?"

Stoner had some information to impart. He had not mentioned his campaign to send the *Free Enterprise* out mining on distant planets. But now the news had to be broken, and to lessen the impact on Betsy, he had already asked Clay and Cindy to come for dinner. "The kids are coming too."

"Good. The more the merrier," Betsy said expansively. "You're home early."

"Had plans," Stoner said, laying a hand on one of Betsy's full breasts, "but cake takes precedence, I guess."

"It does when I'm just finishing mixing and getting ready to put it in the oven." She looked at her button watch and winked. "I can work you in in about ten minutes."

Later, holding her close, relaxed and fulfilled, loving the way she seemed to curve into the convexities of his body, Stoner said sleepily, "Who says old married sex is boring?"

"I dunno," she purred. "Who?"

"Some dummy," Stoner said.

"Well, there's a certain sameness. You do this, and I do that."

"But think how long it's taken us to perfect it. No wasted this or that."

She laughed. "I'm sold."

"Good. I'd hate to have to take the time to train a new one," Stoner said.

She jabbed him in the gut with an elbow, and he grunted, although he'd known it was coming and had tensed. She felt his solidity, the hard ridges of his abdominal muscles. "You're still as firm as a young boy," she commended.

"Who are you kidding?" Stoner asked, looking down.

"Your *muscles*, idiot."

"Oh."

He followed her into the kitchen after they had showered and dressed. The cake was sending out delicious smells. He beat the icing for her, eating only three or four tablespoonfuls before she jerked it out of his hand, telling him there wouldn't be enough for the cake.

"All right," she said as she spread the creamy icing onto the cake, "you can tell me now."

"Huh?" he asked, trying to look innocent.

"What's up?" she asked, looking at him and daring him to deny that something was on his mind.

"Oh, I just thought it would be nice to have the kids here for an evening, now that their fire has cooled to just below the temperature of a sun flare."

"Stoner . . ."

"Well . . ." he said, sounding somewhat like Dexter Hamilton.

"Well?"

"We'll be gone about three or four months at the most," he said, looking away, unable to meet her eyes.

"And where are we going?"

"Not we, honey," he said, putting his hands on her shoulders. "Not you. I know you're all involved with Derek in getting the new educational system set up and going."

"Where?" she asked grimly. "And who are we?"

"Out toward Vega," he answered.

"Damn you, Stoner," she said, eyes flashing, although she had to fight to hold back sudden tears.

"I'm the only one for the job," he explained. "We've got to have metals."

"Oh, hell, I know," she said. "We. You're talking about Clay?"

"And Cindy," he said. "Wouldn't dare separate them this early in their marriage. There'd be a total meltdown both on the planet and in space when they had been apart for a day and a night."

"Both of them?"

"Ito says Cindy is as good an astronavigator as he is, and with quicker reflexes."

"Stoner, what will *I* do?" she asked, and now the tears did come.

"Do your job, woman, just like the rest of us."

"Damn, damn, damn!" she said, and then wiped her face on her sleeve as the door chime announced an arrival. The door burst open, and the vibrancy of youthful excitement preceded Clay and Cindy into the kitchen.

"Hey, Stoner," Clay shouted, "I'm getting the *Belle Jennie* for the trip. She's the newest and hottest scout ship *Free Enterprise* brought out."

Clay paused and gulped, seeing Betsy's reddened eyes. "You did tell her?" he whispered.

"Good thing I did," Stoner mumbled.

"Well, the *Belle*'s the best we could get for the trip," Clay continued as Cindy looked at Betsy, full of concern, until Betsy smiled lopsidedly.

"Yeah, I'm pleased," Stoner said.

Cindy took her mother's hand. "I didn't know until today," she said. "I'd have told you."

"I know," Betsy replied.

"No one knew. No use worrying about something until we were sure it was going to happen," Stoner explained.

"Well, I'm sure the three of you can handle it," Betsy said. "Want to set the table, Cindy?"

"Sure, Mom. You men get out of the way."

Stoner and Clay went into the living room. Cindy looked at her mother carefully. "We'll be all right," she soothed. "And you will be too. I know you'll be lonely, but we'll be back before you know it. It's a great opportunity for me."

"I'm proud of you, honey. Ito says you learn quickly."

"Well," she said, shrugging, "sometimes my brain is about ready to burst."

"You'll get the ship there and back," Betsy assured her.

The door chimed again. "That's Derek," Cindy said, recognizing the voice when Stoner had let the guests in. "You'll have *him* for company, and you two seem to enjoy working together." She heard a laugh and recognized it as having come from Mandy Miller. She smiled. "Playing Cupid, Mom?"

"I believe in doing my part," Betsy said stoically.

"Still trying to make an honest woman of Mandy, huh?"

"She deserves a little bit of happiness."

"Yes, she's lost two men."

Betsy frowned.

Cindy laughed. "Don't give me the disapproving stare, Mother dear. You think the same as I. You're afraid if she stays unattached—"

"We do not gossip in this family," Betsy said.

"Not even among just us girls?" Cindy asked. "Mom, you're not the only one who notices the way she and Duncan look at each other. Isn't it too bad that the captain married Jackie just before Rocky got—"

"Think it, but don't say it," Betsy said.

"Okay. But that's what you think too."

"I'm afraid so," Betsy admitted.

Table talk began with Derek describing his reactions to the lovely countryside near Hamilton City, and when it was evident that he had seen that countryside in company with Mandy, Cindy and Betsy exchanged meaningful looks. Mandy, Cindy thought, looked a bit more lively than usual, with good color to her face and her eyes looking alive for a change.

Well, well, she thought.

Romance, Stoner McRae thought. But he felt that Derek and Mandy would make a good pair.

It was Clay who brought up the subject of the expedition, and after that, it dominated the conversation.

"Maybe we should apply, Mandy," Derek suggested, only half in jest. "I wouldn't mind seeing a bit more of this universe."

"Thank you, no," Mandy said. "I've seen all I want to see," and for a moment there was darkness in her eyes as she lowered her face and had one last bite of Betsy's cake.

II

THE BRAZILIANS

NINE

In her journal, Evangeline Burr considered the year 2040 to have been the true beginning of the Age of Space, for in that year three great starships had left Earth. Two of them, the *Spirit of America* and the Soviet Union's *Karl Marx*, had chosen a common destination, the neighboring stars 61 Cygni A and B. Evangeline liked to think it was more than chance that the American ship had landed safely, while the Soviet ship had been destroyed in space with only one survivor.

The third ship, the *Estrêla do Brasil*, had chosen an independent direction, so that the diverging paths into the stars had brought Captain Gilberto Francisco da Lisboa's starship to planetfall parsecs away from the Cygni stars. The *Estrêla*, built to prove that Brazil's industrial and technological might equaled that of the other two superpowers, had, like the American ship, found an apparent answer to that age-old question regarding whether or not intelligent life existed in abundance or if humankind was alone in the universe. True, the combined exploration of three starships had resulted in locating only three planets spinning in that narrow band of a star's influence that allowed the existence of water in a liquid form and the formation of tiny plant life in the oceans, with its resulting production of free oxygen. However rare, two of those three "life-zone" planets had been inhabited by intelligent humanoids. The third had been seeded with a deadly virus.

The captain of the *Estrêla do Brasil* was a product of a society that still was influenced by conquistadoral thinking. Due to that philosophy, the Brazilians had fought a small war with a race armed with spears, maces, and longbows, and to the shame of the memory of the captain—who happened to be a fatality in the final battle—the South Americans had lost.

And now it appeared that the new captain, Antonio Villa-Lobos, would suffer the next humiliation, for, after five years in space and the examination of a dozen stars for a possible new settlement, only three had had planetary systems, none habitable. The *Estrêla do Brasil* would soon be forced to admit defeat and make the long journey back to Earth.

The Brazilians who had survived war on the first planet visited by the *Estrêla do Brasil* were demoralized, restless, and often near mutiny. And yet Villa-Lobos, a mulish man who was determined to squeeze glory for himself from this ill-fated mission, sent the ship outward, ever outward, so that the black distances merged into a sameness, one working day like any other.

Antonio Villa-Lobos was not a scientist; he was a military man. The universe, the galaxy—both were continuing puzzles to him. When, as first officer, Villa-Lobos had stood proudly on the ship's command bridge as the tame scientists and technicians sent the *Estrêla* burning outward, away from Earth's orbit, it had all seemed so simple. There were so many stars up there, it would be child's play to find a planet that glowed a healthy blue from near space.

But the distances! Space was not, as it appeared from Earth, a nest of closely packed stars. Villa-Lobos's brain stored the figures: the nearest star to Earth was four-plus light-years away, and a light-year was no Sunday stroll, being on the order of almost six *trillion* miles. And four light-years' separation, Villa-Lobos had found, made stars close neighbors. His astronavigators talked in parsecs, a measure consisting of 3.26 light years.

True, trillions of miles could be covered by the

Estrêla do Brasil in the blink of an eye as the Shaw Drive—the design stolen by Brazil's very efficient intelligence service from the hapless Americans—did some semimagical trick, causing parsecs to vanish in an instant. It was then that the frustration began to grow, for the Brazilians still believed that Shaw Drive, used in close proximity to a body of planetary size, would cause a massive explosion that would destroy the starship and everything around it. (There were no Brazilian intelligence agents on Omega to discover that Max Rosen and Grace Monroe had proved otherwise, and the dictatorial atmosphere aboard the Brazilian ship eliminated any chance of experimentation by on-board scientists.) It took time to move the starship near enough to a planetary system to allow the astroscientists to make readings. Time and distance.

To make matters worse, the *Estrêla do Brasil* stank. The growing plants in her large green areas absorbed carbon dioxide and released oxygen. The regenerators gave plenty of oxygen to breathe and the air scrubbers ran constantly, but it stank. It seemed to Villa-Lobos that one would eventually get used to the ever-present odor, the staleness, but that didn't seem to be the case. People dreamed of standing on a beach, on a wide plain, on a mountain, drawing pure, fresh, sweet air into their lungs, but when they awoke, the staleness was there and their thoughts turned with sheer hatred to Villa-Lobos, their captain. And then, at the breakfast table was the same reconstituted food, molecules they had eaten before, many times, and their thoughts turned again to the captain.

In a junior officer's mess Major Bento Mattos, Army of Brazil, lifted a spoonful of what was intended to be *vatapá*, a native dish made with rice flour, fish, shrimp, and red peppers, sniffed it, grimaced, and then chewed with a look of distaste before swallowing. Bento Mattos, like most of the people of Brazil, was of mixed blood. His family history could trace his original Brazilian ancestry back to Italian immigrants, and the family

historians sometimes chose to overlook that the original
Italians had married mestizos, that there was *pardo*—
brown—in the family. He himself was a physical throw-
back to his distant ancestry, with his black, tightly
curled hair, strong, almost Roman nose, and the full
lips of his Mediterranean origins. He was, he knew, a
handsome man. He was an even six feet tall, and he
kept physically fit by regular workouts in the ship's
gyms.

Major Bento Mattos was third in command of the
army security forces aboard ship. He had narrowly escaped death while watching many of his soldiers die at
the hands of the savages on a planet for which the
Brazilians did not have a name. When Bento thought of
the planet, he mentally labeled it the Planet of the
Savages and burned with hatred for the traitor Astrud
Cabral, the anthropologist who had become a bleeding
heart and betrayed her own countrymen to the savages.
He felt that her death had been, if anything, too merci-
ful. Captain Villa-Lobos had ordered the traitor bound
and left under the *Estrêla*'s outboard rockets before
takeoff. Bento had no way of knowing that she had not
died, that at the last minute before the ship's rockets
were fired, she had been saved from cremation by her
native lover.

"Is it that bad?" The inquiry about Bento's breakfast came from a very attractive Brazilian air force lieutenant, one dressed in regulation blouse and skirt, her
bare legs showing the swarthy tone of her smooth skin.
She, Lieutenant Judit Alvarez, thought that Major Mattos
was indeed quite handsome. She had been just twenty-
one when the *Estrêla do Brasil* began her voyage, and
she still had the freshness of youth. She wore her hair
at regulation length, and it had enough body to hold
form, to swing delicately forward toward her high cheekbones, which told of her own mestizo blood. But Ger-
man blood had given her startlingly green eyes, wide
and well outlined with makeup, so her pretty face had

an appearance of continued enthusiasm. She did not, however, feel enthusiastic.

Bento's lip curled distastefully as he said, "Perhaps it is only that they did not bathe Portinari before he was recycled."

"You're very terrible," Judit said, lowering the spoon that she'd lifted toward her mouth. Portinari was the latest to die. She did not know for a fact that human bodies fed into the recycler became a direct part of the food they ate. It was said that such material was used only to nourish the green plants, but just the idea took away what little appetite she had for the synthasized food. The synthashrimp in the so-called *vatapá* had a rubbery consistency.

"Sorry," Bento said. "No, it isn't that bad, really."

One had to eat. Judit closed her eyes as she chewed, as if that would cut off her sense of taste as well as her vision. It did not.

"I have been promised a change in the time of my watch," Judit said, after they had eaten in silence for a while. Bento smiled at her. "It will mean that I will have to do twelve hours straight in order to change watches."

"I will rub your back and legs to banish the tiredness," he offered. For a year now, ever since he had convinced Judit to share his quarters with him, they had been on conflicting watches. It meant that one of them was sleeping at least half the time the other was awake, and it meant that their lovemaking was often inhibited by tiredness.

"*Ummm,*" Judit said. "I will hold you to that promise."

Judit Alvarez was on the engineering staff of the *Estrêla do Brasil*. Her duties took place toward the nonrotating core of the *Estrêla*'s giant wheel, where the artificial gravity generated by the spinning of the wheel was almost nonexistent. She primarily spent her on-duty hours monitoring the ship's life-support systems, but she was a key member of the team that activated the Shaw Drive.

Hours later, when Judit finished pulling two watches in a row, she was tired. She would have twelve free hours, and she'd need to sleep for at least six of them. She had found that she needed less sleep on board ship, perhaps because spending her six on-duty hours in gravity only one tenth Earth's normal did not cause her to burn energy as swiftly. Bento had just come off his watch and was in the shower when she entered the quarters. She quickly stripped off her uniform and fell into bed, covering her head with the sheets to discourage Bento from disturbing her.

When she awoke, he was watching an old movie, using earphones so the sound would not awaken her. He wore only a pair of battered old gym pants. Seeing the nicely toned muscles of his torso and his manly profile, she felt an immediate melting and then the inevitable moment of guilt. Although she was a self-confirmed member of Brazil's new order and accepted the government's view that religion was the opiate of the people, she had been indelibly marked by her early training in Catholicism. What she did with Bento was her choice, but deep down inside her, that old voice still cried, "Wrong, wrong."

Bento caught movement out of the corner of his eye as she sat up, letting the coverlet fall to reveal her firm, youthful breasts. "The sleeping beauty awakes," he said.

She stretched languorously, smiling an open invitation. He came to her, put his hands on her breasts, kissed her, then pulled away and stood upright. It was unusual for either of them to withhold when the other indicated desire, so she knew immediately that his thoughts were elsewhere.

"The astronomers have detected free oxygen and water vapor in the atmosphere of the second planet," he said.

She got out of bed and drew a lounging coat over her nakedness. "So?"

They had been cruising at sublight speed toward the planetary system of yet another sun for months. They had more months of boring travel ahead before they could go into orbit around the planet.

"You show as much enthusiasm as the others," he said. "During my watch I was ordered to spread the word that this planet shows great promise. When I told this news I met blank stares, or comments such as yours."

"Well, it is something," she conceded. "How I would like to stand under a kind sun and breathe real air."

Bento sat down and looked at her as she walked to the dressing table and began to brush her hair. "How would you assess morale in the engineering section?"

She didn't answer for a moment. "No worse, no better than in other sections. We are all service people, and we understand the necessities of the situation better than some of the settlers. At the moment I don't think anyone would advise giving up."

"And if the planet toward which we are headed proves unsatisfactory?"

She shrugged. "I can only speak for myself. I feel imprisoned. I long for open spaces and fresh air."

"Would you be disappointed enough to oppose the decisions of the commander of the ship?"

A chill swept through her. "Mutiny?"

"I personally think that the emotional climate for even so drastic an action is growing. Have you visited the sick bay? There are dozens of patients there suffering from various forms of stress-related ailments. Have you noticed that there has not been a baby born in the past year? Women choose to prevent or terminate pregnancy. In the past year we have had to control dozens of incidents of violence. There are more than twenty people in the ship's brig on various charges—dereliction of duty, insubordination, and"—he paused to give his statement emphasis—"ten of them for actively advocating an overthrow of authority in order to take the ship back to Earth."

"And if the planet ahead proves to be uninhabitable, what will your position be?" she asked.

"My father fought with Carlos da Lisboa from the Matto Grosso to Brasilia," Bento said. "He received medals of honor from da Lisboa's own hand. Before I left home for the academy, my father told me that he did not approve of everything that da Lisboa had done, but he said, 'Son, give him a chance. He is a great dictator, and he brought equality and opportunity to everyone.' I suppose I feel the same way about our captain. Villa-Lobos inherited a terrible situation after our first captain was killed. But as he is our new captain, I pledge him my honor. This arm will fight against anyone who questions the captain's authority."

"But wouldn't you like to go home?" Judit asked.

"Not now. I would like to make planetfall. I would like to have a role in planting a small part of Brazil on the virgin soil of a beautiful planet, to help nurture that planting into something that will enhance the greatness of my country."

"And if our country no longer exists?" She felt herself go pale. That possibility was seldom voiced.

"Then it is more important than ever for us to find a new world and make it the new Brazil."

"We found a world," she reminded him, "and we looted and killed."

He whirled to face her, his face showing quick anger. "You sound like the traitor Cabral. Would you have had us adapt to the savagery of the inhabitants? Would you, as she did, become breeding stock for savages and have the entire colony absorbed into the native population in a matter of just a few generations?"

"I can't help but feel that there could have been some middle course," Judit said evenly. She smiled. "Such talk is heavy going for me, my love. We have time for a workout in the gym, or—"

"I like the sound of that *or*," he said. "Then we'll see if there's still time for exercise in the vertical plane."

The *Estrêla do Brasil* was essentially a germfree environment. Medical advances on Earth had exterminated the diseases that had once scourged humankind, sending germ after germ, virus after virus, into extinction to join the AIDS virus, which had been effectively eliminated from Earth by the end of the twentieth century. In the closed confines of the ship, virucides had wiped out even the relatively few rapidly mutating cold viruses and viruses of like type that had been brought aboard, inevitably, by the crew and settlers. In spite of this, however, the sick bays were overcrowded. Psychosomatic ailments that mimicked a variety of diseases were treated with tranquilizers and soft, commonsense counseling by members of the medical staff. The epidemic of stress-related maladies came to a peak in the weeks before the *Estrêla do Brasil* went into a low but stable orbit around a world whose great oceans gave her the wonderful, beautiful, and astoundingly appealing blue of a water world.

Now the sick bays emptied. The viewscreens were all in use as people crowded around to see the swirls of cloud, the overtinge of blue, the darker outlines of land masses. The ship's instruments observed, measured, and recorded. Men and women bent to their tasks of analyzing the results, and the results pleased them, inspiring wide, toothy smiles.

"Beautiful, oh, how beautiful," Judit Alvarez enthused, standing before the viewscreen with Bento Mattos during their off-watch time. "I will wade the beach of that ocean. We will take long hikes in the forests. We will *breathe*."

There was no sign of intelligent life. The ship's big eyes scanned every square mile of land area from polar orbit as the planet obligingly rotated to reveal her secrets, her waters and mountains, plains and forests. Reports from the scout ships were glowingly positive. The atmosphere was heavy with pure, sweet oxygen.

The seas were rife with life, devoid of any pollution. The forests had life, as did the plains. Life seemed to be the rule instead of the exception on any world where free water and oxygen existed. But there were, apparently, no bipedal toolmakers, no armed savages, no sign of intelligent building. The *Estrêla do Brasil* had found a home.

Captain Antonio Villa-Lobos, tired of reading report after overly cautious report stating that the world below was apparently suitable for habitation, called a conference of department heads. Major Mattos's two superior officers had availed themselves of opportunity and the privileges of rank to be off the ship, riding as observers with scout-ship pilots who were scooping up samples of air, water, and soil for analysis on board ship. Bento was at the meeting early, representing the army and security. He found a seat at the back of the captain's mess and watched the scientists file in, one and two at a time. There was a general air of well-being, many smiles, and animated comparison of findings.

Captain Villa-Lobos was in formal uniform when he entered. He stood, frowning out at the gathered department heads. "How long?" he growled. "How long must I wait for you to give me the information I need?"

There was no answer.

"You say you *think*. You say you *believe*. You say *it seems that*. Are you scientists or are you frightened children?" His finger stabbed toward a distinguished senior member of the medical staff. "You. You have searched. You have tested hundreds of samples, and you have found no frightful germ, nothing more than the soil bacteria. And yet you say we must wait. Wait for what?"

"Captain," the medical chairman said, "we must be sure. If we land and there is some disease against which we have no natural immunity, no countermeasures—"

"Have you found such a threat?" Villa-Lobos roared, and the chairman was silent. "Nor have you found any ogres in the forests. Just animals. We can handle animals. Can there be any doubt now that this planet is devoid of intelligent life?" He glared at another man, who shook his head.

"Good," Villa-Lobos said. "I am tired of waiting. I am tired of dealing with frightened people. I have selected a landing site."

There was a stir among those gathered. Villa-Lobos motioned, and an aide pushed buttons to lower a viewscreen. A computerized representation of the planet appeared on the screen. For a moment the captain watched the simulated movement of a living world, and then he motioned for the globe on the screen to be stilled. He pointed. "There."

The landmass indicated was in the southern hemisphere. It was a continent with approximately the land area of North America, shaped roughly like a flattened circle. Villa-Lobos nodded to his aide, and the image was enlarged, focusing on the west-central coastline. A magnificent, winding bay penetrated hills, reminding Bento Mattos of the geography of Rio de Janeiro. Bento nodded. It seemed an excellent choice. The climate, he knew from having listened to the scientists, would be much the same as that of Rio de Janeiro, and, in all, the continent had many of the features of his native country: wide rivers, jungles, *llanos*, and snowcapped mountains inland.

"Concentrate your exploration on that continent," Villa-Lobos ordered. "I want detailed surveys of the land around this bay."

"We will need time to test local vegetation, the availability of water, and so on," the chairman of medicine said.

"Three days," Villa-Lobos ordered.

"A week, Captain," the chairman said respectfully. "We need at least a week."

"A week, then!" the captain shouted, throwing up his hands. "No more. In one week I myself will land on the beach of that bay and personally test the air if I do not have your clearance by then."

Just as Villa-Lobos was turning to go, the communicator carried by his aide registered a call from the bridge. The aide listened, hurried to Villa-Lobos's side, and whispered in his ear. The captain looked around the room, saw Bento's peaked military cap, and shouted, "Major Mattos, come with me."

Bento had to trot to catch up with the captain and his aide. He was on Villa-Lobos's heels when the captain entered the bridge and went immediately to the communications bank. "Where is this madman?" he demanded.

A screen showed the outline of a northern hemisphere landmass. A blinking red dot was moving swiftly inland from the sea. Bento recognized the dot as a signal sent by the homing device on a scout ship.

"His name?" Villa-Lobos demanded.

"Lieutenant Heitar Lobato," the communications officer said. "The observer is his wife, Lieutenant Marta Lobato. I play for you his last transmission." He pushed a button, and a male voice, somewhat strained, filled the space of the bridge.

"*Say again,* Estrêla."

The voice of the communications officer, amplified, said, "You are out of position. Check your computer and return to your assigned course."

"*I do not read you,* Estrêla."

"Radio trouble?" Bento asked the communications officer.

"Wait," the officer said.

The communications officer inclined his head toward the recorder: "You are below your assigned altitude, Lieutenant Lobato. You are out of your assigned area."

"*Please, Heitar,*" a female voice pleaded.

"*Be silent, Marta,*" Lobato said.

The communications officer turned off the recorder and looked up at the captain. "He has refused to acknowledge further transmissions."

"May I?" Bento asked, reaching for the communicator. He pressed the transmit button and said, "Lieutenant Heitar Lobato, this is Major Mattos speaking. You are in violation of orders. I order you to acknowledge your orders and return to your assigned duties."

The red dot on the screen blinked out.

"He has disconnected the transponder," the communications officer reported, incredulous. "His intention seems to be to fly among the mountains and lose himself."

The communications officer pushed buttons, and a faint blip appeared, blinked out, then reappeared. "I have him on metal detection now, but he can evade the detector by flying among the peaks and valleys of the mountains."

"But why?" Bento asked. "Has this man showed signs of instability before? Is he in any trouble?"

"No more instability than others," the communications officer said, with a look up at the glowering face of the captain. "He has not been in trouble."

"Until now," the captain responded darkly. "I want the ship back. I want that man punished."

"Sir," Bento said, standing at attention, "with all respect, sir. We can find the ship at any time once we are planetside."

"The man is a deserter," Villa-Lobos said coldly.

"Sir," Bento said, "it is the stress. He has broken under the stress, that is all."

"He's always been a good man, sir," the communications officer added.

"I want him, now." Villa-Lobos seized the communicator. "All scouts, this is the captain speaking. I want you to assemble . . ." He gave the coordinates of the area into which Lobato's ship had disappeared. "Search for and locate scout ship number five. Give the pilot a chance to follow you, escorted, to the *Estrêla*. If he disobeys orders, destroy him and the ship."

"Sir!" the communications officer protested. "We can hardly afford to lose a scout."

"We can *not* afford to condone mutiny and desertion," Villa-Lobos said quietly.

Heitar Lobato, one of the youngest pilots, thought of his ship as the *Marta*, although policy allowed for no private naming and referred to Lobato's ship only as number five. His marriage to Marta Ramos had been the first such ceremony to be performed aboard the *Estrêla do Brasil*. Marta had forgotten to take her injections—or at least she said that was what had happened—and now she had a three-month-old fetus growing inside her lovely little body.

Simply put, Heitar had had enough. He was sick of breathing the stinking air aboard ship, repulsed by eating recycled carbohydrates and protein. He was sure in his own mind that he would go mad if he had to spend one more hour aboard the *Estrêla*. He had been flying low and slow over a beautiful, fruitful world for days now, waiting for the order to land, an order that had never come. And each time he had to take Marta back to the stinking closeness of the ship, she had to rush for a sanitary facility and he could hear her straining, gagging, as she vomited up whatever was in her stomach and then continued to retch even after she was empty.

"We must go back, Heitar," Marta implored as her husband held the scout low and fast, zigzagging up a narrow valley toward the snow-covered mountains. "Please, Heitar."

"No. We will not go back. You know that no more than three hours ago we opened the hatch. We breathed *air*. You have not been sick since."

"It is natural for me to be sick at this stage of my pregnancy," she said. "Please, I beg you. Turn the ship. Climb out of this valley and I will tell the captain that you were momentarily disoriented. He will not punish you if we go back now."

"We will find a place, and we will land. When the ship comes down, if it ever does, then we will go back."

"They will come for us. You know Villa-Lobos. He will take this as mutiny."

"He will have to find us, then," Heitar said, swooping the ship up and over a line of tall trees on a ridge.

Something flashed by, high, and was gone. Marta knew that it had been a ship. "They're close," she warned. She tried to pull Heitar's hands off the controls. "We must go back," she cried, tears coming as he pushed her hands away with his superior strength.

"Number five, number five," a voice said from the ship's communicator. "Lieutenant Lobato, we have you in sight. You are ordered to return to the *Estrêla*."

Heitar uttered an obscenity and sent the ship curving around an outthrusting bluff. Marta gasped as he narrowly missed the bluff on the opposite side of the narrowing valley.

"Heitar," the voice said, "I have orders to shoot you down. I don't want to do that."

"That's Jorge," Marta said. "He's our friend. We must go up."

"I don't think Jorge will shoot us," Heitar said. "But if he wants to shoot, he will have to catch us first."

The ship soared, leaped a ridge with the boughs of alien trees swishing in the wind of her passage, then ducked down into a canyon that angled upward, upward. Great bluffs of oddly colored rocks made a blur as Marta looked out the port. She caught the sight of snow ahead.

"Heitar, have you gone totally crazy?" the voice asked from the communicator. "Listen to me. Slow down. Gain altitude."

"I will breathe," Heitar vowed, his eyes wide, darting back and forth as he threw the scout into a hard port turn to avoid smashing into the rocks.

A blinding flash of a laser weapon came from a hundred yards in front.

"Oh, God," Marta moaned.

"He was not even close," Heitar told her. "Jorge would not shoot us."

The next laser impact was just to their starboard side. Blinded by the glare, Heitar raised his hand to rub his eyes, saw the bend in the canyon coming, threw the ship to port directly into the top of a lone, tall, oddly needled alien tree. He tried to control the sudden change of attitude in the ship, but number five impacted directly into the bald, blank face of a stone cliff.

Two scouts zoomed up and came to hover over the site as smashed bits of metal and rock showered down hundreds of feet to the canyon's bottom.

"*Estrêla*," the pilot named Jorge said into his communicator. "Number five will not be coming back."

The hydrogen-powered scout ship, weighing just over ten tons, had disintegrated. The resulting explosion of unused fuel had been quite visible to those on the bridge of the *Estrêla*. Captain Villa-Lobos grunted in satisfaction. "A commendation for the pilot who followed my orders," he said, assuming that number five had been destroyed by laser blasts from one of the pursuing scouts.

"Why?" the communications officer asked softly. "Why would he do such a foolish thing, now that we are so near, so near to being alive again?"

"I want all scouts aboard," Villa-Lobos ordered. "We will have no more incidents." He waited until the communications officer had sent the orders, and until the red dots on the screen indicated that all scouts were climbing to orbit altitude on the way home to the ship. "Come with me, Mattos," he said.

Bento followed the captain into his quarters. Villa-Lobos whirled to face him. "In a time of crisis, when they were needed, where were your superiors?"

"The colonel and the general felt that it was desirable for them to have an advance look at the planet, sir," Bento answered.

"So, they were joyriding when I needed them," the captain said.

Bento did not express his opinion. He failed to see

how either the colonel or the general could have done more than he himself had done.

"When they come aboard, confine them to quarters," Villa-Lobos said. "Inform them that they are deprived of rank and that you are now the senior army officer."

Bento's face flushed. "Sir, may I speak?" Villa-Lobos nodded grimly. "I don't know, sir, how the soldiers will behave. They are very fond of—"

"I don't care what the soldiers think," Villa-Lobos shouted, and there was something in his eyes that prevented Bento from speaking further. He saluted, did a snappy about-face, and left the captain's quarters thinking that it had not only been Lieutenant Heitar Lobato who had been crazed by the years of inactivity aboard ship. The army contingent was the only armed force on the *Estrêla*. Its members were fiercely loyal to General Joaquim de Assis, and no one knew better than Bento Mattos that it was only de Assis's force of personality, his rapport with the men, that had limited dissatisfaction among the men to mere grumbling. Many of their comrades had died following Captain da Lisboa's orders. They had wanted to stay on the Planet of the Savages and avenge the deaths of their comrades with the weapons of the *Estrêla do Brasil*, including thermonuclear blasts.

Bento was at the scout pods when the ships began to land, one by one. General de Assis was on the third ship to land. "Sir," Bento said, "an urgent matter. If I may talk with you and the colonel in privacy?"

"Of course, Bento," de Assis said genially.

They waited until Colonel Carlos Luz joined them. Bento led the way to the general's quarters. Luz went immediately to the private bar and poured three drinks. Among the three senior officers, in privacy, there was little display of rank.

"It's a beauty of a world, Bento," Luz toasted, hoisting his glass.

"A scout pilot went berserk," Bento said. "Villa-

Lobos ordered him to be killed. He then ordered me to confine you, sir, and the colonel, to your quarters and tell you that you are stripped of rank."

Bento drank, allowing his words to sink in. Luz's face went pale, then red with anger. De Assis pouted, tasting the good Brazilian brandy. "I must say, Bento, that you followed your orders gracefully."

"Sir," Bento said, "I am merely informing you of the captain's orders. I have no intention of trying to carry them out."

De Assis removed his coat and tossed it onto a chair. "Oh, but you have already done so, Bento. And I have just stripped myself of rank."

"Sir?"

"The egomaniac has gone over the edge this time, Joaquim," Luz said. "It's time we put him in his place."

"Gentlemen, I am tired," de Assis said, sinking into a contour chair. "Our glorious leader is still captain of this ship, and we are still under the rule of Brazil as long as we are aboard this ship."

Luz's glowering face brightened. "As long as we're aboard."

"Exactly," de Assis said.

"Now hear this," the communicator boomed. "This is the captain speaking."

De Assis closed his eyes. Luz and Bento looked toward the speakers, not knowing what to expect.

"All personnel are to take their assigned positions for landing," Villa-Lobos's voice said. "We are at fifteen minutes and counting for retrofire."

"The son of a bitch is going to take us down before the eggheads give the okay," Luz said. "We've got to stop him, Joaquim."

"Didn't you find our new world to be beautiful?" de Assis asked.

"Yes, but—"

"It's all right, Luz," de Assis soothed. "The scientists are old nannies. It is a good world—a clean, healthy world. Let us not discourage our good captain from giving us a chance to get an early start toward building our new world, under the command of the army of Brazil."

De Assis opened his eyes. "I hadn't told you, Bento. We'll be taking over once we're on the ground."

"Sir!" Bento snapped, grinning, feeling much better. "I therefore defer to your authority, resign my promotion, and await my orders."

"I suppose, Bento, that you should go to your station and strap in. That lovely lady of yours is going to be throwing a switch in less than fifteen minutes, and the retrorockets will give us quite a kick."

In the blackness of space the *Estrêla do Brasil* rotated on her horizontal axis. Stabs of flame from twenty-five percent of her huge rockets burned the darkness, then subsided. She rotated again. Half an hour later, as her mass of thousands of tons obeyed the pull of the planet's gravity, her leading edge began to glow in the buildup of heat as metal pushed through the thickening atmosphere at several times the speed of sound. The rockets fired again, and the ship's forward motion altered, became more vertical, rockets firing in careful, balanced sequence. Inside, over a thousand people lay on their couches or sat in their chairs and felt the g forces build as the massive ship slowed, fell, slowed, and fell again.

Judit Alvarez's station during landing was at the computer screen. The firing sequences were automatic, governed by the computer, which, of course, could react much more swiftly than a mere human. Her job was to monitor the firings, to watch the sequence of glows on the control panel. Beside the main screen a smaller screen showed a layer of soft-looking, billowy white clouds. Then the screen was milky as the massive ship plunged through, and suddenly there was the blue of ocean, the green of land, a lovely, winding bay, and hills.

The computer's voice was feminine, speaking in the soft, musical vowels of Brazil's modified Portuguese.

The voice was calling out altitude: "One hundred thousand feet, ninety thousand feet . . ."

Judit, seduced by the beauty of the landscape below, took her eyes off the monitor. Her head jerked back as the ship lurched and an alarm pulsed with a shrill, blood-chilling sound. The speed of the ship's fall increased, jerking out of the optimum landing attitude so that she was falling with one edge of her massive wheel tilted downward. The thrust of air against her tilted bottom was drifting her toward the sea.

"Systems failure," Judit reported, surprised to hear the cool, matter-of-fact statement coming from her own lips. She did not feel cool and matter-of-fact. "Rocket pods twenty-nine through forty-four." And even as she spoke, the long hours of training sent her fingers flying. She overrode the computer and began to punch the manual firing buttons for the rockets whose engines had shut off. She sensed, as if in her bones, the minute jarring caused by the firing of rockets and felt the ship jerk slightly, then begin to regain landing attitude. Even as she worked, the computer was reducing thrust on rockets on the opposite perimeter of the giant ship.

Slowly the ship righted.

"Fifty thousand feet," the slightly metallic voice of the computer said.

"Instituting emergency correcting program," Judit said. Her fingers flew. The computer was now back in control of the ship, and the deceleration forces were building again as all rockets fired to reduce the speed the ship had picked up during the malfunction.

Judit's eyes flew to the fuel indicators. The rockets were being forced to consume more fuel than had been originally programmed. There was no great danger of running out of fuel, but it was critical to conserve, for she had to admit that there was the possibility that the ship might have to leave the beautiful, blue planet whose surface was coming up toward her so rapidly and continue the search.

"Good, good," said the chief engineer from his

cubicle where he was overseeing the entire landing operation.

"Thirty-five thousand feet," the computer said.

"Speed of descent nominal," Judit reported, her voice belying the swiftness of her heartbeat.

Other officers reported that all systems were nominal.

"Twenty thousand feet," the computer said.

Then the rockets numbered twenty-nine to forty-four in the bank cut off again. Judit refired them manually.

"Ten thousand feet," the unperturbed computer said.

The ship had not yet righted itself when another bank of rockets malfunctioned. The *Estrêla* lurched and took on a wobble. Judit punched the computer override and began to play the console, her fingers flying from one blinking red button to the next. A rocket or a group of rockets would fire, and she would fight for control, calling on the computer for aid in balancing the ship in landing attitude.

On the bridge Antonio Villa-Lobos had a splendid view of the landing site he had chosen. The ship was to land in a small meadow about three miles inland from the cliff-lined coast. To the north the land sloped gently downward into a cozy, beautiful valley that merged with the winding, blue, picture-book bay in smooth, white, sandy beaches.

"What are you doing?" Villa-Lobos screamed at his bridge crew when the *Estrêla* lurched and tilted and her rate of fall increased even as she drifted eastward toward the cliff and the sea. Then the engineering reports began to come in, in calm, reassuring voices, and the ship righted herself. He knew, of course, that control of the ship was now in the hands of the engineering crew and the computer, and that his bridge crew were, in effect, merely passengers and observers.

"Can't you handle even a simple landing procedure?" he asked in an icy voice.

And then, suddenly, the ship began an obscene dance, tilting to one side and then the other. The control board showing rocket firings began to blink and cavort like a game machine, and Villa-Lobos lost his footing and sat heavily on the deck.

In the engineering spaces the crew was performing as the professionals they were. Judit's movements showed that she had been trained well and had unusually swift reaction time. She was, in effect, flying the *Estrêla* manually, with some assist from the computer. Perspiration beaded her forehead.

"Five thousand feet," the serene voice of the computer said, as the faulty bank of rockets cut out once more and the *Estrêla* knifed down in a gliding swoop that covered three thousand feet before Judit could correct.

A glance at the screens on either side set Judit's heart to pounding faster. To the east she saw the sheer cliffs, four hundred feet high, and below them the incredible blue of the sea. The ship, tilting toward the cliffs, was sliding inevitably eastward. In desperation she cried out, "Fire all steering rockets in quadrant three."

"Aye, aye," said the officer to her right, and the ship quivered as the rockets fired. The slide toward the cliffs slowed. The *Estrêla* was, once again, fighting back to landing attitude.

The computer began to count off the altitude in hundreds of feet as the *Estrêla* dropped below one thousand feet. It was, Judit saw, going to be very close. There was no longer any choice of landing site. The terrain at the top of the cliff was a mixture of boulders and low-growing vegetation. Now and then an erosion gulley showed raw earth and stone.

"Four hundred, three hundred, two hundred," the computer counted.

The *Estrêla* quivered. All her rockets were roaring at maximum thrust in an effort to make the moment of touchdown coincide with the moment of zero fall rate.

The steering rockets were still blasting, but in atmosphere they did not have the power to move the vast mass of the ship. Judit thought for the last chilling seconds that the *Estrêla* was going to drift over the brink of the cliffs and, catching the western edge of the wheel on the land, tumble out of control into the sea.

"Sixty, fifty, forty," the computer sang out happily.

With an explosion that thudded through the hull, one of the tortured rockets in section twenty-nine through forty-four destructed. Like distant artillery fire the bank exploded, one and two at a time, the failures feeding on the fires of others. People died even before the *Estrêla* tilted inland, all lift lost on the western side, and smashed into the earth at an angle of about twenty degrees.

Judit's fingers were pushing buttons even as she realized that not only would the *Estrêla* never fly again, but that within seconds she herself would probably be dead.

The ship impacted with a force that smashed the edge of the wheel inward. A great rent in her hull spread toward the control bridge at the center of the ship. Yet the *Estrêla* seemed to settle slowly, for there were still rockets firing on the side next to the cliffs.

Surprisingly, Judit's monitors were still working. She could look at one screen and see directly down into the blue sea, where great waves humped and then flung themselves in a smashing of white against the unyielding stone of the cliffs.

In all the years in space the *Estrêla* had not heard the eerie wail of an alarm that had only one meaning: Abandon ship. Had it occurred in space, a selected few would have run toward the scout-ship pods; for the majority, there would have been no hope. Now the alarm wailed.

Bento Mattos was at his assigned landing station in that section of the wheel that extended a full quarter of her mass over the sheer cliffs as the *Estrêla*, moaning her death song, sank on the still-firing rockets.

An oxygen tank burst as the explosion of rockets continued. The oxygen-fed fires rushed inward and, as luck would have it, found a direct path to the control bridge just as Antonio Villa-Lobos opened the door in panic, the sound of the abandon-ship alarm screaming in his ears. He stepped into a holocaust of flame and had time only to scream once. But that single intake of breath drew fire into his lungs.

The chief engineer had no contact with a large portion of the ship, since the fires and explosions had destroyed whole sections of the monitoring and communications equipment. He issued crisp orders. His crew began to try to save at least parts of the ship, moving efficiently to cut off all rockets, scram the nuclear generating plant, and activate manual and automatic fire-control measures.

"Chief, the fire is eating along the perimeter, in the fuel bays," Judit reported. "The bulkheads are not holding."

That was evident to anyone who had a basic knowledge of the structure of the ship. Every few seconds the *Estrêla* jumped or quivered, and there was the sound of a distant explosion as another fuel bay was breached.

"People are already getting out," another officer reported, flashing onto the big screen a scene being recorded by a sensor set at the *Estrêla*'s highest central point.

Judit glanced up and saw streams of screaming, panicked settlers running away from the *Estrêla*. The high sensor rotated, and the eastern edge of the *Estrêla* was a sea of fire. Even as Judit watched, the rounded dome of the control bridge seemed to swell and then burst into explosion.

"Fire-control automatics are operating," an officer reported.

"Chief," Judit said, "that fire at the core will reach the weapons storage area soon."

The chief nodded. "All right," he said, "everyone out. If there's anything left after all the fuel bunkers go, we can come back and salvage it."

There was no panic among the engineering crew.

They moved out in an orderly manner, many of them taking time to gather weapons or personal items. The evacuation route led them down a broad corridor. The ventilators were still running, bringing with their airflow a scent of burning rocket fuel.

A group of settlers came running down the corridor, going the wrong way. The chief engineer yelled at them to stop and, with the help of his crew, managed to turn the flood and get it going the right way toward an outside hatch.

Judit turned away from the broad corridor, angling toward the portion of the ship that hung over the cliffs, for Bento's section and station were there. He took his responsibilities seriously and would have no way of knowing that the fires were so badly out of control, that the starship would be ripped soon by the blast of the main magazine. Then the explosions in the outer ring of fuel bunkers would continue until they circled the ship and very probably ate inward to ignite the oxygen-storage tanks.

She ran lightly, glad, for once, of the long sessions in the gym, for she was now in gravity that felt just a bit more than Earth's normal.

Another group of settlers joined her, coming from a side corridor. "No, no," she screamed at them, "you can't get off this way. You must go there." She pointed. A few took her advice. Most, however, continued toward the edge of the wheel that jutted out into empty air over the cliffs.

She heard loud voices ahead and increased her pace. Some of Bento's men were herding settlers back from the corridors leading to the suspended area of the ship.

"Where is Major Mattos?" she yelled, seizing a soldier's arm.

"Chemistry lab," the soldier said, jerking away to wrestle with a panicked man who was trying to get past.

Judit fought her way down the corridor, her uniform giving her passage past the soldiers who were trying to steer the settlers toward a safe exit. The door to the chemistry lab was open, and from it she heard screams of agony. With her heart leaping she entered. Bento was playing a water hose over a writhing, screaming woman on the floor. The woman's clothing was steaming, and parts of the cloth and her skin were being eaten away.

The floor of the lab was wet and hot. Judit looked down and saw the soles of her service shoes beginning to smoke. Then she saw a large, broken container, and the label caused her to suck in her breath. The screams of the woman who writhed on the floor were heartbreaking, but there was only one thing to do. She drew her laser pistol and put her hand on Bento's arm. He turned, his eyes wild, saw the laser in her hand, and started to form a question as Judit aimed the beam of her weapon to slice into the dying woman's forehead. It was over in a moment.

"God, no," Bento moaned.

"She could not live." Judit pointed to the container.

"I know, it's acid. I was washing it off," Bento said.

"There was no hope for her," Judit said. "You must get your men off, Bento. There is little time."

Bento seemed dazed. She looked down. His shoes were steaming. She led him out of the lab. "Remove your shoes. Be careful not to touch them where the soles are wet." She did the same, then they moved down the corridor. The men had succeeded in moving the settlers in the correct direction. Several fuel bunkers exploded at once, and the *Estrêla* groaned and shifted. For a moment Judit feared that the ship was going to slide off the cliff.

"We're going to lose the whole ship?" Bento asked as she led him on the run toward the exit, far away.

"There'll be general damage when the magazine explodes," she said, "localized damage when the heat begins to ignite all the hydrogen engines of the crawlers, scout ships, and stationary equipment. If the explosions don't breach the container of the nuclear reactor, we can come back and salvage something."

"We must go back and help settlers get off," Bento said.

"There's no time," she yelled at him as another group of bunkers exploded, throwing both of them sprawling.

"Close," he said. "All right, let's get the hell out of here."

She knew the ship well. She had surveyed and checked every space, every corridor. She led him down shortcuts he had not known existed, and then, with Judit panting and leading the way, they burst out of an open hatch and were blown forward by a great gust of air as bunkers erupted close behind them. He scrambled to his feet, lifted her, and they ran as the entire world seemed to go up behind them in smoke and fire.

They leaped one erosion gulley and then came to a deeper, wider one. The chief engineer crouched at the bottom.

"Judit," the chief shouted. "Down here."

Judit leaped down. She looked up and saw Bento leap, and even as he fell toward her, there was a roaring flash behind him as the *Estrêla* was gutted by the largest explosion of all.

She had to see. She crawled up the bank and peered over the edge. It seemed that the *Estrêla* loomed directly atop her, so near were they. Flames engulfed the ship from rim to rim. A man stumbled toward her, his clothing aflame, his mouth open in soundless agony before he fell. And then the magazine went, the force of it lifting the ship, and in a sea of roaring flames, the air filled with flying debris and smoke making the day dim, the great starship grated metal on rock as she slid slowly, slowly, to fall into the sea.

The cliff was only four hundred feet high. The huge starship would, Judit felt, lie there, one edge in the sea, while her upper lip, the most damaged one, leaned on the cliff. But Judit had no way of knowing that the ship had slid onto an ancient volcanic plateau, and that the sheer cliff that extended four hundred feet above the water extended downward for well over a mile.

"Bento, look!" Judit gasped.

He came to her side. Around them things began falling. The air was heated by the *Estrêla*'s flames. Neither noticed, for the *Estrêla* was still sliding.

Judit ran down the length of the erosion gulley, which ended with a sheer drop off the cliffs. Bento stood with her, each with one hand clinging to rocks as they leaned over to witness the crushed edge of the *Estrêla*'s wheel slowly sink into roiled, steaming water.

An explosion showered them with warm seawater. And then, with a mighty rush of bubbles that continued for a long, long time, the *Estrêla* was gone.

In the silence Judit began to hear the cries of the wounded, the weeping of men and women. Bento's face was pale.

"My God," he whispered.

A wave of sheer, hopeless loneliness swept over Judit, and she shuddered. The sky above was fair. Far out over the ocean there was an area of fluffy clouds. The sun was pleasantly hot, the air balmy and, as the ocean breeze began to clear away the smoke and fumes, deliciously sweet. Yet the sky looked alien, unfriendly. They were alone. Only the navigator, if he lived, would know how many trillions of miles separated them from all they had known, from others of their kind, from home. She wondered if Bento was thinking similar thoughts. He squeezed her hand and looked at her, his eyes wide.

"It's gone," he said.

"Yes."

He shook his head, and then his eyes narrowed with resolve. "There is much to do."

Over five hundred people had died with the *Estrêla do Brasil*. Among the dead was Captain Antonio Villa-

Lobos. So it would not be necessary, Bento thought as he and his men completed a roster of the survivors and as the medical personnel who had escaped used pieces of clothing to bandage wounds, to depose the incompetent captain. Moreover, those who were to have led the coup were also dead, apparently, for the general and his second in command were not among the stunned groups of survivors. Of the ship's service crew, only a few were alive, most of them from the engineering section. Major Bento Mattos was the senior living officer.

Using the engineering staff as a cadre, Bento began to organize those surviving service personnel. They gathered in a group near the cliffs. His first order was to Judit, to take inventory of the group's assets. Eleven had carried a weapon off the ship, the standard service-issue laser. One man had a small screwdriver in his pocket. A quick survey of the non-service survivors revealed that those who had carried something off the *Estrêla* had chosen mostly personal possessions, pictures of relatives left behind on Earth, items of clothing, and jewelry. Tools, Bento soon found, were the last things anyone had considered during the moments of panic.

It was early afternoon when the quick inventory of assets was concluded. "I don't think I have to remind you," Bento told his group of just over thirty Brazilian military and space service people, "that the eleven lasers we have will become useless once the charge is depleted. Therefore, no laser will be fired except in the defense of life or upon my specific orders when being used as a tool."

"We would need weapons only against animals," the chief engineer offered.

"There are animals, quite large," another warned.

"Our most immediate need is for water," Bento said, "and there is water in the valley." A pretty little river fell in a foaming cataract into the valley's western end. "We must move everyone down the slope. Our next need will be food. Chief, will you inquire among the settlers for those skilled in the natural sciences to begin a search for edible fruits, nuts, and plants. It's going to be a process of experimentation at best, but we can at least have the best advice available before we risk a life by eating anything."

Bento did not state his sure knowledge, nor did he have to, that if the native fruits of the planet were poisonous to humans, there was no hope.

"Since there is animal life, there will be flesh, but that can wait. We will not use laser charges in hunting for meat except in a case of dire emergency. How many of you attended the Brazilian Armed Services Survival Training School?"

To his surprise, Judit was one of a half-dozen who responded affirmatively. They had never mentioned the subject during their time together.

"Excellent," Bento said. "You six, with Lieutenant Alvarez in command, will search for metallic fragments at the crash site, and if you find suitable material, we will use stones to grind the fragments into cutting instruments. Then you will fashion spears and bows as you were taught in survival training. The rest of you will work with me in moving everyone into the valley before darkness."

Some had died before the slow march down the slope into the valley began. A small group was left behind to inter the dead in cairns of stone, since there were no tools for digging in the hard clay of the plateau. The strongest volunteered to carry the wounded.

In the wooded valley there was deadwood for fires, and before darkness fell, Bento remedied an oversight, sending a few people to collect all cigarette lighters. A fire-making committee was chosen from among the scientists, and they were entrusted with the lighters.

Judit and her detail, laden with odds and ends of metallic and plastic fragments, returned from the crash site at dusk, when fires were glowing along the south bank of the little river. Judit found Bento standing beside the stream, looking out toward the bay.

"We'll be able to fashion knives from some metals," she said. "We will not be able to work the fragments of the hull at all."

Bento nodded. Judit, shuddering, put her arms around him. "Perhaps we should have died with the ship," she whispered.

"We're alive. This is a rich land."

"And we will become as our native ancestors were when the white man came," she said. "Savages, hunter-gatherers. The culture of which we are products will be forgotten, for we will be too much occupied with mere survival to teach it to our children."

"No," Bento insisted.

"We have no way of recording the knowledge in the minds of the survivors. Memory is fickle, Bento."

"We will have to make a way," he vowed. Then he sighed. There was so much to do, and he secretly felt much as Judit felt. It had taken humans hundreds of thousands of years to reach the point of building the first hut, of fashioning the first tool from flint. In this group of survivors, fewer than five hundred, was knowledge of all Earth's scientific disciplines. Would it be possible to save that knowledge? Would it be possible, starting with a few lasers, a screwdriver, and a few cigarette lighters, to come all the way back to a technology that would once again put a ship in space? He himself would be long dead before the society passed beyond wood-burning technology . . . if it ever did . . . if any of them survived. He was fully aware of the fact that the captain had ordered a landing before much had been learned of the planet. The nature of the animal life, for example, was a total mystery. There had been no testing at all for toxicity in the planet's vegetation or animal flesh.

Perhaps, he thought as the darkness came and the sky overhead glowed with its billions of stars, it *would* have been best to have died with the ship. But he was a man, and he was alive. As long as he was alive, he would strive onward.

"There is a pleasant little glade in the forest," he said gently, "with soft leaves for a bed." He led Judit there, gathered the fallen leaves, and held her closely to him until, at long last, he fell into an exhausted sleep.

III

EXPLORATION

TEN

The two most pampered residents of Hamilton City had spent a good portion of the beautiful summer day at the clear, rocky creek named for one of them. Now they trotted along side by side toward the outskirts of town, furry little critters, but one with biological hair, the other with a sleek coat of tensile, flexible fibers that represented another of Grace Monroe's achievements.

Jumper the dog had been the only native earth animal alive aboard the *Spirit of America* and, until recent months, the only one on Omega. The sleek and beautiful Abyssinian cat that ran at Jumper's side was the oddest of Grace's artificial creations, possessing, on a smaller scale, the same amazing artificial brain that made the admiral seem so human. Furthermore, Cat was endowed with an ability that not even Grace could explain fully: Cat could alter his form. Within the limits of the adaptability of the odd materials that formed him, Cat could assume any shape. He had been perfecting his present form for over a year, and he could well have been chosen the recipient of Best in Show at any cat competition back on Earth.

Jumper, the fuzzy little dog that had been smuggled aboard the *Spirit of America* by his master, Clay Girard, was seven years old and in his prime; but he was not the happiest of dogs. Clay's duties and his preoccupation with Cindy often left Jumper on his own. It wasn't all bad, for, as the only dog on Omega, he had hundreds of friends and never lacked for a tasty tidbit, but he missed Clay.

Cat, on the other hand, was a loner. He seemed to enjoy going to the creek called Jumper's Run, where he perched in a tree and observed the splashings of the colonists' children and Baby's family of little Omegan dragons. He disdained joining them, although, unlike a real cat, he did occasionally enjoy a swim. His artificial fur dried quickly and returned to its sleek neatness.

Cat's brain, although not large enough to accumulate even the logic and knowledge of Mopro, was in many ways superior to the brain of the little dog. But Jumper was the closest thing to Cat's size, and Jumper liked to romp with Cat, giving Cat a chance to exercise and perfect movement skills.

Jumper's claws clicked as the two gained the paved plastic streets and entered the city. Jumper's destination was his new home, which had been built for Clay and Cindy as near to Jumper's Run as possible, but tantalizing aromas and the beautiful weather led Jumper into a rambling approach, so there were blocks of houses to be passed to reach his own home. Progress slowed when a woman who had been working in her garden looked up, smiled, and whistled. Jumper's ears pointed. Cat paused, sat down, and straightened an imaginary displacement of a few hairs on his foreleg with his red tongue.

"Cookie, Jumper?" the woman asked.

Jumper lolled his tongue, trotted over to accept a pat on the head and a sweet, fruit-filled cookie, and then was off again. Twice more he detoured to wag his tail and accept friendly words and pats. Cat, who was not in the mood for petting—he liked it most of the time, but on that day there seemed to be something in the air that called for more serious activity—went his own way, heading toward the *Spirit of America*. He had his own favorite private places aboard ship, and he was often seen slinking into odd nooks by changing his body shape. There he would investigate, check, and report any rusting or abnormality to the admiral.

Jumper was delayed quite a while at the Howard

house. Seven-year-old Webb had returned early from the creek to be sure that his mother was, as promised, making spaghetti for dinner. Satisfied by the delicious smell of the simmering sauce, Webb was tossing a ball against the pastel plastic wall of the house. Jumper liked nothing more than a good game of chase the ball, so some time was spent in that pleasant activity. Jumper liked Webb very much, perhaps because Webb reminded him of a younger Clay Girard, back in the Chicago junkyard.

Jumper retrieved the ball once more, dropped it, wet with his saliva, at Webb's feet, and threw himself down onto the grass with a happy sigh.

"Tired, boy?" Webb asked, rubbing the dog's head. Jumper licked his hand and panted, tongue dripping.

"Come back tonight and I'll give you some spaghetti," Webb promised. He sat beside Jumper, wishing that Jumper was his, or, alternatively, that Captain Rodrick would relax rules and let the scientists use the frozen embryos to grow enough dogs so that he could have one of his own. Already there was a small herd of growing calves out in the newly fenced pastures. Soon the colony would have fresh milk. In the past, Webb knew, people killed beef cattle to eat steak. Webb had never had real steak, and he wasn't sure he would be willing to see a living thing killed to have one, when synthasteaks tasted so good and his mother's meaty spaghetti sauce was so delicious.

He didn't notice Tina Sells and Lyndon West coming down the street, returning from the beach. Tina had started taking Lyndon to the less frequented places, because the kid was a real monster.

"Hi, Webb," Tina said, pausing. "Hi, Jumper."

Jumper wagged his tail.

"Filthy animal," Lyndon said, in that surprising voice that seemed far too old for a two-year-old child.

"Oh, shut up, Lyndon," Webb said disgustedly.

"How are you adjusting to Omegan life?" Tina asked.

"It's great," Webb told her. "I wish I had a dog like Jumper."

"Maybe soon," Tina said. "The labs are hatching chickens for real eggs now, and there's a new litter of pigs." She laughed. "Some litter. Two hundred squealing little piglets."

Unnoticed, Lyndon had picked up a stick with a sharp end. He moved casually to stand beside Webb and suddenly jabbed the stick directly toward one of Jumper's eyes. Jumper jerked his head, and the sharp stick punched his nose painfully. Jumper had friends of all ages, and he knew young children. He liked them and would never, ever hurt one of them simply for having pulled his ear or having tried to cut a tooth on him. But he knew, also, that human children had to be taught that a dog has feelings too. He nipped Lyndon on the hand. His teeth left white dents in the skin but did not bring blood.

Lyndon screamed. "That filthy animal bit me."

"He should have torn your hand off," Webb said, "trying to hurt his eye."

"My mother will have this beast destroyed," Lyndon said.

"Your mother wears army shoes," Webb shouted, angered.

Tina jerked Lyndon out of the Webb yard. Jumper, with a final tail wag at Webb, went on his way. He pushed open the small access door that Clay had installed for his comings and goings and sniffed to assess the food possibilities for the evening. Nothing was cooking. Instead, Clay and Cindy were packing. Jumper had seen that happen just once before, when they were packing to move out of the McRae house. He knew only that such activity indicated change, and he didn't like change. He whined and began to follow Clay's every step, once getting in the way and causing Clay to stumble over him.

"Go lie down, Jumper," Clay said sternly. Jumper's ears drooped, and he crawled under a chair, his head turning with each of Clay's movements.

"He senses that something's going on," Cindy noted, kneeling to pat Jumper on the head. "Do you suppose we could take him with us?"

"I don't think that would be a good idea," Clay said. "He'll be good company for your mother while we're gone."

"He's taken quite a liking to Webb Howard," Cindy said. "I'm sure Webb would be glad to watch him during the day while Mother's at school."

"Good idea," Clay responded. "That Webb is all boy."

"Like you were when you stowed away on the ship," Cindy agreed. "I'll talk with Webb and his mother tomorrow."

ELEVEN

It took only hours for the news to spread throughout the colony that the *Free Enterprise* was to make a voyage of exploration. Almost all the space service people either came to Rodrick in person or submitted a written request to be included on the crew list, and one by one Rodrick responded to them. For example, he told Ito and Emi Zuki that although they were the most qualified for such a trip, they were needed more at Hamilton City. With the data stores of the ship's computer being transferred to the land-based facilities in Hamilton City, the Itos could not be spared.

The duty roster for the *Spirit of America*'s return voyage was complete, and many of the volunteers were eliminated simply by checking that list. Rodrick interviewed others, while Jackie, at his side, asked questions now and then. They both agreed that the best selection for an engineering officer was Gage Fergus, who had worked under Harry Shaw on the *Free Enterprise*. Fergus was an energetic little man with an unruly mass of red hair and, although he was an American citizen, the charming accent of the Scot. He was single, not yet forty, and as Jackie learned when she put through a call to Harry Shaw, a thoroughly dependable space engineer.

Both Jackie and Duncan smiled when the next volunteer came into the interview room.

"Don't laugh," Jean Roebling pleaded with a dazzling smile. "Please." She had deliberately put aside her own adaptations of the standard service garb and was dressed in the neat, functional fatigue uniform of a space rating, a one-piece jumpsuit with neatly buttoned pockets.

"Hear me out," Jean said, as Jackie and Duncan exchanged glances. "I want to do something useful. I know my limitations. I'm not qualified to use any weapon, and I have no technical or scientific skills, but I know about food and its care. I can be the ship's housekeeper. I know I can do it, and I'm asking you, please, to give me the opportunity."

Jean Roebling reminded Duncan of frills, feathers, and whipped cream, but there was a poetic and lovely delicacy about her.

"Jean, thank you for coming," Rodrick said. "We'll consider it."

"That means no," Jean said, her shoulders drooping.

"Jean, what if one of the food servers malfunctions?" Rodrick asked. "Could you repair it?"

Jean spread her hands.

"Commander Fergus could repair the server," Jackie said, looking at Rodrick. "I've tasted the results of Jean's work with standard ship's rations. I rather like the idea of having something that tastes good while being nutritious."

"I can get someone to give me a crash course in light weapons," Jean offered brightly, looking at Jackie in hope.

"Does the captain of this expedition recommend Ms. Roebling?" Rodrick asked.

"I do," Jackie said, with a wink at Jean, who beamed happily.

"Then I bow to the desires of two beautiful explorers," Rodrick said. Jean dashed forward, bent over the table, kissed Rodrick on the cheek, then withdrew and stood at what she imagined to be attention. Rodrick grinned. It was rather difficult to give Jean's curves a military look, even when they were so well fitted by a singlet and drawn up in a shoulders-back pose. In fact, that shoulders-back pose merely emphasized Jean's obvious female attributes.

He had agreed to assigning Jean to the crew because he knew the capabilities of the others, and he had one more crew member definitely in mind.

The firepower of the *Free Enterprise* would protect the ship in space. Stoner would be at fire control, and he was a good man. For small ship action, Clay Girard was as good as any pilot in the service, and he had proven himself during the assault on the city of Suses. Jackie could maneuver a starship with the best of them and had a fine command of military tactics. Then there was the additional firepower of Mopro and the sergeant. Actually, the only weakness of the *Free Enterprise* would be that it had but one scout ship aboard. The addition of a dozen or more trained men or women wouldn't have made her more formidable without additional scouts, and it was not within his means to spare more scout ships. He did, however, want one more stabilizing influence aboard, and the person he had in mind was not on the list of volunteers. When he and Jackie had finished the selections, he left Jackie to the many details of organization and planning and went in search of Leslie Young. He had to go all the way to Suses to find her.

*   *   *

Oscar Kost had been long aware that Leslie Young, formerly Lieutenant Colonel Leslie Young of the National Service Corps, was an exceptional woman in many ways. From the time Leslie had managed security for the Utah site where the *Spirit of America* had been built in secrecy—at least secret from the American people, if not to the intelligence services of the Soviet Union and Brazil—Leslie Young had never disappointed Kost. They had watched the huge ship leave the desert and diminish into the upper atmosphere: Oscar because his neck ached and he had no intentions, at that time, of ever leaving Earth; Leslie because she loved the ever more scarce wild areas of the Earth over which the National Service Corps stood guard and, just possibly, she began to realize years later, because Kost was not going.

In those years before the second American starship left the solar system, Leslie had seen some of America's prime wilderness areas destroyed under the heavy earth-moving equipment to give living space to the ever-growing population of nonworking poor. It had taken no persuasion at all to convince her that she should be aboard the *Free Enterprise*.

On Omega Leslie had found her niche quickly as a security officer, with the help and advice of Oscar Kost. She had taken a close look at the security arrangements for Hamilton City and had visited the firing range—nothing more than a secluded valley in the highlands—with Mopro and the admiral and had been impressed with the combined firepower of the robots. She herself had impressed the admiral; manning a number of weapons, she had showed the admiral that he would want her on his side in the event of trouble.

When Oscar went to the city on the Great Misty River, Leslie accompanied him. By that time Rodrick had given orders that Leslie's word regarding safety and security was his word. Although the Eeperan residents of the city of Suses had apparently recovered fully from the brief but destructive battle and were content to continue their lives of indolence and pleasure, Leslie had given the American security forces on the river a quick shake-up to provide a wall of defense around the work sites—after all, Oscar was working in the pyramid. She often led patrols into the city of Suses, just to keep an eye on things.

Leslie was a small woman, just five-feet-one-inch tall, wore her ebony hair short and brushing her high cheekbones. Her brown eyes could be stern, or they could laugh. Leslie was from the South and usually soft-spoken, but she could, if provoked, give vent to a chewing out that would have done credit to a space service sergeant major.

Off duty, dressed in something cool, it was evident to the least observant that Leslie Young was a woman of nearly perfect proportions. Like any Earthwoman, she was the object of stares and open invitations from what most everyone had started calling the studs, the magnificent Eeperan men, and she also got her share of attention from the members of the American teams who were working along the river.

More than one single man taken with Leslie's beauty puzzled over his failure in attracting her attention and wondered just what was going on when she spent a great deal of her time with Oscar, a man old enough to be her father.

Leslie enjoyed Oscar's company. Of all the men she had ever known, he had the most active mind. In her years in the National Service Corps, Leslie had served in some isolated places, such as the Utah site—which, before it became a construction site, was a radioactive waste dump—and she had spent her time reading in a number of fields. Oscar was the only man she'd ever known who could converse with her on any subject and follow her often lightning-fast changes of direction.

If, at that time, someone had asked her if she was in love with a man twice her age—a man who, in spite

of modern medical science, insisted upon having a stiff
neck and, worse, claimed it to be the result of a disease
long since conquered—she would have looked at the
questioner coldly, and then, perhaps, she would have
laughed. She just liked being with Oscar, and he liked
being with her. She saw to it that Oscar had a bodyguard
—herself—whenever she had the slightest suspicion
that he needed one, so they were often together when
Oscar was working.

They were together when Rodrick arrived, blowing
desert sands with a hot landing, then emerging from
the scout with Jumper the dog leaping ahead of him to
see some of his friends who had been away from Hamilton City for a while. Jumper had begged for a flight
with Rodrick, and since Clay and Cindy were busy with
preparations for the prospecting expedition, Rodrick
had given in. Now he handed a leash to a space service
enlisted man and told him to keep Jumper out of trouble.

Oscar was having coffee with Leslie. She was taking the opportunity to ask his advice on a matter that
had been concerning her: Although she had not caught
anyone at it, she knew that some of the guards were
making off-duty visits to the city to take advantage of
the hospitality of Eepera.

"The fruits of victory?" Oscar asked. "It's been that
way for a long time, Leslie."

"I wonder what the soldiers will think of the fruits
of victory when I start making random drug tests,"
Leslie said.

Oscar frowned. "Any foundation for that worry?"

"Not yet, not as far as I can tell," she admitted.

Oscar rubbed his neck. "Wouldn't want . . ." He
paused. The drug that was so much a part of Eeperan
life, and probably the main reason for their total stagna-
tion over thousands of years, was an insidious one—the
most potent aphrodisiac ever discovered, at least on
two known planets.

"We almost lost civilization on Earth in the twentieth century because of drugs that had not even a fraction of the appeal of this one," Leslie said.

"Have you spoken to Duncan about this?" Oscar asked.

"Not yet. As I said, I've seen no evidence of drug use, but if the fraternization continues, it's inevitable."

Oscar was pouring a fresh cup of coffee when Rodrick entered the room. "Well, speaking of the captain . . ." he said.

Rodrick wasted no time in stating his purpose. Then he leaned back in his chair and wondered why Leslie was being so obviously indecisive about his request that she join the prospecting expedition. "Is there some problem of which I'm unaware, Colonel Young?" he finally asked.

"It's more a potential problem," Leslie said. She told Rodrick of her fears that continued socializing between the Americans and the Eepera could create a drug situation among the soldiers who were stationed temporarily in the encampment atop the bluffs.

"If that's your only concern," Rodrick said, "I think I can ease your mind." He picked up a pen and a sheet of paper, wrote quickly, and handed the sheet to Leslie. On it he had written an order. Any colony member who, by twice-weekly drug testing, was shown to have taken the Eeperan aphrodisiac would be confined to a hospital in Hamilton City for treatment.

"I'll have Max oversee the testing," Rodrick said. "Is there any other reason why you would not want to go with the *Free Enterprise*?"

There was. Leslie looked quickly at Oscar and felt a surge of loss, thinking of not seeing him for months. It was at that moment that she first began to suspect that her feelings for Oscar Kost were more than admiration and friendship.

Oscar cleared his throat. "It's a fine opportunity, Leslie," he remarked.

"Come with us, then," Leslie urged with a smile.

"I'd love to," Oscar said, his eyes just a bit more revealing than usual—softened, perhaps, by the way Leslie was looking at him. "But I'm needed here, and I'm too old for gallivanting around the galaxy."

TWELVE

Lance Corporal Vic Wakefield was twenty-four years old. He was an always neat six-footer who had been in line for promotion before leaving the space service to sign on with the *Free Enterprise*. He was a man of wiry strength, even temperament, and good sense. He had a sharp eye when it came to women, very much like other young men, and he had the looks to be eyed in return. His face was handsomely craggy, his nose strong, his mouth sensuous. He seemed to be handy anytime Colonel Leslie Young felt it necessary to run a patrol through the city of Suses, below the bluffs.

It had been on a regular patrol that he had caught the eye of an Eeperan woman. She had looked down into his eyes from a second-floor window, and her eyes had widened in appreciation as Vic returned her smile. He had nodded only slightly when the Eeperan woman made an inviting, come-hither motion with her hand, but he was smiling widely when in the early darkness of a cooling desert night he found the building from which the Eeperan woman had beckoned. It was the same woman who opened the door.

"I had so hoped that you would come," the woman said, taking his hand and leading him into a service-man's erotic dream. Several times during that first night Corporal Wakefield had said, "Hey, who needs it?" For he didn't need a drug to make him appreciate the most sensuous woman to have come into his young life, and then the most sensuous *two* women.

Vic had been extremely careful. For the first few nights he went alone and was pleased by his expanding circle of . . . acquaintances, mainly Eeperan females. Vic had had an uncle who had been a marine during the last incursion of the American military into a foreign nation, when President Tony Healy decided to clear the Cuban military out of Panama, and he had heard some rousing tales about the willing acceptance of American marines by the local belles. Vic was sure, at the time, that his uncle was exaggerating. But not even old Uncle Jack's wildest dreams could have matched what Vic found in Suses.

Vic's best buddy, PFC Tom Wing, was getting a little suspicious. Vic wasn't participating in the nightly poker games anymore, and there was only one thing Vic loved more than poker. If it was what he thought it was, then Tom Wing wanted to be a part of it. When he finally convinced Vic to confess that he had friends in the city, Tom went along in great anticipation and soon discovered that he had not had enough imagination even to begin to anticipate the juicy realities of Eeperan women.

After a while, although neither Vic nor Tom were tiring of fleshly delights, it did add a little interest to an evening to join in one of the Eeperan gatherings. The Eeperan studs were sometimes a bit arrogant, but after Vic had laid out one particularly obnoxious fellow with a quick right jab, there was no more trouble. Some of the Eeperan studs were bearable, almost likable. One courteous fellow, named Yanee, seemed to go out of his way to be friendly. He was constantly offering Vic and Tom a hit of the drug that all the Eepera used, but he didn't push when both Vic and Tom said, "Thanks, but there are rumors circulating that we might be tested for drugs." Besides, who needed more of an aphrodisiac than acres and acres of smooth, dreamy, warm, willing Eeperan feminine flesh?

Vic always took along a jug of gin from the still back in Hamilton City, and that was enough for two space marines. Yanee took a liking to gin and drank with them, while steering them to the wildest of the women at any particular party. Yanee was a pretty good guy. The only time he got out of line was one night when he hinted that Vic and Tom should bring along one or two female members of the American contingent guarding the pyramid area and revealed that he had had an Earthwoman.

Vic was feeling no pain. He looked at the Eeperan stud and said, "You're lying, boy."

"No, no," Yanee said. "For it was I who saved the life of the woman called Theresita."

Vic got a little warm under the collar. He knew about the Russian broad, how she'd been doped and knocked up before Jacob, flying *Apache One*, had found her. He frowned. "Listen, boy," he said, "I'd suggest you forget all about that. One thing we Earthmen are selfish about, that's our women. We don't like to hear that someone dopes 'em to get 'em in bed."

Yanee held his peace. As the evening wore on, however, he found Tom, in a mellow mood, taking a rest. He asked carefully couched questions.

"Yeah," Tom said, "the Russian broad did have a kid. He's a real little monster, precocious as hell and as mean as a snake."

Yanee managed to keep Tom talking about *his* son, Lyndon West, for ten minutes, laughing as Tom told of some of the boy's antics. He sounded very much like a full-blooded Eeperan boy, and Yanee suddenly felt himself yearning to see him.

Neither Tom nor Vic took a hit of the drug until after the twice-weekly drug tests had started.

"With a light dosage," his friend Yanee assured him, "it will be out of your bloodstream and totally undetectable before dawn."

Vic told Tom that he was going to take a light hit, that if there were a surprise test the next day he'd need Tom's help to fake it. Within a half hour Vic would not have traded places with a hero in Moslem paradise, which, he understood, was totally chauvinist and filled with delights for the male.

So it began. The junior officer in charge of security ran his drug tests predictably. A man could take a hit on a Saturday night, secure in his knowledge that he'd have all day Sunday and until evening on Monday to work it out of the bloodstream and, as the Eepera said, the drug left no trace after a few hours.

When Lance Corporal Celia Hadley rotated to the river post for a tour, Vic gave her a little hit of the drug one night in his quarters and found that it turned an old friend—they'd made connections on the voyage out aboard the *Free Enterprise*—into the equivalent of one of those Eeperan tigresses. He did, however, put his foot down firmly when, after a couple more private parties with Celia, she asked to join him on one of his excursions into the city.

"You go. Why can't I?" Celia demanded.

"I don't know the Eeperan men well enough," Vic said. "I can't guarantee your safety."

"Vic, don't be silly. You and I underwent identical military training," she said.

"Well, you're not going with me. I'm not going to line you up with one of those fancy studs."

"Then I'll go alone," she threatened.

"Oh, no, you don't," he said. He frowned, knowing that, having introduced Celia to the drug, he was in some way responsible for her. "All right. We go together."

THIRTEEN

The admiral waited until Grace and Evangeline were taking a break from their translation work. "Hi," Grace said when he came in. "Sit down. What's going on out in the real world, where the sun shines?"

"The *Free Enterprise* is almost ready to go," the admiral reported.

"What worries you about that?" Grace asked.

"I'd like to be going along," he said, his handsome face showing no emotion, as usual.

Grace knew her creation. She smiled. "I think the sergeant is dependable, don't you?"

"He is quite capable," the admiral agreed.

"But?"

"Coming from me, this sounds foolish," the admiral said, with a wry smile. "I remember my early days, that's all."

"Your childhood," Grace said.

"Yes."

"And you think that the sergeant has not had enough experience to have overcome some of his childish ideas," Grace said. The admiral nodded. "This immaturity is mainly aimed at you, is that not right?"

"I think it might be advisable, Grace, to let him indulge his ambition to face me in a contest."

Grace looked at him thoughtfully, picturing in her mind the damage both robots were capable of inflicting. "I'm sure you've thought this out thoroughly."

"I think so," the admiral said. "His desire to prove himself superior eats at him, occupies too much of his thought. In a life-and-death situation, his reaction time might be slowed a fraction by his preoccupation with proving his superiority to me."

"So what do you want to do?" Grace asked. "Let him tear off your arm so that you'll have to be repaired?"

"I don't think it would be psychologically healthy for him to win an encounter with me," the admiral said.

"Would it be healthy for *you* to win?" Grace asked, and was immediately sorry. She knew him better than that, knew that he had conquered his early ego problems, that he truly thought only of the good of the whole.

"It was necessary for me to learn that I was not indestructible," the admiral said. "The miner that bit off my legs taught me that. The sergeant must learn his capabilities. His specifications show that he is stronger and quicker than I, but he must learn that he also has to be able to use his brain."

"I think you're way ahead of me," Grace said. "I might as well tell you to go ahead with whatever it is you've planned, but I have to know what it is so that I can have the shop ready with spare parts when you two dismember each other."

"No parts will be necessary," the admiral said.

"And when will it happen?"

"Before the *Free Enterprise* lifts off."

"And just what sort of contest do you have in mind?" she asked.

"I'll need your help," he said. He told her what he had planned.

She smiled. "I need to get out of this dungeon for a day or so," she said. "I'll fly back with you, and we'll get to work."

The next day the admiral found the sergeant aboard the *Free Enterprise*, inspecting the ship in the company of Mopro. The admiral wasted no time. "Is this all you can find to do with your time before a critical expedition?" he demanded.

The sergeant pulled himself to stiff attention. "I

was not aware that you were put in charge of this operation."

"Obviously someone should be," the admiral said.

"I am inspecting the ship on the orders of Commander Jackie Rodrick," the sergeant said.

"Then you need help," the admiral retorted, "for you are obviously incapable of such a task."

He saw the blow coming, and it was quick, surprisingly quick. He had just enough time to close and allow the force of the sergeant's fist to spend itself as the sergeant's arm wrapped around his neck. Then he was testing the sergeant's strength, tying him up with his arms around him. The sergeant was, as described in the specifications, just a bit more powerful, and he was certainly quick. The admiral felt himself being disengaged and shoved away, then a quick chop of the sergeant's left hand came whistling toward his eyes. The sergeant was not holding back. Had the chop landed, he would have been bent, his nose pushed back, and most probably blinded. He had instructed Mopro in advance, and as he barely avoided the sergeant's blow, the big defense robot lumbered forward, shot out his powerful arms, and held both the sergeant and the admiral. Not even the strength in their bodies could overcome one arm of Mopro.

Mopro was sending and spelling out a message at the same time. "Stop. No damage. There is no time for repair."

"He's right, Sergeant Lunkhead," the admiral said. "And if he weren't, I'd—"

"When I return," the sergeant whispered in fury. "When I return."

"If you're so intent on proving the value of experience," the admiral said, "there is a way that will produce no damage but will give you the opportunity you seek."

"Name it, Fancy Pants," the sergeant said, his eyes red with his anger.

The admiral led his opponent to a gym aboard the

Free Enterprise. Mopro, solid, huge, and silent, kept his bulk between the two.

"We will need witnesses," the admiral said.

"That does not matter to me," the sergeant said.

There was a short delay. The sergeant turned to look in surprise when Grace, Jackie and Duncan Rodrick, and several other people came in and took seats. Grace came forward with two long, slim fencing foils in her hands.

"Well, gentlemen," she said. "I've anticipated this."

The sergeant was glaring at the two feeble-looking weapons with disdain. "You did study fencing for coordination?" Grace asked.

"I did," the sergeant said with great respect in his voice. This woman, he knew, was his designer—his mother, in a manner of thinking. And she had had so little time for him. There were so many things he wanted to ask her. He felt that she would be the only person in the world to whom he could open himself, state his innermost doubts, his feelings. And all she had time for, it seemed, was Fancy Pants. "What can we prove with such weapons, Dr. Monroe?"

"Swiftness, agility, skill, and courage," Grace replied. She nodded to Jackie, who turned a rheostat on a remote box. Grace touched a foil to a metal weight lying on the gym floor. Sparks flew. "The blade will not, of course, do damage to your skin, nor will it penetrate. The electrical charge transmitted, however, when a foil touches either of you will approximate the damage that would be done by a similar contact of foil on human flesh. A light scratch will be painful; a strike powerful enough to penetrate flesh will penetrate you electrically. You both know your internal structure, the vital points where a strike will cause temporary paralysis. A direct jab, both strong and accurate enough to penetrate into a human's heart, will put either of you out of action totally until I revive you by restoring function to the areas affected. You can have your combat to the death' without costing me time to repair you. Is that satisfactory, Sergeant?"

"It is satisfactory," the sergeant agreed with a grim smile. With his lightning speed, he had made his old fencing masters look like rank amateurs. He had spent many hours with a computer-directed fencing robot whose speed matched his own. No training the admiral could have accumulated would protect him. The sergeant stepped back, posed, at the ready. Grace went back to sit among the spectators. The admiral gave the fencer's salute and said, *"En garde."*

The first exchange was so fast that the humans could see only a blur of steel between the two robots. It was apparent from the first that the admiral was on the defensive. Hand on hip, foil making hissing movements, the sergeant, with a grim smile, pushed his opponent back and back until, with a leap, the admiral avoided being pinned against the wall. Then they moved the length of the gym with the sergeant's foil flashing and whistling.

The admiral felt a pain on his chest. He leaped back and looked down to see his shirt slashed, knowing from the pain that the electrical simulation indicated a shallow gash, about four inches long. This did not distract him from his analysis of the sergeant's attack patterns. He had opened a channel to the main computer and was entering every movement of his faster opponent while concentrating only on blocking or parrying the sergeant's foil.

"The sergeant's going to take him," Duncan whispered to Jackie.

"Don't count the admiral out yet," Jackie whispered back.

The sergeant's foil leaped, a living thing, and the admiral felt a stabbing pain in his right shoulder. His entire right arm went numb. His foil was hanging down uselessly, and he could not raise it. The sergeant, seeing that he now had the advantage, pushed in for the kill. The admiral leaped to one side and, as he leaped, transferred the foil from his right hand to his left. He sent an order, and the ship's main computer gave him a series of movements. As he had suspected, the sergeant's patterns of attack were predictable. He retreated, blocking and parrying, almost running from the sergeant's emotional desire to finish the match. Then the computer analysis began to match the pattern of the sergeant's movements, and the admiral began to call off the moves in his mind, waiting, waiting, until one-two-three-four, it was time. He went under a straight thrust aimed at his heart, came up from below, and the charged tip of his foil contacted the sergeant's body directly over the sergeant's main power supply. In a man, the foil would have slipped between ribs and stopped the heart.

The sergeant's eyes went wide, and he stared at the admiral in disbelief as the strength went out of his arms and the foil fell from his hand to clatter on the gym floor. He sank to his knees, made a moaning sound as he tried to overcome the numbness, and then fell with a great *thunk* to the floor. The admiral was on his knees beside the sergeant immediately, lifting him with his good arm, running from the gym to a laboratory. He gently placed the sergeant on a table, and Grace was beside him, tools in hand.

"Wait outside, Admiral," she said.

She used a special tool to cut into an invisible seam, then rolled the protective skin away from the sergeant's power supply. It took only a minute to demagnetize the system. The sergeant's eyes opened. He lifted his head and looked down at his exposed interior, then up at Grace, and the look of shock and sadness made her want to weep.

"He beat me?" the sergeant asked in a soft, weak voice.

"Of course," she said.

Damn it, robots were not supposed to have feelings. She still didn't understand how they had turned out to be so human. The look of hurt in his eyes made her almost ashamed of herself.

"You say 'of course'?" he asked. "How can that be? Have you modified him since you've been on Omega?"

"No. He has learned, that's all."

The sergeant was watching without interest as Grace used a heat tool to reseam the protective covering, the skin on his chest. "I'm faster and stronger," he said, as petulant as a little boy.

"Yes," she said. "I know. I've studied your schematics. I approve of the changes Roebling made in my design." She smiled. "I did design you, you know."

"Yes," he said. "I had so looked forward to—"

Grace felt a stab of remorse. She should have taken time to speak with him, to get to know him.

"Will it help if I say I'm sorry?" she asked. "I am sorry, sorry that I haven't had time to spend with you, to talk with you. You must have a million questions. The admiral did, when he was young."

"I—I would—" He couldn't speak.

Grace finished the seam and pulled the sergeant's slashed shirt across his chest, then leaned against the table. "You're not supposed to have feelings or emotions, but you do, don't you?"

"That is one thing I need to know," he admitted, thinking that Grace must be the most beautiful thing, animate or otherwise, in the universe. "May I touch you?"

"Of course," she said, and his hand moved. One finger pushed lightly against the back of her hand.

"You are flesh and blood, and you designed me," the sergeant marveled. "I have read everything there was to read about you. I have tried to reconstruct your thinking processes."

"I've tried that myself," she said, with a little laugh. "But I can't. I can't tell you how I arrived at the basic working of that brain of yours. Accident? Divine inspiration? One day it was just there, in my head. I said, 'Grace, if you add this and that and do this and that, it will live.' And it did. I was designing a chemical-fueled

computer, and I came up with the brain that is now in
Juke, and then the brain in Mopro."

"And then *him*."

"Yes."

"Roebling could not improve on that," he said.

"No, you two are very much alike. Your early
programming was a bit different. I'm not sure if that
accounts for the difference in the way you and the
admiral think, or whether it's just a matter of personality, as it is in humans." She put her hand on his cheek.
"There are a lot of answers we might come up with
together, the three of us. Do you think that we can all
work together now?"

His lips pouted, and he looked so much like a little
boy that she wanted to take him into her arms.

"I know," she sympathized, smiling. "You're faster.
You're stronger. The admiral himself told me so."

"Then how did he best me?" he asked.

"With this," she said, tapping him on the forehead.
"By thinking."

"Am I inferior in thinking ability then?"

"No. Or, to be honest, I don't see how you could
be. But the admiral has had more time to discover the
power of his brain."

The sergeant sat up, legs dangling. "Roebling said
that I was to be more practical. He said that the admiral
began to deviate from his original purpose even before
he left Earth, neglecting his training to study such
things as literature and art and languages." He looked
into Grace's eyes. "How exactly did he beat me?"

"He used the computer to analyze your patterns of
attack," Grace explained. "You see, he knew you were
faster and stronger, and he needed something to overcome your advantage. He used his brain to find it."

"That is unfair," he said flatly.

"Unfair?" She laughed. "Would it have been unfair
if he'd used the computer against, say, a formidable
enemy, something or someone who threatened the entire colony? Wouldn't it have been 'fair' to use any

means to protect those whom he was designed to protect?"

"If he had not used the computer, I would have bested him."

"Most probably," Grace agreed. "But if he had not used the computer, he would have *thought* of some other way to equalize your superior speed and strength. That is the advantage of this." Again she tapped his forehead. "You are the consummate fighting man. You are perhaps the most valuable single individual on Omega, because, in an emergency, you would perform best. That's why the admiral arranged this little duel, to show you that you—regardless of your strengths—are not indestructible. He learned that lesson in a more damaging way, and he felt that you should be made aware of a certain, uh, weakness, before you were entrusted with the safety of a ship and her crew."

"He arranged it?"

"Yes, of course."

"Will I have another opportunity?"

"I should hope not," Grace said sternly. "Don't you see yet how valuable you are? Don't you see that both you and he are too important, not only as assets but as individuals, to be allowed to damage yourselves simply because you need to massage your ego?"

"That's putting it pretty bluntly, Dr. Monroe," he said, letting his eyes fall.

"I meant to be blunt," she replied. "Look, we have a few days before you leave on the *Free Enterprise*. I'd like you to spend as much time with me as possible, without neglecting your duties."

"I'd like that very much," he said.

"And drop the Dr. Monroe stuff," she said, taking his hand and pulling him down from the table. "Call me Grace."

The admiral was waiting outside. He looked at Grace questioningly.

"All right, gentlemen," Grace said. "You've had

your little fling. Now it's time to get down to business. I want you both to remember that, in a way, you're brothers. Now I know all about sibling rivalry, and in times of peace and idleness you can think up any kind of contests you choose, as long as you don't mangle each other. For now, I want you to shake hands."

The admiral was the first to stick out his hand. The sergeant took it, grinning. "You had to use the computer to beat me," he said.

"You were predictable," the admiral said. "If you like, after you return, I'll show you how to be totally random in attacking."

"I think I can figure that out for myself," the sergeant said. "Even if I have to have a computer to help."

Grace rolled her eyes. "Knock it off," she admonished. "If either one of you gets competitive on me again until I give you the word, I'll use an electrical prod on the seats of your pants." She marched off.

The sergeant looked at the admiral, one eyebrow raised.

"That's our mom," the admiral said, with a wide grin.

"Would she?" the sergeant asked.

"I don't doubt it for a minute," the admiral said.

FOURTEEN

Jackie was the last to enter the hatch of the *Free Enterprise*. Cindy, on the bridge, closed the hatch behind the ship's captain and checked all airtight openings as Jackie made her way forward.

The entire colony, with the exception of those who were working to unravel the secrets of the Eepera, had turned out. The ship had begun to come to life hours earlier, as Engineer Gage Fergus activated her systems. Through her hull one could feel something—a charge, an awareness of power.

Duncan Rodrick stood at a safe distance, a considerable distance, for the wash of fire from the ship's rocket exhausts would be formidable. He stored the last image of Jackie in his mind. She had paused at the hatch, turned, and waved, a slim, graceful figure in uniform.

"It's damned inefficent to build 'em to land on the surface," Max Rosen said.

"We can lighten starships by megatons," Grace agreed. "Have to have the proper shuttle system first, though."

"The shuttle systems exist on Earth," Rodrick pointed out. "Colonizers can be built for less than half the cost of one of these birds, even less than the Russians and Brazilians spent by building their ships in orbit. With the Shaw Drive, and with the economy in fuel you two worked out, we could move a million people here in a few months."

"Gad," Delia Howard said, "I thought we left Earth to get away from the millions." She had just watched her husband board a starship bound for an unknown destination. At her side their son, Webb, cradled a whining Jumper in his arms. Jumper had seen the two people he loved best go into the great ship, and he knew what happened then.

Aboard ship the skeleton crew was busy as the prelaunch checklists neared completion. Cindy, in the astronavigator's seat, was a bit nervous, although she would have little responsibility during the launch.

At Cindy's side Clay punched buttons and threw switches. "You're almost as good as those first chimps who rode the rockets from old Cape Canaveral," Cindy whispered to him. Clay winked at her.

From deep down in the power spaces the Scot's burr of Gage Fergus came, beginning the countdown.

"Go, baby," Clay whispered as he felt the ignition of rockets. The ship shivered and seemed to become heavy and inch upward on columns of multiple fire. An ocean of sound roared over the plains and fields of Eden. Those who were closest to the pad were grateful for their earplugs.

Mandy Miller glanced around at the assembly of people, saw several hundred heads lift as if they were controlled by a common source, then turned her eyes back to the ship as it rose and grew smaller and accelerated into and through a layer of low cloud. The sound was now bearable. She removed her earplugs and let it wash over her. She never lost her awe at a rocket takeoff. She had heard the sound, in various forms, many times. In the early days of her marriage to Rocky Miller, she'd watched dozens of takeoffs, and each time there had been the thrill and pride and an emotion approaching joy as machinery functioned perfectly and the great, rumbling, thundering sound announced still another conquest of gravity.

She let her eyes fall again. Rodrick stood straight and tall, not twenty feet from her, and his face was unreadable as it tilted up to catch the last glimpse of the ship. Then he lowered his head and, as if he felt her eyes on him, turned to stare at her for a brief moment. She felt a tingle of awareness, a jolt as if she'd grabbed a live wire.

"Quite a show," said Derek Roebling, at her side.

"Impressive," she agreed, wondering if he'd noticed that exchange of glances between her and Rodrick. At the back of her mind there pounded one central fact: Duncan's wife was on that ship, going far, far away, and there was always the chance, God forbid, that she would not come back.

"Watching great ships lift off makes me hungry," Derek said. "May I offer the lady one of Amando Kwait's garden salads and a broiled lobster, or whatever you call those great, spiny things that Allen Jones's boys bring up from the sea?"

"Thanks, Derek," she said, still shaken by the heat of Rodrick's glance. "But I have work to do."

Derek followed her and caught her elbow as she stepped onto the street leading into the city. "Walk you home?"

"To the lab," she said, smiling. Why couldn't she simply accept things? Most women, she felt, had only one chance at a man of the caliber of Derek, some no chance at all. And she had had three men who loved her. Rocky, and it had been good, in the beginning. Duncan. Now this man, who showed a patience that was touching, a patience she would not have been able to manage were she in his shoes.

"On second thought," she said, "I just happen to be one of the finest broilers of lobster on Omega."

"Good," he said, grinning and taking her hand.

He had altered one of the standard designs and had personally supervised the building of his house. One room was perched on the northern cliff overlooking Stanton Bay, cantilevered over a drop down to a pebbly beach and the blue waters. The covering was a quarter dome, rigged to slide back into the roofline of the house proper and open the room to Omega's summer. He kissed Mandy there, with a soft sea breeze ruffling her hair. At first her lips were still, unanswering, then they moved, moistened, searched, and finding something, became soft and heated.

It was not, of course, the first time Derek had kissed an attractive woman. But as far as he was concerned, it was the most outstanding kiss of his life. He held it for a long time, and then, as she pushed away, he looked into her eyes. She turned away, and he felt the chill in the set of her shoulders.

"If it's too soon, I'm sorry," he said. "I can wait."

She felt hopeless. For a moment his kiss had warmed her. For a moment she had felt safe in his arms.

"When you're ready to talk about it . . ." he said,

coming to put his hands on her arms, pressing his face into her hair from the rear.

Talk? she was thinking. She *could* talk about what he meant, about her husband, Rocky, now dead. What she couldn't talk about was the guilty semiwish that Jackie would not return. And that guilt was souring her. She turned. "You promised to feed me, sir," she said.

FIFTEEN

Radio contact with the *Free Enterprise* ended quickly as the Shaw Drive was activated and the ship lightstepped to a predetermined point some light-years away in the direction of Vega. There were too many things to be done on Omega for the Americans to spend time wondering about the explorers. Betsy McRae and Derek were involved in comprehensive testing of all the colony's children, and Betsy was grateful for the work. Rodrick, meanwhile, was concerned with preparations for the lift-off of the *Spirit of America*. Max's and Grace's work separated them again; Grace was back in the pyramid with Evangeline, at the boring work of translation, with both of them beginning to wonder if they would ever find anything of significance in all the many volumes of priestly writings. Harry Shaw was studying the outer casing of the Eeperan power plant, looking for a way in without risking the possibility of releasing what he had come to know was a very potent converter of energy inside the housing. Along the Great Misty River the desert nights, which were always cool, were now growing chilly. In Eden, Amando Kwait and Dena Madden divided their time between preparing the agricultural cargo of the *Spirit of America* and supervising a harvest so bountiful that it would, with proper storage and preservation, feed the population of Omega for years, with a surplus to be loaded into the empty cargo bins of the starship.

Meanwhile the exploration of the huge planet continued. With a surface area four times that of the Earth, the planet was a continuing wonder and challenge to scientists. Her jungles were still largely unknown, and not a week went by without the discovery of some new and often awesome species of animal life in those steaming, fertile, teeming, vast areas. Because of her experience in survival in the jungle areas, Theresita West had taken a great interest in jungle exploration, an interest shared by her husband, Jacob. As a result, Lyndon West celebrated his second birthday in the care of his baby-sitter and earned himself an energetic spanking when he thrust a full plate of cake and ice cream into Tina's face when she refused to let him detonate a model spaceship, a gift from Jacob, with a vial of rocket fuel he had somehow stolen.

Delia Howard had found suitable lab space in Mandy Miller's Life Sciences section. The admiral, true to his word, had delivered a printout of Grace Monroe's notes, translated from Grace's personal shorthand. After she had seen Webb off to bed with a motherly kiss, Delia spent some interesting nights poring over Grace's work. She had not yet had an opportunity to talk directly with Grace, and she had a million questions. There was, for example, no logical reason why the Monroe brain functioned as if biologically alive.

Delia's area of interest had its roots in the questing science of late twentieth-century students of the human brain. In the 1980s it had first been said—by scientists, not by preachers or teachers of that semimystical regime loosely called positive thinking—that emotions and mental attitude had direct connections with certain diseases and illnesses. It was then that people first began to understand that the human brain and the human immune system formed a kind of closed circuit and that the brain could consciously be caused to send a signal along nerves to enhance the body's defenses.

Sixty years later the field was still wide open for study. Although the neuropeptides, those small, protein-like chemicals made by the cells in the brain, could be readily synthesized and were used in the treatment of many abnormal conditions, the human brain was still as relatively unexplored as the deepest jungles on Omega.

Delia's early work on Omega centered on trying to understand how Grace Monroe had created a thinking, feeling organism like the admiral without the use of chemical messengers, such as those manufactured by the human brain. At the same time, she was working with Eeperan cadavers taken after the battle on the river. She had been requested by Mandy Miller to make an effort to explain the precocity of Lyndon West. That, as it turned out, proved to be relatively simple. She could draw on work done shortly after the turn of the century, a study of children with genius level IQ, and she had the cadaver of a three-year-old Eeperan girl.

Mandy called Delia into her office the day after Delia had submitted a brief but intensely detailed report on her findings. For the first time Delia was introduced to Lyndon West's mother, a big-boned woman of over forty years, hair pulled back in an efficient and easily kept style.

"Delia," Mandy said, "Theresita has read your report."

Theresita smiled. "Since I have no background in medicine, I'm afraid I find it incomprehensible."

"No problem," Delia assured her. "It's easy for those of us who work in the medical field to forget that not everyone learns our mumbo-jumbo words. In brief, it appears that we were right in thinking that the main difference between Eepera and human is a surprising early maturity of certain areas of the brain."

This was a touchy area with Mandy, who had spent

a lot of time, using test results from the adult population of Eepera in Suses, to prove to herself that the
Eepera were not innately superior in brain power to
humans. "Among adults, and juveniles past the age of
sixteen," she said, "there is no discernible difference
between the brain capability of the average human and
the average Eepera."

"Exactly," Delia said. "However, certain neuropeptides are produced in greater quantities in the brain of
the very young Eepera." She spread her hands. "One
might theorize that in the early development of the
Eeperan race it was not feasible for a mother to care for
her young as long as a human mother does. Whatever
the evolutionary reason, certain areas of the brain develop quickly in an Eeperan infant—the centers con-
trolling speech and muscular coordination, for example."

"So Lyndon is sort of a flash in the pot," Theresita
said. She found American slang expressions to be colorful and often amused Jacob by misusing them.

"His development will level out," Delia agreed.

Theresita looked at her hands. "And is there some
chemical or physical reason for his, uh, aggressiveness,
for his tendency to be antisocial?"

Delia, rather liking the larger woman with the
handsome, serious face, had been wondering how to
approach that very subject.

"Well," she began, then looked at Mandy, who
nodded. "It isn't necessarily a lack of development in
logic, sensitivity, or social awareness. It's just that the
development of certain skills runs so far ahead. When
you combine, in one brain, some characteristics that are
typical of a human child of twelve with those of a
two-year-old child, you get an imbalance."

"Theresita," Mandy said, "Dr. Allano has been
studying Eeperan children in Suses. You can read his
report if you like. Briefly, either the Eepera don't like
their own children or they have the same difficulty
you're experiencing. They have a very effective program of zero population growth, so there are relatively

few children, but none are permitted in open society until they reach the age of about ten. They place all children in a care center under the control of specially trained Whorsk slaves."

"Am I to build a prison for him, then?" Theresita asked miserably.

Both Mandy and Delia were silent.

"I should spend more time with him. . . ." Theresita said.

"You will *not* feel guilty about this!" Mandy said. "As your doctor, I forbid you to blame yourself for something over which you have no control."

"And yet I carried him. He's half-mine," Theresita said.

"Mrs. West," Delia asked, "would you say that the boy has a normal attachment to you?"

Theresita smiled. "He is my first child. How can I tell?" Then she sighed. "No, I am lying to you. I have wondered about this. He needs me, of course, for he is not capable of caring for himself totally, and he would be lonely. And yet . . ."

"Does he ever direct any of his aggression against you?" Delia asked.

"Not so much anymore," Theresita said, with a grim smile. "You see, although we were not allowed to read the teachings of the ancient Jewish philosophers in my country when I was young, we were aware of some of the basics, such as the admonition that to spare the rod is to spoil the child."

"I think I understand," Delia said. "Then he has had to be punished by you?"

Theresita nodded. "Once, when he didn't want to go to bed, he struck me with a heavy toy. I bear the scar here." She touched the back of her head. "At other times his actions were less direct. Once, when I had punished him for abusive language, he poured honey over my bed."

Delia wanted to reach out and touch the woman. She felt great pity. To have a son and not know the warmth of his love, as she had always enjoyed the love of her own son, Webb, was a terrible thing.

"But there is hope now?" Theresita asked. "I can expect him to become more, uh, normal as he grows older?"

"I wish you had told me about those aggressive actions against you," Mandy said. "We might have been able to do something. I suggest that we start a program of psychostudy, under Dr. Allano."

Theresita sat proudly. "As you know, I, a woman, rose to the rank of marshal in the Red Army. I sat at the right hand of Yuri Kolchak during the most dangerous time in the history of the world. I have killed in battle. I have suffered wounds. It is not a matter of pride to me, Dr. Miller, to have to admit that I can't control one small boy."

"We'll help," Delia said, feeling tears form in her eyes. "One thing we can do is to see that he has a normal role model. My son, Webb, knows him, and although Lyndon is not among Webb's favorite acquaintances, he doesn't *really* dislike Lyndon. Webb's a pretty solid-minded little boy, and if I talk with him and explain Lyndon's problems, he might be willing to spend some time with your son and, just maybe, teach him how to be a boy."

"I'd be very grateful," Theresita said. "But I still feel that I'm neglecting my responsibilities by working when I should be at home with Lyndon."

"The work you're doing is valuable," Mandy reminded her. "We've barely begun to know the jungles, but look what we've gained: We have the Omegan dragons and their fantastic scales. Through the study of certain jungle vegetation, we have made a great advancement in weapons development. I told you, Theresita, knock off the guilt. Do your work. Of course spend what time you can with your son, and meanwhile we'll see what we can do to help in his development."

*   *   *

That night Delia had her talk with Webb. "Roaring rockets, Mom!" Webb exploded. "You want me to hang around with that little monster?" But Webb listened as his mother explained, and in the end, making a face of disgust, he agreed that it wouldn't really strain his brain to spend some time with the little monster. The next day Webb sought out Tina Sells and her small charge. Tina had taken Lyndon to a spot on Jumper's Run north of the swimming and wading hole. She had found it impossible to keep close enough watch on Lyndon when numbers of other children were around and was afraid that sooner or later Lyndon was going to hurt someone seriously. She'd had a talk with her parents, telling them she was considering telling Theresita that she could no longer tend the boy; but she was, after all, a part of the colony, and she looked upon her duties with Lyndon as her contribution. By watching the boy during the day, she freed an adult for more important work.

"Hello, Puke Face," Lyndon said when Webb approached, Jumper leading the way, tail high, but pausing warily when he saw Lyndon.

"Can it, you midget terrorist," Tina ordered.

Webb swallowed his dislike and said, "If you can keep your big mouth shut for a little while, I'll take you for a hike, Lyndon."

"Anything to get away from her," Lyndon said, trying to catch Jumper's tail as he came to accept a pat from Tina.

Tina didn't say that she felt the same way about him. "Don't go far," she said as Webb waded into the creek, the water cool and clean on his bare feet.

Lyndon hurried to catch up. Webb led the way out of the water, pointing out interesting plants to a silent, brooding Lyndon. The opposite bank rose sharply and just to the north formed a rocky brink overlooking the creek. Webb walked well away from the drop into the water. There was a little pool just below the rocks, and as Webb came to seize Lyndon's arm to pull him away from the edge, he saw two large fish lying with heads to the current.

"See that?" Webb asked, pointing.

"So what?" Lyndon challenged. "Dumb fish. That's all."

"Is everything dumb to you?" Webb asked.

"Mostly," Lyndon said. "Especially girls and pukey seven-year-olds who think they know everything."

"Why do you always have to be such a barf-head?" Webb demanded impatiently. "Come on, get away before you fall."

"I'm not spastic," Lyndon said, jerking away and darting to stand on the very edge. He grinned back at Webb. "Do heights scare you?"

"No," Webb said. "Go ahead and fall. Jump if you want to. It'd solve a lot of problems."

Lyndon pretended to lose his balance as he stood on the edge of the drop, his arms windmilling. Webb leaped forward, grabbed him, and Lyndon sat down, legs dangling over the brink. "Let's watch the dumb fish."

Webb saw that a larger fish had joined the two who were almost motionless, except for tails that waved gracefully to hold them against the gentle current. He sat down next to Lyndon. "You know," he said, "it doesn't take much to be a nice kid instead of a monster. All you gotta do is control that mouth of yours and realize that other people have feelings too."

"Who cares?" Lyndon asked, slinging a rock that fell near the three fish, causing them to scatter.

"Come on, let's go back," Webb said.

"I'm not ready."

"Well, maybe you want to stay up here by yourself," Webb said, rising. Jumper came scampering forward as he saw Webb stand, and as he sensed the drop he halted, legs stiff, tail dropping. With one lightning motion Lyndon caught Jumper by the front leg and jerked him, yelping. Jumper's claws splayed. He fell twenty-five feet and landed with a mighty splash.

"You little jerk!" Webb yelled, rushing back to look down. "If you've hurt that dog—"

Jumper surfaced and with all four legs moving furiously, swam to the opposite bank, climbed out onto a rock, and shook himself.

"He's not hurt," Lyndon said, rising and moving behind Webb. He shoved with all his might, directly into the small of Webb's back, and as Webb screamed and fell, he said, "But *you* will be."

SIXTEEN

For the third time Prince Yanee of the Eepera had an Earthwoman. This one was not as beautiful as the first, but fueled with the aphrodisiac, she was interesting. He had almost missed her. She had come into the city at night, following the two space marines who had been next to no help in making it possible for Yanee to satisfy what had at first been a whim and then, for lack of fulfillment, an urgent desire. At first the woman had refused the drug. Without it she was only moderately interesting to Yanee, good for not much more than novelty value. With the drug she was almost the equal in passion of the larger woman who had borne his child.

As a space marine, Lance Corporal Celia Hadley performed the same duties, carried the same weapons, and drew the same pay as her male counterparts. She also had the same freedoms. During her training on Earth she had pulled liberty with the men, had drunk beside them, and had participated in one great free-for-all with some space-jock trainees. But she had mostly confined her sexual activities to men she knew in the unit. Cohabitation in a private room in the barracks was frowned upon in basic training, but once she was on station, things eased up, and when she was promoted to corporal, she found that no one paid attention to the marines' night life as long as they were discreet.

Now and then the media—especially those units operated by conservatives—decried the lack of morality in the defense services, where men and women shared the same barracks—with private rooms, of course—but Celia hadn't let it bother her. She had no desire to be married, to have kids, to spend her life being some man's private punching bag. She knew that her attitude was counter to current morality in the United States, where the ever-dwindling middle class had returned to counting the family unit as the basic foundation of society, but she didn't care. She did her share of chicken-shit duties, earned her pay, and figured that gave her the right to do what she pleased, as long as she broke no laws or regulations. She had volunteered for the *Free Enterprise* because she was bored with spit and polish, guard duty, close-order drill, and the day-to-day crap of the space marines. For a while things had been interesting. She met a couple of nice men on the trip, and it was sort of neat, getting laid aboard a huge spaceship so far away from Earth that you couldn't even see the sun, but then there she was, pulling guard duty and routine patrols in a frigging desert with the same type of horny jerks she had known ever since she enlisted.

Her first night with Yanee introduced her to a man unlike anyone she'd ever dated, and the first time she popped the dope and had sex with the Eeperan—well, she'd never realized her body had so many nerve endings. "I think maybe I'll just stay here with you," she'd told Yanee, still feeling things more powerfully than she had ever felt them.

Yanee had said, "Is there not more to life than one continuous orgasm?"

She had approached the adventure with some trepidation. She'd heard a lot about the Eepera studs, and how one of them had doped and ravished the Russian broad. After the first night, however, she knew that the studs were no different, really, from your average space marine, in that all a male wanted was sex. Yanee valued her as a person, always getting her to talk about her life in the colony. He was a sensitive guy, and it just wasn't fair for anyone to keep him from seeing his kid. Hell, he'd saved the Russian broad's life, hadn't he? How was he to know that Earthwomen, or at least some of them, felt that their bodies were sacred or something? How was he to know that Theresita was fertile? Eeperan women had to work at getting pregnant, and there were never any accidents.

"You really would like to see your kid, huh?" she asked one night, after the initial flush of the drug had been worn off by strenuous activity.

"What would it hurt for me to see him, to speak with him?" Yanee asked. "Perhaps you could make a request for me to those in charge, my darling, and tell them I mean no harm and will offer no problems."

"I can't do tht, Buster," Celia said. "I'm off limits coming here, and if they find out I've hit on that drug of yours, they'll put me in the hospital and fry my mind."

But Yanee looked so sad that she put her brain to work, no easy task under the influence of the drug. "Look, I'm on duty at the guard post directly atop the bluff. Come up tomorrow. Put your request in writing. I'll pass it on and put in a good word for you. You never know, the commander might just give you permission to see the kid."

Yanee appeared at the guard post the next day dressed in the gleaming white regalia of an Eepera prince. Corporal Hadley was formal, even cool, as she listened to his request. She agreed formally, for she was in the presence of two space marine privates, to pass Yanee's petition along to the commander. She did it through the proper channels, so it took two days for it

to arrive on Max Rosen's desk in the room where Grace
and Evangeline continued their translations. It was evening before Max opened the envelope and read Yanee's
request.

"Yanee . . ." Grace mused when Max let her read
the petition. "He was the spokesman who came to the
dam, right?"

Max nodded. "A prince. He was the one who led
the Americans into the ambush in the city."

"Is there more to this than appears on the surface?" Grace asked. "From my observations the Eepera
are not that fond of their young."

Max had on his thinking look, which was one of
total agony. "We're going to have to live with these
peacocks for a long time. They've still got the cities
downstream, and they're fully armed. I guess it wouldn't
hurt to have a few friends, at least someone with whom
we can have a dialogue now and then. I wonder what
Theresita would say to his request."

"Shall I ask her?" Grace asked.

"Do that, would you?" Max answered, but before
Grace had the opportunity, there was disturbing news
from Hamilton City.

The Earth colony on Omega numbered under two
thousand people, and it was a closely knit community.
Gossip traveled faster than news. When the news about
Webb Howard came, Grace remembered one statement in Yanee's request, in a paragraph near the end:

> Due to the early development of intelligence
> in Eeperan children, they go through a period of
> extreme belligerence. From what I have been able
> to learn, this is not true with children of Earth-
> people. Perhaps I might be of aid in guiding the
> rearing of my son.

Grace, after the news from Hamilton City, wished
that she had read the letter more closely, that she had
sensed the warning in Yanee's statement about Eeperan
children.

SEVENTEEN

The *Free Enterprise* was a mote in emptiness. She rested while Cindy did her work, matching the known star charts that viewed the galaxy from a point parsecs away, from old Earth. Even with the aid of the computer to transform the charts, it was not an easy job. The ship had lightstepped twice, on the first search attempt having found a sterile star, a planetless thermonuclear furnace spewing its matter into empty space.

Two weeks had been consumed in examining the four planets of a second star. And now Cindy was choosing the next target, selecting, with the help of the ship's instruments and the computer, only those stars with the characteristics of old Sol, Earth's sun. There were several choices, all at medium range—as space distances go.

"I just can't decide," she said to Clay. They were alone on the bridge, the others taking advantage of the time to catch up on sleep.

"Put their numbers in a jar and draw one," Clay suggested.

"That would probably be as good a method as any," Cindy said. "But we can't afford too many more fruitless lightsteps."

"I know," Clay said. "But someday we'll have all the fuel we need to go stepping all over the place, and you won't have to rack your brain trying to find just the right kind of star."

Jackie Rodrick came onto the bridge, her eyes still sleep-swollen. "How's it going?" she asked Cindy.

"Several candidates, Jackie," Cindy said. "It's just a matter of choosing one."

"All G-type suns?" Jackie asked, drawing a cup of coffee.

"Yes," Cindy replied. "And two of them so much like Sol, it would be difficult to tell them apart without measurements."

"Number them one and two and draw straws," Jackie said, seating herself and throwing one shapely leg over the arm of the command chair.

Clay laughed. "See? There's nothing to knowing how to command."

"No," Cindy said. "I'll make the choice." She used the ship's optics on highest magnification. The distant star was a sparkle of light. "When I was a kid and watched space operas on the screen, there'd be all these pretty globes swimming around in space. Like you could see all the planets of a solar system as planets, not tiny little stars. It's so different out here. Everything's so tiny and so far away. It takes us days to look at just four planets, because when you're near enough to one to see what she's like, the next nearest one is millions of miles away and is nothing more than a dim star in the viewers."

"Are you talking just to delay making a decision?" Clay asked with a smile.

"I guess so," Cindy admitted. "Okay, let's go for one."

"No pressure," Jackie said. "We can search about three more systems before we're down to enough fuel to get home."

"This one," Cindy decided, enlarging the chosen star on the screen until it was a blob of light, grainy, fiery.

She rechecked her navigation calculations three times before sending them down to Gage Fergus. Then there was a period of waiting while Gage, working shorthanded as he was, programmed the Shaw Drive.

Leslie Young and Jean Roebling joined the little

group on the bridge. Clay showed them the chosen star.

"It's so small," Jean said.

"Slightly larger than Earth's sun," Clay said. "And a little bit hotter. If we find a water planet there, its orbit should be more than one standard astronomical unit from the sun. We'll check that band first, when we get close."

"Let's get lucky," Leslie wished.

"I guess that's what it will have to be," Clay said. "Pure luck."

"Ito says that the odds of finding two suns like 61 Cygni A and B, close together and each with a life-zone planet, are about a billion to one," Cindy said.

"Well, we haven't seen that many suns close up," Clay responded, "but the Russians sent out three probes and found no planets, and only one of our probes did. We know that out of the billions of suns in the galaxy, a sizable number will have developed planetary systems, at least statistically, but when you consider the volume of space occupied by the galaxy and the distances involved . . ."

Jackie was listening to their conversation with musing interest. Clay and Cindy, although married and doing responsible, skilled work, were still kids. She and Duncan had had a talk just recently about one challenge posed by Clay and Cindy specifically and the other young people of Omega in general: In some areas Clay's and Cindy's development had been abnormal, their skills formed in a rush by necessity. But their overall education was not nearly complete. Clay could fly the skin off a scout, and he had quickly picked up what he had to learn to handle the huge *Free Enterprise*, but his foundation of scientific knowledge was far from complete. It was the same with Cindy. Sometimes, when Jackie heard them talk, she was saddened, because they sounded like two kids full of awe and wonder but without understanding. If the colony was to retain the level of technology now in existence and build on it—and they had both been considering the possibility that there would be no further influx of Earthpeople—some way would have to be found to give Omega's young people time to develop, time to learn, before pushing them into working.

When the moment came to engage the Shaw Drive, there was silence on the bridge during that timeless, almost unfelt instant when the *Free Enterprise* ceased to exist at one point and occupied another space at a far distant point. Everyone felt the suspense as Cindy began her scan of the space ahead, the space immediately around a sun that now showed as a disk on the ship's optics.

"All *right*," Cindy said, as she enlarged two tiny dots of light past the point of fine resolution. "Two big ones, at approximately the distance of Uranus and Pluto from Sol."

"Where there are outriders like that, there are probably others, closer to the sun," Clay said.

Cindy's fingers began to fly over the keyboard. "I'm figuring a step to a distance of three astronomical units from the sun," she said. "From there we'll be able to scan the entire life zone."

"Isn't this exciting?" Jean bubbled. "I know we're going to find a beautiful one, with vegetation and water and all the good things."

"And no Whorsk or Eepera," Clay added.

"I think it would be wonderful to meet a truly intelligent species," Jean said. "Kind and peaceful, with all sorts of neat scientific secrets."

"Hah!" Clay said. "Fat chance."

Leslie, who had been largely silent, lifted her communicator and contacted Stoner, who was buckled into the sealed compartment where the weapons-control unit was housed. "Stoner," she said, "we'll be stepping in close to this sun in just a few minutes."

"I've got all my eyes and ears turned on," Stoner said.

"You're not expecting trouble?" Jean asked Leslie.

Leslie smiled. "Not expecting, just guarding against unpleasant surprises."

Clay, who had nothing to do while waiting for Cindy and Gage Fergus to figure the lightstep, looked up and grinned at Leslie. "Remember how, back on Earth, the scientists used to get on the screen and agonize over whether or not there was any life out in the galaxy? It was as if everyone was afraid we were alone in the whole universe, that humans were the only intelligent life, that Earth was the only planet where life had formed. Sometimes, now, I wish they'd been right."

"I know what you mean," Cindy said, "after meeting the Whorsk and the Eepera."

"Maybe it's just cosmic coincidence that Omega has a native intelligent species," Clay suggested. "But I wonder. The Eepera have their legends about their home planets and their native race, and there are hints in their folklore about other races. What if the development of life on planets with air and water is the rule and not the exception?"

"Then I'd wonder what we're going to find down there," Cindy said, for the *Free Enterprise* had light-stepped and quickly located a planet one-and-a-half standard astronomical units from the sun—now a blazing disk the relative size of Earth's sun. As the ship's optics gathered the reflected light from the planet and analyzed it and formed a color-corrected image on the screen, they saw the unmistakable blue of oceans and the hint of white clouds indicating atmosphere.

In the awed silence, Jackie leaned forward in her chair.

"I'm getting very good readings," Cindy said, trying to keep her voice professionally calm but failing. "Free oxygen. Water vapor."

What would they find? How would they fare? Jackie wondered, taking a quick look around. Leslie Young looked competent in uniform with a weapon at her side. Gage? Jean? Jackie shrugged mentally. Clay was as good as anyone with a scout. And she had Stoner on weapons control. "Colonel Young," she said, her voice taking on the ring of command, "please alert Mopro and the sergeant."

Leslie spoke into her communicator quietly and then said, "The defense robot is positioned to act as an auxiliary space battery, firing from an open lock. The sergeant is assisting the chief in the power room."

"Very well," Jackie said.

Jean Roebling's eyes were wide. She was beginning to realize that she had not volunteered for a sightseeing excursion, and her imagination began to work. Based on her limited knowledge, she envisioned weirdly shaped spacecraft making roaring, growling noises as they did in space-opera thrillers, closing on the ship. "Is there something I can do?" she whispered to Leslie.

"I'd love a cup of coffee," Leslie said. She smiled to herself as Jean hurried toward the ever-present coffee machine. Jean had needed something to do, however simple, to keep her mind off the possibilities that were being imagined, all quite different but equally vivid, by everyone on the bridge. Everyone, even Jean, knew that if they had stumbled into a nest of those fierce and terrible creatures who had once pursued the Eepera to Earth, there would be no help available. The multiple light-years that separated them from Omega prevented any communication. If the *Free Enterprise* did not return, there would be no one to send to look for her.

Jackie ordered Cindy to make one small lightstep almost within rocket-access distance of a blue planet of this unnamed star. Clay blinked. During the time taken by that action, the planet exploded into his vision screens, a globe slightly flattened at the poles, showing the gleam of ice, the brilliant blue of oceans, and the darker masses of land partially obscured by cloud. He had seen it before, from the space near Earth, from the space near the life-zone planets of 61 Cygni A and B. With the shape of ocean and landmass undefined, all the water planets he had seen looked alike; and they were all fantastically beautiful, for they were the colorful promise of life surrounded by an immensity of hostile, cold space, where a person could die in a hundred ways.

"Oh, yes," Cindy whispered as she began to scan, sending the ship's electronic probes penetrating through the clouds. She sang out the readings as they were recorded: the oxygen and carbon dioxide content of the air, the pleasingly low ratios of those gases not compatible with human life, and surface temperatures. Finished with the initial readings, she turned, face glowing. "Perfect," she said.

"All right, Clay," Jackie ordered, "get on your horse."

Cindy's smile faded. "Commander," she said, "can I please go with him?"

Jackie's face was stern, and she didn't bother to answer. They had been over that question before. Cindy was the only astronavigator aboard. In a pinch, Jackie herself could handle the ship, but without a navigator she would have to use up weeks or months to figure out where to go.

Clay patted Cindy on top of her head and left the bridge. Minutes later, on Clay's instructions, Cindy popped a hatch on one of the ship's pods, and the *Belle Jennie* leaped out into space, engines engaged, and fell away—a tiny, disappearing brightness—toward the planet.

The *Jennie* was sending back excellent telemetry as she penetrated the atmosphere. Clay slowed, allowing the instruments to gather atmospheric samples for analysis on board, the pleasing results relayed almost instantly to the orbiting starship. *Jennie's* cameras were showing a large, green continent below, with a blue sea curving away to the horizon. The air contained no industrial contaminants, nothing more than the products of combustion, which could be reasonably expected, for any planet with vegetation and atmosphere would experience wildfires.

Since the products of an industrial or technological society would have been detected in the air, Clay relaxed a bit and sent, "Going down to one hundred thousand feet, starting circumpolar run."

At that height and speed it would take a highly sophisticated detection system to see the *Jennie,* and some very advanced weapons to do her harm, but it was not possible to study every detail as *Jennie* flashed over the surface with the planet rotating under her. It was possible to determine that there were no large scars on the surface made by intelligent beings, no cities, no roads, no electromagnetic radiation. In the hours required for that preliminary survey, there was an expectant tension aboard the *Free Enterprise.*

"Outstanding," Clay sent. "Time for a closer look."

Now Clay concentrated on the landmasses, flying at slightly reduced speed, *Jennie* trailing a sonic boom behind her, her instruments working. "Hey, it's looking very, very good," he sent. "Large metallic deposits."

Stoner McRae was now on the communicator, watching the readouts from *Jennie's* instruments. "Give me a slower orbit around the area of rolling hills," he said, and Clay slowed, went lower, and watched as the geodetic instruments recorded an ore field of impressive size.

"What have we got, Stoner?" Clay asked.

"Iron ore," Stoner replied, "at least equal to the old Lake Superior deposits in the United States and Canada, and that was enough to build two great industrial nations."

"So we've got iron," Clay said.

"Fly onward, Mr. Girard," Stoner said.

Clay spent several days prospecting, flying low and slow at times on Stoner's orders. And, in a computerized model aboard the *Free Enterprise,* the new planet began to look better and better to Stoner.

"I'm just about ready to recommend that we move

here," he told the others, who were gathered on the bridge to watch the digitally re-formed images of the surface on the screen. "Apparently this planet was formed just as the Earth was formed, with the heavy metals boiled up from the interior and caught near the surface during cooling. You name the metal, and she's got it."

"The platinum metals?" Jackie asked.

Stoner didn't answer for a moment. "Deep, and scarce, just like on Earth," he said. He winked at Jackie. "But we've only looked at two of the landmasses so far."

Clay accelerated the *Jennie* across an ocean. There were life signals from near the surface of the water, but nothing large. The life detectors were capable of penetrating only to a shallow depth. The *Jennie* made planetfall approximately at the center of a South-American-sized continent and flew over a coastal mountain range that gave way to a semiarid desert.

"Whoa," Stoner yelped as *Jennie*'s ore detectors blipped. "Give me a slow circle over that erosion slope."

After a quarter hour he said, "Clay, let's you and me file a claim to that slope."

"What have we got?" Clay asked.

"There's a reef of gold in there that would make the old South African mines look poor," Stoner said.

Clay flew on. The desert was beginning to give way to a rolling transition zone when Stoner whooped and gave Clay an order to orbit, but Clay's eyes were glued on something up ahead.

"Hey," Stoner yelled, "what are you doing? I just got a blip of platinum ore back there."

"Take a look at the visual monitor," Clay said, his voice tense.

Jackie had already seen it on the screen. As the rolling countryside steepened into foothills, a sizable plateau rose and flattened. Atop that rise was an array of gleaming, glittering, light-shattering shapes.

"All right, Clay," Jackie ordered, "get out of there."

"There's no radiation of any kind," Clay said. "Look, there are triangles, circles, obelisks, and trapezoids."

He was slowing, playing all of *Jennie*'s sensors and detection instruments on the glittering constructions.

"Like diamonds," Jean whispered.

"These couldn't possibly be natural formations," Clay said.

"I agree," Jackie said. "I told you to get out of there. Come straight up, and fast."

"Commander," Clay said, "we're going to have to take a close look. Why not now?"

He brought *Jennie* closer to the top of the plateau. The material of the geometric constructions broke the energy of the sun into its component colors, making flashes of brilliance in rainbow colors, and the designs took on unearthly beauty from all angles.

"No life signals," Clay reported. "The things are nonmetallic."

He made one more orbit of the plateau to record the construction from all angles. "All right," he sent, "I'm coming up."

Jackie was waiting beside the pod that housed the *Jennie*. Clay stepped out and starting stripping off his gear.

"Lieutenant Girard," Jackie said, in a tone of voice that made Clay straighten, "I gave you a direct order, which you disobeyed."

Clay had been chewed out before. Being human, he had made mistakes while he was being trained as a scout pilot. He had been reprimanded by experts—by Jacob West and Renaldo Cruz, the two Apache scout pilots, and by Duncan Rodrick himself—but the scolding he got, standing in an empty service area beside *Jennie*'s pod, made his face burn. Jackie Rodrick, a commander in the space service, second in command on Omega, and captain of the *Free Enterprise*, set him back on his heels.

"If such a thing ever happens again," Jackie concluded, "I'll ground you. I'll bust your ass." She paused.

"Yes, ma'am." Clay gulped.

"And I might even spank it," Jackie concluded angrily. "Now get your gear off. We've got work to do."

EIGHTEEN

Freed, for the moment, of the constant need to watch the little monster, Tina Sells lay back on the bank of Jumper's Run. She was thinking about Cindy and that Cindy was now married, while she, Tina, didn't even have a real boyfriend. Of course, she had not yet had a chance to get to know all of the boys who had come out on the *Free Enterprise*, one of whom was very handsome. She was, after all, only a few years younger than Cindy, and it was high time she had something in her life more exciting than baby-sitting for Mr. and Mrs. West's little terrorist.

She let her eyes close and didn't pay any attention to a splash from upstream. Lyndon could swim like a fish, and Webb was old enough to take care of himself. *Probably just one of them throwing a rock into the creek*, she thought, but then heard a frightened scream and a bigger splash. She leaped to her feet.

"Lyndon!" she yelled. "Lyndon, where are you?"

"Up here," the boy answered.

She ran across the stream and climbed up toward the cliffs. She found Lyndon sitting on the edge, feet dangling. "Where's Webb?" she asked.

"He fell," Lyndon replied quietly and calmly.

Tina rushed to look down. Her hand went to her

lips to stifle a scream. Webb lay half in, half out of the little pool, the clear water darkened by blood. Jumper was licking Webb's face.

It took Tina some time to go back downstream and then wade up to the pool. Jumper, sitting beside Webb's still form, was whining. Tina could not determine the source of the blood. Webb's face was white, with a large bruise beginning on one cheek. She took his arms and pulled his lower body out of the water. He was breathing shallowly. "Lyndon," she screamed, "go get help!"

Lyndon, still sitting on the rocks above, looked down at her blankly.

"Get help, you little bastard," Tina yelled, leaping to her feet. "Jumper, you stay with Webb," she ordered. She ran down the stream, slipping once and banging her shin on a rock. When she heard the voices of the children playing in the shallow pools below, she began to yell, and two boys ran up to meet her. "Get back to town quickly," she told them. "Have them send a doctor and the medical crawler."

"What's going on?" one of the boys asked.

"Just go," Tina said. "Webb Howard is hurt badly."

She ran, panting with exertion, back toward the upstream pool. As she neared it, she heard Jumper growling. She rounded the last bend in the stream and froze for a moment. Lyndon had come down from the cliff and was holding a large rock above his head as he tried to approach the motionless Webb. Jumper was prancing around, dashing in to nip at Lyndon's legs, keeping him away from Webb.

"What do you think you're doing?" Tina shrieked.

Lyndon whirled, the rock still poised over his head. "This animal was attacking me," he accused.

"You were trying to hit Webb with that rock," Tina said, running toward him. He spun around, amazingly agile and solidly built for a two-year-old, and threw the stone at Jumper, who scampered out of the way. Tina reached Lyndon and slapped him hard. He fell into the water, then jumped to his feet, glaring with pure hatred at her. After a moment he fled downstream.

Tina was sitting on the wet rocks, holding Webb's head in her lap, when the medical crawler screamed up and jolted to a halt as near to the wooded stream as possible. She heard people running through the trees, and then Mandy Miller, face flushed from exertion, was coming toward her, leading other medical people.

Mandy dropped her medical bag beside Tina and knelt on the flat rock. She jerked open the bag and applied a vital-signs monitor quickly and expertly.

"What happened, Tina?" Mandy asked.

"I—I think he fell," Tina said. "From up there."

Mandy was stripping away Webb's shorts. She had seen quickly that his right leg was badly broken. That was the source of the blood.

"Did he land where he's lying?" Mandy asked.

"I pulled him—he was partly in the water."

A coloring bruise on Webb's stomach confirmed Mandy's worst fears. She slapped an automatic intravenous module onto Webb's arm. "You see the leg," she told the two assistants who had arrived with a litter. "Probably internal bleeding. I'm administering the standard antishock IV. Let's get him to the vehicle."

Tina trailed along behind the running men. Mandy leaped into the driver's seat of the medical crawler. "If you're coming, get in," she told Tina.

"I have to find Lyndon," the girl said.

"He was with Webb?"

"Yes."

Mandy's eyes narrowed, but there was no time to waste in speculation. She got on the communicator to locate Theresita and Jacob. They were far to the south, deep in the equatorial jungle. When their base camp reached them, they were two hours by foot from the camp and the nearest scout ship, and it was not possible to retrieve them from under the dense canopy of the jungle by air.

Mandy's next call was to Duncan Rodrick. "Request scrambling," she said when she heard his voice.

It was an infrequent request, but Rodrick did not question her. The colony's business was done in the open, and there were few secrets, at least few requiring voicing on the air. "Scrambling, channel two," he said, and waited.

"Captain," Mandy said, "I have only a moment. You can ask questions later. I think Lyndon West pushed Webb Howard off a cliff. The West boy has disappeared along Jumper's Run. I'd like you to investigate. I'll be at the hospital." She clicked off then and concentrated on making speed.

Rodrick met Tina and Lyndon walking slowly back toward the outskirts of the city. He halted his crawler and told them to hop in. Tina's face was tearstained. Lyndon looked at Rodrick coldly.

"Want to tell me what happened?" Rodrick asked as he turned the crawler.

"Webb was taking Lyndon for a hike," Tina said. "He says"—she looked at Lyndon—"that Webb just slipped and fell."

"How about it, Lyndon?" Rodrick asked. "How, exactly, did it happen?"

"Well, sir," Lyndon said, with great respect in his voice, "we were standing on the bluff watching some fish in the pool in the stream below."

Rodrick hadn't been around Lyndon much. He could not get used to hearing such a mature use of language from a boy so small.

"And then the dumb dog ran between Webb's legs and tripped him. They both fell."

"He didn't call me or anything," Tina said, looking at Lyndon angrily. "I wouldn't even have known anything had happened if I hadn't heard the splash."

"Why didn't you call Tina?" Rodrick asked.

"I don't know. I guess I was shocked," Lyndon explained. "I was going to call her, but I just couldn't seem to get my mouth open."

"I told him to go get help, and he just sat there, grinning," Tina said. "I ran down the creek and sent some boys for help, and when I got back he was trying to hit Webb with a great big rock, and Jumper was keeping him away from Webb."

"Are you sure?" Rodrick asked.

"Sir, she's lying," Lyndon said calmly. "The animal tried to bite me when I came down to see if I could do anything for Webb. I was simply trying to protect myself from a vicious beast."

Rodrick's face was grim. Jumper was hardly a vicious beast.

"Then why were you trying to move toward Webb with the rock held over your head?" Tina demanded. "Tell me that."

Lyndon crossed his pudgy arms over his chest. "I have made my statement," he said.

The crawler was now on the main street. When Lyndon saw that it was headed for the hospital, he asked, "Where are you taking me?"

"I want to check on Webb's condition," Rodrick said.

"You can do that by radio. I want to go home. I'm hungry."

"I want you to talk to the doctors," Rodrick said. "Perhaps you can help them by describing the accident, just how Webb landed."

"Oh, no, you don't," Lyndon said. "That's just an excuse to turn me over to the brain fryers. You think I'm lying."

"That possibility had occurred to me," Rodrick agreed, and felt immediately belittled. It was not logical for a mature man to dislike a child so intensely.

"I want my mother," Lyndon said.

"She's been notified," Rodrick said. "It will be a few hours before she gets here. In the meantime, you *will* talk with Dr. Allano."

Lyndon fell silent. He had talked with Allano before, and the man was easy to fool. He saw no problem there. He marched beside Rodrick into a treatment room, climbed onto a table, and lay down. There was, he knew, no way to prove that he was lying. Their attempts at probing his mind had been laughable. All he had to do was act like a punk human child with people like Dr. Allano to set them to scratching their heads. He did not, however, hear Rodrick's orders to Allano when the doctor arrived. He let out one big squeak of surprise when, without so much as a word, Dr. Allano put a mister on his upper arm and pressed a trigger to send a mist of compressed medication into his flesh and into his bloodstream. He felt a momentary dizziness, and then he felt great.

"Of course I shoved the dumb bastard off the cliff," he told Allano. His smiling face and disdainful words were being recorded. "Why? Why not? He is, after all, retarded, a useless lunk." There was more, enough to make Robert Allano feel that perhaps Mandy was right in half wishing that all of the Eepera could be destroyed. When he had the complete story, Allano misted the boy into a deep sleep and had a nurse remove him to a security room.

Rodrick was with Delia Howard outside the room where Mandy and her staff were fighting to save the life of a seven-year-old boy. Allano pulled Rodrick aside and told him of the results of the truth serum Lyndon had been given.

"For the moment," Rodrick said, "I don't want Mrs. Howard to know."

"Of course," Allano agreed.

Rodrick took Delia a cup of coffee. "I'm sure you have your duties, Captain," Delia said.

"If you don't mind, I'll wait with you," he said.

"Thank you."

Two hours later both of them, having exchanged only some small talk during the period, jumped to the sound of Mandy's amplified voice coming from the speakers.

"Delia," Mandy said, "your son is going to be all

right. We're closing now. We've done the internal repair, and he's reacting strongly. We're going to do some preliminary work on his leg while we have him here."

Now, for the first time since the boy had been brought in, Delia wept. Rodrick, feeling helpless, paced the waiting area. He turned when a door opened and Theresita rushed in, followed closely by Jacob. Both were filthy and stained with sweat, not having had time to change from jungle garb. Theresita ran to Delia and took her hands in hers.

"He's going to be all right," Delia said, sniffing back tears. "Mandy just told us."

"I'm so glad," Theresita said. "He's such a fine little boy."

"Your son is here," Rodrick said. "He was a bit, uh, upset, and Dr. Allano sedated him."

"He's not hurt?" Theresita asked, her face going white.

"No, no, he's fine," Rodrick said. "Come along and we'll have a chat with Dr. Allano. Delia, if you need anything . . ."

Allano began to look thoroughly uncomfortable the minute Theresita walked into his office. He was grateful when Rodrick took over. "Jacob, Theresita, sit down. This is going to be very rough, especially for you, Theresita, but it's something that has to be done. I think the best way is to tell you fast: Webb's fall was no accident."

Theresita sighed. Jacob took her hand and squeezed it. "We feared as much," she admitted.

"On my authority Dr. Allano used a truth serum," Rodrick said. "I think you have to see the result."

A tear escaped from Theresita's left eye as she watched the screening of Lyndon's statements while under the influence of the barbiturate that prevented lying.

"What are we going to do?" she asked when it was over. "He is only two years old. What can we do?"

"There's something else," Rodrick said. "Prince Yanee has filed a petition with Max to see the boy."

"No," Jacob replied angrily.

"Now wait, Jacob," Rodrick said. "In his petition he states that all Eeperan children show extreme aggression when young. They're placed with Whorsk caretakers in special facilities. Apparently Lyndon shows Eeperan characteristics, and since the Eepera know more about taking care of Eeperan children than we do, maybe it wouldn't be all bad to have a talk with Yanee about it."

"Get the information from some other Eepera," Jacob snarled. "If I come face to face with that Yanee bastard, I'll kill him."

"Please," Theresita pleaded. "There is my son to consider. He is in trouble, and I haven't done very well with him. If Yanee can help, if he can give us some idea how to control Lyndon—"

"Damn," Jacob said, stomping to his feet.

"I did not choose my son's father," Theresita continued, "but I did carry my son. He is mine. I am his mother."

"All right, damn it," Jacob said.

"You do not have to meet with Yanee," Dr. Allano said.

"I'll be there," Jacob snarled. "I will be there."

NINETEEN

"With about two or three weeks of strip mining, I think we can get into some very worthwhile ore," Stoner said.

The entire crew was in the captain's mess on board the *Free Enterprise*. Mopro and the sergeant were on alert, the sergeant manning the ship's detection instruments from the bridge, and Mopro in battle position, ready to use his self-contained arsenal of weapons from an open port.

"The ore fields are within five miles of the plateau?" Jackie asked.

"Yep," Stoner answered.

"I think someone mentioned luck before we found this planet," Leslie said. "It seems more like bad luck to find the metallic ores we need right under the nose of something obviously built by intelligent beings."

"We're just going to have to find out what those constructions are and what or who built them," Clay said.

"Is there going to be an intelligent life form on every habitable planet?" Jackie mused. "I'm considering the possibility of leaving here to look for a planet with metals and no problems." Clay started to speak, but Jackie raised her hand to indicate that she wasn't finished. "I know. We're low on rhenium. We might or might not find something worthwhile with the limited amount of traveling and searching we can do with the remaining fuel."

"I've looked at the tapes a dozen times," Clay said.

"There's no movement around the constructions. I think we could take a closer look without any danger. It's unlikely that they'd have weapons that could do much harm. If they had the technological capacity to manufacture anything that might be potent enough to threaten us, there'd be some evidence of it in the atmosphere or signs of exploitation of the planet's metals."

"That makes sense, Jackie," Stoner commented. He was concentrating on the evidence of a field of ore that showed traces of the platinum metals. If rhenium were present in that ore field in about the same percentage of occurrence as on Earth, after refining the ore on Omega he could load enough of it on the *Free Enterprise* to provide enough rhenium to send a ship to search a hundred solar systems.

Jackie felt she had earned her rank in the space service. Counting her time on the *Free Enterprise,* she had more deep-space experience than any other officer, including Duncan, and had participated in fighting a lively little war. But never before had she been faced with ordering people out to face possible death. It was a natural decision—although not necessarily the best one—that she would not ask any of those under her command to do something she herself was unwilling to do.

"All right," Jackie said. "We'll take a look from the ground."

"I'll start getting ready," Clay said.

"Not you," Jackie said. "You, Cindy, and the chief engineer are indispensable to the ship."

Clay started to protest; then he remembered the chewing out he'd had down in the pod area. He glanced at Cindy glumly.

"Stoner, you'll be in command. You'll keep the fire-control systems active. Chief Fergus, you will have the ship ready to lightstep at an instant's notice."

Leslie Young nodded. It seemed that by process of elimination she would lead the ground exploration.

"We'll take both robots," Jackie said. "Mopro for firepower, the sergeant for mobility."

"I'll go," Jean offered, although her hands were trembling.

Jackie started to say something tart about the value of fluff in the event of trouble, but she was not an unkind person. "Thank you, Jean," she said sincerely, "but I think you'll be of more value here on the ship. Colonel Young will accompany me."

"And I," Shag Howard said.

"That won't be necessary," Jackie said. "There's no need to risk more than two lives."

Howard, ordinarily a quiet, introspective man, stood up. "Commander," he said, "so far I haven't been much use on this trip. For all the good I've done, I might as well have stayed at home with my wife and son. It seems logical that my medical skills might be needed if you run into anything with teeth out there."

Jackie nodded. "All right, Shag. Light armor. What weapons do you know?"

"Light arms," Shag said. "I belonged to a sports club back on Earth. We had competitions with antique projectile rifles, but the principle is the same as shooting a laser rifle."

"Good," Jackie said.

It took only a short while to outfit the ground party. The scout ship's cargo hatch had to be left open a crack to accommodate Mopro, but the vacuum of space didn't bother the big defense robot. Jackie and Leslie occupied the *Jennie*'s seats. The sergeant and Shag were folded into the small space behind the seats. The trip would be a brief one, so the discomfort could be endured.

"Once we're on the ground we'll check in every five minutes," Jackie told Cindy, who would be at the communications bank. "And if things get interesting, I'll leave the broadcast channels open. Stoner, this is a direct order: If we should encounter anything hostile and find ourselves in so deep that we can't get out on our own resources, you're to take the ship back to

Omega. I can't imagine anything that would be too much for Mopro and the sergeant to handle, but . . ."

The thought was left unspoken, but everyone knew what she meant. Stoner felt that the unknown threat to which Jackie was referring would hang over the heads of all humans in space until someday, somewhere, man would face that terrifying society called the Masters, which the Eepera feared. They were alone, eight people and two robots, with the blackness and emptiness of space around them, and with the unknown facing them on the surface of a beautiful planet. The crystalline constructions on the plateau in the heart of a great desert were undoubtedly the product of intelligence and of great technical skill. If they were the work of that parent race that had been traveling in space long before the Egyptians had begun the construction of their first pyramid, then only God knew what kind of weapons the ground party would face.

"I understand," Stoner said. Priorities. The ship was more valuable than three human lives and two robots, even though, in practical terms, Mopro and the sergeant were of more potential value for defense than Jackie, Leslie, and Shag.

The *Jennie* dropped away from the *Free Enterprise*. Cindy kept the scout on visuals until it landed on the edge of the plateau, a few hundred yards from the nearest construction. Clay chafed, wanting to be down there. It bothered him to know that three good friends of his faced the unknown dangers on the surface alone.

Mopro extricated himself from the *Jennie*'s cargo bay and rolled, weapons at the ready, to stand between the scout and the nearest blaze of reflected light coming from the simple but beautiful constructions. The sergeant, at last doing something that he had been designed to do, leapfrogged past Mopro and hit the dirt, a laser rifle pointed, searching for any movement among the constructions.

Jackie told Leslie and Shag to spread out. Mopro rolled. From the ground the transparent shapes loomed high overhead and seemed to grow larger as the group approached cautiously.

The sergeant sped past Mopro, a bit contemptuous of the big defense robot's relative lack of speed and mobility. He darted between two tall triangles, then circled them, but saw nothing except the odd constructions and undisturbed sand around them.

"I see no opening in the constructions," he radioed back to Jackie. "I see no evidence of any living presence."

Jackie was making her regular reports to the orbiting ship. "Scout ahead with Mopro," she told the sergeant.

Leslie circled around a gleaming square that soared sheer and clear to a hundred feet over her head. She could look all the way through the material and see Jackie's outline, distorted and taking on the colors of the prism. Leslie also heard the sergeant's continued reports as he moved swiftly through the towering constructions, covering twice the ground investigated by Mopro. Shag was with Jackie, walking about ten feet to her right, his eyes searching, rifle held at the ready.

The field of structures covered a square of about twenty acres. It took time to search it. It soon became apparent to the sergeant that they were wasting time. He could see through the structures all the way to barren sand outside the area. His specialized search instruments gave no readings. No heat, other than that reflected by the clear material, activated his sensors. It was the same with Mopro.

"Commander Rodrick," the sergeant reported, "I have covered or observed every inch of ground. There are no life signs, no heat, no radiation, no indication that anyone or anything has been here for a long time."

"Very well," Jackie said. "Mopro, I'd like a small sample of that material for analysis. Don't do any great damage in getting it."

There seemed to be little danger of doing damage to one of the constructions, short of using some high-powered weapons or tools. Mopro tried to cut out a small piece at the sharp corner of a rectangular construction. It took him some time to discover that it took a molecular cutting torch to separate a small piece. Meanwhile, the sergeant was making a second search.

"Whoever built them," Leslie said as she and the others watched Mopro's attempt to obtain a sample, "they're not here."

"I think these structures are an art form," Shag said. "They blend with the surroundings and are visible from the air only because of the color they refract."

"A mad artist, traveling parsecs through space to build a masterpiece that no one would ever see?" Jackie asked.

"Stranger things have happened in the world of art," Leslie said.

"They could be listening devices," Jackie said. "I know we can see through them, and there doesn't seem to be any machinery or electronics involved, but the Eepera say that their race set up listening posts at various places. We have no idea where the science of the original Eepera race has led them since our bunch fled to Earth."

"Well, if that's the case," Shag said, "we should be expecting company. But I think you're wrong. If these were technical gadgets, they'd be concealed. It's hard for me to imagine that there's something concealed inside these things. We can look directly through them."

"The material distorts slightly, and the flare of colors makes it hard to distinguish details on the other side," Leslie said. "But I think they're just what they appear to be—hollow, with relatively thin shells."

"What's inside?" Jackie asked.

"Air or a vacuum," Shag guessed.

Mopro finished his cutting and cooled a piece of the material in his hands before extending it toward Jackie.

"It's thicker than it looks," Jackie commented. "Mopro, could the construction be solid?"

Mopro printed out his findings on the band of light

around his head: "Soundings indicate that all constructions are hollow."

Jackie thumbed the switch on her communicator. "Cindy," she said, "tell the chief to be ready to land the ship at local dawn. Let Stoner pick out the landing site. Tell him we're going to camp here tonight and keep an eye on things. If it's still quiet in the morning, Stoner can start his preparations to begin mining as soon as the ship is on the ground."

The balance of the day was spent in further exploration. The sergeant explored the steep, sloping walls leading to the plateau, searching for caves and evidence of intelligent activity, but all he found was rock and some hardy desert vegetation. He ranged outward three miles in a circle. The barren ground was free of any sign of life except for a few species of lizardlike reptiles.

Field rations were heated by Mopro's torch. It was a fireless camp. Each of them had only one thin thermal blanket, which came in handy when the sun went down and the temperature began to drop sharply. Since neither the sergeant nor Mopro needed sleep, they took the watch. The sergeant, still contemptuous of the bulky defense robot, exercised his authority. He gave Mopro orders to spend the night hours digging down beside one of the constructions, to find out how deeply it was embedded in the sandy soil. When dawn came and Jackie saw the huge excavation, exposing over ten feet of material below ground level, she felt a moment of guilt for not having thought of it herself. At least the job was done. She could see through the material to the soil on the other side.

She didn't like it. Mopro had dug down over ten feet and there was still no indication of a foundation. The material seemed to extend much deeper into the soil.

"There could be machinery down there, down the shaft," she said.

"No indication of metals other than natural, minor amounts in the soil," Mopro printed.

"Well, we've spent a day and a night here," Jackie said. She contacted the ship and told Cindy to bring her down. She told Mopro to keep digging.

It was always impressive to see something as large as a starship come lowering, thundering, down, down, through sparse clouds and then into a great cloud of dust as the ship's multiple rockets seared the soil surface. Then she was down. Jackie called Stoner to the plateau and told the others to stand by. Stoner hummed and mused as he examined representative structures and then stood beside the hole Mopro was excavating. The robot had dug down another five feet, and the going was easy in soft, sandy dirt.

On board the *Free Enterprise* Clay was getting impatient. He kept the sergeant in constant conversation, asking questions, demanding descriptions, getting reports of the action as Mopro dug deeper, deeper.

"We're wasting time," he said to Cindy. "Stoner and I could be unloading the big earth movers."

Deep within the excavation Mopro's hands finally contacted solidity. He lifted his head and printed, "Rock. Natural."

Stoner slid down into the hole. He brushed aside dirt with his hands. "Natural bedrock," he said. "No sign of being worked." He brushed dirt away from the side of the construction. The natural bedrock seemed to continue across the shaft of the structure, rough and uneven. There seemed to be no way of fastening the material to the bedrock, but the edges of it were contoured to match every irregularity of the rock.

"It seems to have been poured," he shouted up to the others. "Otherwise it would have been one heck of a job to cut the lower edges to conform to the rock the way they do."

Stoner got an assist from Mopro to clamber out of the hole, showering dirt down behind him. The big robot stood mutely, waiting orders.

"That's enough, Mopro," Jackie said.

"A lot of work and a lot of material went into these things," Stoner said.

"What's your opinion as to the nature of the material?" Shag asked.

"I dunno," Stoner admitted. "Some kind of plastic?"

"It took a molecular torch to cut off this sample," Jackie said, handing the small piece to Stoner. Stoner sniffed and rubbed it across his front teeth. "If it's plastic, it's a damned tough plastic."

"Is there any possibility that these constructions only seem to be transparent all the way through?" Jackie asked, addressing the question to anyone who wanted to venture an opinion.

"An optical illusion?" Shag asked.

"Mirror tricks," Jackie said.

"They'd have to know more about bending light than we do," Stoner said. "Not that that's impossible."

"I don't like it," Jackie said, feeling her responsibility.

"If it would ease your mind, we can have Mopro blast a hole in one," Stoner suggested.

"Oh, no," Leslie said quickly. Then, "Sorry, I was just thinking of their beauty. Seems a shame to deface one of them."

Mopro, his drive units humming, rolled and pulled himself out of the excavation to stand on level ground.

"It is a shame," Jackie said, "but I'd feel better if we knew for sure that they're nothing more than hollow space inside."

"Mopro, see if you can drill a hole in this one," Stoner said.

"I suggest we all put on our helmets and go on internal life support until we see if there's something noxious inside," Shag said.

"Yes," Jackie agreed, donning her helmet. They checked each other, and Jackie gave the signal to Mopro. He rolled a few feet away from them, faced the side of the square, and opened a port to reveal his laser cannon.

"Hold on, Mopro," Jackie said. "Let me report to Cindy what we're doing. She did so, then left her communicator open as she nodded to Mopro. The defense robot's laser cannon extended itself, but before he could fire, a cry of warning from the sergeant caused him to turn ponderously toward the humans.

The sergeant's weapon had been jerked away and was dangling in the air on an almost invisible, very fine line. The sergeant himself was struggling as loop after loop of the fine, hard-to-see line pinned his arms and legs. The humans were faring no better.

Leslie felt the first of the lines loop down over her body, and then her arms were jerked to her sides and she was being lifted. A small loop wrenched the weapon from her hand.

Jackie's only thought was to warn the ship. She tried to lift her communicator, yelling, "Blast off, *Enterprise*. Blast off." But then the communicator flew from her hand and went flying upward to disappear, seemingly right through the transparent wall of the structure. Jackie was slowly being drawn up toward the point of the communicator's disappearance.

Below, Mopro was fighting what seemed to be hundreds of the small, almost invisible lines.

"Fire, you metal-brained idiot," the sergeant yelled as he was being drawn slowly up toward the top of the square construction.

Mopro fell to his knees. His massive strength served only to stretch the hundreds of lines around him. He opened the ports of his kneecaps, exposing two deadly cannons ready to fire explosive projectiles. But above him Jackie was disappearing into the construction, sinking through the transparency as if into calm water. To fire, Mopro reasoned, would endanger his human charges.

"Fire, fire," the sergeant yelled as, still struggling, he followed the humans through the side of the square into inky darkness.

TWENTY

Lance Corporal Vic Wakefield felt wonderful. The great thing about an Eeperan party was that you never had a hangover. Oh, for a while during the morning you had a funny feeling, as if your entire body craved something—food, water . . . something. Nothing seemed to satisfy that craving, but it gradually wore off. By the time Vic was called in to see Commander Max Rosen, he was functioning perfectly and looking forward to the night.

"Corporal," Max told Vic, "I want you to escort Prince Yanee to Hamilton City. There'll be a scout on the pad in about fifteen minutes."

Vic hadn't seen his buddy Yanee standing in the shadows. He repressed a grin. So old Yanee had done it. He had obtained permission to go to Hamilton City to see his son.

"Yes, sir," Vic said.

"Since you're due for rotation tomorrow," Max said, "there's no need for you to come back with Yanee. Your replacement will escort the prince back."

Vic started to protest. He'd been looking forward to one last night with the Eepera tigresses, one last hit of that drug that had no name, even among the Eepera. But to protest would have been revealing. He was a good space marine; he knew when to keep his mouth shut. "Yes, sir," he said. "Permission to pack, sir?"

"Right," Max said. He looked up at Yanee. "There's a pretty tense situation over there," he said. "I hope you don't do anything to make it worse."

"On the contrary," Yanee replied smoothly, "perhaps I can give some suggestions about rearing an Eeperan child."

Yanee walked beside Vic to Vic's tent, where the packing was done swiftly by dint of long training. Yanee pretended not to see when Vic secreted a small packet of the drug in a rolled-up pair of socks. He had not expected such a favorable development so quickly. He had, he realized, overestimated the intelligence of these Earthpeople. Soon the drug would be in the enemy's stronghold, and the Earthpeople had no resistance to its habituating effects, as did the Eepera.

Vic and Yanee were waiting when *Apache One* came in with Jacob West's usual flair. Jacob opened ship and came out the hatch to face the tall, handsome Eeperan. Yanee met the dark-faced man's gaze questioningly.

"I don't believe we've met," Yanee said.

"That's fortunate for you," Jacob growled. "Get him aboard, Marine, and put him in cargo. I won't have him soil my cabin."

"Sir," Vic ventured, "may I remind you that Prince Yanee is on official business with permission from the commander?"

"Cargo," Jacob snapped. "And you with him."

"I get the distinct impression that the pilot does not like me," Yanee said with a disdainful smile as the ship lifted with a stomach-sinking lurch. "And he doesn't even know me."

"He knows of you," Vic said with a grin. "He married the big Russian broad."

"Ah," Yanee said, "yes, I see. But he is so wrong in thinking that I am not his friend."

"Yanee, I guess I'd better warn you that Jacob West is not the only one who doesn't think much of the Eepera."

"But we are a defeated people," Yanee said. "We have surrendered. We are in your hands."

"Being a prince, you must know all this protocol

junk," Vic said. "But I'd suggest that you be friendly but formal, and talk as little as possible."

"Oh, I know how to crawl," Yanee said.

"You won't have to crawl," Vic responded. "You can be honest and open with Captain Rodrick. He's a good man, a straight and honorable man, and he wants peace here on Omega."

"Until *they* come," Yanee said.

Vic, who would not have faltered facing any number of known enemies, shivered. The idea of some unknown danger looming down from the blackness of space spooked him. "You really think they'll come?"

"Oh, yes," Yanee said. "One cannot say when, but they will come. The Masters will be in no hurry, for it will be but the work of a minute or two to wipe out everything that you have built and all of our cities, even if they don't choose to smash the entire planet."

Vic looked glum. Yanee clapped him on the back. "Don't worry. It could be years. Meanwhile, there is life to live, eh, my friend? There are beautiful women. There are the passions of the night and the means to intensify them."

"Yeah, sure, eat, drink, and be merry," Vic said.

"Our magic potion has a profound effect on Earth-women," Yanee said.

Vic thought of that crazy Celia Hadley, who now participated in the nightly Eeperan parties as wildly as any Eepera woman. And he thought of a juicy little teenager he'd had his eyes on ever since he landed on Omega. She was young but stacked. He wasn't quite ready for a permanent attachment, not yet. He'd pull more guard tours over on the Great Misty River, and he didn't want a young wife back in Hamilton City to prey on his conscience, but it wouldn't hurt to talk to the girl, to lay the groundwork. After all, it was understood that every single man and woman should marry. Vic wouldn't mind breeding a few little space marines with Tina Sells.

Vic was feeling better, no longer shivering at the

thought of Yanee's ogres from deep space, when *Apache One* landed on the Hamilton City pads and he delivered Yanee into the hands of a space service officer he had known on the *Free Enterprise*. He went to his private quarters.

Omega wasn't a bad duty post. He had his own house. A little expansion, and it'd be big enough for a wife and a couple of kids. He unpacked, placing the pair of socks containing the drug at the bottom of a drawer. He felt just a little doubtful. Over there, in Suses, it seemed to be all right; here, just knowing the drug was in his drawer made him nervous. On one of his tours on a weapons satellite he'd seen a marine have a bad drug experience. Vic had been one of the men who subdued the marine and carried him into the clinic. And he'd seen and talked to the marine after a rush series of psychotreatment. He didn't know exactly what the fellow had undergone, but he didn't want any part of it. The guy was never normal after that, and he went back planetside on the next shuttle. Scuttlebutt had been that he was given a medical discharge.

Well, he was back in civilization, or what passed for it on a new planet. He luxuriated in a long, steamy shower, dressed in his best casual uniform, and found himself walking toward the home of Tina Sells. He barely knew the girl, but he liked the way she had looked at him when they met. His luck was with him. When he knocked on the door, Tina, dressed in cute little shorts and a skimpy knit thing that came just above her naval, answered.

"Hi," he said. "I'll bet you don't remember me."

"I'll bet I do," she said. "You're Vic Wakefield."

"Outstanding," he said. He shifted his feet. "Look, I just thought—"

"Wanta come in?" she asked. "Since we're all Omegans now, I think we should all know each other, don't you?" Tina was more than pleased to have a handsome young man standing on her doorstep. She had been brooding over her carelessness in almost getting Webb killed and wondering what they were going to do with Lyndon. And, after all, everyone over the age of fifteen or so already had at least one boyfriend.

"I thought just that," Vic said, stepping into a comfortable, neat living room. "And of all the first settlers of Omega, I thought, well, I want to know this pretty Tina."

Tina flushed with pleasure. She served Vic a drink, being careful not to pour too much. Her father might have noticed just how full the bottle was, and she was not allowed to drink as yet. She didn't particularly want to have to explain missing liquor.

It was just beautiful. Vic sat there on a couch, all straight and handsome, talking softly and complimenting her. He asked all sorts of interesting questions about what she liked and the things she'd done as a little girl back on Earth, and it was absolutely perfect when he finally said, "Look, I guess I'd better go, but I'd like to take you out sometime."

"I think that can be arranged," she said, trying to sound witty and adult.

"Should I speak with your father?" Vic asked.

"No," she said quickly. Then, with a shrug and a smile, "Well, to tell the truth, that would be good. He'll hum and grunt and look you over from head to toe, but then he'll feel that he knows you and he'll say"—she deepened her voice—"'Vic, as you know, Tina is not quite sixteen, and that's very young, even for Omega.'"

"And I'll say, 'Sir, my intentions are nothing but honorable,'" Vic said, taking her hand, his touch sending a thrill through her body.

True to Tina's prediction, Tony Sells hummed and looked Vic over from head to toe. Tina had invited Vic to dinner. Before the meal, while Tina and Vic were in the living room listening to some of Tina's favorite music, her mother pulled Tony aside and said, "Honey, we knew it was coming."

"But a space marine?" Tony asked.

"It's just a date," Trisha Sells said. "She's young. She'll date several of the young men before—"

"Yeah." Tony snorted. "She has such a wide choice."

They had, of course, discussed that very problem before deciding to come to Omega. They had been told then that boys of Tina's age group would be scarce. But Tony had envisioned Tina falling in love with the son of some illustrious scientist, a boy of education and breeding. Not that there was all that much wrong with Vic Wakefield. He was a nice enough lad, handsome and polite. And Tony knew that there was a continuing education program for the service people. When and if their duties as protectors and fighters were no longer needed, they'd be taught useful skills. But a space marine?

Tina volunteered to do the dishes after a pleasant meal during which Vic, sensing the doubt in Tina's parents, tried to convince them, without being too obvious, that he was not just a space-head marine. He had been taking courses ever since he finished basic training and was well on the way toward an accredited degree in electronics repair. He helped Tina clear the table and put the dishes in the washer.

"Mom, we're going for a walk," Tina said, coming out of the kitchen ahead of Vic.

"All right, dear," Trisha agreed, with a look at Tony.

"We're going to walk through the fields down to the river," Tina said. "Vic hasn't seen Amando Kwait's miracles yet."

Vic took her hand as they walked away from the city. By the time they reached the river it was growing dark. They sat on a patch of grass and watched the first stars appear.

"Do you like sailing?" Vic asked after a long silence.

Tina had been sure that he was working up his nerve to kiss her. "I haven't done any," she said.

"I did some back home," he said. "We can check

out a little sailer tomorrow, and I'll teach you everything you need to know." He had not intended a hidden meaning, but the idea flashed into his mind with
the words. If a guy sailed around the southern point
of Stanton Bay, he'd be just about as much alone with a
girl as a man could be. Only the eyes of a ship in the air
could see them.

Not that he was going to move on this one. No.
She was the marrying kind. As they walked home through
the velvety Omegan night, her hand in his, he began to
like the idea more and more of having this one in his
home permanently.

"Back so soon?" Tony asked when Tina came into
the living room.

"Vic had an early duty call," Tina said.

Trisha came into Tina's room after Tina had showered and was in the T-shirt she slept in. Tina smiled.
"You came to ask me questions, didn't you?"

"No, not really," her mother said.

"I don't mind. It was a lovely evening. Vic is such
a gentleman."

"Really?" Trisha asked, trying to sound casual.

"He didn't even try to kiss me," Tina said. "He
held my hand."

Trisha felt a sharp pang of nostalgia, and concern.
She remembered how she'd felt when she and Tony
were dating. Of course, she had been older, in college.
But this was Omega. Cindy McRae and Clay Girard
had been married at the age of sixteen.

"Do you like him, Mother?" Tina asked.

"Yes, very much," Trisha said. "He does seem to
be a nice boy."

"He wants me to go sailing with him," Tina said.
"He knows all about it."

Trisha sat down beside her daughter on the bed.
"Tina, I'm pleased that you have a friend like Vic. I'm
not going to preach to you. I think we've instilled the
proper values in you. But you and I are both aware that
the situation here on Omega is not like it was on Earth.

There you'd have had years to go to school, to date and meet different boys. All I'm going to say to you is this: Don't think that you have to fall in love with the first boy who holds your hand. There'll be other young men here. They'll come out from Earth. You're young. You have time. And soon our school system here will be good enough to allow you to continue your studies."

"I won't do anything hastily, and I won't do anything yucky, not that Vic would ask me to."

"I know you won't," Trisha said, kissing Tina on the forehead and leaving the room.

In his own little home Vic prepared for bed, whistling, feeling fine. He'd felt a real sense of loss when he'd left Tina. He was sure that she was the one, and the nights in Suses with the Eepera tigresses didn't seem to have as much appeal as they had previously. He turned off the lights and got into bed, smiling in the darkness, remembering the way she smelled. Clean, young, human. Not perfumed and, by late night, slightly soiled and soured like the tigresses.

"Tina," he said aloud. He liked the sound. He said it again, grinned widely, and closed his eyes—only to experience a gut-wrenching ache that quickly spread through his entire body until he trembled. He leaped out of his bed, walked to turn on the light. His hands were shaking. Something was happening to him. He reached for his communicator to call for medical help and then froze as a thought came to him. He remembered Celia Hadley and the way she'd been acting lately. Celia took heavy, heavy hits of the drug and kept it up throughout most of the night. And in the mornings she shook and had to hide her hands to prevent others from seeing. He'd suspected that Celia was getting addicted to the drug. The big Russian broad had been hooked, or so it was rumored.

If he called medical and they found he'd been hitting on the drug—

But something had to be done. He had to know if the trembling, the frantic crying out of every cell in his body was a call for the drug he had been taking just about every night for weeks. He went to the drawer, retrieved the packet, measured out a small dose, and washed it down with a slug of Omegan white wine. Within minutes he felt fine, and as he lay on his bed, he could picture the tigresses in his mind, dozens, *hundreds*, all willing, all so perfect and beautiful. He wouldn't be back on the river for a full rotation, a full week. It was going to be tough, being able almost to feel the smooth, sweet skin of the Eeperan women but not being able to go to the playground in Suses.

He found himself thinking of Tina. The drug was no real problem. He'd never been beaten by anything. Maybe he was getting to be just a little dependent on it. But he could whip it. The Russian broad had been force-fed the drug for maybe months, and she whipped it. What she could do, he could do. He went to sleep *knowing* that Tina's body would be smoother, sweeter, more endearing than that of the most sensuous tigress in Suses.

TWENTY-ONE

Sitting in Dr. Allano's office at the hospital, Theresita faced the man who had saved her life and then used her sexually while she was under the influence of the Eeperan drug. Jacob was with her, standing with a glowering frown at her side. Theresita had to admit to some curiosity. Her memories of the time she had been kept in the city of Suses by this Eeperan were hazy, but in spite of herself she felt a warm glow inside as she remembered. Yanee was indeed handsome, golden, his muscular chest exposed by the robes of an Eeperan prince.

Yanee bowed. "I see you are in health," he began.

"Yes, thank you," Theresita replied.

"I cannot apologize for my nature, nor for the ways of my race," Yanee said. "I do regret that there is misunderstanding between us and our peoples."

"We're not here to make speeches," Jacob said.

"You want to see the boy," Theresita said.

"I do," Yanee said. "There has been some trouble involving him?"

Theresita explained the situation briefly as she walked with Yanee down the hall. Jacob trailed behind. Yanee shook his head. "Yes, he would do exactly that. He would have done the same to an Eeperan child, given the opportunity. You see, all children are nothing more than animals. The mental and physical development of an Eeperan child runs far ahead of his acceptance of social behavior. To the child, only *he* exists. Others are nothing more than objects meant to be of service to him. If something is not of immediate value, for selfish purposes, he has no hesitation in ridding himself of it, and that attitude would extend to a larger child. The smaller would resent the larger for his strength, if for nothing else, or for his very presence."

"When does this antisocial behavior cease?" Theresita asked.

"At about ten years. Omegan years."

"Good Lord," Theresita said. "And by the time he's eight or nine—"

"He'll be stronger than an Earthboy of his same age, and completely capable of and willing to kill you if you displease him in some small matter," Yanee said.

"Here we are," Theresita said, opening a door. Lyndon was watching a tape of a low-level flight over the southern jungles. He turned when Yanee and Theresita stepped into the room.

"Who's this?" he asked Theresita.

"I am Yanee, prince of the city of Suses."

"Big deal," Lyndon said, but he switched off the screen, obviously interested.

"I am your father," Yanee said.

"Thanks for nothing." Lyndon spat. "If you're so great, why did you leave me here with these mental pygmies?"

"I have come to look upon you," Yanee said. "I am pleased. You have the body and the look of the Eepera."

"And thanks to your choice, I'm half-human," Lyndon said, sneering at Theresita.

"I think that your mother cares for you. I know that she has not been harsh with you."

"All right, you've looked upon me," Lyndon mimicked. "Now why don't you go? I was watching some interesting scenes of my planet."

Without a further word Yanee turned and swept past Theresita into the hall. Theresita, left alone with her son, said, "Would you like to come home?"

Lyndon's face contorted. "It's as boring there as it is here. And you'd just go off with the Indian and leave me with that dizzy little broad."

Theresita remembered Mandy's stern order. "Don't feel guilty for something over which you had no control." But that was just words. With a feeling of helplessness she left the room, closing the door behind her. In the hall Yanee and Jacob were looking at each other coldly.

"What will be done with him?" Yanee asked.

"I don't know," Theresita admitted. "He almost killed a boy. We can't have a repetition of that."

"There is a solution," Yanee said. "But it is radical, so I am hesitant to mention it."

"We're open to any sensible suggestion," Theresita said.

"I will take the boy to Suses. He will be placed with the others. There he will be tended day and night by specially trained Whorsk. They know the characteristics of our young, and they have tended many generations. I myself spent my first ten years with them."

Theresita turned away, knowing now that she had dreaded such a suggestion all along but not knowing what else to do. Allano had been trying mild psycho-treatment without success. Lyndon's will was strong, his mental development advanced. Psychotreatment was not the horrible thing that some feared, but the use of chemicals inside the human brain was, to her, fearful. It was said, and Mandy had reassured her repeatedly, that psychotreatment did not cause damage, but it often revealed damage in development. Often the eradication of some undesirable mental aberration seemed to leave a blank in the mind, and from that arose the scary stories. No one could tell her that Lyndon would be the same if the doctors used psychotreatment in an effort to curb his aggression, his—yes, she had to admit it, had to use the word—psychopathic tendencies.

"Not a chance," Jacob said. "We won't turn him over to a bunch of bugs."

"Do you have a choice?" Yanee did not speak to Jacob but to Theresita. "You can visit him when you like. When he ceases to be an animal, then . . . After all, he is your son."

"But he'd be Eeperan," Theresita said.

"The adult Eeperan is not a savage," Yanee said. "He will be taught to respect his mother."

"No," Jacob said.

"We *don't* have any choice," Theresita moaned. "Treatment? What if, by wiping out that which is natu-ral to an Eeperan child, they take something vital to his development? Would you want him to be a dull, docile thing like a man who has been given a lobotomy? That can happen. We used psychotreatment widely back in the Soviet Union. I have seen the results. If the aberra-tion is minor, there is little change. But the things that make Lyndon different are deep-seated, basic. I will not have him become a human robot."

"Let's take some time to think it through," Jacob urged.

"I have thought," Theresita said. "My God, I'm his

mother. I've known ever since we got the call in the jungle that something like this would have to be done."

"You are a very wise woman," Yanee said.

"They are not mistreated, your children?" Theresita asked.

"No. They are forced to be nonviolent by constant supervision. They are taught by Eeperan teachers. Their punishment is locally painful but not damaging."

"I will see this place," Theresita said.

Yanee bowed.

"Now. Before I change my mind," Theresita said.

This time Jacob allowed Yanee into the cabin of *Apache One*. At Yanee's direction they landed in a large square near the river in Suses. It was a short walk to the fenced buildings where a new generation of Eepera were receiving their early training. Yanee was recognized, and the threesome were admitted through an otherwise impenetrable outer perimeter.

"I've seen prisons less secure than this," Jacob remarked.

In a pleasant garden a half-dozen Eeperan children from the size of Lyndon to boys the size of Webb were paired with uniformed Whorsk. The scene seemed to be peaceful until, suddenly, one of the larger Eeperan boys lifted a stone from the border of a flower bed and with a deadly swiftness and amazing power smashed it down on the head of his Whorsk attendant. The Whorsk's shell cracked, and as it fell, liquids began to ooze. Seemingly from nowhere another Whorsk appeared and seized the boy, who had started to run.

"My God," Theresita said.

"The attendant got careless," Yanee said casually. "They lose quite a few that way."

"What will they do to the boy?" Jacob asked.

"Oh, he'll probably receive a punishment tour of solitude. Perhaps a day or two."

"My God," Theresita gasped.

In a classroom dominated by an aged Eepera woman, Eeperan boys and girls acted quite civilized, reciting their lessons, smiling, trying to impress the visiting prince, scarcely looking at Theresita and Jacob. During the midday meal the children were separated from each other by little partitions on the long tables. The individual quarters were roomy and clean. There was a room and bed alcove in each for the child. The Whorsk attendants slept in their own quarters.

"This is one of several facilities," Yanee explained. "It happens to be the finest. I think the boy would be as content as a child could be here."

Even after seeing the place and knowing it was a virtual prison where violence could erupt at any moment, Theresita knew she had no other choice. She would not submit Lyndon to psychotreatment.

There was one more stop: a pleasant enclosed garden. "This is where parents sit with their children when visiting," Yanee said. "You could come as often as you like."

Theresita was silent on the flight home. She had told Yanee that she would notify him soon of her decision. Actually, she had already made it, and she needed only one brief talk with Mandy Miller to reinforce it.

"Yes," Mandy said, "I fear there would be brain damage if we tried to eradicate Eeperan personality characteristics from the boy."

Theresita flew with Jacob to deliver Lyndon to the children's home. She bent to kiss him good-bye. Fascinated by his new surroundings, he tried to hit her on the nose, saying, "Knock it off."

TWENTY-TWO

Yanee dropped in on a gathering of his friends and enjoyed a meal with them but declined an invitation to stay. He went out into the night. It was still early enough for there to be some activity on the streets, so he made no effort to be circumspect until he had walked out of the central, lighted areas of the city in the direction of the bluff under the softly glowing pyramid. Then he kept to the shadows, pausing now and then to be sure he was unobserved. The regular evening patrol made its way down from the camp atop the bluff and headed toward the river. He waited until it was well into the city before moving slowly and carefully into the shadow of the cliff to make his way among boulders to a dark, hidden nook. As heir to the throne of the city of Suses, he was one of only two men outside the priesthood who knew just where to stand, just which rock to push to cause a hidden door to slide aside enough for him to slip sideways into a smooth-walled passageway that led upward to steps, burrowing deeper and higher into the native stone.

After a considerable climb he encountered a door. Not even he could force it open, but it was opened for him almost immediately when he gave a series of spaced knocks. A young priest recognized him, bowed silently, and led him forward.

"Great Ahmes," the young priest said as they entered a comfortably furnished chamber, "Prince Yanee."

The priest who had only recently assumed the highest position, and the traditional name, rose to meet

185

Yanee with a murmur of greeting. Refreshments were served. Yanee told of his certain knowledge that the drug that so incapacitated the Earthpeople had been smuggled into the enemy's colony. The high priest nodded with satisfaction.

"We have observed that three more members of the enemy's guard force are now participating in Eeperan pleasure," Ahmes said. "The female called Celia is going to be very valuable to us. It is she who has convinced the three new ones to join her. Soon they will all be ours."

"It will not be so easy," Yanee cautioned. "Your priests continue to give the impression of cooperating with their scientists?"

"Of course," Ahmes answered. "And in the process we learn. We have been wrong, Yanee, in depending solely upon the science of our ancestors."

"When most of the Americans cannot continue to function without our drug, we will have total access to their knowledge. When we assimilate their science, using our superior brains, we will possess all their technology."

"And if, in the meantime, *they* come?"

Yanee shrugged. "That is in the hands of the gods." There was a brief silence. "Given some time, I'm not sure that a first encounter with the Masters would be fatal for the Earthmen. They can be formidable."

"They have easily mastered the mystery of the light weapons. Now they work toward understanding the power itself."

"That is the value of a continuing study of science," Yanee said. "While we, in our comfort, have been content to live well and enjoy the security of our ancient machines, the Earthpeople are continually probing."

"Perhaps it is time that we advanced our own knowledge, without further delay," Ahmes suggested.

Yanee showed interest.

"Of all the Earthpeople, the woman Grace is the

most knowledgeable in science. If we had all the knowledge in her mind, we would close the gap quickly."

Yanee pondered. He had grasped the priest's meaning immediately. The priests had an ancient method. . . . "You are, of course, exercising the utmost care in keeping secret this lower level?"

"No one enters or leaves without my supervision," Ahmes said. "The laboratories of our fathers are inviolate and will remain so."

"The risk is great. These Earthpeople set great value on individual lives, and they are especially protective of their women."

"But the rewards would also be great," Ahmes reminded him.

"Proceed with care," Yanee said. "Take no risk."

"Of course," Ahmes replied.

TWENTY-THREE

Cindy had slept little during the night, dozing in her chair on the bridge of the *Free Enterprise*. When the ship was safely down and a thorough search had been made among the gleaming geometrical figures on the plateau, she could finally relax. She listened with interest as Stoner joined the group on the plateau and talked about the way the transparent material was molded to the bedrock; then she had a bit of breakfast. She jerked her head up when she heard Jackie's voice go faint and agitated. She could not understand what Jackie was saying.

"Please repeat," she said into the communicator. Then, more formally, "Commander Rodrick, come in."

At that point Clay came back onto the bridge. "What's up?"

"I don't know," Cindy said, going back to her attempts to raise the ground party. After several transmissions with no answer, she turned to Clay. "Something's happened."

"Try again," Clay said, worried. He used the ship's optics, but the ship was lower than the top of the plateau, so he could see nothing. The only scout was up there, atop the hill.

"Everything was fine. They were going to drill into one of the structures, and then nothing," Cindy said.

Clay leaped to his feet.

"What are you going to do?" Cindy asked.

"I'm going up there to take a look."

"Clay, we have specific orders." She rose and clutched at his arm. "In the event of trouble, we're to lift ship and get her out of possible harm's way."

"We don't know that there's trouble," he said. "It could be simple communications failure."

"Clay, there are four communicators up there, plus the internal systems of the sergeant and Mopro."

"I'm not going to leave them without knowing what's going on," he said.

"Clay—"

He removed her hands from his arm. "I'm going. If worse comes to worst, you and the chief can get the ship home. It's all navigation and power anyhow. The pilot is nothing more than a button pusher."

"Unless things get rough," she reminded him.

"You know which buttons to push."

"I wouldn't," she said. "I wouldn't leave you."

"You have the ship to think of," he said. "I'm going to be all right. I'll be back. I'm sure there's a simple explanation for the failure of communication. But you'll do the right thing if—"

She was weeping silently.

Clay went well armed. He used a crawler to approach the plateau and then had to dismount and climb

the rocks. He covered every foot of the plateau, sometimes following the tracks of the group. Mopro's treads
left a trail that could not be missed.

He found the excavation. The entire area was covered with footprints and Mopro's treads. When he saw
the marks of Mopro's last struggles, Clay went pale. It
was evident that the big defense robot had been fighting something very powerful, for his treads had dug
deeply into the dry soil. There were no tread marks
leading away from the disturbed area, and Clay had
difficulty imagining what could have been powerful
enough to lift the huge defense robot and carry him
away without leaving tracks. The evidence seemed to
indicate that Mopro had been removed by air, but the
Free Enterprise's sensors had been operating all night
long without detecting the approach of any airborne
object.

With his weapon at the ready, Clay made his way
toward the *Belle Jennie*. The scout ship was intact, the
hatch closed. He opened the hatch and leaped back,
ready to fire if something emerged. He entered cautiously, finger on the trigger of his laser weapon. *Jennie*'s automatic systems clicked and hummed at him.
She was empty. He had been making regular checks
with Cindy by communicator. He used *Jennie*'s system
to call again and tell Cindy that he was lifting ship, all
detectors working, to take a look from the air.

He hovered over the plateau. Nothing. He began
to fly in expanding circles, keeping in close communication with Cindy. Other than small animals, there were
no signs of life, no radio emissions.

To the south of the plateau the land sank into a
dry, eroded valley. From the air there was a rugged
beauty to the landscape, but Clay knew that it would be
difficult to try to make a way through the canyons, the
exposed rock formations, and the scattered boulders.

"Clay," Cindy sent, "I think you'd better come
back to the ship."

"Yeah, in a few minutes," Clay said.

"We have our orders," Cindy reminded him.

Clay was feeling both frustrated and a bit panicked. He had fought in the war against the Eepera and done well, but he considered this expedition to be his first real test. While it was true that he had not been in command, he had been the second senior service officer aboard, and he had lost his commander and three other members, plus two valuable robots. He simply could not face the idea of going back to Omega to tell Duncan Rodrick that Rodrick's wife was missing, and that he, Clay, had left without any effort to find her and the others.

He had completed one orbit around the plateau, all instruments searching. Widening the circle, he started around again and looked down with interest at the badlands to the south as they came slowly into view. He was quite certain, however, that the answers he was seeking lay back on the plateau among the structures. He had half decided to go back to the plateau and blast hell out of a couple of the structures to see if he could get some reaction. Someone or something was there, something that defied all the sophisticated instruments for search and detection on both the scout and the starship. Jackie and the others had not simply been swallowed up by empty air.

Or had they?

He was, after all, trillions of miles from anything familiar. If any one fact had emerged with clarity in the age of exploration of the stars, it was that humans could not begin to conceive of the complexity and strangeness of the universe. Since humans had first begun to lift their opticals and other detection instruments out of Earth's obscuring atmosphere in the twentieth century, scientists had been forced to alter many theories that had once seemed so certain. And now humans were just beginning to probe the real mysteries of the universe.

Clay shivered. In all of human history and prehistory, it had been the unknown that was most frightening. And now Clay faced the unknown alone. He tried to conceptualize invisible beings—or not even beings, but things that could not be defined by human standards as alive, things that could not be detected by any known instrument, things capable of causing humans and robots to disappear. He almost wished that *Jennie's* sensors would give him warning of something tangible—a ship, or even the mysterious race that had spawned the Eepera. To have something to see, something against which he could fight, would be better than trying to imagine an invisible, undetectable threat.

Well, it was time to do something. Jackie had radioed to Cindy that they were going to try to cut into one of the structures. Then communications had been broken off. The key to their disappearance was back there among the gleaming, crystalline geometrics. He'd hover there and use the *Jennie's* laser cannon, and, by God, he'd see what was inside.

But what if Jackie and the others were inside one of the structures?

Clay was so tense, he jumped when *Jennie's* systems gave an alarm. He took a deep breath to quiet his suddenly pounding heart and saw that the detectors had picked up a local concentration of metal. There had been just one sharp blip and then silence. He turned *Jennie* sharply and retraced his route, and the alarm sang out again. It took a few minutes to pinpoint the single, sharp blip—a concentrated mass of metal at the bottom of a brushy canyon. He could see nothing from the air. The thing that kept his heart pounding was that the detectors were not picking up just another subsurface deposit of metallic ore; the sharpness of the signal indicated refined metals, and a considerable mass of them.

He reported the situation to Cindy and heard the concern in her voice. He smiled wryly, for only minutes before he'd been almost wishing for something tangible, and now he had it. He lowered the scout and saw, through the dense brush, the glint of something

metallic. There were no life signals. He was now only
fifty feet above the object, lower than the side walls of
the canyon, ready to push the panic button at any sign
of hostility or life and shoot *Jennie* straight up toward
the stratosphere.

"My God," he whispered, as the outlines of the
metallic object burned into his mind.

It was about a hundred feet long, longer than it
was wide, with one squared angle detectable through
the brush. And there, clearly visible as he lowered still
farther, was a turret that could be nothing other than a
weapons' mount.

His finger hovered over the button that would
send *Jennie* shooting upward as he eased the scout
forward, trying to see past the obscuring brush. "Ah,"
he said aloud, as he saw where the metallic hull of the
ship below had been shattered by impact. It was a
starship, and she had come in hard. Her ovate bow was
smashed against a stone reef that crossed the canyon.
Her hull was split open for about thirty feet back from
the bow. And she had been there a long time. Brush
was growing up and out of the shattered hull.

"Cindy," he said, and his voice caused shivers to
run up and down her neck, "someone's been here
before us."

"Come back to the ship," Cindy pleaded. "We've
got to go back to Omega and report, Clay."

Gage Fergus had been waiting on the bridge with
Cindy and Jean. He took the communicator. "Tell us
what you see," he requested.

"It's a ship," Clay said. "Can't be anything else.
About a hundred feet long. Built squarish with rounded
bow and stern. I can't see all of it because the brush has
grown up around it. There's no sign of life, and I don't
think we'll find any because it's been here long enough
for the local vegetation to seed itself and grow up
through rents in the hull."

"And it's not, maybe, one of the scout ships from

the *Karl Marx*?" Gage asked. "It's possible that another one got off without Theresita's knowledge."

"Definitely not of Earthly design," Clay reported. "It has an alien look. I don't know exactly how to describe it, but if you saw it, you'd know that it wasn't made on Earth."

"We need to take a look inside," Gage said.

"I was thinking the same thing," Clay answered.

"Come back here and pick me up," Gage said.

"No," Clay said. "You're to stay aboard. The ship can't fly without you."

"Clay, we can learn a lot from an alien ship," Gage argued, "and you just don't have the engineering and scientific knowledge to know what you're looking at. I've got to get on board that ship. That's all there is to it."

"I guess you're right," Clay said. "I'll be there in five minutes."

Clay was not surprised to see three figures emerge from the *Free Enterprise* when he landed nearby. With the chief engineer off the ship, Cindy and Jean would not be able to fly her. He did not even argue as the three crammed themselves into *Jennie*'s cabin. He was back over the ship in the canyon in minutes and took *Jennie* low for one more check for signs of life emissions. He put *Jennie* down on the rim of the canyon and locked her up. It was hard work to get down into the canyon, and by the time they reached the stern of the ship, they were perspiring freely.

The ship had obviously been designed for space. In spite of her odd contours, there was the look of conquering distances in the design, the potential of flight into the vast emptiness of space. She had come down at a steep angle, so she had left a deep, overgrown trench behind her in the canyon bottom's soft soil before she smashed her bow against the immovable rock dike.

With Clay in the lead they made their way through thick brush to the ship's side, moving toward the bow and the rents in the hull. Clay used a machete to clear away the denser brush. Twenty feet from the bow the hull had been split by impact. Clay began to clear away brush to give himself room to look inside.

"Single-hull construction," Gage Fergus said. "They didn't bother with the added safety factor of a double hull."

"I think I can squeeze through here now," Clay said. He cut away one final growth of brush and stuck his head into the rent, then played his light around inside. He saw a tangle of jagged metal, pipes, and fallen material. About ten feet back the light revealed a bulkhead and a gaping hatch giving way to darkness.

"Cindy, you and Jean stay outside," Clay said.

"Not a chance," Jean said, shivering. "I'm going to be hanging onto your coattails."

Clay laughed. He, too, had an eerie feeling, like a child walking through a cemetery at night. His heart in his mouth, he crawled carefully over the jagged metal and stood, head bent, inside the ship. He played his light around and tensed as the beam reflected from dozens of little points of light. He was still trying to figure out what the lights were when the area seemed to explode into movement and dozens of small, leathery flying things burst toward him, the tips of their dry wings brushing his hair. Behind him both Cindy and Jean shrieked as the flying things swarmed past.

Clay sat down weakly. "Bats," he said, panting, "or the local equivalent."

"I just aged ten years," Jean said, laughing shrilly.

Now all four were inside. Fergus was examining the damaged, twisted pipes. "Maybe part of the life support system," he guessed.

Clay moved toward the hatch. The next compartment was obviously crew's quarters. There was a musty smell of age there. A bunk was open, and on it was a tangle of dry-rotted material.

"Humanoid," Clay said. "The bunk is about six feet long, two-and-a-half feet wide." There were more than a dozen bunks, folding neatly into place on the walls.

The hatch at the far end of the quarters was closed. Clay had to use his laser to cut away the corroded fastener. When he managed to push the hatch open, it creaked on its hinges. The next space was, they guessed, a galley, although not even Gage could identify some of the equipment there. The space behind the closed hatch was in excellent condition. The air was stale and some items dry-rotted, but aside from damage where a piece of equipment had come loose from its fasteners and smashed, everything was intact. Clay pushed on. Two hatches led out of that area. The one to the left led down a corridor close to the outer hull.

"I'd guess the engines are toward the stern," Gage said.

"This one leads to the bridge," Clay reported, having forced open a hatch to look into a space with contoured chairs and masses of panels with instruments and odd protrusions. Light came dimly through ports that had been covered on the outside with dust and vegetative debris. "Let's stick together, Chief; take a look here first."

The bridge area was spacious, with four chairs, pointing again toward humanoid form for the ship's designers. Although there was an alien difference, any human pilot could have spotted the purpose of some instruments.

"The labels are like the Eeperan language," Gage marveled.

"I have a feeling we're aboard a ship built by the people who scare the Eepera so much," Cindy said.

"Here's a computer terminal," Gage pointed out, fingering a keyboard. The keys were odd, pointed instead of flat.

"These screens must be for optical search," Cindy said, "but I can't make heads or tails out of the controls."

"Maybe red for weapons?" Clay asked, examining a separate console with a chair in front of it.

"I wouldn't start pushing buttons at random," Cindy warned.

"It won't take a scientific team long to figure it out," Gage said. "From the looks of things, I'd say that the technology that built this ship was very much like ours. There are only so many ways to channel a functioning electric current. Maybe some different metallic alloys. I think the most interesting things we're going to find will be in the weapons and power rooms."

"Captain's quarters," Clay said, having opened a door at the rear of the bridge. And then, as he stepped in, "Holy—" His voice was odd when he said, "I think you'll want to take a look in here."

He moved inside to allow the others access. The room was spacious, and it gleamed with the softness of a gold and platinum decor. The items that had caught Clay's attention were on the walls: works of art, some done in a technique utilizing metals, possibly sprayed, in vivid, living colors.

It was the content of the artworks that caused a deep silence. The figures were quite human, although their dress was odd, alien. Directly in front of the door was a five-by-five scene, framed in gold, showing two nude women being dismembered by four men in loose, flowing robes. The focus of the scene was the faces of the two women, faces that spoke of agony.

On a table next to a comfortable chair was a small sculpture of unknown material, depicting a man holding his internal organs in his hands and screaming in pain. On another wall a series of smaller works in vivid, unfaded colors presented a study in creative torture and dismemberment.

"Nice people," Jean remarked, her voice muffled.

Cindy looked nervously over her shoulder, as if expecting the appearance of the creatures who looked like the golden, beautiful Eepera of Omega, creatures who had raised agony and torture to a fine art.

"Where are they?" Gage wondered. "What happened to them?"

"They're dead," Clay said. "The ship could have been here hundreds of years."

"They might have been able to get off a signal," Cindy said. "Maybe the survivors were picked up by other ships. We've seen no skeletons."

"If *they're* no longer here, what happened to Jackie and the others?" Jean asked.

In silence the four humans, staying very close to each other, explored the passageway that led toward the stern of the ship. The engine spaces took up the stern, and Gage became immediately fascinated as they moved through an area taken up with neat, enclosed square shapes.

"This is bigger than the engine room on either the *Spirit of America* or the *Free Enterprise*," Clay noted.

"Some of these things could be weapons control or power," Gage said, "but you're right. It looks as if their power plant isn't as small and efficient as the Shaw Drive."

Clay opened a door. It creaked but operated well. He shone his light into the space and felt a chill as the light reflected off a gleam of white. There was a different odor, too, a rank, old, musky scent that made him want to turn away. He moved closer, however, and then froze.

"At least one of them didn't get out," he whispered.

The beam of his light showed a skull with empty, dark eye sockets. The skull was enmeshed in a tangle of wires and equipment.

"Ugh," Jean said as she moved in to add the beam of her light.

The area was filled with racks, wiring, and oddly constructed equipment, but the skull held their attention, for wires penetrated it. By looking in and around the equipment that surrounded the skull, they saw that the entire humanoid skeleton was encased.

"Medical treatment?" Clay suggested.

"Here's another one," Cindy said, having turned her light away. Cindy's find was even more bizarre. The entire top of the skull had been removed. As flesh

had decayed, a metallic plate connected to the surrounding equipment by wires had been bared.

"It has no arms or legs," Cindy said, shuddering.

"I am *not* enjoying this at all," Jean announced.

"There are other connections," Gage said. "This
tube, here." He pointed to tubing running to the neck
area of the legless, armless skeleton. "It could have
been an IV tube going into an artery. These down
here," he pointed, "are evacuation tubes."

There were six other skeletons. As hard as it was to
believe, each seemed to have been an integral part of
the complicated electronic systems. One legless, armless skeleton had been fitted into an area that required
curving it into a tiny space so that the spine was bent.

Gage busied himself tracing the wiring from one of
the skeletons. "I'm beginning to feel a little sick," he
said.

"What is it?" Clay asked.

"I think these people were part of the ship's equipment," Gage said. "This first one had his fingers actually attached to mechanicals. The wires definitely
extended down into the brains of all of them."

"I don't understand," Jean said.

"I think they used the brains of living beings instead of microchips," Gage explained.

"Oh, no," Cindy whispered.

"There's no indication of joints on the armless and
legless torsos," Gage continued. "Genetic engineering.
Making a flesh-and-blood component."

"A living being?" Cindy asked. "Spending its entire life as part of a machine, being fed through tubes,
never leaving that one space?"

"I could be wrong," Gage admitted, "but I don't
see indications of any other source for the computers
that are absolutely necessary for space flight."

"I can understand why the Eepera are scared of
these people," Clay said frankly.

"I want to take a better look at the power plant, if
possible," Gage said, moving back toward the square

forms that occupied one room. "Look for printed material. The labels on the instruments in the control room look like the Eeperan priestly writings. I imagine Grace can translate anything we find. If we can find the technical manuals, we can find out how it all works without having to come back here and tear it apart."

After an hour of searching, no printed material had been found, so the chief engineer made a quick trip back to the *Jennie* for a basic tool kit. Soon he was soiled, sweaty, and totally frustrated, having run into the same problem that had plagued Harry Shaw and Max Rosen in their attempt to analyze the power source in the pyramid at Suses. Each of the square containers in the engine space was sealed, the cases molded, welded, or joined to the floor plates by a method that left no indication of a joint.

"They've not been totally sealed just for neatness," Gage muttered. "For two cents I'd blast one open."

"And maybe destroy the whole ship," Clay said.

"That's the rub," the chief admitted.

Gage settled for a second-best course of action, bringing a portable recorder aboard with a powered light source to make holograph images of everything aboard.

Clay was seriously worried about Jackie and the others. He recognized the importance of collecting as much information as possible from the wrecked ship, which undoubtedly represented the technology of a fearsome potential enemy. But he was imagining that his friends were being held by monsters capable of inflicting terrible torture. The crystalline structures had ceased to be works of art in his mind. Now he wondered if they were some form of collective signaling devices erected by the survivors of the crash.

Nothing made sense. Since the ship had crashed long ago, it did not seem logical to think that either the survivors or their descendants were still around. But four human beings and two robots had disappeared. To think of Jackie, Leslie, Stoner, and Shag Howard being held by creatures who had engineered living beings to be components of a machine made him restless and, in the end, perhaps a bit careless.

"I think the thing for us to do is get back to Omega," the chief said. "We'll let Rodrick and Shaw decide whether to send a study party out here or maybe equip the *Free Enterprise* with a rig to pick the whole shipwreck up and carry it off."

"Do you have all the holo pictures you think you need?" Clay asked.

Gage nodded. "Without starting to tear things apart. I guess I'd better wait for the proper equipment to do that."

Clay closed the hatches behind them as they left the ship. In the *Jennie* he said, "I'm taking the three of you back to the ship, then I'm going to use the laser to open up one or more of those structures on the plateau."

"I'd like to take a look at those things myself," Gage requested.

"We can't risk it," Clay replied. "It's more important than ever to get the ship back to Omega with the information about that alien ship."

The chief engineer, not a service officer, admitted to himself that Clay was right.

Clay set the scout down near the *Free Enterprise* and watched his friends start to walk the short distance to their starship. Jean was the first to fall. Since Clay was watching his wife, who was swinging along briskly, he did not notice Jean stagger. His eyes switched to her as she crumpled to the ground and then, quickly, Cindy followed. She went down as if all life had suddenly left her body. She seemed to land in a heap. Clay leaped from his chair with a shout of alarm as Gage Fergus also went limp.

The pain that Clay experienced was enough to send him screaming from the hatch, weapon in hand, whirling to find the source of the attack. He fell heavily as he ran from the *Jennie*, a fine, almost invisible line having been looped around one foot. He hit the ground rolling, saw a movement, raised his weapon to fire, and felt it jerked forceably from his hand as a dozen other fine, strong lines began to immobilize all his limbs. Darkness came to him with no warning.

TWENTY-FOUR

Paul Warden was tired. He had been working with Harry Shaw for weeks, and that man was a workaholic who never needed rest. Even Max, who was a mono-maniac himself, had stopped trying to keep up with Shaw. Now and then he'd just grunt and walk away, and if you wanted to know where he was, all you had to do was go to the thermatent he shared with Grace, and there he'd be, in his uniform, sleeping so soundly that it took drastic action to awaken him.

Fortunately, the hard work had not been without reward. Warden had rigged a sun gun based on the Eeperan design, powered it with plain old electricity, jazzed it up a bit with some Earth-type microtechnology, and had come up with a weapon that was more deadly and of longer range than the original. The Eeperan secret was in two heavy magnetic arrays that gathered electrons and compacted them inside a force field until the temperature was hotter than the surface of a sun, and then directed that charged energy like an invisible lightning bolt with total accuracy. Warden's adaptation of the sun gun would be a splendid addition to the armaments of a ship, where there was a power source.

Harry and Max, meanwhile, were agreed on a method of getting inside the protective shell of the Eeperan power source. Some basic, totally safe experiments had hinted at the nature of the device. They had discovered a series of highly polished metallic mirrors that directed sunlight down into the power room. The power plant was now known to operate by utilizing solar energy, and as a result, when sunlight was blocked from it for a period of four days—much longer than any natural cloud cover would ever have blocked the sun in a site like the river valley—the lights began to dim both inside the pyramid and in the city. It was evident that, in addition to converting sunlight directly into energy, the plant also had a means of storing energy. That, Harry felt, was going to be very interesting indeed.

Max and Harry agreed that the danger of unleashing unpredictable energy would be lessened if the power were bled from the plant by blocking sunlight until there was no output—that is, until all the lights were out. For the residents of the city to be notified that there would be a power outage, the regular patrols were ordered to spread the news. There was, of course, some grumbling and a formal protest from the city's officials.

For the sake of safety it would also be necessary to evacuate the pyramid. Paul Warden didn't mind that at all. He had been too exhausted lately to have had much chance to pursue his courtship of Evangeline. She and Grace probably could use a break from their seemingly endless translation tasks. He suggested that the three of them hop over to Hamilton City for a rest. It would also be a fine opportunity for Evangeline to consult with Egyptologist Dr. Abdul, who was recuperating in Hamilton City after a long illness.

"Paul," Evangeline suggested, "let's take this opportunity to remove Sage's body from that dismal museum."

Paul had not forgotten that the body of the woman he had once loved was in what the Eeperan priests called their Museum of Life in chambers below the pyramid; he had simply been too busy to do anything about it. He nodded. It was something that had to be done. He rounded up a few volunteers and, with Evangeline and Grace at his sides, descended the secret stairs to stand in the chambers first discovered by Elton and Becky Dark.

Evangeline had been there only once, and she shuddered to think of going there again. But Sage had been her friend. For too long a time now her corpse, so perfectly preserved that she looked alive, had been there, in darkness, among the preserved priests and representative samplings of Earthmen and Earthwomen from the time of the early Egyptian dynasties, when the Eepera were on Earth. Besides, Paul had been so distant lately, and Evangeline wondered if memories of Sage might have something to do with it. If he hadn't yet come to terms with Sage's death, there was no time like the present.

Evangeline looked at the floor to avoid seeing the eyes of the priests and priestesses in the outer chambers. Out of curiosity she did look at a bearded Bronze Age warrior, and then felt tears spring into her eyes as she stood before the glass case where Sage Bryson was on display. Sage wore a filmy Eeperan gown, which was so thin that her nipples and the darkness of her pudenda could be seen. She was smiling pleasantly, and her eyes sparkled.

Evangeline, very familiar with the Eeperan writing now, read the newly incised lettering on a metal plate at Sage's feet. The plate said simply that this was an Earthwoman, and the date from an Eeperan calendar was the date for the past year. There was evidence that someone had examined her, for her clothing was not hanging properly. There had been a few of the Life Science physicians in the chamber. They had been primarily interested in the specimens from the Bronze Age, and further study was planned, to learn about the quality of human life during the various epochs. It still made Evangeline shiver to think that someone had removed Sage's garment to study the incisions through which her internal organs had been removed and the preservatives inserted. It seemed, somehow, to be more of a desecration to have someone looking at Sage's nude body than at the nude bodies of men and women who had been dead for three thousand years.

Sage was still smiling pleasantly when she was eased carefully into a coffin. As the group left the Museum of Life, the lights went out behind them and Evangeline hurried to get in front, rather than look back over her shoulder into the darkness.

Grace went with them as far as a scout ship and waited until the coffin had been loaded into the cargo bay. "I've decided to stay here," she said. "I'll take some material with me to the tent and do some work. Say hello to Dr. Abdul for me."

"Give yourself a break," Paul urged.

Grace smiled. "Well, I will admit that it isn't just the work that's keeping me here. Max won't be working all the time."

Evangeline smiled. She knew why Grace had decided to stay. She, too, had been reminded of her own mortality by looking into Sage's dead, smiling, utterly beautiful face. Evangeline knew that if she and Paul were married and he was staying, she'd stay too.

Grace watched the scout lift off. Soon she would be going back to Hamilton City with Max and all the others for Sage's interment, for Sage had been one of them and deserved no less. Meanwhile, there was a lot to do. She went into the top of the pyramid and found Max and Harry preparing for the final assault on the power plant.

"Thought you were gone," Max growled, but there was a smile in his eyes.

"I can be of help," she said.

"I'm sure you could, Grace," Harry said, "but I'm going to be alone in here when I cut through the cover of this thing."

Grace looked quickly at Max and saw that he didn't like that idea at all, but he made no comment. Selfishly, she was glad. If the power plant went boom when it was opened, she'd rather have Max at her side, miles away, than standing beside Harry. She liked and respected Shaw, but she loved Max.

"I'll be in the library," she said. "When you start out, come and get me."

"Be about a half hour," Max said, winking at her.

The evacuation of the pyramid was under way. Space marines were making a last check. She told Corporal Celia Hadley, who, she thought, needed to be examined by a doctor, that she'd come out with Max. The female marine looked quite ill and had lost a lot of weight. Her eyes seemed to be burning as if from a fever. Grace made a mental note to call the girl's condition to the attention of the next doctor who came over.

Grace had set aside some interesting-looking texts that, with luck, might just contain something other than the seemingly infinite amount of nit-picking about the gods that the Eeperan priests had adopted from the Egyptians. She was selecting a couple of them to take to the tent with her when she heard a footfall behind her and turned to see Yanee. He bowed.

"Yanee, you're not supposed to be in here at all," she said. "And now the pyramid is being evacuated."

He stepped to one side of the doorway just inside the room, made a motion with his right hand, and four priests moved into the room.

Grace began to move slowly toward her own desk. She had a laser pistol in the drawer. The four priests leaped forward and seized her before she could get the drawer open. She did not scream. She knew that there was no one to hear. Her voice could not possibly carry to the top, where Max and Harry were working. She managed to plant one knee firmly into the vulnerable area of a male crotch, but the other three men bore her down, and then she felt the bite of a needle in the fleshy side of her hip, and within a few seconds she could not have screamed at all, as darkness engulfed her.

TWENTY-FIVE

Vic Wakefield had never seen anything more beautiful than his Tina in a bathing suit. She'd come to the door at his knock with a beach jacket over the suit, and she'd kept the jacket on all the way to the docks, where Vic had arranged for the use of a little sailing sloop. She hadn't taken the jacket off until they were well out in Stanton Bay, with the sail billowing prettily before a fair breeze, and when she did, Vic almost let the rudder slip out of his hands.

In years, he thought, she might be just short of sixteen, but in maturity of body, wow. He'd been about three-quarters in love with her, but after seeing her in a bathing suit, he was a dead duck. She came and stood beside him. The bay was running with small waves, and the motion of the boat caused her to sway against his shoulder so that he could feel the heat and feminine softness of her. He looked up and felt tears of sheer appreciation form in his eyes at her smile as she looked out over the blue water toward the shore.

"I'm going to marry you, you know," he declared.

She looked down with a pixie smile. "Oh? Don't I have something to say about that?"

"You have no choice at all," he replied. "When our names were written in the Book of Life they were written side by side, Vic and Tina."

"Is that the way it is?" she asked.

"Absolutely."

"Then I guess I'll marry you."

He reached for her, and she danced away. "When I'm eighteen," she said, laughing.

Vic groaned. But he had to hang onto the tiller and tend the sail. He wasn't going to waste time giving her sailing lessons, not now. His concentration was one hundred percent on getting the sloop around the southern arm of land and out of sight of the town. He wanted to kiss her more than he'd ever wanted anything in his life.

It took almost an hour to clear the bay. She came and sat by him, and they talked—likes and dislikes, deep thoughts and shallow, the talk of all young lovers from the beginning of time, talk interspersed with a touch, a look, a breathy awareness. And then they were in the lee of the southern tip of land that bounded Stanton Bay, and he lowered the sail, anchored the sloop, and walked toward her with his heart pounding.

"You can't catch me," she said gaily, and dived over the side. She sliced into the water neatly, surfaced, shook water from her hair, and swam away. Vic checked the anchor line and dived after her. The water was summer warm and very clear. He was gaining on her when she turned, dived under the water, then surfaced, heading back toward the boat. She drew herself up over the low stern and wouldn't let him board, pushing him back into the water with shrieks of laughter. Then she stood back and let her arms hang at her sides, and her eyes went wide as he climbed aboard, dripping, and advanced on her. She tilted her head to look up into his face, and as his arms went around her, she lifted her arms to his neck and leaned into him, her flesh hot on his, the body heat contrasting to the coolness of her wet, skimpy bathing suit. Vic fell a million miles through space into her eyes, and then there was the heat of her mouth on his, and time stood still.

They lay side by side on a blanket spread on the deck, the sun drying their suits. They kissed until Tina was breathless, and then she pushed him away, only to allow him to return his mouth to hers time and time again.

"Eighteen?" he whispered, when he himself had to stop kissing her lest he implode.

"That's what my mother says." Her voice was deep, throaty, in a way she had never heard herself talk.

"I'm not kissing your mother."

She giggled. "She'd slap your face if you tried to kiss her like that." His tongue was probing.

"Clay and Cindy Girard were just sixteen," he said, his lips brushing hers.

"I know," she said.

"When will you be sixteen?"

"Five months."

"Five months!" He rolled onto his back, groaning.

"It'll pass quickly."

"Five months?"

"And there's no guarantee that they'll let me get married then," she said, her face darkening.

He leaned on one elbow and traced her name on her thigh with his forefinger. "Well, whatever it takes, we'll get married, but I wouldn't want to start off with your mother and father against us."

"No."

"I'll probably wear your lips out kissing you, though," he teased, pulling her down atop him.

It was not the first time she'd ever been kissed, and kissed repeatedly. There'd been a boy on the *Spirit of America*, when she was only thirteen. They'd taught each other how to kiss, and she'd let him experiment with her bared breasts, just once. She was not, however, an innocent. She'd done her study in sex education. She knew that her morality, while the middle-class norm of the time, was not everyone's morality. Nor had refraining from premarital sex been recognized as the proper and desirable course of action throughout history. But she was a solid-minded girl and recognized that she was young and inexperienced. She believed the teachers, ministers, and her parents when they said that, although no discernible physical harm was done by nonsanctioned sex, psychological harm—feelings of guilt and regret—might well result. She was adult in body but not in mind. And, as the day progressed with another swim, a picnic lunch, and then another frenzied session of kissing on the blanket spread on the deck, she would have given herself to Vic, except for two things: Vic did not press the issue, and she had not received her antifertility medication, being too young.

When she realized that Vic truly loved her, truly wanted to marry her, truly respected her and her moral code, she felt like weeping with happiness.

"Thank you," she said.

"For what?"

"For not putting pressure on me."

"Hey," he said, "would I do that to the girl I'm going to marry? The girl who's going to be the mother of my kids?"

"Oh, Vic," she said.

Throughout the afternoon she had not allowed her body to come into contact with that part of him that was so evidently and so arousingly male. Now she threw herself atop him, and he gasped as she put her weight on him and kissed him hotly. "Wear my lips out," she whispered. "I'll help. I love you so, and I feel so safe with you."

There is just so much that an honorable man can take without breaking. After about ten minutes of her body atop his, of softness against aching hardness, he pushed her off and with a croak of sheer frustration dived into the water. She helped him get back into the boat. The cool water had helped. He looked at the sun and said it was about time to head home.

"I wish we could stay here forever," she said.

"Me, too, but I don't want your father after me with a baseball bat." He went down into the cabin for a shirt. It was still hot and stuffy there, and he felt momentary dizziness. He found his shirt and her beach jacket, and then his stomach rebelled and he bent over in agony. Sweat beaded and rolled off his face. He felt panic. He couldn't allow her to see him that way. He fumbled in his carrybag, found a packet of measured doses of the Eeperan drug, and took a swig of water from a jug to wash it down. Then he waited, just seconds it seemed, until he felt not only normal but wonderful. She was waiting for him on deck, lying on the blanket with one knee up.

"We can stay ten minutes longer," she said, reaching out to him with her arms.

The inflaming drug coursed through his veins. In total shock and surprise Tina, crying out, fended off his determined advances. His face was contorted with drug-induced need.

"No, no," he groaned. "I'm sorry." He rose, went to the anchor line, felt a resurgence of his overwhelming need, then left the anchor down and went into the cabin, returning with a glass of wine for each of them. "I'm sorry," he said. "It won't happen again. Let's drink to it."

Tina was confused. All day he'd been so perfect, so gentlemanly, then suddenly he was trying to rip off her bathing suit. She drank to cover her confusion, and within five minutes she was writhing under him, heedless of the initial pain, both of them unaware of the small amount of blood that stained the blanket underneath them.

She went sailing with him the next day to have a chance to tell him in private that she hated him, that he'd tricked her and seduced her into doing something that she'd promised herself never to do. He gave her the drug, in coffee, on the way out of the bay, and by the time the sloop was anchored, she was acting like one of the Eeperan tigresses of the city of Suses. She went with him the next time without protest, still confused but full of anticipation.

TWENTY-SIX

Leslie Young realized quickly that it was useless to struggle against the weblike material. She could hear the others crying out and could see, below her, that even the massive and powerful Mopro was immobilized. It was somewhat painful to be lifted by the fine lines, but the thickness and durability of her protective suit prevented the lines from cutting into her flesh. The question she was trying to answer was: What was the source of the lines? They were too tiny to follow with the eye, but they seemed to lead toward the crystalline wall above her head. She was being dragged toward the wall, and then she was being lifted against its side. At a height of about thirty feet she felt the wall give way, and she passed from the bright sunlight into a gloom that blinded her until her eyes adjusted. She felt herself being touched in several places, and then she felt nothing.

She yawned, opened her eyes, and tried to stretch. She still could not move her arms. Remembering, her eyes popped open. She was lying on her back. She rolled and saw Jackie lying beside her, eyes still closed. Beyond Jackie were Shag Howard and Stoner. The sergeant and Mopro were not in the room.

She managed to sit up, although her arms were secured to her sides by dozens of the fine, transparent lines. The room was bare. There were no doors, no windows. The walls, floor, and ceiling, which exuded light, were of the same crystalline material. She bent her head and could just see the button-watch on her jacket. Over eight hours had passed since Jackie had given Mopro the order to slice into the structure.

Jackie stirred, made a sleepy, contented sound, and tried to move her arms. That effort wakened her. Her eyes opened, darted around, then settled on Leslie's face.

"We've been asleep for over eight hours," Leslie told her. "Shag and Stoner are here, but the robots are not."

It took Jackie a minute or two to sit up and examine the barren room. Then she began to edge toward Leslie. "Let me see if I can loosen your bonds with my teeth," she said.

"I doubt it," Leslie said, "but you can try."

Jackie positioned herself and tried to bite through the lines that held Leslie's arms. The material did not seem to have the hardness of wire, but she could not sever it. A hissing sound caused her to stop and struggle back into a sitting position. A section of the wall had moved to one side, creating an opening. Clay Girard, limp, trussed, came sliding into the room. He was followed by Gage Fergus, then Cindy and Jean.

"They didn't follow orders," Jackie said with more sadness than anger. Mixed with the sadness was self-reproach. She had allowed all of them to be captured. The expedition was a failure, and the loss of the ship and the two valuable robots would have serious effects upon the people of Omega. There was another concern, of less cosmic importance but of intense personal discomfort: She needed, very badly, to relieve herself. It was taking a great deal of her concentration simply not to let it flow.

Stoner came awake with a rush and struggled briefly.

"Don't, Stoner," Leslie advised. "You'll hurt yourself."

"What the hell?" Stoner asked, jerking into a sitting position, then edging backward to lean against a wall. "How'd they get Clay and the others?"

"I don't know," Jackie said.

The door hissed open again, and Jackie forgot even her urgent need to urinate as a shadow fell onto the floor and a four-foot-high cross between a teddy bear and a glamour doll stepped into the room. It was obvious at first glance that the creature was female. She was pleasingly humanoid, slim and graceful, with a beautiful, sleek, silvery pelt on her exposed arms and legs. A ruff of fur around her neck at first looked like a fur collar but on closer examination proved to be natural. A shock of neatly kept fur ran from the center of her well-shaped head to the ruff at the nape of her neck, a streak of vivid scarlet.

"Well, hello," Stoner said, thinking that there couldn't be any real danger from so pretty, so cuddly a creature.

At the sound of his voice the creature looked at him. She had large, mauve eyes. But there were, in her look, confidence and a sense of command. She spoke. Her voice sounded like a combination of cat's purr and the piping, sweet tones of a young girl. Leslie felt that the sounds were designed to soothe their concern.

The charming female was joined by another, this one obviously male, but also very attractive. He stood an inch or so taller than the female and had sleek fur of a slightly different shade. He carried no weapons. They were dressed similarly, in silken garments of simplicity, but a touch of decoration on the female's garment added a bit of color. The male's ruff was brilliant blue.

"We are friends," Leslie said. "We meant you no harm."

The male spoke in that purring, soothing language, his voice that of a young boy. He walked to Leslie and ran his hands up and down her arms. He had three slim, graceful fingers and an opposing thumb. His touch seemed to dissolve her bonds. Leslie rubbed her arms to get the circulation going. She decided that it would be unwise to stand and tower over the creature. "You are both very beautiful," she said quietly. "I can't believe you mean us any harm either."

Both of them listened attentively as she spoke.

The female bent over those who still slept, and there was a sudden scent, a bit acrid, as she waved her fingers in the faces of each. They awakened immediately.

"Easy," Jackie warned Clay as he started to struggle. "Just be silent for a while."

The female had awakened Jean last. She seemed quite interested in Jean's clothing, fingering her jacket. Jean had made some alterations to the standard wear and had touched the neckline with lace. The female's hands seemed to dissolve Jean's bonds.

"Thank you," Jean said.

The little female made a motion clearly indicating that Jean should stand. Jean did so and as the little female motioned, smiled at the others. "She likes my clothing," she said. She posed and turned, causing her short skirt to swirl. The little female nodded, smiled, and tried to caress a wrinkle out of the skirt.

Jean pointed to the female's shift and smiled, nodding. "Very nice," she said. "The material is quite elegant." She extended a hand slowly, smiling. The little female pulled back but halted as Jean fingered the material of the shift, smiled, and nodded.

"I think," Jean said, for the benefit of the others, "that this pretty little one is fashion conscious." She mused a moment, took off her scarf, looped it around the female's waist, and tied it with an ornate bow. "Ah," she said, smiling, and nodded.

The little female posed and turned, smiling.

"Yes," Jean said. "This material would be a joy to work. Look." She fingered the little female's shift and bunched it at the shoulder. "A tuck here, a fold there, wouldn't that be attractive?"

The male had been watching with great interest. He pointed one three-fingered hand at Jean's suggested alteration at the shoulder of the shift and laughed. The female joined in. It was the happy, silvery laughter of children.

"I think we're going to be great friends," Jean said,

reaching out to touch the male's brilliant-blue ruff. He pulled away at first, then smiled. The smile faded quickly, and he motioned Jean to sit. He drew himself up and turned to face the men, who were still bound. He talked for about a minute, his voice stern. When he stopped talking, he looked at Stoner, who was the largest of the men, as if in question.

"Friends," Stoner said. "We'll be very good." He grinned. "How could anyone do harm to sexy teddy bears?"

The male said something to the female, and she dissolved Stoner's bonds. The male motioned Stoner to his feet and indicated that he should walk toward the door. Stoner had taken only two steps when both of the teddy bears raised their hands and pointed their fingers toward him, and jets of the weblike material shot out, wrapping around Stoner so that he was immobilized within seconds.

"All right," Stoner said. "I get the message." He smiled and nodded. "Yes. We understand."

Soon all the humans were free. The female pointed to Jean's mouth and then to her own. "I think she's saying that we must learn their language," Jackie said.

The little female pointed to herself and to the male and said, "Spreen."

"Humans," Jean said, pointing to herself and the others. "Spreen," she said, pointing to the two of them. The female Spreen nodded and smiled.

So it was that the first word of the Spreen language learned by humans was the name of the race. The second was concerned with a biological function, since Jackie was experiencing great discomfort. The word was evoked with shy laughter from the female Spreen, by the simple expedient of Jackie holding her lower abdomen in both hands and making a face of pain. The sanitary facilities were small but practical, and then all of the crew of the *Free Enterprise* were gathered again with the two Spreen in another room with crystalline walls. It was furnished by fairies, or so it seemed to

Jean, who was enchanted by the Spreen and their appreciation of beauty.

The next step was names. The graceful little female was Cee-Cee. The male, Dun-Dun.

"It'll take weeks for us to build a vocabulary for even basic communication," Jackie said. "How can we tell them that we have a machine on board the ship that will make communication easy?"

Stoner tried to get across the idea with loud talk and motions, to the amusement of Cee-Cee. The translation machine perfected by Grace Monroe seemed to be beyond the Spreen's imagination and beyond Stoner's ability to describe in sign language. He did succeed in getting across the idea of a machine, for Dun-Dun held out his arms and moved by shuffling his feet in a good imitation of Mopro. Stoner took the opportunity to find out what had happened to the robots, nodding eagerly. Dun-Dun led him to another chamber, where the sergeant and Mopro were almost covered by the weblike strands. Mopro had used his massive power to stretch his bonds. His knees were exposed, and Stoner saw the muzzles of his cannon extending as he entered.

"Hold fire, Mopro," Stoner said.

"We were about to blast out of here," the sergeant said angrily.

"That won't be necessary," Stoner said. "The natives are friendly. There will be no violence from either of you, is that clear?"

"Yes, sir," the sergeant said glumly. Mopro printed "Clear" on his communications band.

Stoner turned to Dun-Dun and made gestures requesting the release of the robots. Dun-Dun thought for a moment, then nodded. He dissolved the bonds on the sergeant first.

The sergeant stood, tensed and ready for action. Although his primary weapons had been taken from him, he still had a small but deadly laser pistol hidden in the top of his boot. "These things don't understand English," he said.

"No," Stoner confirmed as Dun-Dun began to dissolve Mopro's bonds.

"When Mopro is released, we will seize control," the sergeant said. "I will terminate this one. Mopro, you roll into the hallway outside and blast anything that moves."

Before Stoner could speak, Mopro had radioed to the sergeant. "Those are not the orders of the human in control. Please stop giving contradictory orders."

The sergeant heard Mopro's communication as well as Stoner's spoken words: "There will be no violence. You will take no action."

The sergeant was alert, poised to spring. He had been humiliated. The entire expedition was in danger, all because of small, furry things that looked like some toymaker's creation. As Dun-Dun finished releasing Mopro and moved back to stand by Stoner's side, the sergeant leaped to seize him. Mopro, realizing the sergeant's intentions, moved faster, much to the more agile robot's surprise, wrapping the sergeant in his powerful arms and lifting him from the floor.

"Sergeant," Stoner yelled, as Dun-Dun raised his hands. "If you disobey orders again, I'll have Mopro pull your power supply."

The sergeant relaxed. Mopro lowered him to the floor. Stoner smiled at Dun-Dun and made a motion that had universal application, the forefinger drawing a small circle at his temple, then the finger pointing to the sergeant. Dun-Dun looked doubtful, his hands raised, ready to immobilize the robots again.

It took Stoner some time to convince Dun-Dun to allow the two robots to be released onto the surface. He finally accomplished it by calling attention to Mopro's size and his difficulty in negotiating the passageways built for the four-feet-high Spreen. Dun-Dun signaled agreement that it would be best to get the massive machine out of the crystalline chambers, then led the way through a corridor to a blank, crystalline wall.

"Sergeant, you will remain aboard the *Free Enter-*

prise," Stoner ordered. "Mopro, bring the translation machine in its case. We'll use your power supply to run it. Get back as soon as you can. In the meantime I'll see if I can't get them to give us back our communicators."

Dun-Dun placed his hand on the wall, and a panel slid back. The two robots went out into the sunlight.

There was no difficulty in getting the communicators back. Although the Spreen apparently had no such technology, Dun-Dun was not mystified when Jackie contacted the sergeant and learned that the robots were now aboard the *Free Enterprise*, with Mopro ready to return with the translation machine.

"Tell the sergeant to go into my cabin and get my sewing kit," Jean said. "It's in a pink case."

Jackie relayed the request.

Cee-Cee was working with Jean, laboriously teaching Jean Spreen words. Dun-Dun disappeared for a few minutes and returned with other Spreen and containers of something that looked, to Earthpeople, very unappetizing. The Spreen demonstrated, taking dainty bites of the grayish, lumpy mass and making pleased sounds.

"It looks like some sort of fungus," Jackie said. "I think we'd better stick to field rations." She opened her pack and passed around pieces of a brittle, chewy grain cake. The Spreens examined it, sniffed it, and politely went back to eating the fungus.

Mopro made good time. By the time the meal was finished, he was outside the square structure where there was access to the indoors. Stoner finally made Dun-Dun understand that it was important to open the door. Mopro set up the translation machine in a large chamber that seemed to be at ground level. Cindy, who had been briefed by Grace on the operation of the translation machine, had to make several attempts at adjustment and then, suddenly, as she spoke, the machine's speakers purred and spoke in the soft language of the Spreen. The Spreen laughed delightedly.

It was get-acquainted time, and Dun-Dun's first question told them that the Spreen were not ignorant of the nature of the universe. "What is your planet, and how far away is it?"

Between twenty and thirty of the delightful little people were now in the large chamber. It was evident that Dun-Dun had some authority, for he was the spokesman. His first interest was in the location of Earth. There was a problem with orientation, because each race had different names for the large stars and galactic features. That problem was solved when Dun-Dun sent a young male running out of the chamber to return quickly with several very good star charts. Cindy oriented herself and soon located the position of Omega. There were few pointer stars in the direction of Earth, but she picked a spot near Earth's approximate location, toward the periphery from the Spreen planet, and pointed to it. Dun-Dun and others peering over his shoulder nodded and made sounds of appreciation.

"You travel far," Dun-Dun said.

"Yes, far," Jackie agreed. "Do the Spreen travel among the stars?"

"Of course not," Dun-Dun said. "Our home is here, and here is our happiness. Why should we travel? Such activity is for the Bese and for other odd creatures, such as humans."

It was Leslie who caught the untranslatable word, Bese. "Who are the Bese?" she asked.

"They have not come for a long time," Dun-Dun said. "We had hoped that you were they, for we have many things now to trade, and we miss the sweet goodness they traded with us."

"Are the Bese like us?" Leslie asked.

Dun-Dun looked at her for a few moments. "Like you but unlike you."

"They come in great ships to trade with you?" Leslie asked.

"Not for a long time."

"There is a shipwreck in the valley to the south," Clay said. "Was that a Bese starship?"

"Yes. One by one they died," Dun-Dun said, "for, like you, they could not eat our food."

"Is Bese a name you have for these people, or do they call themselves Bese?" Stoner asked.

"It is their name. They told it to us. They said it means the Masters, but that is a word that has no meaning here," Dun-Dun said.

It had been a long day. Cee-Cee, who had been standing at Dun-Dun's side, yawned and then apologized. "It is time to rest," Cee-Cee mumbled. "We will talk more, with your wonderful machine, tomorrow."

The rooms assigned to the women were feminine, small, and equipped with tiny pull-out pads that served for beds. Because of the group's tiredness and the release from tension, it was not only possible but unavoidable to sleep on the beds, even if they had to curl up to keep their feet from extending off the bed and onto the floor. The men fared equally well. There were sanitary facilities, and the water—tested by portable equipment in Mopro's array—was sweet and good.

The talk began again before they were ready, all of them having been awakened gently by Spreen. When, at last, the Spreen were temporarily out of questions about Earth and its people, Jackie, as spokeswoman, began to try to understand a few things about the odd little teddy bears. Cee-Cee suggested that perhaps the visitors would understand better if they saw, instead of just heard about, the life-style of the Spreen.

The translation machine was mounted on Mopro's back. Larger corridors had to be used to permit passage, and sometimes the halls were too narrow for talk to be translated as they walked. In general, the way led downward along sloping corridors lined with the crystalline material. By the time the group had traveled perhaps two hundred feet into the earth, some facts were known.

The crystalline structures on the surface served several purposes: They offered access to the outside, where Spreen rarely ventured. They were an expression of the Spreen's love of beauty. They were a beacon for incoming Bese ships, which carried cargos of some sweet, good-tasting substance. And they were the Spreen's windows to the stars, for it was in the structures that their observatories were constructed.

Leslie estimated that they had seen somewhere near two hundred Spreen, all attractive, all neatly and handsomely dressed. She had seen a rainbow variety of pelt and ruff colors, and she was beginning to be able to see individual differences in facial expression and characteristics. Cee-Cee, for example, was perhaps the most adorable of the females, and she chose the word "adorable" because beautiful didn't quite seem to describe Cee-Cee. Dun-Dun had an air of command. All the Spreen seemed friendly and curious. Politeness was the rule.

The Spreen were quite open in answering questions. All had the ability to extrude the strong, thin lines from their fingers, a substance that toughened upon contact with the air. They also had the ability to shoot a liquid, which became a gas, from their fingertips. It was with that gas that they put the Earthpeople to sleep instantly, or could, with a minor change, awaken them.

All conversation ceased when Dun-Dun led the party onto a balcony overlooking a huge, airy, well-lighted cavern. The ceiling was a least fifty feet high, and the cavern stretched onward for over a hundred yards. On the floor of the cavern, below them, were what seemed to be thousands of plain Spreen with black, brown, or tan pelts and no ruffs or crests. Without the decorative features of their fur, they looked more than ever like well-shaped little teddy bears.

It took a while for the translation machine to find an English equivalent for the Spreen name for the workers in the cavern. The closest term was "doers." The doers sang as they worked to cultivate the giant fungus that was food for all Spreen.

"Those below are not like you," Jackie commented to Dun-Dun.

"They are doers. We are . . ." It took some more searching to find an appropriate word. The word was "watchers." It did not mean that they looked on and did nothing, Jackie discovered, but that they guarded or directed.

"Can a doer ever become a watcher?" Jackie asked, still trying to clarify what seemed to be a lopsided society with thousands of workers and only a few elite.

Dun-Dun had difficulty understanding the question. When he did, he was amused. Of course doers could never become watchers. Each was born to his or her place, and each would be unhappy if forced to change. Indeed, the workers seemed to be happy. Their songs were gay and lilting. They seemed to play, taking time to swim and splash in crystal-clear pools, chasing, bouncing their young, as much as they worked.

Something about Spreen logic was learned when the entire party climbed the sloping corridors toward the surface again before returning to the depths to see the last and most spectacular surprise in the Spreen's underground home. The trip to the surface took them into the constructions, where Dun-Dun's personal observatory was opened for the visitors' inspection. His telescope was fashioned from the same crystalline substance that was the only building material of the Spreen. The lenses, too, were made of the crystalline substance and were surprisingly good, although not as efficient as the lenses ground back on Earth.

Dun-Dun impressed the Americans as he showed them around, displayed star charts, and demonstrated something of mathematical calculations.

"Did you learn your math and about the stars from the Bese?" Jackie asked.

Dun-Dun showed quick disdain. "We knew the stars and the magic of numbers long before the first Bese landed here."

Soon they were headed downward again. Jackie

realized that if the Spreen leaned toward the practical, it would have been logical to view the observatory first, then descend to the cave of the doers and onward to the workshops. In later discussions, however, it was decided that Dun-Dun was showing them the small Spreen world in accordance with his own priorities: The doers were essential to existence, thus they were shown first. Dun-Dun was vitally interested in astronomy, so the observatory was second. Only then did the Spreen take the visitors to the workshops.

On the way back down, Stoner solved one problem regarding the surface structures. He asked Dun-Dun why it had appeared to the group standing on the outside that they were seeing all the way through the structures when the structures actually contained rooms, observatories, and living quarters. Stoner didn't understand Dun-Dun's explanation, so Dun-Dun called a halt, took out a writing instrument and a pad, and dashed off a series of complicated formulae that neither Stoner nor Gage Fergus understood. But they got the idea that a method of "fracturing" light was used, designed into the crystalline material by a strict formula.

"Mirror tricks?" Jackie asked.

"Not quite that simple," Stoner replied. "They're doing things with light that seem to defy all the rules."

Dun-Dun allowed Fergus to keep the formulae he had written. The engineer smiled. People like Harry, Grace, and Max would have fun trying to figure them out.

Jean and Cee-Cee, who had already formed a firm friendship, led the way into the first workshop, where Jean stopped in her tracks as she caught sight of sparkling, gleaming jewels arranged on a fabric-covered table. The stones seemed to live, to writhe, to glow, to move. And yet they were inanimate objects.

"Nice," Jean said, using one of the few Spreen words she had learned.

"Nice," Cee-Cee agreed, leading her to the table and inviting her to examine the stones.

"Diamonds?" Jackie asked Stoner as the group handled, admired, and fingered the jewels.

"Unlike any I've ever seen," he said.

"They are not beautiful when they are mined," Dun-Dun stated. "Come."

At a workbench a sable-colored doer was extruding an almost invisible filament from his fingertips, wrapping it carefully around what Stoner saw was an uncut, rough gemstone. The stone was about the size of the ball of his thumb, and Stoner was a big man with large hands. He watched as the doer carefully examined the stone before placing another loop of filament around it. When the doer was satisfied, he opened a small door in a crystalline structure in front of him.

"Please do not look directly at the light trap," Cee-Cee warned them, holding up her hand to tell the doer to wait. "Look away from it, and have it only in the corner of your eyes."

When she gave the doer the go-ahead—all eyes turned away, the contraption in front of the doer seen only in peripheral vision—there was a brilliant flash of light that illuminated the entire workshop to multiples of the light of day, and a loud cracking sound was heard.

"Now you may look," Cee-Cee said.

The doer opened the door, and the stone inside had somehow captured the light and glowed with it, moved with it, and danced in a delicate pattern of sheer beauty. The doer, smiling proudly, handed the stone to Jean for her examination.

"The filament wrapping has disappeared," she said incredulously.

"It lives inside the stone," Cee-Cee explained. "It gives life to the stone."

"Do you like it?" Dun-Dun asked Jean.

"I've never seen anything so lovely," she said.

"It is yours," he said.

"Thank you," Jean whispered.

"Do you all like our jewels?" Dun-Dun asked.

Everyone liked them.

"Then you will trade —— for them?" He used a word they had heard before, but for which they had not tried to find an exact English equivalent.

"Just what is it?" Jackie asked.

"It is sweet and good," Ccc-Cee said. "The Bese make it. We had hoped that you made it, too, for it has been a long time since the Bese came, and our supply is old, no longer fresh and good."

"Could you show us a sample?" Jackie asked.

Dun-Dun gave orders. A young Spreen left on the run. While they awaited his return they watched doers instill life into more gemstones, which they began to call fire diamonds. Some were left in their natural state, merely polished. Others had been faceted, and those cut stones seemed to possess the most glowing, sparkling life.

Stoner asked Dun-Dun where the Spreen found the diamonds, and the party was taken lower and deeper into the earth until singing was heard up ahead. They emerged into another cavern where doers worked, mining diamonds from what Stoner immediately recognized as a volcanic core.

"Do you use any of the metallic ores?" he casually asked Dun-Dun, who did not understand. Stoner launched into a long and convoluted explanation, finally making Dun-Dun understand by showing him Jackie's gold wedding ring, the steel of a laser pistol, and other metallic objects.

"We have no use for such stuff," Dun-Dun said.

"Would the Spreen have any objection if we took some of the metallic ore from your planet? If we dug in the valley where our ship now stands?"

Dun-Dun thought for a moment. "Our home does not extend into the regions under the valley. If you have use for the heavy dirt there, you are welcome to it."

"What did the Bese take in exchange for the sweet goodness?" Stoner asked.

"The jewels," Cee-Cee responded.

The young Spreen who had been sent on an errand returned, carrying a small but ornately carved container, which he handed to Stoner. Stoner lifted the lid. There was a small spoon inside, and at the bottom of the jar, a brownish, sugary glob.

"See if you think this is what I think it is," he said, handing the jar to Jackie. She used the spoon and scooped up a small amount of the brownish mass.

"Honey," she said, tasting it.

"Gone to sugar, old," Stoner said. "They said that their supplies were no longer fresh."

"This is your sweet goodness?" Jackie asked Dun-Dun.

"Yes. Isn't it wonderful?"

"It *is* wonderful," Jackie agreed. "We call it honey."

"Do you make it?" Cee-Cee asked excitedly.

"On Omega we make large amounts of it," Jackie answered. "We will be happy to share the sweet goodness with the Spreen."

Cee-Cee clapped her hands happily and sang out the news to those Spreen who were not near enough to the translation machine to hear. A song broke out among the watchers, and down below, the miners halted their work to join in the song, which praised the sweet goodness. The prospect of having a new supply seemed to be the greatest news the doers and the watchers in the cavern had ever heard.

"Isn't it funny," Clay whispered to Cindy, "how a bear likes honey?"

"Buzz, buzz, buzz, I wonder why he does?" Cindy whispered back.

TWENTY-SEVEN

To escape the tedium of living on board ship, a camp had been set up on the banks of the only stream running through the valley near the plateau of the Spreen. Jean was spending most of her time underground with Cee-Cee and the female watchers, for her design talents were much in demand. She had borrowed a portable power supply and set up a tailoring shop in a lovely, beautifully furnished chamber that was a part of Dun-Dun and Cee-Cee's living area, and she was never alone.

The filaments the Spreen extruded from their fingertips were spun into the lovely silken material for their clothing. The filaments were also used as thread, for buildings, and for defense. Jean used her sewing machine to make clothing for the watcher females. Their joy was her ample reward. One of her first designs had been for Cee-Cee—a slinky, simple, classic evening dress that emphasized her lovely little figure and exposed what was, to Dun-Dun—at least at first—a shocking view of her downy breasts. The look on Dun-Dun's face—after his initial shock, and Cee-Cee's pride—were all the reward Jean could have wanted. When Dun-Dun presented her with a handful of lovely Spreen fire diamonds, she protested.

"Take them," Dun-Dun urged, "because you have given us good things. You have made our women happy and even more beautiful. Value must be exchanged for value, for a Spreen cannot take a gift that is not returned value for value."

"I'm building up a king's ransom," Jean told Leslie one evening when they were visiting with Cee-Cee, who had put aside her dislike for the outdoors to come to the landing party's camp on the river. "I don't ask for them, but it's their code."

"With what those would bring on Earth, you could be a very rich woman," Leslie said.

"Hell, I was born rich," Jean said. "I've always been rich. When I was back home, I could wear only one dress at a time, sail only one yacht at a time, drive only one ground vehicle at a time, live in only one mansion. What does wealth mean? For a long time to come, everyone on Omega will have all they can eat thanks to old Amando Kwait, and thanks to Baby there are dragon scales for everyone to wear pretty jewelry. When we come here with a load of honey, we'll have enough Spreen jewels for everyone, plus enough to trade on Earth for things we need. I just can't get excited up here about having more of something than I need or than anyone else has."

"Well, I was never able to see it just that way," Leslie said, laughing, "since I wasn't born rich."

"Have some of my wealth," Jean said, handing Leslie a half-dozen jewels.

Cee-Cee, a bit uncomfortable at first from being out in the open, was sitting on a blanket near an open fire where Clay, Stoner, and Shag were telling her about life on Earth. In turn she told them more about the life of the Spreen. They had been able to garner a lot of information in the past few weeks, while Stoner's big earth-moving machines worked day and night, stripping the soil and surface rocks away from what was proving to be a very large and rich deposit of molybdenite—bluish, rich in both molybdenum and the noble platinum metals, including a pleasing richness of that rarest of all metals, rhenium.

They listened with pleasure to Cee-Cee's soft, pleasant voice and the translation coming out of the machine. Then, after Cee-Cee had gone off with Jean to sleep in the *Jennie* because, even with her new friends, she was not yet ready to spend the night in the open air, the men mused over what they knew about the Spreen.

"The only written language they have is mathematical symbols," Stoner said. "And that's odd, since they've found ways to study the stars, know celestial mechanics, and have formed, apparently on their own, theories covering the formation of stars, gravity, and light. What they do with light is going to keep our theorists busy for years. And yet they're totally static."

"Just as the Whorsk and the Eepera are static," Gage commented.

"So we've encountered three intelligent species," Stoner said, "each of them with myths or legends or tribal memory to take them back thousands of years. But not one of them, not even the Eepera, who have a form of written history, have made any scientific advances for thousands of years. That brings up a couple of interesting questions. Why are *we* different? Why do *we* continue to seek, to strive for advancement or change?"

"Or is it that we simply have not yet reached our threshold of achievement?" Gage Fergus asked. "Maybe, in a couple of centuries or a thousand years, we'll become static too."

"With all that out there?" Clay asked, waving at a sky across which the disk of this distant galaxy spread in a display far brighter than the Milky Way seen from Earth. "No way. As long as there are humans with the means to explore, or inquire, they'll be trying to see what's beyond the next star."

"There were racial units on Earth that never advanced," Gage pointed out. "The bushmen of Africa, some tribes in New Guinea—they never changed, not even when they came into contact with so-called modern humans."

"And what about the Bese?" Shag asked. "We don't know whether their science and thinking have gone static. We won't know until we come nose to nose with them."

"Then why have they not been here to Spreen for so long a time?" Stoner asked.

"The use of living components in their ship implies that they'd come to a dead end in microtechnology," Gage said.

"But how far had they advanced in the biological sciences to be able to utilize those living components?" Stoner asked, leaning forward to toss deadwood onto the fire.

There was a silence. The muttering roar of the diggers, carried on a breeze, came to them. The machines were being supervised by Mopro and the sergeant, tireless, efficient.

"Isn't it most important that the Spreen are happy?" Clay asked. "They're content in their home. They seem to breed just often enough to maintain a stable population. Do you suppose it's because they are content—maybe because they have no competition on this planet—that they're so devoid of any of the cruelty we've seen in the Whorsk and the Eepera, and why there's no violence in their society?"

"Well, I don't know," Stoner said. "One man's paradise is another man's endless boredom. The Spreen have their duties. The doers work. The watchers keep order and maintain organization. There's no incentive to change, no outside threat to cause them to develop better defensive measures. They'd change if, for example, invaders came here and saw how cute they are and started carrying off their young ones as pets."

"We can never let that happen!" Clay said, indignant.

"Will we be able to prevent it?" Stoner asked. "When and if the starships start pouring Earth's surplus population out into space, it may be the Earthmen who'll be guilty of such crimes. Think about the poaching that wiped out elephants and rhinoceri in Africa."

"Then we'll have to do something," Clay said.

"Yes, we'll have to try," Stoner agreed.

"Sometimes I wish we could just forget about Earth," Clay said, then quickly added, "Oh, I know we can't. It's going to be up to us to show them that there's more to life than looking up and wondering when the bombs are going to start dropping from the weapons stations. We can show them that there's plenty out here in space, enough land and good things to make life wonderful for everyone. But I, for one, will fight to see to it that they don't do to Omega what they did to the Earth."

"Or what we're doing here?" Stoner asked. "Ripping away the surface, changing the ecology of this valley to get at what we need?"

"We can replace the earth we've removed," Clay said.

"But we've still changed it," Stoner persisted. "There's always going to have to be some balance struck between thoughtless exploitation that does serious and long-term damage and the inescapable need to get at a planet's resources."

"We should lay down some rules," Clay decided, "before we bring people out from Earth."

"Good idea," Gage commended. "When we get back to Omega, why don't you discuss that idea with Dexter Hamilton and Rodrick?"

"I'm not a politician," Clay said.

"Someone has to be, or you'll end up with the kind of men we had in power on Earth," Gage said. "Earth is going to need us. We've learned how to survive out here. If I know Harry Shaw, we're going to have some pretty impressive resources and some very deadly weapons once he's worked on and expanded Eeperan technology."

"If we had something more powerful than their nuclear weapons and missiles and all the rest," Clay said, "we could go back and lay down the law to them, tell them that greed and the lust for power are going to be left behind on Earth, or they can stay there and kill each other off."

Stoner laughed. "Good luck with that, kiddo."

Shag yawned. "I'm going to turn in," he said.

"I'm with you," Stoner said, rising to move out of the light of the fire to his sleeping bag.

Clay lay awake for a long time. Cindy, at his side, made a soft little buzzing sound in her sleep. He put one hand on her and experienced anew the wonder of her, felt his love for her swell inside him until he wanted to laugh for joy. One day they'd have children. One day maybe children of theirs would climb into a state-of-the-art starship and go flashing off to a distant galaxy. Would they find a sameness? Would they find the same old violence, greed, and power seeking? What kind of world would he, Clay Girard, want for his sons and daughters? He pictured Omega a couple of decades in the future—the big, sprawling continents dotted with cities and fields, but with vast tracts of undisturbed wilderness. Yes, he would fight, for Omega was his world, and none of them back on Earth had the right to come out to his world and start tearing it apart or to bring their silly racial, religious, and philosophical differences.

He slept, and he dreamed that Cindy was walking toward him on beautiful grass, through a parklike setting. A little girl who looked like her was holding one of her hands, and a boy who looked like him, the other. He awoke with Cindy kissing him awake and the sun up and Stoner clumping around to rekindle the fire. A pot of coffee was brewing over the open fire within minutes, and Clay approached the day with optimism and a deep-seated resolve to see that the evils of Earth stayed there.

Jean and Cee-Cee were ready to return to the Spreen's underground home after breakfast. Clay dropped them off on the plateau. He and Gage flew on to the wrecked Bese ship. Fergus had been working hard to figure out the control system of the ship, and he had made a lot of progress. Using a portable power source, he had activated a weapons turret. Feeling certain he knew how to fire the ship's oddly constructed weapon, he had found the controls to open the turret, and on that morning he was going to push the button. Clay was positioned on the rim of the canyon to observe. He took cover behind large rocks when Fergus said he was ready. A flash of light came from the turret. On the canyon wall a section of bare rock was blasted as if by lightning.

"It's the Eeperan sun gun," Gage radioed after the noise of falling rock had ceased.

"These guys can't be so tough if that's all they've got," Clay said. He went back down and joined Gage in the ship.

"Remember when we were talking last night about the lack of advancement in the three races we've encountered?" Clay asked. "I may be wrong, but it seems to me that there is a possibility that all three of them took what science they had from the Bese. We know the Eepera did. That's all they have—machines that they took originally from their home planet. The Whorsk's only technical development beyond stone tools is the airship. The Spreen's science all deals with light. It could all have come from the Bese, couldn't it?"

"Sounds logical," Gage agreed. "I'm betting that when Harry gets the power plant open in the pyramid, and then later, when we open up the power plant on this ship, we're going to find the same thing, some means of converting light energy into usable power."

The diggers droned on with their work. They were into the ore field now, and the holds of the *Free Enterprise* were slowly being filled with the rich, blue molybdenite. Jean's store of Spreen jewels continued to grow. The Spreen mined several separate volcanic cores, all rich in diamonds. They were so generous that Jean felt guilty and promised herself that she was going to raise holy hell if the *Free Enterprise* didn't make a quick turnaround after returning to Omega, with a cargo of the honey the Spreen loved so well.

"The doers work so hard making the jewels," she

told Cee-Cee one day. "And you seem to put so little value on them."

"We do value the jewels," Cee-Cee said. "But we like to share beauty. We like to trade."

"Why don't you keep any jewels for yourself?" Jean asked. She had become quite fluent in the simple Spreen language and could converse without the translation machine.

"We do," Cee-Cee said. She led Jean to a small room adjacent to her bedroom, opened the door, and pressed a section of wall. "These are mine," she said as a cascade of light struck Jean's eyes, living light coming from a half-dozen jewels, the largest of which was the size of Jean's doubled hands.

"This one is my favorite," Cee-Cee said, handing Jean a jewel that glowed with a rich, green light.

Awestruck, Jean held the green fire diamond in her hands. It was almost perfectly round and had been multifaceted. It was the size of a golf ball and incredibly beautiful.

Cee-Cee laughed. "You see, we do allow ourselves just a bit of selfishness. We keep the best for ourselves."

"Everyone has jewels like these, all the watchers?"

"Watchers?" Cee-Cee laughed. "The doers have the choice stones, for they are the ones who discover them."

"The doers have better than these?"

"Oh, yes. And that is only proper, since they do the work. But they are not greedy. Why does one need more than a few, when each is so beautiful? This, the green one, was the prize in an old doer's collection, until he found another green one that was larger and more brilliant. Then he gave this one to me, and I was happy to have it."

"Cee-Cee," Jean said, "don't ask me why, but take my advice. If the Bese ever return, don't show your private collections to them. If other Earthmen come here in the future, show them only the stones you wish to trade."

Cee-Cee laughed merrily. "Show this to barbarians?" She held the green stone in front of her eyes, moved it to make it live. "No, we would never show anything like this to the Bese. I show it to you because I know you are my friend."

"And not a barbarian?" Jean asked, curious, for that had been the first time she had heard a Spreen use a disparaging word about either the Bese or humans.

"I hope not," Cee-Cee said seriously. "Are you?"

"I pray not," Jean said, but she knew that she could not speak for all Earthpeople, and she prayed, too, that there would be some way to limit access to the Spreen planet. Otherwise she dared not think what would happen if humans saw the Spreen jewels, especially those in the private collections.

TWENTY-EIGHT

Without Jackie the pleasant house overlooking Stanton Bay was too quiet. Rodrick was amazed to discover that he had become fully adapted to married life. It was odd how the house and all things in it seemed to be changed. Before Jackie had taken the *Free Enterprise* outward to the stars, there had been times when he was alone in the house, for they were both busy people. But being alone and knowing that she would soon be coming in the door was totally unlike being alone and knowing that only weeks had passed since the ship lifted and that many more weeks—maybe months—would pass before a radio message from near space announced the return.

He had always liked music, although he had not

always had the time to enjoy it. During the first evenings alone, he played some of his favorite works and at first enjoyed them. He also watched a few of his all-time favorite movies, which he had not seen in a while because his taste was for epic action and Jackie's preferences were for artistic or dramatic films. It took only a few evenings for it all to pall: The music merely emphasized the emptiness of the house, and he found himself being inattentive when he screened even his favorite epic.

One night after he had worked late helping Amando Kwait finish his catalogue of Omegan plants to be taken back to Earth, he found himself almost alone aboard the *Spirit of America*. He knew that there was a man on duty in the engine spaces and another on the bridge. He had accompanied Amando to the hatch and watched him walk away into the night. Rodrick stood there for a long time, looking up at the stars and wondering where the *Free Enterprise* was at that exact moment. When he closed the hatch and started walking the ship's empty corridors, he knew that he was simply delaying the return to his empty house.

The old girl was in beautiful condition. She'd had a paint job to repair the damage done to her exterior when she had almost lightstepped into the heart of a star. All her internal systems had been kept in good working order. The fusion-generating plant, even when working at low output, provided much more electricity than the ship needed, so her lights were on at all times.

Oddly enough, he didn't feel lonely there. There were only three people in all of the ship's vast areas, but he felt at ease. He took an internal transporter in toward the core of the ship, identified himself to the duty man on the bridge—a space service rating named Ellis—and was admitted.

"Lonely duty, eh, Ellis?" he asked as he seated himself in the command chair. Soon, now, he'd be sitting there with the ship in space again.

"Not bad, sir," Ellis answered. He was a young

man, still in his twenties. "I'm taking courses under Derek Roebling, and my duty nights here give me a chance to get in some concentrated study."

"Are you on the crew roster for the return?" Rodrick asked.

"No, sir. My wife had twins a couple of months ago, so I'll stay on Omega. There are plenty of single guys from both crews, or husband-wife teams."

"Don't blame you for wanting to stay," Rodrick said.

"I used to look forward to the trip back," Ellis said. "I thought of it as going home, but . . ."

"You don't think that way anymore?"

"No, sir. I think of this as my home now. Ruth and I have a great house. We picked the spot. The house sort of sprawls on three levels on the hill just inland from the power station. We have a view of the fields and the river. We decided against building on the bay because Ruth grew up in farm country—even if she did live in a high-rise—and we both liked the feeling of looking out at wide open spaces. Now that we've got the twins . . ." He fell silent.

Rodrick drew off a cup of coffee and sat in silence for a while. Ellis, seated at the console, opened a textbook. All the lights on the ship's control panels were normal. Her eyes and ears were on, aimed at space, and that readiness was the only hint of anything unpleasant in Rodrick's thoughts. He was comfortable in the command chair. He liked the smell of the ship, the soft, muted sounds of her. He felt pleasant anticipation, knowing that she'd lift and blast her way into the freedom of space.

"Good night, Ellis," he said after a while, rising to leave the bridge. He considered visiting the duty man in the engine spaces but instead found himself walking toward the observatory. His palm print opened the limited-access door, and the lights glowed dimly, just enough to light his way to the comfortable chairs before the large screens. The ports were closed, the power to the screens off. Not bothering with the screens, he opened the big ports instead and lay back to gaze up into Omega's cloudless, star-filled night sky. He turned the lights off, and after a few seconds his eyes were adjusted to the view from the port, and he let his mind go back over the events of the outward journey. That, of course, brought Mandy to mind. Quite often they'd sat together here in the observatory, to talk quietly or just to sit and look at the stars. She had been a comfort to him, stability when things were rough. She alone had really understood his loneliness, a loneliness compounded by the responsibilities he carried.

Rocky Miller had been alive then, a good officer but with weaknesses. In spite of the mutual attraction between Rodrick and Mandy, she'd been loyal to her husband, as he was now loyal to Jackie in everything but his yearnings, for just the remembrance of those times with Mandy brought such a need for her that it was almost painful.

He closed his eyes and brought his thoughts up to date. He'd need to fly over to the Great Misty River in a day or so to check on the progress of Harry's investigation of Eeperan technology. It was going to be necessary to bring Max back to Hamilton City soon, to supervise the final readiness of the ship. So, as he thought of his current responsibilities, he put Mandy far back in his consciousness, and when the door opened, almost noiselessly, and he turned his head to see *her* familiar figure outlined against the light of the corridor, he thought that he was either dreaming or hallucinating.

He sat quietly, not even his head visible to her as he slumped in the big, comfortable chair. She closed the door behind her and, although he had overridden the automatics and the lights did not come on, she made her way toward the seats and the screens in the dimness of starlight coming through the port. He caught the scent of her perfume. He knew that she was going to be startled when she realized that she was not alone, but he remained silent. She sat in the chair next to him. Her eyes had not yet adjusted to the dimness. She leaned back and looked up at the stars.

He could see her face faintly, the proud, perfect nose in profile, the soft mass of her hair, the slim line of neck.

It was as if she became aware of him gradually. She did not start or cry out. She turned her face toward him, and he heard her breath catch. "Duncan?"

"Sorry if I startled you," he said.

"No. I felt your presence before I saw you."

"Do you come here often?"

"No," she said quickly. Then, her voice almost inaudible, "Yes, yes I do." After a long pause she added, "I didn't know you were here."

"I know," he said. "It's nice to see you."

"Busy times."

"Yes," he said. His hands were tense on the arms of the chair.

She rose. "I think I'd better go."

There was no reason, no honor, left in him. He leaped to his feet and seized her arm as she started to walk past his chair. She was wearing a light sweater over her uniform. He could feel the warmth of her through the soft material. For a moment she pulled against his grasp, and then stopped. He reached around her, put his hand on her other arm and turned her to face him. In the starlight he could see that she was crying, the tears reflecting the dim light as if they were jewels.

There was no need for words. It was a moment whose time had come. Her full lips were slightly parted, her breasts heaving with her rapid breathing. He felt the force of exploding suns in his blood as he drew her toward him and bent to find the moist softness of her mouth. He had kissed her only once, briefly, and that kiss had brought disaster, for it had been witnessed by Rocky and quite possibly had been the final increment of Rocky's decision to lead two hundred colonists away from the settlement into the Whorsk ambush that had killed them all—all except the woman in his arms. But Rodrick was not thinking of the past or the possibility that his love for this small, compact, wonderfully sweet woman in his arms had brought disaster. He was pure emotion, the capable, always calm, confident commander swept away by a need that had been building for so long, so long.

Her posture from the time he began to pull her slowly toward him and to lower his lips to hers was total surrender, for she, too, was desire; common sense, conscience, all the strength she had expended in the past to deny her consuming need for him shed from her through the tears that had come as she started to walk away. An odd, inexplicable attraction had brought sudden awareness to them years before, when, as strangers, they had first glanced at each other across a room filled with people. That chemistry of nature was denied, but constant exposure intensified it. As they fought against it and thought, perhaps, that they had defeated the mysterious force, they became more vulnerable. Now, this accidental encounter erupted in an explosion of passion that swept everything before it.

His arms had a force that drove the breath from her lungs. One of his hands, after he initially clutched her, lowered without conscious bidding to rest on her womanly rump, to apply the proper force that positioned sensitivity to sensitivity and signals the true beginning.

There was no need to delay, for their passion had been building for years, and it demanded quickness, not tenderness—shared lust, not love. Like two teenagers with no more than ten minutes allowed, with need having been built by hours of mutual exploration, they parted, and in her hurry to rid herself of her sweater, she caught him directly on the nose with her elbow, and he laughed as he himself bared his body with a haste that, in a bedroom farce, would have been comical.

There was nothing comical from their viewpoint. Nothing mattered other than the fact that at last they were there, together. A pile of hay in a barn or a forest glade blanketed in leaves and pine needles would have served as well as the soft, full carpeting in the observatory. Had they been in a house, or Rodrick's quarters, or in any situation where a bed was near, they would not, could not, have waited long enough to find it.

He lifted her and placed her on the carpet. There was a scramble, and then in frenzied haste—like the union of two cells that takes place quickly, magically, when maleness and femaleness meet in the rich, dark, moist confines of the origination of life—they were one, and she began to moan of her fulfillment immediately.

"Duncan?"

"Ummm."

"That was damned undignified."

"Thoroughly ridiculous."

"Juvenile."

"Beautiful."

"Yes," she whispered, touching his lips, his face, with pouting, feathery lips. The euphoria had not yet begun to fade. "Now what?"

"Get dressed."

She dressed with her back to him, giving him a glimpse of her rump, so beautifully feminine, so dear. He led her down the corridors to his quarters, palmed the door opened, adjusted lights to a pleasant dimness, and held her until the need resurged; and once again, but less precipitously, they were undressing.

Now they took time to explore, to know, to experience. In the union there was little of the previous frantic haste, but the deep need and lasting hunger still enveloped them.

It was late, but there was a feeling of space, of timelessness, of the absence of night and day, for they were in the captain's quarters aboard a great starship with little or no danger of discovery. She had freshened herself and put on one of his uniform shirts. It came to just below the joint of her splendid, smooth, lovely thighs. As she swung one leg up onto the bed and sat

on it, holding a glass of Amando's very good white
wine, he caught a glimpse of the darkness into which he
had totally submerged himself.

"Well, we've done it," she said.

"Sorry?"

She smiled. "I'm telling myself that it was inevitable."

"I think so," he responded seriously. "God knows I
fought it."

She laughed. "Sometimes I felt you fought it too
hard."

"There's no way I can give you up now, you know,"
he said.

A bit frightened by his seriousness, she tried to be
light. "Sir, was I that good?" The lightness didn't quite
come off. "Should we talk about it now?"

"Not now," he said.

"We have to, sooner or later."

"In the light of day," he said. "I had already decided, before you came into the observatory, to move
back into my quarters here on the ship. The house
seems too . . . inhospitable."

The implication of his statement caused her to take
a deep breath, for it opened the door for them to be
together here on the ship every night.

"How have you been boarding?" he wanted to
know.

"Through a cargo port, on the side facing the bay,"
she said. "I like to come to the observatory to think, to
be alone. Away from my office. When I go out the back
way, after everyone has gone home, there's no one to
see."

He nodded.

"Duncan, I think we can both safely say that what
just happened was inevitable, that old Mother Nature's
magic was just too strong for us. But to plan, to be
deliberate about it, that's a different thing."

"I don't want to talk about it yet," he said. "I'm not
ready."

She rose and walked to the bar but did not refill

her glass. Standing with her back toward him, she said, "If you want to say to hell with everything and be together, then I'll do it."

"All right," he said, "but not until Jackie gets back."

She turned. There was a sad little smile on her face. "Yes, damn it, neither of us could do that. We couldn't stab her in the back."

"No."

"I won't be back," she told him.

"I can understand that. But there's no need for you to give up the inner sanctum you enjoy. I won't move onto the ship, so you'll still be free to come to the observatory."

She laughed. "Men used to say that women were an alien species. I think it's the other way around. Duncan, I won't be coming to the observatory. My God, don't you know why I went there?"

"Yes, I guess I do," he confessed.

"I've loved you from the first time I saw you. If we both hadn't been so damned honorable, I'd have thrown myself into your bed before we were two weeks away from Earth."

"Yes," he said.

She began to unbutton the shirt, revealed herself to him as the shirt fluttered to the floor. "Well, since we've done it, let's make the most of it, because this is it. Do you agree that that would be best?"

"Yes," he lied. It hurt to think of Jackie. It hurt him to realize that he'd done the very thing he had promised himself never to do, but to think of having known her and then to say no more was even more painful. She threw herself onto the bed and into his arms, and when she left, the sky was beginning to lighten in the east.

He knew that she would honor her vow; she would not come back to his quarters or to the observatory. It was over. What they'd had was something, but it was not enough. He moved his terminal and his personal effects back into his quarters aboard the *Spirit of America* the next morning, for now the house seemed to be less hospitable than ever. He had a busy day and was working into the evening in his quarters when he heard a knock on the door. His heart leaped. There were only the two duty men aboard. He ran to the door and threw it open. She had been weeping. Her eyes were swollen and red, and that made her even more beautiful, for he knew that she'd been weeping for him.

"I can't," she whispered. "I can't . . ."

He swept her into his arms.

On the following night there was no weeping.

TWENTY-NINE

Max left Harry alone in the room that housed the Eeperan power plant. He'd insisted upon staying, but Harry had been equally insistent upon his going. The reasoning was not new: There were only two men left on Omega who fully understood the mechanics and operation of a Shaw Drive, and it was not practical to risk both their lives.

"Let *me* do it, then," Max had said. "I'm a better mechanic than you. You can be all thumbs."

But Harry had won. "You're a newlywed, Max. Get the hell out of here and join that lovely wife of yours."

Max was already brightening, as he did any time there was a prospect of spending some time with Grace, when he entered the library. She'd told him she'd wait for him there, but the place was empty. "Hey!" he yelled, thinking she might be among the stacks somewhere. "Hey, Grace!"

His voice echoed off the stone walls. He made a quick examination of the work area. Her equipment was all in order, the translation machine turned off.

He lifted his communicator. "Harry, hold off a minute or two. I can't find Grace."

"Right," Harry sent. "I'm still setting things up."

Max was not concerned. He wandered around in the pyramid and then made his way to the entrance. The space marine guards were in place at the foot of the ramp. The camp had been cleared, with all personnel removed to a safe distance.

"Hey," he yelled, "has Grace Monroe come out?"

"No, sir," a guard yelled back.

"One of you come in and help me look for her," Max called.

He still wasn't worried, not even when he and the marine had searched the lower levels and had almost finished searching the midlevels where the library was located.

"Max," Harry called, "what's the holdup?"

Now Max was beginning to worry. "No sign of Grace," he sent back. "You're going to have to wait, Harry. I'm going to send for some help."

A group of space marines arrived on the double and scattered to search the pyramid from the tip—which still showed damage from Clay Girard's attack during the brief war—to the sublevels where the ancient mummies stood row on row. After an hour Max was not only worried, he was frantic. His always mussed hair was standing out in a hundred directions, and his uniform had surrendered helplessly to his inspired untidiness. Harry had come down from the power room.

"I don't like this, Harry," Max said, his face contorted in agony. "I've sent for the admiral."

"Have you questioned any of the priests?" Harry asked.

"They were all evacuated early," Max said. "The three of us were the only ones in the place." They were in the large chamber of idols at ground level. Around them ancient Egyptian gods with animal and bird heads stared out at them with blank, lifeless eyes.

A space marine officer came striding in. "Dr. Rosen, we've turned this place upside down. She's just not here."

Max ran a hand through his wild hair. And at that moment he saw a figure enter the chamber, and he brightened. "Admiral," he said.

"I came as quickly as I could," the admiral said. He had been in Hamilton City, supervising the final transfer of data from the computer on board ship to the permanent facilities in the city. "What's happened?"

Max explained. The admiral's handsome face was attentive. To Max it seemed that more and more the admiral was taking on human characteristics. Once he would have had the same expression on his face whether he was being chewed in half by a miner or answering a child's questions about arithmetic.

"You have not questioned the priests?" the admiral asked.

"They weren't here," Max said.

"Where are they?"

"The priests are housed in a villa just below the cliffs," the marine officer answered.

"Please come with me," the admiral said. "Bring four men."

"I'll go with you," Max said, for lack of anything else to do.

The party filed down the stone steps carved into the face of the cliffs. The city of Suses spread before them, impressive and beautiful. In the streets below they could see few Eepera but many Whorsk. The gleaming white villa where the priests had been housed until they could return to their work in the pyramid was half-sunken into the base of the cliff. White-robed junior priests stood guard at the gates. When the admiral led the group around the corner of the building and was first seen by the guards, one of them broke from his post and ran toward the villa's veranda.

"Stun gun," the admiral barked to the marine at his side, and the man, trained to obey orders without question, dropped the running priest with a well-placed stun charge. "Secure the other guard," the admiral ordered.

Max's eyes went wide. He himself would not have ordered the stunning of the priest, but he had great respect for the admiral's judgment and thus made no protest.

"Four men," the admiral said, "surround the villa. Keep watch on all exterior openings." The men scattered on the run. The admiral spoke to Max: "When we get inside, stay close to me, please. You, sir," he said to the officer, "would you please cover our rear and stay close."

The veranda was shaded and tastefully decorated with green plants. The entry door was not locked. Inside, there was splendor. Max had not taken the time to see too much of the city, and he was impressed. The floors were of beautiful, perfect white marble. The statuary and decor had the look of ancient Egypt. The foyer branched into two hallways. The admiral hesitated for a moment, then took the right branch. He had walked only a few paces when he heard a wild cry from behind an ornately carved door. He threw open the door.

Lance Corporal Celia Hadley had taken the opportunity of being relieved of duty at the guard post to visit her Eeperan friends. She had brought with her two male marines. With them were two Eeperan women and one male, and the cry the admiral had heard was Celia's response to the ministrations of the Eeperan man. When the door burst open, Celia looked up, angry because the interruption had lessened the quality of terminal pleasure, then her eyes went wide as she saw the admiral and a space marine lieutenant. She tried to push the Eeperan off her. The two male marines were continuing with their activities.

"Stun, please," the admiral commanded, and when the officer hesitated, the robot grabbed the stun gun and one by one, starting with the woman and the Eeperan male, used a two-hour stun charge on all the occupants of the room. He handed the stun gun back. "Sir, would you please call the camp and have a hospital unit with litters sent?"

Max said, "Those marines were drugged."

"Yes," the admiral agreed. He went back into the hall and continued his exploration. The villa had over a dozen rooms, but all were empty. The rear rooms were windowless, for they had been constructed underground, set back into the cliff.

"No priests," Max commented.

The admiral was examining a rear wall closely. It was well-decorated with Egyptian-style painting and seemed to be solid.

"Where the hell are the priests?" Max growled, his gut aching with worry.

The admiral raised his laser pistol and blasted the wall, the beam charring and then penetrating a beautiful scene of serving girls in attractive brief costumes. A shout of fear came from the hole. The admiral ran directly at the wall, flattened his chest against it, and burst through. In the chamber beyond, a group of Eeperan priests wailed in fear. The admiral held his laser weapon trained on them. The lieutenant was ready with his stun gun, and Max stood helplessly, looking around frantically for Grace.

"Where is the chief priest?" the admiral demanded.

The priests shrank back from the threatening face and remained silent. The admiral took three quick steps forward and seized a priest by his robe, bunching it below the priest's chin and lifting him from the floor.

"Where is Ahmes?" he demanded.

"I don't know," the priest gasped. "We were told to stay here in the villa until we would be allowed to return to our duties."

The admiral threw the priest away from him roughly,

and the priest landed on his feet, then fell. The admiral faced the others. "Dr. Grace Monroe, whom you all know, is missing. So is your chief priest. If any of you know the whereabouts of Dr. Monroe, tell me and you will live. If you don't know the whereabouts of Dr. Monroe, tell me where Ahmes is, and you will live."

The priests, although they had paled and some of them trembled, were silent.

"Lieutenant," the admiral said, "you will begin with this one." He pointed. "You will kill him, and then we will give the others a chance to speak. If they do not, then you will kill the next, and the next, until one of them speaks."

The lieutenant was holding his stun gun, which was not a killing weapon. He recognized the admiral's strategy. He lifted the stun gun and fired. A few of the priests screamed as the Eeperan fell. A moment passed as the admiral scanned the other priest's faces.

"Next," the admiral said, and the stun gun hummed again.

From the first moment of his arrival the admiral had sensed a deadly threat to the woman who had created him, who had been his mother during his infancy, the woman who meant more to him than anything else in the universe. He had the feeling that he was battling time. He had no time to waste coaxing information from the priests. What he had seen in the front room of the villa—space marines under the influence of the Eeperan drug—had not been needed to convince him that, without anyone noticing, something had been going on among the Eeperan priests.

It was, of course, against the admiral's programming to harm a living being needlessly, but he had, after all, been originally designed as an instrument of war, programmed to kill designated enemies. He now saw the priests as enemies, as a threat to his Grace. Had there not been a stun gun available, he would have used a laser actually to kill, for his computerlike brain told him that time was running out. Grace had been missing for almost three hours.

He was human enough to know regret. Since it seemed improbable that Grace had left the pyramid without having been seen by the guard, that meant that she was still somewhere inside or below the structure. His regret came from not having been more persistent in searching for hidden entrances, secret passageways, and buried chambers. He had assumed—as had the others—that with the discovery of the Museum of Life, all the pyramid's secrets had been revealed. Now there was no time to search for hidden doors.

"Now will someone speak?" he asked, with two more priests crumbled onto the floor. A priest was sobbing hysterically. No one spoke. The lieutenant pointed the stun gun and gave the intended victim time to speak, but he merely fell to his knees and began to pray. The stun gun hummed. In quick order ten of the twenty-plus priests were sleeping. They'd awaken in two hours with a slight headache. The others, the admiral was sure, thought that the fallen were actually dead. And still no one spoke.

THIRTY

Grace regained consciousness slowly. She had a vile taste in her mouth and could not move. She opened her eyes to bright lights and the face of the high priest, Ahmes. She was strapped into sitting upright, and there was something on her head. She resisted the urge to scream or to demand to know what was going on.

"Ahmes," she said in the Eeperan language, "greetings."

"Greetings, Dr. Monroe," Ahmes replied.

"I do not recognize your costume," Grace said. She could see that bands around her wrists secured her hands to the arms of a chair. She could feel similar bands at her ankles. There seemed to be a band around her forehead as well. She could see a shadow of it and could not move her head.

"It is the costume of the medical laboratory," Ahmes said.

"We are still in the pyramid?" Grace asked.

"Far below it," Ahmes answered, "in chambers, the laboratories of our forefathers, cut from the living rock."

A chill caused Grace's skin to crawl. She thought of Sage Bryson. Damn, they'd all been so busy, they hadn't even stopped to investigate the methods of Sage's preservation. Looking back, she realized that that had been a serious omission. It had been so evident, if only she had thought of it, that Sage's preservation had to have been done in some kind of laboratory.

"Am I to become an exhibit in the Museum of Life?" she asked, fighting hard to control her horror.

"Perhaps that honor will be given to you," Ahmes replied.

"It's time to ask you about your intentions," Grace said.

"And it is time to tell you," Ahmes agreed with a little bow. "It is nothing more than a practical application of Eeperan science," he said. "We are unhappy with your desecration of our sacred temple. We think it very unwise to have you meddle with the secrets of our great ancestors. And yet we are helpless against your weapons and your science. In self-defense we must learn all your secrets."

"And how do you intend to do that?" she wanted to know.

"It is evident to us that you are among the most

knowledgeable of all the Earthpeople," Ahmes said. "With your knowledge, we will have a beginning. In our laboratories we will put your knowledge to work to construct the magic weapons with which you bested us."

Grace felt tendrils of fear. Her head was held by something reminding her of the antique rigs with which mental patients were treated with electroshock. Were these superstitious morons going to start messing around with her brain?

"As a fellow scientist," she said, "I'd be very interested in an explanation of your methods."

"Of course," he agreed. "Although there has been little need for it during our centuries of peace here, we have retained the science of deep-brain probe. The last time it was used was over two centuries past, when the leader of a misguided uprising against priestly authority had to be corrected. Certain portions of his brain were treated, to remove his aggressive tendencies. Prior to that, however, we transferred his memory into the sacred brain-probe receptacle. There it remains, to be studied. In your case, we must transfer your knowledge."

"How is this done?" she asked.

"It is quite painless," he assured her. "The brain itself feels no pain."

Grace swallowed. It was as she feared. The bastards planned to go into her brain.

"Wouldn't it be simpler, and safer for you, if I merely taught you what you want to know? After all, we're going to have to live together on this planet. I assure you that if you do me harm, my fellow humans will not take it lightly."

"I regret that what we do is necessary," Ahmes said. "I have come to respect your scientific knowledge. But unfortunately, we have no time to spare, and in all truth, why should you tell us the secrets we need to drive you from our city and exterminate you from our planet?"

A wave of hopelessness caused Grace to feel dizzy.

She felt the chair tilt and realized with growing panic that she was being positioned so that the priests, who had about as much real medical knowledge as Baby, the Omegan dragon, could begin to drill holes in her skull through which they clearly intended to thrust things into her brain. Without realizing it, she was thinking, *Admiral, help me. Admiral, help me, please.*

"It will not be necessary to shave away your hair," Ahmes was saying behind her. "The drills and the probes are quite small, and we would not want you to be disfigured, in case we do have the chance to place you in the Museum of Life."

"You're saying that this process will kill me?" Grace asked.

"It may," Ahmes said, "although the leader of the uprising survived. He was kept as a curiosity, well fed and content, although it was quite a chore to tend him as one has to tend a newborn infant."

"Help me, Admiral," Grace whispered as she heard the whirr of a drill near her ear and felt the bite of a needle into her scalp. "Admiral, hurry." And then she felt a dull vibration, no pain, as a drill began to enter her scalp. When it encountered bone she could hear it, a vibrating, grating, whirring noise. Her skull was less than one-half inch thick at that point. Within a few seconds the drill would punch through and then continue into the gray matter of her brain.

THIRTY-ONE

"It's not going to work, Admiral," Max said. Twelve priests had felt the stun gun. The others cowered but remained silent. "Maybe they don't know."

"They know," the admiral said. But he, too, was beginning to think that one of two conditions existed: Either the priests were so indoctrinated that they would die before they gave up the secrets, or they truly did not know what had happened to Grace or Ahmes. He was feeling a desperation new to him, an emotion so human that he almost wished for the innocence of his youth. And he was getting odd, strange flashes of thought. At moments he could almost see clearly, at others a blur: a room, men in white lab smocks, banks of equipment.

A scout was landing outside. Reinforcements were coming. They, however, would be of no help. He was more sure than ever that time was short. How he knew, he would not have been able to say, but he felt it, amid those odd flashes of inner vision of a room with men in white, of equipment, bright lights, the hum of . . . what?

He was also thinking of Sage Bryson. He had seen her, mounted, a beautiful lifelike specimen in the Museum of Life. What was . . . something trying to tell him? He saw convoluted whorls, and for a flash the picture was complete, a brain, exposed, so delicately fragile and susceptible to irreversible damage, and there was only one thing left for him to do, a desperate measure, a method that came to him generated by his inner vision of a human brain, by his ability to "plug into" the most complex computer.

He leaped forward, seized a priest, and bore him down to the floor.

"What are you doing?" Max gasped as a small drill emerged from the admiral's finger. It was easy to forget that this so human-looking robot was not a man but a machine, with a body designed for many purposes, with an artificial brain powered by small atomic batteries.

The admiral did not answer. The priest screamed as the drill pierced his scalp and snarled through his skull. The drill disappeared.

The marine lieutenant's face turned white. He was trained to kill and had killed during the war against the Eeperans, but to stand by and see a robot drill into a living skull was different. He looked at Max. Max's face was grim. He sensed the admiral's desperation. To him the life of his wife was more important than a hundred Eeperan priests. That was just the way it was.

A fine filament sought out a particular spot in the priest's brain, and a very small electrical current went through it. The priest began to babble words that made no sense. The admiral adjusted the filament and let his consciousness flow down, down, through his finger, down the fine, sterile filament, and then he was seeing images, hearing words. It was very much as if he were connected to the ship's main computer with billions of items of information available to him. He could not, however, direct access as well as he could with the computer and had to file through personal memories, impressions, hoards of data regarding gods and rules and sex and hunger. And then he was seeing the room, a laboratory, Eeperans in white lab smocks, banks of electronic equipment—and suddenly he received the seed of it all, a machine that would literally drain out all contents of a mind into a complicated electronic reservoir, leaving . . . nothing.

"Where," he was sending. "Where?"

He saw the cliffs, quickly oriented himself, and

then, with care, removed the filament. "Get this man medical attention," he said, leaping to his feet and leaving the room so swiftly that Max and the lieutenant were left behind. He was outside, running past space marine reinforcements who were moving in rapidly. His motions were a blur as he ran toward the cliff with the speed only a machine could attain. And then he saw the place, thundered into it with his laser blasting to smash the rocks, found the door, and aimed his beam to lance through it. He backhanded the priest inside the door, not having time enough to pull the blow, leaving the priest falling, his cheek crushed, blood spouting.

His footsteps rang into echoes as he sped down the tunnel leading deeper under the cliffs. Ahead was another door, less sturdy. He hit it on the run and burst into the lab. White-smocked priests scattered. He lanced a group of them with his laser, for they stood between him and Grace, who was tilted backward in a chairlike contraption, a thing with wires running from it to her skull, the high priest standing beside her head.

Priests fell, flesh and garments smoking.

As the door burst open, Ahmes had started to pull the drill from Grace's skull. It was in his hand, still turning, as the admiral's laser flared. Ahmes's head was severed at the neck to fall with a solid thud to the stone floor.

"Admiral, help me!" Grace cried, and he was leaping to her side, using his great strength to rip away her restraining bands. A few of the surviving priests were running from the lab, but the admiral paid them no attention. He heard the hum of a stun gun from down the tunnel and knew that the lieutenant and Max were there.

". . . were going into my brain," Grace was saying as he examined the contraption on her head, saw there were no direct connections, slid it off, and set it aside.

"Did the drilling, Admiral, get to my brain?"

He saw the small area of blood, gently examined the tiny wound, and saw flakes of bone from the drill.

He had sterilized the fine probe he'd used on the priest with internally stored fluid and heat. He extended it again and said, "Be very still."

She felt odd. She knew—had felt—that the bastards had penetrated her skull, that the drill had sunk, spinning, into the very seat of her being, the soft, vulnerable, irreplaceable tissue.

"Damage?" she whispered, a tear sliding from the corner of her eye.

The admiral was being very, very careful. When the filament reached the bottom of the hole and encountered bone, he knew elation. He, too, had feared that Grace's brain—that unique, genius-filled brain—had been tampered with, but the drill had not gone through the skull.

"It didn't go through, Grace," he said.

"Thank God," she said. "But I feel a little funny."

Max came panting into the room and skidded to a halt.

"Hi," Grace said.

"She's all right," the admiral told him quickly. "I got here in time."

Max moved forward. Grace held out her hands, too dizzy to try to rise. "You all right?" Max asked gruffly, his throat constricted.

"She has a small wound in her scalp and skull, but there's no serious damage. We must get her out of here," the admiral said. He slowly returned the chair to a vertical position. Grace put her hand on her forehead and said, "Whew."

Max took her hands. His eyes were leaking. "Get a team down here, Max," she told him, beginning to feel very, very sleepy.

"Yeah, we will," he said.

"Wanta talk to my—my—" She seemed unable to speak, then, ". . . my son."

"Who?" Max asked, worried again, for she had no son.

"Admiral," she whispered.

Max withdrew. The admiral put his ear close to her lips. "Calling you," she said.

"I heard. You were saying, 'Admiral, help me.' "

"Yes. You heard?"

"At first I wasn't sure."

"Have to investigate—" she began, and then she was asleep, her body, her strength, giving way to shock and the results of her extreme tension. The admiral carried her through the tunnel to a waiting medical crawler. Within an hour she was in one of Mandy's hospital beds, her small wound sterilized and the hole in her skull filled with synthetic bone. Max sat at her side and watched her sleep.

THIRTY-TWO

Harry got knocked across the room and had his hair singed—not from removing the cover from the Eeperan power plant but from removing, carefully, with the help of Max, a very complicated series of metallic mirrors and panels of geometrically arranged tubing containing nothing more mysterious than liquid mercury.

The city and the pyramid were without power. Although there was no energy radiating from the power plant, Harry was still very careful as he reached the small black box at the heart of the power plant. An odd but strong field surrounded the box, extending no more than inches beyond its seamed corners. The box was held by a pair of clamps, and it seemed that it could be opened easily simply by loosening the clamps.

"Why so careful?" Max asked as they studied the

box. "Take off those nuts, remove the clamps, and it comes apart."

"Before we do that, I want to know why we're getting a heavy flow of free electrons in the air around it," Harry explained.

Later, when Harry touched the box with a highly insulated probe, energy discharged with a boom and a flash that again singed his hair and sent him tumbling head over heels to bang against the far wall. Ruffled but not seriously hurt, he sat there on the floor and said, "Now that *was* exciting."

The rest was anticlimactic but humbling. Just when they were beginning to lose their awe of Eeperan technology, just when everyone had decided that the society that had spawned the Eepera hadn't been so tough, after all, Max and Harry—being very, very careful and leaving the city and the pyramid without power for over a week—opened the black box to find literally nothing: a vacuum. They put it all back together, let the sun come to the assembly, and within minutes the lights began to blink back on.

It was all done with mirrors and some ingeniously generated magnetic fields formed by several strategically placed electromagnets. The electronic components were so deceptively simple that at first neither Harry nor Max would allow themselves to believe that not only had the Eeperan scientists harnessed the energy of the sun over three thousand years ago, but that they had worked out a wonderfully simple way of broadcasting the sun-generated energy. There were no wires connecting anything with the power station.

The mirrors, thought to be metallic at first, were layers of crystal, and what happened to sunlight inside the layers was still a puzzle when Harry re-created the effect in a lab. Moreover, inside the black box, in a vacuum into which was injected a stream of superheated electrons, something happened that allowed for storage of megavolts of electricity for an unknown—

pending experiments to measure the exact interval—but ler ثthy period.

There was also some interesting information being discovered in the underground chamber where Grace had been the intended victim of the first brain-probe experiment to be conducted by Eeperans in over two hundred years. In contrast to the genius of the sun generator and broadcast power, the Eeperan brain-probe technique was somewhat primitive—nothing more than the control of the function of each area of the brain by means of small electrical currents applied directly to the area. Delia Howard, called in to work with Grace in the Eeperan lab, said that it was like trying to repair a modern computer with a sledgehammer. You could control an individual with the techniques, but you'd do some pretty horrid damage in the process.

Ironically, had Ahmes succeeded in gaining access to Grace's memory areas, his efforts would have been wasted, for the receptacle into which her knowledge was to have been drained had an amino-acid base, and that biological material had long since atrophied. The receptacle was similar to, but not nearly as sophisticated as, Grace's electrobiological brains.

Of greatest value, however, was a scientific journal found in the hidden lab. Dated by an Eeperan calendar, it showed that certain experiments had been conducted by Ahmes, High Priest, one hundred years after the Eepera had landed on the planet that the Earthmen called Omega. Apparently, this Ahmes of almost three thousand years ago had not been successful in his attempts to store the wisdom of aging priests. Thus, the so-called receptacle had never worked, and that left Eeperan science work on the brain at the level of surgical and electrical manipulation. Obviously, the most recent Ahmes, whom the admiral had killed during his rescue mission, had not bothered to read the journal.

So it was that Grace came to realize her own overwhelming superiority in the study of brains when compared to Eeperan work, and Delia Howard determined that the Eepera—and presumably their ancient ancestors—had not understood the function of chemical messengers within the brain. Harry and Max, on the other hand, were made to feel a little bit stupid, because of the sheer genius and simplicity of the power generator and the techniques of broadcasting power. Shaw felt that some Earth scientist interested in working with the properties of light should have conceived the system. Grace, a religious woman, did not voice her opinion that all scientific discoveries were the result of a slow, steady accumulation of knowledge and a dose of divine inspiration.

All the scientific resources of the colony were now concentrated on the study, refinement, and the mutation into other forms of the Eeperan technology. Shaw was in charge. There was no denying the credentials of the man who had invented deep-space travel, and in addition to being a superb theoretician, he was an able administrator. Grace had little time to think of her narrow escape, for she had dived into an intense research program at Shaw's suggestion. She had always intended to study the Eeperan force field, which had hidden the cities along the Great Misty River behind a mist, and now she took the time, accepting as her challenge the construction of a field that not only would shield against electromagnetic radiation, but unlike the Eeperan mist, would itself be invisible. For in the semiweekly sessions of Rodrick's variable membership advisory group, a plan was slowly emerging, a plan that was more hope than possibility.

Paul Warden had been selected to head an antidrug task force to control the disturbing problem that had arisen in recent events. The job was not to his liking, but it had to be done. He started by administering drug tests to all personnel assigned to duty along the Great Misty River, and the result caused great concern. Over twenty people, mostly young service people, showed varying degrees of addiction to the Eeperan drug.

A shock wave of anger rolled through the colony.

The most seriously addicted were hospitalized, and of all of them, Celia Hadley was suffering the most. Mandy, having heard and seen Celia scream for relief and beg for the drug, asked that Theresita be called back to Hamilton City from the jungle research base to sit in on one of Duncan Rodrick's breakfast conferences.

"I asked Theresita to be here," Mandy said, "because she has experienced the effects of the drug and of withdrawal."

"Once, in the African desert, my unit was stranded when our helicopter was damaged by an enemy missile," Theresita said. "We had to walk for six days, with little water and no food except what we could find in the form of roots and, once, a small antelope. Those hardships were nothing when compared with what I experienced in that Whorsk village when I was withdrawing from the drug. I think we must be most compassionate."

Dr. Robert Allano, who wanted to treat the addicted with drugs that altered brain chemistry, said, "*You* had no choice in the matter. *These* people took the drugs voluntarily."

"They will suffer enough," Theresita said. "In the Soviet Union we used psychotreatment extensively, to render dissidents harmless, to rehabilitate criminals, and to make political enemies impotent. In all the cases that I witnessed, the result was harmful. If you want simple laborers, then use chemicals. If you want to salvage useful human beings, be patient, confine them in hospitals, and do what you can to make their suffering bearable."

"You also had enough self-esteem to want to recover," Allano pointed out. "I'm not sure about some of these. The woman, Celia Hadley, admits that she conducted herself like an Eeperan woman, in complete abandonment of all moral codes."

"That's something I'd like to discuss," Mandy interjected. "We're talking about treating the symptoms, not the reasons why. In my opinion we should be concerned with why this all happened, and not just the drug problem itself. I think Robert brought up an excellent point—the basic moral system of the Eepera. I'm not a historian, but from what I have read, it seems to me that morality, like water, tends to seek the lowest level. When two different cultures are interfaced, morals tend to level out at, or slightly above, the more permissive code of the two. In our earliest writings, the ancient Jewish prophets documented what happened to the children of Israel when they were exposed to the debauchery of other peoples. I think such examples can be found throughout history—when Europeans first encountered the free-sex societies in the South Seas, for example. And, somewhat spectacularly, when a segment of our population not far removed from slavery, the victims of generations of poverty and oppression, were suddenly yanked into the mainstream by social legislation, then drug use, alcoholism, crime, and illegitimacy rose to epidemic proportions. The family units that had been the basic building blocks of our nation were severely threatened. And now we're in contact with a hedonistic society that makes the advocates of the if-it-feels-good-do-it school in our past look like saints."

"What would you suggest, Mandy?" Hamilton asked.

"Eradicate the plant from which the drug is derived, first," Mandy said.

"That's a tall order," Amando said. "The plant from which the drug is distilled grows all over the Eeperan continent. It would grow very well here in Eden."

"I think we should make the punishment for using the drug so unpleasant that fear alone would keep our people away from it," Allano declared.

"If we learned one thing back home in our experiments with democracy," Hamilton said, "we learned that morality cannot be legislated."

"There's another aspect that we're all overlooking," Grace said. "The Eepera, admittedly slothful and hedonistic, have redeeming values aside from being a very physically attractive people. They're artistic, they create beautiful buildings—"

"With slave labor," Mandy interrupted.

"—and with the proper motivation, I think they could become worthwhile, productive allies," Grace finished.

"That's something for the future," Rodrick said. "At the moment we don't even have an exchange of dialogue with the majority of the Eepera population, the cities downstream from Suses."

"Maybe it would be a good thing if a few ships from that big, bad empire *did* appear off Omega," Oscar Kost suggested. "There's nothing like an outside threat to bring about swift unification."

"I had hoped," Hamilton said with disgust, "that we had left behind on Earth all those problems that have plagued us for thousands of years—that different cultures and different values bring war. And here we are, facing the same problems. What we need is a new approach, but for the life of me, I can't come up with one. God help us if we don't." He sighed. "I would agree with Theresita. We must not risk wasting our most valuable resource, people, even in small numbers. In a short time the *Spirit of America* will return to Earth, and we don't know what we're going to find there. If we find the worst, if the bombs have been used, every man, woman, and child here will take on immense value—not that they don't have that value now. To be brutally practical, and to take one specific example, Celia Hadley will be one of our most indispensable assets: a woman capable of bearing children."

There was something reassuring about listening to Hamilton. Everyone around the table could remember when, in times of crisis, his face, his manner, and his voice coming from the viewscreen had been the primary symbols of hope. None of them stopped to analyze their feelings. Only Oscar recognized the phenomenon, the eternal reaching out for reassurance in the form of parental leadership. Each person in the room was an outstanding individual, and still they looked for an answer to their problems from someone else, a leader.

After a pause, Hamilton spoke again. "As to Grace's suggestion that the Eepera have redeeming features, I stand mute, for lack of knowledge."

"With all respect to Theresita," Mandy said, "we've seen one result of contact with the Eepera that, it would seem, could not possibly have long-term advantages for us."

"You're speaking of my son," Theresita said grimly.

"Yes," Mandy answered. "I'm sorry. A close association with the Eepera would lead to more mixed children, and I'm not sure we could withstand that. Would we give all the mixed children over to the Eepera, thus strengthening their population while squandering what you, President Hamilton, describe as being indispensable, our breeding women?"

"I think we could go round and round about this forever," Paul Warden said, leaning forward, elbows on the table. "I, for one, will leave long-term decisions to those better able to make them than I. In the meantime I'd like agreement to search the area immediately around the city to see if someone has brought the drug-producing plant to this continent. If there are no objections, I'm going to widen my drug tests. There was a lot of going and coming from Suses before we discovered that some of the personnel stationed there were experimenting with the drug. I'll want to test everyone who spent time on the river."

"Yes to both," Rodrick said. "We simply cannot have that drug available in our general population."

"Then you can start, Paul, by giving me the drug test," Grace said.

The implication of that statement caused a startled silence.

"Or are we in this room to be considered an elite, above the rules?" Grace asked.

Oscar Kost laughed dryly. "I think, my friends,

that we've just seen an example of equality in action. Hell, yes, I'll take your test, Paul."

"Well," Hamilton said, "when I was in the Senate and the White House, there were many who would have liked to give me a truth serum, but I've never been asked to take a drug test before." He winked at Paul. "Lay on, Macduff."

"I would like to submit some topics for future deliberation," Rodrick said. "We've been busy, and we are few, but these are problems we're going to have to solve, and not necessarily in this order: the Whorsk problem. We don't allow overseers with whips in the fields anymore, but the Whorsk still act like slaves. What can we do about that?"

"The Whorsk are incapable of development," Mandy said. "They're happy doing just what they're doing. Those who work the Eeperan fields would starve if they were returned to Whorsk communities."

"Mandy, that statement has been made before about people in similar circumstances," Grace said gently.

"I'll stand by it," Mandy retorted heatedly.

"I said for future consideration, not current debate," Rodrick said. "Secondly, how do we live with the Eepera? Can we get their cooperation in eliminating the drug from the planet?"

"Since they are immune to its addictive qualities," Max said, speaking for the first time, "and since it's been a part of their lives since shortly after they landed here, that's going to be a good trick."

"Still, that would be the only permanent solution," Theresita said. "We've never in our history been faced with so appealing a drug. It enhances sexuality and intensifies sexual satisfaction. It's the ultimate aphrodisiac, and that's something people have been looking for since before the days of the alchemists."

"We'd better not ever consider the solution that we applied to alcohol and drug problems in the twentieth century, then," Oscar said. He grinned. "Although

I'll admit that legalizing the drug might have some appeal."

"Never," Mandy said fervently. "That's exactly what has happened with the Eepera. It's been proven time and time again that animals with stimulators inserted in the brain will push the pleasure button until they're exhausted. The Eepera have been pushing the pleasure button for thousands of years, and their thought and science have become totally static. The aphrodisiac effect of the drug is the greatest danger."

"Are you afraid, Mandy, that we'd all go on one endless sexual orgy?" Grace asked. Grace liked Mandy and worked well with her, but she had been aware for a long time of Mandy's almost irrational hatred for both Whorsk and Eepera, and she also knew that Mandy had no little bit of influence with Duncan Rodrick, who, under military law, was still in charge. Grace didn't want to see any hasty action taken against either Whorsk or Eepera.

Mandy, faced flushed, opened her mouth to reply, but then she caught Rodrick's eyes and flushed internally as well, for that glance reminded her of the nights in his quarters. Here she was preaching morality, and she could hardly wait until the cover of darkness to creep into the bed of a married man.

"I don't think there's any great danger of a drug epidemic among the people who make up this community," Grace said. "We all *are* an elite, handpicked. I can't imagine any of us neglecting our work or responsibilities for a kick in the pants from a drug."

But, although Grace had the last word at the breakfast conference, Mandy, in effect, topped her, and not by anything that she herself did.

Vic Wakefield was not the only man who had served on the Great Misty River who had used the drug or had the drug actively in his bloodstream. He and the others joined those already in the hospital, to undergo the torment of withdrawal, and his detention left a shamed, frightened, conscience-stricken teenaged girl to fight the battle alone. Two days after her last date with Vic, Tina Sells was writhing on her bed, helpless to do anything about it, unable to see Vic, cut off from his supply of drugs, and incapable of going to anyone for help. When her mother came into her room and saw that Tina was ill, the girl tried to convince her mother that it was nothing, but Tony Sells had his daughter in Mandy's office first thing the next morning.

Mandy immediately recognized the symptoms of withdrawal, but administered the drug test to be sure. Tina, weeping out of control, begged Mandy not to tell her parents.

"You're asking me to do something I can't do," Mandy said, angered and horrified that anyone would give the drug to a young girl. "You're going to have to be hospitalized."

It took Mandy over an hour to extract the whole story from Tina. When Tina did at last confess everything, Mandy administered one more test and found that Tina was in the first trimester of pregnancy.

After Tina was all cried out and admitted to the hospital, Mandy stormed into Rodrick's office.

"Tina Sells is only fifteen," she said, "and she's having withdrawal symptoms and she's pregnant. What are you going to do about that?"

Rodrick thought for a moment. "I don't know. What would you suggest?"

"One small nuclear bomb for every Eeperan city," she seethed. "Now."

"That would solve one problem and create others," Duncan said, knowing that she didn't actually mean it.

"We have no idea what effect the drug will have on an unborn child," she said, cooling off slightly.

"It didn't seem to have any effect on Theresita's baby."

"*He* was Eeperan. *They* do not become addicted."

"Abortion?" Rodrick suggested.

"I already suggested it. She says she loves that

Wakefield bastard and wants to marry him and bear his child." She whirled and paced. "Goddamn all men."

"Hey, take it easy," Rodrick said. "You're just upset."

"You're damned right I'm upset!" she shouted. "Tina's not the only one. One marine gave that junk to his wife. To his wife! Why the hell do men always think with their genitals?"

Rodrick was silent.

"You don't deny it because you know I'm right," she said.

Thinking to calm her, he said, "I'll admit that I do a lot of below-the-belt thinking when I'm around you."

"Yes," she said, her voice rising, "you went around broadcasting passion, pouring it all over me, washing me with it, taking advantage of an unfortunate attraction, call it chemistry or whatever. You never gave me a day's peace, with your lovesick eyes and your obvious yearnings."

Rodrick, his pride ruffled, responded before thinking. "Lady, you didn't exactly give me the ice-maiden treatment."

She glared at him for long moments, then slammed out of the office.

He did not expect her that evening. He understood how Tina's misfortune and Vic Wakefield's irresponsibility could upset her. He could not even deny that he had, as she'd accused, poured his need and his desire for her all over her. He wasn't feeling very fond of Duncan Rodrick when her knock came, the familiar quick taps, and he opened the door. She was still in her whites and smelled faintly of that scent common to all hospitals. She didn't speak, but pushed past him and disappeared into the bath. He heard the sound of the shower, and then she came out in one of his shirts. He was lying on the bed, having already completed his preparations for sleep, wearing pajama bottoms. She sat on the side of the bed.

"I said some pretty rough things today," she began, with a downturned mouth.

"No problem," he said.

"Want to just hold me for a while?"

"With pleasure," he said, reaching for her. She put her head on his shoulder, threw one warm, soft, feminine leg across his thighs. When she spoke, after a long time, her voice was soft.

"I realized today that I am a hypocrite," she said. "There I was, condemning the Eepera for enjoying screwing, and all the while I was looking forward to this time with you."

"Don't be too hard on yourself," Duncan soothed.

"I hadn't been with a man since Rocky was killed," she added.

"I know."

"He had his faults, but bed was not one of them."

He didn't know what to say, so he said nothing.

"How I *would* twitch every time I saw you, every time I thought of you. Mandy the sexpot. I dreamed of how good it would be to be in your arms, and damn you, it was even better."

"Hmmm," he murmured, and started to pull her atop him.

"No, wait," she said. "I want the truth: Why didn't this happen before Jackie went off into space?" She put her hand over his mouth before he could answer. "Because she's one helluva woman, Jackie is, and because you're happy with her, right?"

Rodrick was slow in answering.

"When did you have your first woman, or girl?" she asked.

"I'll have to think about that for a minute," he said with a laugh. "Why?"

"Well, maybe you don't even remember her, but can you remember how shivery, how intense, how all-consuming it was?"

"Very well," he said.

"And then, with your first wife? The same, at first, all shivery and intense and all-consuming. What happened?"

"Total incompatibility."

"Even in bed?"

"No, I guess not. Not in bed."

"And with Jackie? I know I'm being very personal, but I have reason. Was it shivery and all-consuming with Jackie?"

"Intense. Mature."

"Ah," she said. "And there we have it. Mature. Or, not as intense as it was when you knew your first girl. Nature gave us both one last shot at that all-consuming, youthful, intense passion. We took it. I'd lie if I said it wasn't great. It was. But now?"

"I think I understand what you're getting at," Rodrick said. "But it gets better, not lesser."

"I submit, sir," she said, lifting her head from his shoulder to look into his face, "that we mature adults, we two, Amanda Miller and Duncan Rodrick, forgot the difference between sex and love and went chasing after our vanished youth. Guilty or not guilty?"

"I don't know."

"Truth," she insisted.

"Mandy, if I'd met you first—"

"Truth. We all know that physical attraction can become love."

"Maybe."

"Think it's time we stopped acting like kids?" she asked.

Was that actually relief he felt? Where was the loss he did not feel, for she was obviously in the process of ending their relationship. "Yes," he said.

"All right." She kissed him. "Let's make this one last. Let's tease and do everything the fertile sexual imaginations of man and woman have ever fantasized. Let's make it last and last, all night, so that we'll both have dark circles under our eyes tomorrow from lack of sleep and maybe make people wonder."

"And then?"

"And then," she said, "I'm going to start giving a certain gentleman a rush unlike any rush he's ever experienced. I'm going to sweep him off his feet, stop taking the conception inhibitor, and have a child as quickly as possible."

"You seem very sure."

"I am, Dunc. I am. I took a good, close look at this man who has been interested in me—"

"Roebling?"

"Yes. He's unlike either you or Rocky. No offense, but he's sophisticated, undemanding, witty, gentle, and still he's a man. One of my problems has always been that I'm a romantic. I wanted glamour. I found it in a space jock, and you know as well as I that there were some disappointments there. And you—you were an ideal. I don't think I thought of you as a man, at first—just an ideal, manhood embodied, handsome, strong, confident. And this is probably the most important —unattainable."

She kissed him again. "I'm not sorry, Dunc. My God, it's been great. And I'm going to keep a great big, huge chunk of you locked up right next to my heart for the rest of my life, but I'm going to marry Derek, and I'm going to be happy and have half a dozen kids."

"You hit me right in the gut with one thing," he said. "That part about an ideal. To me you're Joan of Arc, Aphrodite, that first girl—her name was Dorothy, by the way—all rolled into one."

"Remember me?"

"With sweet and private pleasure."

"Just to be sure," she said, and began.

THIRTY-THREE

Stoner McRae had a problem. The *Free Enterprise* was only half-loaded with ore, and it looked as if he would have to settle for that. The weight of the ore was causing the ship to sink into the soft soil of Spreen. The rocket nozzles were within four feet of the ground, and he could not allow them to get any closer lest they overheat from the fiery exhaust when they were fired. He discussed the problem with the others. No one could offer a solution. The ideal thing would be to construct a solid launch pad, but that was not possible. There were no materials aboard ship for such a project, and to manufacture cement on the Spreen planet was beyond the immediate capacity of the small group there.

The concentration of rhenium in the molybdenum sulfide ore was relatively rich by Earth standards, being twenty-five parts per one million, and with the *Free Enterprise*'s cargo area full of the ore, there'd be enough refined rhenium to have made the trip very much worthwhile. Half a load would provide enough refined rhenium for several trips to Spreen, but Stoner didn't want to give up.

Jean Roebling, that frivolous female who had been the first to establish friendship with the Spreen through a mutual love of beauty, was instrumental in solving the problem. Jean was spending most of her time with Cee-Cee and a bevy of happy, laughing little teddy-bearlike dolls. She and Cee-Cee had devised a system whereby Jean's fashion designs were turned into completed products by the Spreen females, since their seamless method, using the material extruded from their fingertips, was faster and more lasting than a dress turned out on Jean's sewing machine.

Cee-Cee and other Spreen had become more willing to spend time in the open, often visiting the *Free Enterprise* or the open-air camp on the river. Cee-Cee and Dun-Dun were visiting when Stoner gloomily announced that he didn't dare load another ton of ore on the ship.

"That means you'll be leaving," Cee-Cee said sadly.

"I'm afraid so," Jean said, "but we'll be back."

Dun-Dun, who often visited the strip-mining site with Stoner, mused for a minute. "The optimum situation would be for you to fill completely the ship with this blue dirt that you need?"

"Yep," Stoner confirmed. "She'd hold as much again as we've got on her, but she'd be sitting with the rocket nozzles on the ground and would blow up when we tried to lift."

"The earth is soft," Dun-Dun said. "If you had a firm surface under the ship, then you could load more of the blue dirt and stay with us longer?"

"If we had a few thousand yards of cement and a way to work it," Stoner said.

"Tell me the weight of the ship," Dun-Dun said.

In a few minutes Stoner and Dun-Dun had withdrawn from the others, and Dun-Dun was using his writing implement to figure furiously. At first Stoner was not hopeful, but as Dun-Dun talked, in that young boy's tenor voice, Stoner began to be interested. He brought Dun-Dun aboard ship, where the little Spreen had his first look at a computer. He was astounded. When he saw the computer at work, checking the figures he had laboriously put down on his writing pad, he went silent, almost sullen.

"Is there a problem?" Stoner asked.

"My life's work has just been invalidated," Dun-Dun moaned, his face expressing a sadness that touched

Stoner. "Since I was a child, I have spent my spare time figuring perfect numbers."

"Ah," Stoner said, understanding immediately. A perfect number is an integer, the sum of whose divisors including one but not including itself is equal to itself, as in the example, $1 + 2 + 4 + 7 + 14 = 28$. The computer could effortlessly crank out endless series of perfect numbers, going into many digits. Stoner could understand Dun-Dun's chagrin to discover that all of his tedious figuring by longhand could be bested within seconds by a machine.

"Dun-Dun," Stoner said, "when we come back, would you like to have such a machine for yourself?" A small computer, with an atomic battery as a power source, would keep Dun-Dun busy for years, and also give him an excellent tool for his astronomical calculations.

The little Spreen brightened. "For such a machine I would trade my personal collection of jewels."

"That won't be necessary," Stoner assured him. "While you're here, I want to show you something else." He took Dun-Dun to the ship's bridge and demonstrated the ship's optics. Dun-Dun was more excited than ever.

"Your instruments are fine," Stoner said, "but we can provide you with a telescope of greater magnification and clarity."

"Then we will make a down payment for such wonders by building you a hard place on which your ship will rest," Dun-Dun decided.

Stoner was doubtful until the next day, when a small army of doers, singing merrily, marched to a site not far from the ship, bringing with them large, crystal containers of material like that used in the Spreen buildings and tunnels. It took only two days for them to build a pad. Since rocket fuel was no problem, the ship was lifted, drifted a bit to the side, and lowered with its huge legs seated firmly on the unyielding hardness. The roar of the mining machines continued, and the ore continued to be moved by crawler into the holds of the ship. The date of departure drew nearer.

Everyone was in love with the delightful little Spreen. With lift-off less than a week away, Jean organized a farewell party aboard the *Free Enterprise*. She had been saving a special treat for her friends. The ship's company was dressed in their best. Cee-Cee and other Spreen females wore Jean's creations and posed prettily as Leslie operated holograph cameras. The Spreen had brought a supply of the fungus that was their only item of diet. The meal was held in the captain's mess, and there was gay singing. Dun-Dun tasted a glass of Omegan wine and had to spit it out. When Jean brought out her treat, however—two gallons of Omegan honey, the entire ship's supply—the Spreen were childlike in their pleasure, each accepting seconds and thirds until the two gallons were consumed.

"I think it makes them drunk," Clay whispered to Cindy, grinning at the antics of the Spreen. They had lost all inhibitions, and Cee-Cee and another pretty little female climbed onto the table to do a dance as graceful and suggestive as anything the Earthpeople had ever seen. When the Spreen left the ship, escorted by Jean, Mopro, and the sergeant, they were still under the influence of the honey, singing happily all the way back to the plateau.

Now the ship was ready, heavy with ore. Dun-Dun, Cee-Cee, and a small group of Spreen came to bid them farewell. The occasion was formal. Dun-Dun made a speech, then Jackie made a speech. Jean, after the ceremonies, took Cee-Cee aside. Stoner and Dun-Dun followed as Jean and Cee-Cee walked away from the ship, along the river.

Although it had been somewhere between one hundred and two hundred years since a Bese ship had landed on Spreen, Stoner was concerned for the Spreen. "Dun-Dun," he said, "we can supply you with weapons for defense."

"We are not helpless," Dun-Dun said.

"I know, I know," Stoner said, laughing. "You took us quite easily, and that sleep-inducing gas of yours is handy, but would that be enough to face an enemy with weapons such as ours?"

By coincidence, Dun-Dun's answer came in the form of a demonstration. A large reptilian thing with six legs, a wicked-looking head, and a large mouth opened to show a set of long, venom-dripping fangs darted from under a low bush on the riverbank. It seemed intent on eating Stoner, or at least his foot. From Dun-Dun's extended fingers jetted liquid that, upon striking the reptile, vaporized. The animal jerked, shuddered, and collapsed. There was no doubt in Stoner's mind, but he asked, "This one is not asleep? . . ."

"No," Dun-Dun said calmly. "You see? We are not helpless. I believe you are thinking of the Bese, are you not? That they might come again? Perhaps they will. When they first came, long, long ago, we reluctantly killed many of them, but then they saw the fire diamonds, and they realized that to neutralize us, to destroy us, would end forever the supply of the stones that they prize as much as you. You don't have to worry about us, my friend. Not only can we defend ourselves, we are simply too valuable to be harmed."

"If, by any chance, a Bese ship comes before we return, would it be too much to implore you not to mention that we have been here?"

Dun-Dun mused. "It would be good for trade to let the Bese know that they have competition, and that you have offered more than honey." Then, after a pause, "But if you feel that such a disclosure would endanger you or your planet—"

"It could," Stoner said.

"Then we will, of course, honor your request," Dun-Dun promised. "I think I understand. When you conducted me on a tour of your ship, I saw no men living as machines, as on the Bese ship."

"We value each individual."

"That is admirable. When we first encountered the

Bese, we lost many watchers. It took several generations to rebuild the population. I think there is a difference between you humans and the Bese, and we have
come to value your friendship."

Meanwhile, Jean was asking Cee-Cee to accompany her for a visit to Omega. Cee-Cee seemed to like
the idea, but before giving her answer, she asked how
many days would pass before she could be returned.

"It could be months," Jean responded. "We'll have
to process the ore on Omega and extract the metal
needed to fuel the ship."

"I'm sorry, then," Cee-Cee said. "To be away from
my source of food for so long would be fatal to me."

"We could find a way to preserve your food," Jean
suggested.

"Perhaps in the future," Cee-Cee said.

In spite of their fondness for the Spreen, everyone
was ready to get back to Omega. Jackie burned with
her need to see Duncan. Leslie had found that, as she'd
expected, she missed Oscar's dry wit, his ability to
listen, and his calm presence. Shag was eager to see his
wife and son.

The ship was heavier than when she'd left Earth,
and her lift-off was slow and ponderous. Once the rockets had her moving, however, she accelerated upward
while the Spreen watched and cheered from their plateau. In space, weight no longer mattered. There was
more than enough rocket fuel for the landing on Omega.
"It will sure be nice to be home," Cindy said, deter-
mining the settings for the lightstep.

"She does look good," Clay agreed as the *Free
Enterprise* materialized within a two-day sublight cruise
to Omega orbit.

THIRTY-FOUR

It was depressing to many that the first law passed on Omega, having to do directly with conditions on the planet, was a repressive measure.

"It's a sad commentary on the human condition," Grace told Max.

"It's a matter of survival," Max growled.

The law stated simply that any person using, possessing, growing, gathering, distributing, or otherwise trafficking in the Eeperan drug would be subject to immediate psychotreatment. The treatment would remove any knowledge or memory of the drug from the person being treated. If the one receiving treatment was suffering from withdrawal at the time, the withdrawal symptoms would continue to run their normal course, but the subject would not know why he or she was suffering. Removing specific memory was impossible without damaging other memory areas, and the degree of brain damage was not totally predictable. Psychotreatment was a severe punishment.

Every member of the colony had been allowed to vote for or against adoption of the law. The results were overwhelmingly in favor of its implementation. Vic Wakefield voted for it, and Tina Sells would have, had she been allowed to participate. Both Vic and Tina were thin and pale but beginning to recover from their ordeal.

There had been a very heated family conference in the Sells house, with Vic present, when Vic and Tina were released from the hospital. The outcome of the conference saw Tina, in a simple, pastel dress, and Vic, in uniform, standing before Duncan Rodrick for a civil wedding ceremony. Tina's stomach bulge was not noticeable, but the Omegan community was somewhat like a small village; after all, there were fewer than two thousand people, including children. Everyone knew about her pregnancy, and that caused Tina's parents some chagrin.

The building machines were working, expanding Vic's house, when he carried his bride over the threshold and closed the door behind them, closing all the others out physically but not mentally. There had been none of the happiness and excitement that young girls anticipate when planning their own wedding. It had been quick, grim, and, Tina felt, a bit sordid. She was fully aware of the new life in her womb.

At least one of her worries had been eased: Extensive examination of the fetus showed a normal baby, healthy and forming perfectly.

There was to be no honeymoon. Tina explored the house, examined the well-planned kitchen, and began to prepare a meal. Vic sat in the kitchen with her. There was hardly any conversation, and no rush, as usual with newlyweds, to find a bed. In spite of everything, he still thought that she was the most beautiful thing he'd ever seen.

"Hey, you're a great cook," Vic said after sampling the meal.

"Thank you," she replied. "I like cooking. I did a lot of the cooking at home."

When he'd helped her clean up, he said, "What would you like to do now?"

"I don't know. Nothing. I'm tired, I guess."

They watched a holomovie. It was a period piece, quite romantic, and the female star was young, pretty, virginal, and very much in love. Vic pretended not to notice that Tina was weeping. It was as if both of them wanted to postpone going to bed, for they watched other things on the holoscreen until it was one o'clock in the morning. Vic had to report to duty early that day, so Tina changed to a nightgown in the dressing room and came to the bed with her head down. Vic was already under the sheet.

"Tina, you'll never know how sorry I am that it happened this way," he said. She was lying on her back, looking at the ceiling.

"If I wanted to blame you," she said, "I'd blame you for taking that stuff the first time. After that you couldn't help yourself."

"Still—"

"I would have married you without . . . things being the way they are," she went on. "It could have been so beautiful, with flower girls and all my friends there, and my mother weeping with happiness instead of shame."

"Hey, I know it's been rough," he said, rolling over to put his arm across her. "We're just going to have to tough it through. I'll work hard. I'll study and get my degree. We weren't the only ones who got messed up."

"That's no consolation," she said, her throat closing.

"We can make it a good life," he told her. "We'll have an early start on a family."

Tina smiled. That was the only bright spot in her life, the baby. "Yes, we have that," she said.

"When will I be able to feel it kick?"

"Soon," she said as his hand rubbed her stomach. She felt a stirring inside her. *Well,* she thought, *you learned your lessons well, didn't you? Here you are, hot to trot.*

She answered his kiss. When it happened, she responded, but opening her eyes, she saw him looking at her, a puzzled expression on his face. They would not find the courage to confide mutually that it was not great for weeks. By then they both would realize their punishment: that without the drug, sex seemed hardly worth the trouble.

The return of the *Free Enterprise* brought Tina out of a lethargy that seemed to grow deeper day by day.

She joined almost every member of the colony near the landing pads to watch the ship lowering, to thrill once more to the thunder of it, the awesome size of it.

She didn't get a chance to talk to Cindy for a couple of days, and when she did, Cindy was wide-eyed and happy, asking her question after question about how it felt to have a child developing inside her.

"We're going to have one some day," Cindy said. "Clay thinks it's a good idea to wait, because we're going to take the *Free Enterprise* back to Spreen as quickly as possible, and Clay still hopes that he can get us on the crew of the *Spirit of America* for the return. So I envy you, getting to start your family so soon."

Cindy had, of course, heard the full story from her mother, and she didn't bring up the subject of Tina's experience with the drug. It was Tina herself who did. "If anyone ever offers you any of that stuff, don't take it," she advised.

"It must be something," Cindy said, "the way everyone talks about it. Since you mentioned it, can I ask you a question?"

"Sure," Tina said.

"Does it really make everything, uh, you know, so much greater?"

Tina could not help smiling at the still-vivid memories of being with Vic with the drug coursing through her body. "You wouldn't believe it."

"If making love were any better with Clay than it already is," Cindy said, with a little giggle, "I don't think I'd *survive*."

Tina suddenly burst into tears. Cindy tried to comfort her, and finally Tina blurted out that after the drug, nothing was the same, that lovemaking was just work and a tiny little twitch.

"I can't believe that," Cindy said. "But even if it wasn't great, I'd still love it, just being close to Clay, just being one with him and holding him and going to sleep with his arms around me—"

"That's what I've been robbed of," Tina said, still

weeping. "Oh, those bastards. I think Mandy was right in wanting to nuke all of them."

"Tina, don't you love Vic?"

"Yes. Of course."

"Then just enjoy being with him. Enjoy getting to know him. It's great to have someone you know is your best friend and thinks you can do no wrong. Why don't you forget about sex for a while and just love him?"

"I'll try," Tina promised.

The ore had been unloaded from the *Free Enterprise*, and the processing of the ore was going swiftly, with a pleasing yield of rhenium. Meanwhile, Amando was gathering honey. Fortunately, there was a surplus, and much to be gathered.

Duncan Rodrick had moved his personal effects back into the house. His reunion with Jackie, who was the first to step down the ramp after landing, had been rather formal, with just a little hug and a whisper, voiced almost at the same time and in exactly the same words. "I am so glad to see *you*," they'd said, and then she laughed, and they pulled apart to be the formal captain and commander.

Webb Howard, fully recovered, had outdistanced his mother and had thrown himself into his father's arms with a whoop. Gage Fergus, single, didn't bother to leave the ship until he had her shut down. Leslie Young saw Oscar standing at a distance and waved; then, at the first opportunity, she went to him, put her arms around him, and said, "I need to have a long, private talk with you." Then she kissed him, to his surprise and pleasure, directly on his mouth.

"Don't do that again," he said.

"Why not?" she asked.

"Because it made my neck stop hurting, and I need that hurt to remind myself that I'm alive."

She kissed him again. His face altered, softened, and looked ten years younger. "Do you know what you're doing, young lady?"

"I think so," she assured him. "Let's talk about it over dinner."

Of all those who greeted the crew of the ship, not one was more excited or more demonstrative than Jumper. He leaped high, and Clay caught him in his arms and, laughing, took a severe face licking. Then it was Cindy's turn with Jumper, and after that Betsy had her turn with Cindy and Clay, after hugging Stoner fiercely.

The returning explorers found there was little time for celebration. The *Spirit of America* was loaded and waiting. Duncan Rodrick had been putting off her leaving on one pretext or the other while secretly hoping that Jackie would return before he was forced to depart. Oddly enough, his guilt over what had happened with Mandy was quickly submerged in the sheer goodness of having his wife in his arms again. It would have been nice to be able to tell her that he was cured, that never again would Mandy come between them, even in his thoughts, but he was too mature to ease his own conscience with a confession that he knew would be painful for the woman who had become such an important part of his life. No, what had happened would be his and Mandy's secret. They'd been lucky. Their meetings aboard the ship had apparently gone undiscovered. The reunion was made more poignant by the shared knowledge that it would be relatively brief, that Rodrick would soon be leaving for Earth.

The holopictures of the Bese ship on Spreen were shown on a channel available to everyone. Rodrick and members of his primary advisory group had seen the pictures at a private showing. Harry and Max huddled with Gage for hours; then Max came to Rodrick to say, "No question about it—we need to get that Bese ship now and bring it back here—before the *Spirit of America* goes back to Earth."

Only Amando objected to postponing the *Spirit's* departure. The seeds and the plants he'd already loaded aboard ship were in no danger, but he was eager to begin his work on Earth with food plants that promised to end famine forever, and drought-resistant ground cover that would help reclaim land lost to the Earth's deserts.

Rodrick, on the other hand, was relieved. He would be with Jackie a few weeks, until the refinery cranked out a supply of rhenium. Meanwhile, nothing was pressing. A group of the more liberal members of the colony were discussing offering the Whorsk who worked the fields along the Great Misty River an opportunity to be relocated to places of their own choosing, possibly to join the Whorsk communities along the coast. Rodrick had no objection to that. He and Jackie even went with the delegation, equipped with a translation machine, since Whorsk speech was not suited well to the human vocal chords. He stood by while a well-meaning woman spoke into the machine, and her speech, translated into the clicks and grunts of the Whorsk language, poured out in high amplification over a gathering of about a thousand of the sticklike Whorsk.

At first, when the would-be emancipator finished, there was silence, then a growing mutter of sound that rose to a crashing, moaning protest.

A Whorsk in brown robes made his way to stand in front of the human delegation. "Who are you," he demanded, "to tell us we must leave our homes?" The woman was astounded. "Here, in this valley, we came from the egg. Here we have the delicious, rich grain. Who are you to tell us that we must go into the wilderness to live with the savages of our race who must subsist on what they gather from the wilderness, who live in huts, who think only of roaming in their airships?"

"But they are free," the emancipator pointed out.

"We are not ungrateful," the Whorsk spokesman said, "for you have removed the overseers, those who interfered with our work, from the fields."

"But you work without pay, you slave to produce food for the Eepera."

"Our fields are so rich that there is enough," the Whorsk said.

When the Whorsk, with whistles and clicks, began to scatter back to their fields, the woman said, "It's horrible. They don't even realize they are slaves."

"Maybe Mandy is right," Jackie said. "Maybe they have reached the limits of their capabilities."

"We must educate them," the woman protested. "We must teach them democratic values."

When Oscar heard the result of the well-meant effort to change the lives of the Whorsk along the river, he chuckled. "Dexter once said he had hoped we'd leave all the evils behind. It's obvious that we didn't. It starts when some person decides he or she knows best how other people should live. Teach the Whorsk democratic values? Hell, our so-called democratic form of government never worked properly in the United States, and we damned sure never succeeded in getting it to work anywhere else on Earth."

Rodrick allowed himself the luxury of going with the *Free Enterprise* to Spreen, on the pretext that he needed a little flight time in space to hone his skills. He told Jackie that she was still in command, that he was, in effect, supercargo. There was a larger crew this time, including Max and Grace. Max had rigged a pair of huge lifting arms, and a dismantled crane was stowed in a cargo area. By the time the *Free Enterprise* had touched the pad constructed by the Spreen, it seemed that every watcher on the planet was congregated. Cee-Cee ran to Jean Roebling and hugged her. The trading began shortly after landing, honey exchanged for Spreen jewels.

Max and the crew rigged a carrying harness for the wrecked ship, lifted it with four scouts working together, and set it down, to the exclamations of Spreen and man alike, close to the ship's largest cargo hatch. Even by using the largest hatch, it took a week to cut the opening larger and then weld the cuts.

Stoner set up the new computer for Dun-Dun in the little Spreen's observatory, and then, working together, they mounted the telescope Stoner had brought. Though Dun-Dun quickly understood the computer's proper operation, Stoner knew that the Spreen would not have mastered all there was to know about it by the time the *Free Enterprise* had to leave. There was no instruction manual for Dun-Dun, since the Spreen had no written language, so Stoner decided to concentrate on teaching Dun-Dun the mathematical processes best suited to his interests.

At the same time, Stoner was digging again. He had reached the richest part of the deposit, so it took only one month to load all available space on the *Free Enterprise* with ore.

Harry and Max were already tearing into the bowels of the Bese ship when the *Free Enterprise* lifted off after another memorable farewell party, at which most of the Spreen got tipsy on the sweetest, richest honey they'd ever eaten.

"It's becoming almost routine, isn't it?" Jackie asked. The *Free Enterprise* was in orbit over Spreen, waiting for Cindy to give the go-ahead for lightstep. "We cover trillions of miles without even thinking of it. We've now made two successful cargo hauls—or we will have when we get back to Omega. Someday ships like this will be stepping all over the galaxy, and they'll be carrying all sorts of exotic cargo."

Rodrick didn't voice his thoughts. *Unless we run into the Bese.*

It had been a very pleasant trip. He had enjoyed watching Jackie handle the ship so coolly, so professionally. He felt as if he were on vacation, and when he was alone in the captain's quarters with Jackie, as if they were on a second honeymoon. It was a time of reduced tensions, spent with good friends. For the first time since Rodrick had been assigned captain of the *Spirit of America*, he didn't seem to be weighted down with responsibility. And then they landed on Omega, and nothing had changed. He was Rodrick, and he was in command, and others looked to him for leadership.

It was time to get cracking. The addition of Spreen diamonds to the *Spirit*'s cargo was a definite gain. It had been decided to take only a few of the stones, so as not to devalue them. There were people on Earth who would pay dearly for something so uniquely beautiful, and it would have taken the entire store of the Spreen to satisfy the demand if the jewels were sold at the price of quality diamonds. With only a dozen, all perfect, all living with inner fire, however, the price could be set at astronomical levels. The fire diamonds alone—not counting the food and plants aboard, plus jewels fashioned from the dragon scales of Baby and her family—would load the *Spirit of America* with the tools, equipment, and everything else currently needed on Omega.

In spite of a continual effort to get their names added to the *Spirit*'s crew list, Clay and Cindy were going to stay on Omega. There was one last-minute crew change: Mandy Miller's name, which had been added shortly after the first night that she encountered Duncan so unexpectedly in the ship's observatory, was removed. She had other plans, and Derek Roebling was well pleased when she said that she'd decided to stay. He had thought that she had taken a look at him, measured him, found him to be lacking, and tossed him back. When she stopped him on the street and asked him to have dinner with her at her home, he was pleased. He had been even more pleased when she had made it clear, through those looks and actions only a woman can fully express, that she wouldn't mind being kissed.

Max and Harry appeared one day in Rodrick's office aboard the ship. They were greasy and mussed but beaming.

"You two look as if you've been up to something," Rodrick said.

"Into something," Max corrected, for once not looking like a bear in agony. "Into the power plant on the Bese ship."

"Without blowing anything up! Good for you!" Rodrick said.

"What does this look like to you?" Harry asked, holding out a small brick of dull metallic sheen.

"Is it what I think it is?" Rodrick asked. "Rhenium?"

"You know how, throughout history, all the important discoveries seem to have been arrived at independently but simultaneously by scientists working in different countries, without contact with each other?" Harry asked.

Rodrick nodded. "It happened with the airplane, for one thing," he said. "But there was a body of work that preceded it, work that everyone had access to."

"But in physics, chemistry—all the sciences, in fact—it happens time and time again. As you say, new discoveries are based on previous work to which everyone had access. Well, I don't think that the people who built that ship had access to the work of twentieth-century Earth scientists, but they arrived at the same place we did."

"Don't tell me the ship is powered by the reaction of rhenium to bombardment with antimatter," Rodrick said.

"Yep," Max said, beaming. "The power to accelerate particles comes from one of their sun generators instead of a nuke plant, but the end result is the same. And they didn't have a shortage of rhenium either. The stuff's stored inside one of the mountings, to be fed down automatically as a brick is used up. There's enough to take a ship halfway around the galaxy."

"Have you finished investigating the ship's weapons?" Rodrick asked.

Harry nodded. "Sun guns and projectiles. Small but not smart. No missiles, because that takes on-board computers, and their computers were biological—the brains of those poor devils built into the ship itself."

Max grunted and actually smiled. "Hell, those monkeys aren't so tough."

"What about the planet destroyer that the Eepera speak of?"

"That concerned us a little," Shaw admitted. "Nothing like that on board, but this, apparently, was a trading ship. Lots of cargo space."

"And it was built at least two hundred years ago?" Rodrick asked.

"At least," Shaw replied. "But remember that the power plant is almost the same as the plant in the Suses pyramid. No refinements at all, and if we're right about the ship's age, that plant was built almost three thousand years later than the one in Suses.

Max had his agonized thinking look on again. "Of course, the modifications and improvements *we've* made may be incorporated into *their* new stuff. We haven't had time to carry the research to its limits, and they've had two hundred years or so to work on it. What we've done is pretty elementary."

Rodrick knew what Max was talking about. Since his return from Spreen, he had been watching closely as weapons were mounted not only on the *Spirit of America* but on the scout ships she'd take to Earth. These were needed to carry out his daring plan to bring peace to the Earth . . . if it wasn't too late.

"Can we say that we're now ready to go?" he asked.

"I'd like to have a few more weeks or months," Shaw said frankly, "but we're ready. We might spend a year trying to improve on what we've got and draw a blank, and we're not sure Earth has another year."

"That's it, then," Rodrick said. "I'll put out the word for everyone to say good-bye. Lift-off at 0700 day after tomorrow."

That gave him just two more nights with Jackie. Without being morbid about it, he resolved to make the most of them. If conditions on Earth were still as tense as ever—unless the politicians had found their senses, and he doubted that—what they had planned to do didn't just have risks, it was downright dangerous.

IV

THE RETURN

THIRTY-FIVE

No, it had not become routine. Lifting something as big and as heavy as the *Spirit of America* would never be just another day at the office. Millions of moving parts had to operate smoothly without a single malfunction. Hundreds of rockets had to be fired in exact sequence. Only a computer as sophisticated as the on-board machine could handle all the macrosecond decisions.

The good-byes had been said. The entire colony had turned out to watch the lift-off. Rodrick could see them with his naked eye, standing a mile away on a rise, with Hamilton City gleaming its multicolored beauty behind them. With the ship's optics on low magnification, he saw Jackie's face, tears wetting her cheeks. There was Mandy leaning on Derek Roebling's arm, and Clay Girard and Cindy, with Clay looking glum. Jumper was sprawled in the grass, his red tongue dripping.

He had a feeling that he'd lived the moment before, as indeed he had, back on Earth. There was only one difference: Instead of the slim, fair beauty of Jackie at the communications console, there was the larger, mature dark beauty of Theresita West. Ito and Emi Zuki were at their places. Old Max was down in the engine room, with Grace at his side, working the computer console.

"Engines to bridge," Max's voice said.

"Bridge."

"We're ready when you are."

Well, something else had changed. There was a certain lack of space service formality.

"I'm ready when you are," Rodrick said, winking at Ito Zuki.

Max snarled. "We're ready anytime—" He broke off.

"Max," Rodrick said, chuckling, "why don't we just dispense with this countdown stuff and push the little red button and light this thing's candles?"

"You got it," Max said, and immediately the ship groaned and a vibration began, followed by the muffled bellow of the mighty rocket engines. She swayed, seemed to sink for an instant, and then there was a slow, slow movement, and the Omegans on the hill were blanked from view by a powerful swirl of dust and smoke.

"That's it, baby, go," Theresita said in Russian, then looked around quickly. She had never experienced a starship lift-off from planetside, having boarded the *Karl Marx* in orbit. She saw that Emi and Ito were almost as tense as she. Rodrick alone looked relaxed.

"Two thousand feet," Ito reported, his voice carrying to all spaces in the huge ship but heard by only fifty men and women. "Three thousand. All systems optimal."

On the ground Clay shaded his eyes. Then he looked at Jackie. "You never get tired of that, do you?"

"Just routine," she said. "Just routine." But she was lying. She didn't take a deep breath until the *Spirit* was nothing more than a sun-highlighted dot. People were beginning to meander to the city. Cindy was walking with Tina Wakefield, who was carrying a large stomach.

"Jackie," Clay said, "I mean Commander Rodrick—"

"Jackie is fine," she said.

"You're the boss now, right?"

"Temporarily."

"Can I ask you a big favor?"

"I think you've earned that privilege," she said. He was a boy who would probably grow another inch as he filled out. And that boy was an Omegan warrior who had fought well, who had as much time in space as anyone living.

"Well, it's Jumper," Clay said.

Hearing his name, Jumper came scampering back and pranced, tail high, looking up at Clay and Jackie.

"He's lonely," Clay said.

"You wouldn't notice it," Jackie said with a smile. "*I* should have as many friends and admirers as that mutt."

"For his own kind," Clay elaborated.

"Ah." She smiled again. "He told you that?"

"Well, he's getting pretty old, for a dog, and I'd hate to think that he'd be the last of his kind. I mean, on Earth he'd have had a chance to reproduce, to add his genetic material to the gene bank of greater dogdom." His light way of putting it did not disguise the concern in his voice.

"I think it would be very difficult to find a dog exactly like Jumper in our embryo bank," Jackie said.

"Well, she wouldn't have to be just like him."

"Clay, you know that there's a standing policy to hold off on breeding animals not useful in the production of food."

"Yeah, but you're the boss now."

"Let me think about it," Jackie said. The way she said it—that vague, adult way of begging the issue—gave Clay the impression that there was not a chance. He told Jackie he'd see her later and fell back to join Cindy and Tina.

Immediately he had the feeling that he'd walked in on the middle of a private conversation. "Am I interrupting something?" he asked.

"Yes," Cindy said.

"I don't mind," Tina said. "You probably tell him everything anyhow."

Cindy winked at Clay. She had, of course, told him of her conversation about sex with Tina. "I plead guilty, Tina," she said.

"Yeah, she told me," Clay said. "I wouldn't mind

trying that junk if it didn't have lasting effects, like you said. It must have been something."

"I was just telling Cindy that things are better," Tina confided. "After a while you seem to forget how it was with everything intensified."

"Hey, that's great," Cindy said.

"If I had it to do over, I'd wait a couple of years to get married. Gee, I'm going to be all of sixteen when our baby decides to make its debut." She rested her hands on her protruding stomach. "Sometimes I'd still like to have my mother rub my head the way she used to and say, 'Baby, don't worry, it's going to be all right.' And here I'm just a couple of months away from having to rub some kid on the head and say, 'Hey, don't worry, it's going to be all right.'"

"But things are better, huh?" Cindy asked.

"Much."

"Can you still do it when—" Clay fell silent, looking at Tina's greatness.

"We'll have to stop pretty soon. Vic says he's storing up for hard times."

Clay felt himself blushing, and he looked away, then bent to pick up a stick to throw for Jumper.

"I just thought you'd like to know," Tina said. "Mrs. West—Theresita—has been a great help to me. She came and talked to me a lot. She said that sex was disappointing for her when she first married Jacob. But she says it wasn't long before she couldn't really remember how it was with the drug."

"I'm glad," Cindy said.

Clay was relieved when he saw Webb Howard running back to meet them. Jumper, seeing his buddy, ran forward, and Webb made a flying leap and rolled with Jumper on the grass before Jumper wriggled out of his arms and ran around him, barking and frisking.

"Hi, tiger," Clay said.

"Can I have Jumper for the rest of the day?" Webb asked.

"What do you say, Jumper?" Clay asked.

Jumper said, "Arf," and nipped at Webb's heels, trying to get him to play run and chase. "Just you have him home before dark," Clay said sternly.

"Sure thing!" Webb yelled, breaking into a run with Jumper at his heels.

"What did Jackie say?" Cindy asked.

"Nothing. She'll think about it. You know what that means."

"I don't know. Jackie's a good person."

"I think she's worried about what the captain would say when he gets back and finds puppies all over the place," Clay said.

"Did you promise her choice of the first litter?" Cindy asked.

"Heck, I forgot." He remedied that omission when he got home. He contacted Jackie in a crawler, going out to take a look at the rocket-fuel plant where production was going on twenty-four hours a day in order to replenish the *Free Enterprise*'s empty bunkers.

"I forgot to tell you," he mentioned, "that I'll give you pick of the litter."

"That's nice of you, Clay," she said. "I told you I'd think about it."

Communications put the last message from the *Spirit of America* on the alert channel, so that it broke into all programs and activated communicators that were turned off.

"Citizens of Omega," Rodrick's voice, quite formal, said, "three minutes from now we will go into lightstep. We will reach Earth orbit in two stages, stepping first to a point near the orbit of Jupiter, then to within a hundred miles of the Earth itself. We don't know what we'll find there, but we are hopeful, as I'm sure you are. Whatever we find the conditions to be on Earth, we will be back. In the meantime, carry on, and God bless you."

After a moment of carrier wave hiss, the communicator went silent.

*   *   *

"Captain," Ito Zuki said aboard the *Spirit of America*, "we are ready for lightstep."

"Activate, Mr. Zuki," Rodrick ordered, and then looked out the port at old Jupiter, the sun that had failed, so near that the planet's bulk filled all viewscreens.

"Radio check, Emi, please," Rodrick requested.

"We have activity on regular broadcast channels, Captain," Emi said. "Standard entertainment programs."

"Well," Rodrick said, "so they haven't pushed the buttons yet. Very good, Mr. Zuki, program lightstep and stand by. Theresita, all ship's channel, please."

When Theresita was ready, she nodded.

Rodrick said, "All personnel, captain's conference in the captain's mess in one-quarter hour. No exceptions. We are now in the solar system, at the orbit of Jupiter."

Ito and Emi were already putting the *Spirit*'s systems on automatic. She'd be able to take care of herself for a half hour while Rodrick explained to the fifty members of the ship's complement what lay ahead. He wasn't looking forward to it. He had been in favor of putting all the cards on the table before leaving Omega, but not until mere hours before lift-off had he known definitely that Grace Monroe had completed the project that would enable them to implement Dexter Hamilton's plan for the future of humankind, and Earth, with any hope of success.

THIRTY-SIX

In a small, cheerless room on the third story of a plain, stone building in the city of Suses, Lyndon West beat his pillow with all his strength. But he would not cry. They were not going to make him cry. At first he'd been pleased to be away from the dumb kids of the Earthpeople and from human adults who thought they knew so much. That was before he'd been told that he would have to learn two languages—Eeperan and Whorsk—before being allowed to participate in any activities.

Learning the languages hadn't been all that difficult. His Whorsk teacher seemed to be emotionless, reacting the same whether Lyndon did well or not, but the aging Eeperan who instructed him in his own language was entirely different. If Lyndon did not show proper attention, the teacher reminded him of his duties with a small, keen rod. He had been spanked by his mother many times, but there was a decided difference between Theresita's hand and the teacher's rod.

Still, it hadn't been too bad. But then, as he became fluent in Eeperan and could get along in Whorsk well enough to communicate with his keepers, he had encountered Eeperan children. He had been looking forward to it, and when he was first allowed to mix with a group of boys ranging from his own age to about eight, he said, "It is good to be with my own people."

It was at that moment that he got his first indication of what his life was to become.

A larger boy spat at his feet and said, "Don't equate yourself with me, you mongrel son of an alien whore."

Lyndon attacked immediately. Being smaller, he tried to equalize the fight quickly with a kick to the opponent's groin, but he missed, the older boy being surprisingly quick. Lyndon was pushed to the ground with his nose bloodied while all the others laughed and called him names.

He was ostracized from the beginning. After a few unsatisfactory attempts to speak to other Eeperan children, he gave up and then was limited to the company of slaves—the emotionless Whorsk slaves, giving him orders, telling him when to eat, when to bathe, when to study, when to go to bed. He was frequently pummeled by larger boys. For survival's sake he learned to avoid the recreation areas. On those rare occasions when he was alone, without the supervision of a Whorsk—such as when a Whorsk teacher ordered him to go to the library for a particular book—he darted from concealment to concealment, looking around corners fearfully lest one of the larger boys was lying in wait.

When he complained of his persecution to the old Eeperan who was his adviser, the adviser said, "Your mother was an Earthwoman, an inferior being. You cannot expect true Eeperan children to accept you as an equal."

"Then why am I here? I am Eeperan in my heart, and the son of a prince. But if I'd known that my own people would reject me, I would have stayed with the Earthpeople."

"You are here because Prince Yanee wanted you here," the adviser replied.

"I will return to Hamilton City and to my mother, then," Lyndon declared, standing as tall as a boy going on three years old can stand. "You will make the arrangements."

The reward for that arrogance was a rodding across the back of his legs, and as he danced out of the adviser's office, the rod making quick little slapping sounds on his legs, he experienced true hopelessness. He went to his room, defied the Whorsk attendant, ran into his bed alcove, and slammed the door. He threw himself onto the bed and, in frustration and misery, drove his small fists into his pillow.

Exhausted, he finally lay on his back and gazed at the undecorated, grim ceiling as he thought, *She said she would come to visit me. When she comes, I'll have her take me back with her.* Even living with stupid and inferior Earthpeople was preferable to this. He had no way of knowing, then, that his mother would be leaving Omega to return to the Earth. He waited and hoped. He inquired for his father. He was told by a new adviser—no adult Eepera wanted to spend too much time with the savage children of the race, so the mercifully short duty was a universal obligation, and each adult took his turn—that Prince Yanee had been forced to flee the city and was, most probably, in one of the cities downriver.

"I request, sir, that I be allowed to return to my mother, with the Earthpeople," he asked the new adviser, in a carefully controlled voice full of politeness.

The new adviser was a younger man. "I was briefed on your peculiar situation," he said, not unkindly. "You are not in an enviable position, being the son of an Earthwoman. I'm sure you know that if your father had been anyone less than Prince Yanee, you wouldn't be here at all. You are here, however, and you must bear it."

Encouraged by the new adviser's friendliness, Lyndon said, "In the history I am studying, I have learned that when our people were on Earth, many Eepera took Earthwomen to their beds."

"So many that the purity of the race was threatened," the adviser said. "So we left the alien planet, and for thousands of years our priests have preached against the sin committed by our ancestors on Earth. To dilute the Eeperan blood will never be allowed again, and yet Prince Yanee has done it, and you, I fear, must bear the consequences."

"What am I to do?" Lyndon pleaded, nearer tears than he had ever allowed himself to be. "The others hate me. They beat me when they catch me. Am I to hide in my room for the next nine years?"

"If there is enough of Prince Yanee's blood in you, there is another course of action," the adviser said. "If you are more Eeperan than Earthman, you will fight them."

What else was there to do? He went to the play areas and was immediately surrounded by a group of taunting boys. He selected one, got in one good lick, and then was swarmed over. Foolhardy courage was not a point of admiration for Eeperan boys, he decided while nursing his bruises in his room, nor, in the interest of his health, was it advisable. After days of brooding, on the other hand, he discovered that hatred was a very potent force. Hatred sharpened his brain. Hatred made his blood run fast and stimulated his thinking.

He made a list of the last group of boys who had beaten him, having to learn some of the names from his Whorsk keepers. Stealthily, in the dark of night, he scouted the school, located the bed alcoves of those on his list, then drew little maps and laid his plans. He would need a weapon, for he was quite small and his strength limited. He came to hate his weakness, to hate the small body, even though it grew daily, if fractionally. His hatred was a force that washed over his physical surroundings, so that even his Whorsk attendants came to notice something different about this small Eeperan boy, something that seemed to command a respect they did not feel for others.

For lack of power in his limbs, Lyndon turned to cunning, becoming a polite, considerate boy in the eyes of the Whorsk who taught him, guarded him, and tended him. One Whorsk female, whose name was a click and a hiss, Tlocksee, seemed to be especially sympathetic, if the cold-blooded Whorsk could be called that. She

was the most attentive, and spent time with Lyndon
when it was not required of her, answering his questions about Whorsk life—duty in the school was preferable, at least in Tlocksee's mind, to working in the
fields—and allowed Lyndon to watch, one night, when
she coupled with a male Whorsk in the slave quarters
next to Lyndon's room. Lyndon thought that bit of
Whorsk life was comical, but he didn't tell Tlocksee
that, for he was depending upon her to provide him
with information and a weapon.

Due to the inclination to violence in all Eeperan
children, relatively small, portable objects that could
inflict physical damage were hard to find. There were
stones in the decorative borders on the grounds, but
any attempt to carry one into quarters was thwarted.
Eating utensils were forbidden. A section of the head-
board on Lyndon's bed would have made a fine club,
but the bed was well constructed and he could not find
a way to separate the rounded posts from the frame;
and if he had been successful, it would have been
noticed immediately.

He had talked with Tlocksee about his problems,
had told her about how he was pounced upon by Eeperan
boys at every opportunity. She'd witnessed several attacks and had interceded on his behalf before he could
be hurt too badly.

"It is not worthy of them," Tlocksee said.

"I need a way to overcome my handicap of being
small," Lyndon told her.

"That will come, as you grow."

"I need it now," Lyndon said desperately. "What I
need, Tlocksee, is a club, not too large, about this far
around"—he made a circle with his hands—"and about
this long."

"Weapons are not allowed," she told him.

"Look, Tlocksee," he said, pushing his face into
hers to show her a purple bruise around his left eye. "If
you were beaten each time you encountered one of

your kind, would you be willing to endure it and wait until you grew?"

Tlocksee brought the club to him hidden under her garments. It was of resilient hardwood that had been smoothed and shaped at one end to fit Lyndon's small hands. "Keep it well hidden," she warned. "If it is discovered, I will disclaim all knowledge of it, call you a liar if you tell anyone I gave it to you, and afterward I will be among those who hate you."

"I will not be caught with it," he said coldly. He found a place for it under his sleeping pad and, to a casual glance, it seemed to be a part of the bed frame. For two nights he practiced with the club, whirling, striking, lunging, venting his hatred and frustration on empty air as the club whistled with the force of his blows.

For two more nights he postponed his vengeance, hoping that his mother or Prince Yanee would come and remove him from an intolerable situation. But no one came. The woman who had given him life had forgotten him. His hatred, never as intense for her as for others, began to encompass his mother. He was alone in the world, and his survival was in his own hands.

He began his revenge in the darkness. It was not difficult: Whorsk attendants slept soundly in their quarters, and bed alcove doors were not locked. He started with the largest and most virulent schoolmate who had beaten him, finding him sleeping peacefully. Lyndon sent him into a different kind of sleep when the club hissed through the air and cracked against his forehead. He left marks without breaking bones, but the boy required hospitalization. He found three others that first night, and the results were the same. An investigation was begun the next day, but there seemed to be no real concern among the school's part-time administrators. Violence was the rule, not the exception, so he was free to punish seven others the next night, working into the morning hours and getting back to his room with the light glowing in the east.

After the second night he secreted his weapon in a dense flowerbed, so when his room was searched he stood confidently at attention, and, of course, nothing was found.

There was no doubt in the minds of the other Eeperan boys as to who was responsible for the stealthy attacks under cover of darkness. Three of the older boys caught Lyndon in the open.

"The idiot adults won't punish you," he was told, "so it is up to us."

He managed to get in one good kick, landing his right foot solidly in the groin of the largest boy and sending him, writhing in pain, to the ground. But his small fists made little impression on the other two. Before Tlocksee could rescue him, he was bleeding and one of his eyes was slowly swelling shut. The boy who had been kicked in the genitals was on his knees, holding his stomach.

"Mongrel," the boy snarled, "I am not through with you."

"I think," Lyndon said, his nose streaming blood onto his uniform tunic, "that I will kill you. Then perhaps my message will be understood."

The boy did not reply. He was hurting. He had seen the welts and bruises left on others by the night-time beatings.

It took a long time for Lyndon to reach the last three who had beaten him. Everyone was alert now, and items of furniture were pushed in front of alcove doors at night. Twice more he was the victim of minor poundings. Meanwhile he had been studying the habits of the three older boys. When the Whorsk attendants were at their evening meal in quarters, he had his opportunity. He had pinpointed the library study time of one of them and now stepped out behind him in a dim hallway as the boy returned to his room and struck without warning from the rear. The boy went down and fell on his face, dazed. Lyndon used a foot to turn him onto his back. The boy looked up, and his eyes went wide.

"It is not you I will kill," Lyndon said. The club whistled, bone snapped once, twice, and the boy lay screaming with two broken arms as Lyndon faded away to walk boldly into the room of another of the three, who was twice Lyndon's size.

The boy saw Lyndon and grinned. "Well, this is convenient," he said as he advanced.

Lyndon had been holding the club behind him. He let the boy get close and then lashed out, low, to cut the boy's legs from under him. Again he left two broken limbs.

It was the third, the leader, the first one to call him the son of an Earth whore, whom he had saved for last. He caught the boy in the hallway outside his room and once again struck from the rear without warning. He intended to kill this time, but his blow at the base of the boy's neck was not quite powerful enough. Death was dealt by a blow to the throat, which smashed the larynx and left the boy fighting for breath, his body flapping like a dying fish.

Lyndon was already running. He hid the club in the flowerbed and went to his room. Tlocksee was coming out of Lyndon's alcove. "I was looking for you," she said. "It is time for your evening meal."

"Listen to me," Lyndon told her, and there was something in his eyes that compelled her to be silent. "I have been here since my last class, with you. You have been helping me with numbers. Do you understand?"

"What have you done?" the Whorsk asked.

"That is not your affair. Someone will come soon, and you will tell him exactly what I have said. Do you understand?"

Frightened, not as intelligent as her small charge, Tlocksee could do nothing but agree. The Eepera came. They searched the rooms. Tlocksee told them that

Lyndon had not left the room since he returned from his last class.

"You are not fooling me," said the man who was currently the adviser for Lyndon's section. "Two boys are hurt and one is dead."

"Sir," Lyndon said, "while I admit that I hold no fondness for those who are dead or hurt, I submit that it is highly unlikely that I, being so small, could do such damage."

As it happened, the adviser who had told Lyndon that he must defend himself was serving a tour as chief administrator for the facility. He heard the statements of the advisers, visited the two boys with broken arms, heard their direct accusations, and pondered.

"We will watch this small one for a while," he told the advisers. "We have no direct evidence that it was he, and indeed, it seems unlikely that one so small could have done this."

He was watching when Lyndon next entered the play area, his female Whorsk attendant a few paces behind. He walked directly toward a group of boys, and at first it seemed that the small boy would be attacked. The administrator, however, could not hear the exchange that took place on the grassy field.

"Get him," one of the boys said. "He killed Ran. Get him."

Two boys started to move toward Lyndon. Lyndon squared his small shoulders. "I grow weary of this," he said. "Be warned. I grow weary."

The two boys halted. There was a silence. Lyndon walked forward, passed within reach of several, then walked on, alone. From his window the chief administrator smiled with a raised eyebrow. This small one, he thought, has become formidable. He pulled Lyndon's file and saw that his work was exemplary, his marks among the highest ever recorded for his age. Yes, he thought, this one should be carefully observed.

There were no more beatings. "He is insane," it was said of him. "Don't bother him, for he is allowed to get away with killing," it was said. "He must have magic," a small boy said, "for he can appear in your room in the dark of night."

Still alone, Lyndon at least no longer had to face almost daily beatings. He could lose himself in his studies for long periods. He concentrated on history but did not neglect the rich literature of poetry. He had only Tlocksee as an audience for his thoughts. Some of them he did not voice even to her. Once again he had shown himself to be superior. Single-handedly he had cowed hundreds of larger boys. He would grow and mature, and he resolved that by the rigorous physical training available to him, he would be strong and fit. Then one day, when he was adult, he would terrify many, as he had done already; he would rule Suses, unite all Eepera, then take his revenge on those most responsible for his loneliness and misery at the school.

"Tlocksee," he said, on the night of his third birthday, "tell me why you perform that silly nightly ritual with the males."

"For pleasure," she said.

"Is this just a Whorsk thing?"

"Our way is different, but it is not merely a Whorsk thing."

"I would try it," he said. "Can it be done between Eepera and Whorsk?"

"I have heard of such," Tlocksee confessed, "but not often."

"Show me how," he said.

Tlocksee made the sound that was a Whorsk laugh. "You are much too small."

"Show me," he ordered, and she took him to his bed.

Tlocksee's orifice was large and wet, and for a while, as she laughed fondly, he was puzzled. But then, as he found a certain position, his eyes narrowed, he became quite intense, and with suddenness he knew pleasure.

Tlocksee's faceted eyes seemed to glow as she looked

at him. He patted her shell-like head. "Each night you will come to my bed," he said, "before going to your quarters. And when I leave here, I promise I will take you with me. Would you like that?"

"You speak of the far future, little one," she said.

"Of what do Whorsk women dream?" he asked.

"I am content."

"This life, this work are all you desire?"

"A house of my own, a mate, a sunny place to hang egg sacs."

"You will have that, and more," Lyndon vowed. "As large a house as you want, as many mates as you want. How many?"

Her eyes gleamed. "Two. No, four."

"Four, then," Lyndon said, motioning her to go.

She left, believing him but without understanding why. Her dreams stimulated by a three-year-old Eeperan boy, she envisioned the future.

In his bed alone Lyndon felt no shame. He had heard, from the distance of course, other boys speak of the unspeakable—of coupling with a Whorsk female. It was a matter of laughter, of forbidden shame, but he felt no remorse. It had been a pleasant experience, and he would repeat it. And one day, when he was strong and powerful, he would have his own mates, more than four perhaps—including, he thought, smiling, a few of the Earthwomen, carefully selected to survive.

THIRTY-SEVEN

For a man schooled at the Space Academy and indoctrinated with the need for cautious and extensive testing of any new system, Duncan Rodrick had come a long way. When the *Spirit of America* had left Earth, he had, against his better judgment, lifted off in a ship that had never been test-flown. Now he was returning to Earth, depending upon other untested systems.

The last conference was over. Everyone was at his or her post. The ship was ready to take a small lightstep to a precisely calculated Earth orbit. Each man and woman had been briefed. Those who had not been privy to the plan devised by Dexter Hamilton and made possible by the quick, improvising work of people like Shaw, Monroe, and Rosen, now knew why they'd been given the opportunity back on Omega to decline the offer of a berth on the *Spirit of America*. Using the Eeperan technology, refined by the Earthpeople, the team on the *Spirit* were about to give the governments on Earth the shock of all time.

"Systems check," Rodrick ordered, and from various points in the ship voices sang out their readiness.

"Well, Mr. President," Rodrick said, "here we go."

Hamilton was on the bridge with Jennie. He had tried to convince her to stay on Omega, but she'd told him she had been at his side too long not to be with him during his most dangerous moment.

"But Jennie," he had said, "if things go wrong, in

312

that last second I'd be able to think of you here on Omega, safe and alive."

"And I'd go through the next decades cursing the medical science that gave me long life," she had said. "No, I will not stay."

Another woman on board the *Spirit* had been asked to stay on Omega by the man she loved. Evangeline had had little contact with Paul since the time in the pyramid of Suses when he clearly let her know that he was more interested in his work than in being with her. Thus it was with misgiving, but finally with grim determination, that she had accepted Duncan Rodrick's invitation to perform an important mission on Earth. She was determined to show Paul Warden, who would be aboard, too, that she was not merely going to sit around translating dry, inane Eeperan priestly writings while waiting for him to find time to talk with her. Thus, she'd been surprised when Paul sought her out aboard the *Spirit* while last-day preparations for lift-off were being made.

"Vange," he'd said, "can I talk with you a minute?"

"How novel," she said.

He looked down at his feet. "Vange . . ."

She waited. Her heart went out to him. He was so like a small boy in so many ways. "What is it?"

"Vange, don't go."

"What?"

"I don't want you to go."

"Can't stand my presence, Paul? The *Spirit* is a big ship. We won't have to be under each other's feet."

His voice hardened, and there was steel in his eyes. "Now you know better than that," he said, no longer the bashful lad but the man she had come to love. "We're taking one hell of a gamble, and you know it. One missile getting through our defenses and—"

"I have the right to be here," she retorted. "I, too, can contribute."

"I know," he conceded. "I have no right to ask, but I'm asking. Vange, when I think of what could happen—

when I think of you—" He swallowed. "Vange, if something does happen, I'd feel a lot better knowing you were safe back on Omega."

"Isn't this concern rather sudden?" she asked, hating herself for continuing their unhappiness.

"No, and you know that too."

"Why am I supposed to be so wise?" she demanded. "Why am I expected to read your mind? For months now all you've done is nod in my direction when we pass each other."

"Vange," he said with pain in his voice, "I can't turn it on and off like some people. I know that if I . . ."

"What?"

"If I so much as kissed you, I wouldn't turn you loose," he said. "I'd say to hell with everything else, but—"

"There's work to be done," she finished for him. She moved toward him, and his eyes widened. He didn't put his arms around her at first, not until she'd pushed her mouth demandingly against his, whispering, "You sonofabitch."

Then he clasped her and held her and felt her mouth melt into his. "I look at Max and Grace," he said, lips brushing hers.

"So do I," she whispered, "and I wanted to hit you, or something, because we could have that."

"Not in small pieces," he said.

"What about me?" she demanded. "Don't I have a say? What if I want small pieces—a minute here, a minute there. Did you think of me at all?"

"All the time. I didn't want to put you through it either."

"Listen, dummy," she said, smiling fondly, "we have a few hours before this ship lifts. We're going to spend it together, and we'll have our communicators off. Your place or mine?"

"Wherever," he said, wondering if he'd ever understand women.

*   *   *

Within a few hours the ship had lifted off and the lightstep activated. As the *Spirit* settled toward Earth, Rodrick contacted Paul in weapons control.

"If it becomes necessary, give them all you've got," the captain ordered.

"No problem," Paul answered evenly.

"Grace, one final check," Rodrick said.

"Ready," Grace said.

"Well, Max, let's push the button."

In weapons control Paul had on his military-developed helmet, which was so sensitive to his thoughts that, while operating the conventional weapons manually, he could direct sun gun fire merely by looking at his target. His eyes were searching as his steady hands rested on the grips that would guide the *Spirit*'s conventional weapons. The automatic missile system was at the ready, the motion, metal, and heat detectors already functioning but finding nothing except empty space until the ship lightstepped and the monitors began to show the space stations and a soaring shuttle. Paul held his breath. The orbit had been planned to be near a Russian station bristling with missiles for surface attack and for defense in space. Paul had his visuals focused on that station. Seconds seemed to be hours. A minute passed.

"I think it's working," Grace said to Max, who was standing near the computer console from which Grace was monitoring a force field adapted from the Eeperans. The force field, which hid the settlements along the Great Misty River under a blanket of fog, now effectively concealed the *Spirit*.

"So far," Max confirmed.

Three scout ships, including *Apache One* and *Apache Two*, had also been equipped with force fields. The crews had been selected on the basis of the languages they spoke. Theresita, with Jacob as her pilot, was, of course, the delegate to Russia. Evangeline's study of Portuguese had made her an unlikely choice—she seemed too cerebral, too gentle for such risky business—to board *Apache Two* with the other American Apache, Renaldo Cruz. Their destination: the superpower of Brazil. Dexter Hamilton had wanted to be aboard the third scout, but he bowed to general opinion that he would be more valuable aboard the *Spirit of America*. Oscar drew the Washington assignment, and his pilot was Leslie.

Invisible to the bristling space defenses of the three major powers, the first scouts to be deployed from the *Spirit*'s pods, armed with computer-controlled sun guns, moved past the huge, nuclear-armed space stations, then maneuvered around the many laser satellites and detection satellites—all the complicated and costly defensive and offensive weapons that had been placed in space by the Soviet Union, the United States, and Brazil. To those who waited and watched aboard the *Spirit*, it seemed eerie. The *Spirit*'s scouts were visible to her own instruments, and it was almost beyond belief to think that the many sophisticated devices that cluttered space around old Earth could be so blind and deaf to the scouts as they positioned themselves in stationary orbits that gave them a field of fire covering all the possible trajectories of any strategic weapon fired either from the surface or from one of the space stations.

It was early morning on the east coasts of the United States and South America when the three specially equipped scouts left the *Spirit of America* and, made invisible by their fields, moved swiftly down toward the chosen landing areas. The markings identifying the scouts as American had been replaced by a pattern designed on Omega by Jean Roebling. On gleaming black hulls hundreds of fluorescent stars had been painted. Once the force fields had been turned off, there would be nothing to identify the ships except Jean's design, which was somewhat disguised by the effect of gleaming dots of light on black. The first impression would be that of looking at the night sky to see stars against blackness.

Moscow was in the time of the long days when *Apache One* drifted down, down, hovering over Red Square. "How does it feel to be home?" Jacob asked, reaching over to squeeze his wife's hand.

"I'm nervous," Theresita admitted. "I hope all these gadgets work."

"They're working," Jacob assured her. "We've just flown through the most intensely protected area on Earth without so much as putting a blip on a radar screen." He was checking below. Red Square was empty, the city slept. He set *Apache One* down in an area that was, by day, lined with people who came to walk past Lenin's preserved body in its glass case. "Ever occur to you that the Russians have their own miniature Museum of Life in there?" he asked, pointing toward the tomb.

"I hadn't thought of it in that way," Theresita said.

Apache One still hummed with power. She had one sun gun mounted. The generator that powered the force field required that her engines be kept going, but the sound did not escape the field.

"Ready?" Jacob asked.

"Ready," she said. "Just as soon as I have one very fierce kiss from my husband."

"No problem," Jacob said, granting her request with an intensity that told her he was not as calm as he seemed.

Theresita turned the radio to the frequency that had been used by the city's defense forces when she was at the right hand of Yuri Kolchak.

"This is Marshal Theresita Pulaski," she said. She repeated it three times, then listened. There was only silence. "They must have changed the frequency," she said.

"Give it another try."

"This is Marshal Theresita Pulaski, and I will speak with the commander of the Moscow Defense Committee," she requested.

"You are broadcasting on a restricted frequency," a deep male voice said.

"Aha," Theresita said to Jacob, then, into the radio, "You will put the defense committee commander on this frequency as soon as possible."

After a pause the male voice said, "State your position."

"My position is Red Square." She left the radio on monitor and raised one eyebrow at Jacob. "I'd say no more than three minutes."

It took two and a half minutes. Armored ground vehicles burst into the square, converging from three points, then slowing as they saw nothing. "Now," Jacob said, momentarily turning off part of the ship's field. This would render them visible, but no weapons could penetrate the remaining field to the ship. Two of the ground vehicles jerked to a halt, and their weapons turrets turned until laser cannon muzzles pointed at the now-visible *Apache One*. Other vehicles started an encircling movement.

"You, you who are listening," Theresita sent. "It is necessary for you to fire upon the black spaceship. You might as well do it now."

"Who are you?" asked a different voice, coming from the radio.

"I have told you. I am Marshal Theresita Pulaski. Listen closely: In fifteen seconds I will disable the tanks that are moving into the square from the west. The personnel inside will not be harmed. Is that understood?"

"Five, four, three . . ." Jacob counted, then sent the disrupter beam to play briefly over three deadly, low-slung tanks grinding toward them. The tanks jolted to an immediate halt. A turret opened, and a tank commander stuck her head out to gaze in awe at the star-sparkling black ship.

"Now you will fire lasers," Theresita sent.

Two Russian laser cannon flared, and the beams

splattered into glowing fire as they encountered the force field.

"Well, Harry, the field works," Jacob West said into the open communicator. Aboard the *Spirit of America*, Dexter Hamilton, among others, breathed a sigh of relief.

"I would prefer that you did not use explosive projectiles," Theresita sent to the Russian's defense network. "I would not like to see you damaged."

A tank fired armor-piercing rounds. The projectiles exploded upon impact with the field and sent shrapnel shrieking around Red Square.

"But you had to, didn't you?" Theresita said sadly, as Jacob used the disrupter beam to stop all engines and electric currents in the offending tank. "Now I will ask you to put me into radio contact with the Premier. First, however, I would like to know his name. When I left, it had not been decided who would succeed Premier Kolchak."

"Stand by," the radio said. In a moment another voice, old, quavering just a bit, said, "Can you offer some proof that you are Marshal Pulaski?"

"Mikhail Simonov?" Theresita asked. "Is it you?" She was both surprised and pleased. She would not have guessed that the aging marshal would have survived the power struggle that would have inevitably followed Yuri's death.

"I am Marshal Simonov, yes."

"On the night that Yuri Kolchak died, I spoke with you and others before leaving to board the *Karl Marx*. I told you to contact President Dexter Hamilton immediately and seek mutual assurance not to use nuclear weapons. Your answer ignored that statement, and your exact words were these: 'You sound as if you are not to be included in this selection.' "

"Comrade Pulaski! What of the *Karl Marx*?" the aging marshal asked.

"Later there will be time for me to explain that," Theresita said, "and how your movement toward war contributed to the destruction of the *Karl Marx*. Now I want you to listen. In something less than three hours there will be, in various parts of the world, a demonstration of power. But prior to that, there will be a broadcast from space on this frequency and others. During that broadcast demands will be set forth to the Soviet Union, the United States, Brazil, and to any other country that possesses strategic weapons. I emphasize to you that we do not want to kill a single human being. To protect this planet from its own destructive stupidity, we will kill if that is our only choice. I will be standing by on this frequency, but I will not speak to you further until after the events I have mentioned."

She turned the volume down as Simonov asked questions, demanding that she answer, and then went silent. Jacob reactivated the full force field, making *Apache One* invisible, and lifted her to a forest glade to the north.

Meanwhile, on a hot, sultry August day, the Mall in Washington, D.C., was crowded. Full force field activated, Leslie hovered over the Mall, looking for a place to land. Oscar, who still couldn't believe that this young and vibrant woman enjoyed the company of a man of his age, tore his attention from Leslie's intense face and looked into a viewer.

"I see they still feel as if they have to get as nearly nude as possible in the summertime and that the overall attractiveness of the American people has not improved," Oscar said wryly.

"It's going to be difficult to find an area not cluttered with people," Leslie said.

"I can fix that," Oscar said. "Get down to about fifty feet and let 'em see us. Give me a hailer."

Leslie lowered the scout and altered the field. The scout blinked into existence, and it was a few seconds before anyone noticed. Then a small boy saw the black, light-glimmering shape hanging directly over his head and yelled. In seconds others were looking up, pointing, and beginning to scatter, leaving the area directly under the ship cleared, save for debris, chewing-gum wrappers, newspapers, and abandoned picnic baskets. The scout's landing gear crushed a couple of baskets.

They had landed between the Washington Monument and the grassy area called the Ellipse. Oscar was having a little trouble. He had figured that the easiest way to get through to the current President was by telephone, but apparently the radio-telephone frequency had been changed since the *Free Enterprise* left Earth. A police car came whooping and wailing down Fourteenth Street and violated the Mall's lawn, coming to a stop a hundred feet away from the scout. Two policemen got out, stun guns in hand, and stood gaping at the ship.

Leslie helped Oscar with a frequency search, and Oscar finally got an operator. He was patched into the White House switchboard within a couple of minutes and was arguing with the switchboard operator as the two policemen, eyes wide, began walking cautiously around the ship, bumping into the force field now and then and leaping back. Other police cars were wailing toward the Mall from various points.

"Look, damn it," Oscar yelled, "just get someone to tell Richard Phillips that Oscar Kost is on the phone."

He slammed the communicator down. "No luck?" Leslie asked.

"The bastard hung up." Oscar fumed. He got the operator back, and this time it was a different voice from the White House. "Son," Oscar said, "I'm having a little trouble getting the President on the telephone. Now here's what I want you to do: Have Tom Watts—is he still chief of the White House secret service detail?—take a look out toward Constitution Avenue. In about a minute we'll stop all traffic there. If you can see down toward the Washington Monument, you'll see us. We're that black thing with the stars on it. Tell President Phillips that I'll be standing by on VHF channel four."

He winked at Leslie. "Well, we have to get their attention. Let's frustrate a few motorists."

Leslie aimed the disrupter at the traffic moving along Constitution Avenue. Within a minute the avenue was blocked by stalled vehicles, and the traffic jam was growing, with horns blowing and windows being rolled down to allow the drivers' angry voices to add to the din. Several police cars had turned off Fourteenth Street, and the scout's monitors warned of the approach of an armored attack helicopter, which moved silently over them and hovered. Other helicopters were coming. Two landed on the Mall, and an assault team with laser rifles began to pour out.

The radio came to life. "Tom Watts calling the person calling himself Oscar Kost."

"Tom, how in hell are you? Still having trouble with your bad arches?"

"You *sound* like Oscar Kost," the voice conceded. "Are you aboard the unauthorized vehicle on the Mall?"

"That's me," Oscar told him. "Tom, tell your people down here to be careful. If they fire at us, they might hurt some innocent folks. And will you kindly get Richard on the radio?"

"Your vehicle has been tentatively identified as a space scout of the type carried by the *Spirit of America*," Tom Watts said.

"Congratulations," Oscar commended. "Quick work. Now see if you can be as quick at putting the President on."

"This is Richard Phillips," a different voice said. "If you are Oscar Kost, this frequency is an open one. The world could be listening."

"Well, Mr. President," Oscar said, "that's all right, because the world is going to hear it all anyhow. By the way, congratulations. I wasn't sure you would win."

"Thank you," Phillips said wryly.

"Mr. President," Oscar said, looking at his watch, "in less than three hours there's going to be a broadcast on VHF channel four. Certain conditions are going to be set forth, after which there will be a demonstration to show that we mean business and can back up our word. I'd suggest that you hear the broadcast with your Cabinet and leaders of Congress, because you are all going to have to make some solid decisions quickly."

The President was still talking when Oscar turned off the radio and Leslie lifted the scout, still visible, and circled the White House. Two fighters flashed past. Helicopters kept pace with them. Then the scout disappeared.

In Brazilia Evangeline was discovering that her Brazilian Portuguese was rather good. She required less time than Oscar—after the *Apache Two*, protected behind her force-field screens, withstood both laser and explosive-projectile attack, during which several innocent bystanders were killed—to be put in touch with the country's ruler, Brazilian dictator Carlos da Lisboa. Renaldo had to use the disrupter beam widely as armored vehicles tried to reach *Apache Two*. To his regret, he used the disrupter beam on an attack aircraft that fired two missiles, which were quickly destroyed by the ship's sun gun. The fighter then came in strafing with explosive rounds, but *Apache Two* could withstand the explosions. When it appeared that the overly eager pilot was intent upon crashing head-on into the scout, Renaldo dropped him with the disrupter beam, cutting off all power so that the craft smashed into the square and burst into flames.

"We told you that we did not come to kill," Evangeline said angrily. "What we have done, you have forced us to do."

Da Lisboa was not accustomed to being defied. He screamed at his military adviser to do whatever was necessary to destroy the invading ship in his square. The adviser tried to calm him and finally succeeded in getting him to attend to Evangeline's promised demonstration and message.

"It is a trick by either the Russians or the Americans," da Lisboa snarled after he had listened to a recorded playback of the conversation with Evangeline. "The woman had a foreign accent. We must be prepared for any eventuality. Put all forces on alert. Have General Cardon sent to me."

Cardon, chief of the Brazilian Joint Chiefs of Staff, was in da Lisboa's office within minutes. "I want you to be prepared to institute Operation Victory upon my order," da Lisboa said.

Cardon, tall, thin, not quite sure that his sanity would last until it was time for him to retire honorably and live on his ranch in the Mato Grosso, tried to hide his panic. He had been ordered to direct the joint chiefs to plan Victory, but he had prayed that not even a man as mad with power as da Lisboa would dare order its execution.

"Sir," Cardon said, "surely we must wait to hear this broadcast and to see whatever demonstration of power these people have."

"Yes, we wait," da Lisboa said. "How long will it take to get all elements of Victory in position?"

"Per your orders, our underseas forces operate at all times with the capacity to take Victory positions within six hours."

"Then get them moving," da Lisboa commanded.

The time passed quickly in the three major capitals of the world. Intelligence and military personnel were frantically busy. Scientific advisers shook their heads, unable to explain how a craft could land, unseen, undetected, in Red Square, on the Mall, in the main square in Brasilia. The armed forces of the three most dangerously armed nations were on red alert, poised to strike or retaliate within an instant. In the Kremlin, Premier Mikhail Simonov rejected a fervent plea from younger men to strike, since the whole thing was obviously a trick of the Americans. In the White House, President Richard Phillips calmed his own hawks. "How do you suggest," he asked, "that we destroy a ship that can become invisible?"

VHF channel four had long been reserved, in most countries, for military use. With the advent of holopicture broadcast, the channels that had once been used by commercial and public television had become available for other uses. It was relatively simple to stop military use of the channel in all three countries at the appointed time.

So it was that Dexter Hamilton appeared once more on screens, flat, one-dimensional, but looking calm, rather handsome, and fatherly.

"I speak primarily to Premier Mikhail Simonov, President Carlos da Lisboa, and President Richard Phillips," he began. "However, I'm pleased to say hello to the rest of you who, for one reason or another, happen to be watching. I'm speaking to you from Earth orbit, aboard a great starship. Your instruments will not be able to detect this ship. Later, we will allow the ship to become visible, so that you may see it.

"Before I continue, let me say honestly that there is no reason for fear or panic. We are not an alien intruder here to take over the Earth. We do have our weapons to enforce the conditions I will set down, but we mean only goodwill, and we beg you, the leaders of the Earth, to listen, then cooperate with us, for we bring to Earth the means to end war, famine, and poverty. We bring the wealth and the freedom of all the galaxy to you.

"Should any one of you fire an offensive weapon with strategic capabilities either from planetside or from space, that weapon will be destroyed immediately. If we are forced to take such action, there may be damage to facilities other than to the weapon itself.

"I feel that some demonstration of our capacity is necessary. Within a few minutes our ship will become visible to your detection instruments. Since it's quite large and will be within the range of the American space station *President Healy* and the Russian space station *Yuri Kolchak*, it will be hard to miss. We will allow you to fire missiles at us. We suggest you not use nuclear missiles because when we destroy them the radiation might affect your own facilities. President da Lisboa, since we are not within easy range of your space stations, we will allow you to see a smaller craft, in stationary orbit directly over Brazil. The *Apache Two* will be within easy missile strike distance. We urge you to fire missiles."

After the *Spirit of America* altered her force field and became visible, it took the Russians only fifteen seconds to fire a twelve-missile volley. *Spirit*'s sun guns, under the operation of Paul Warden, took out all twelve missiles in under three seconds. The American space station, *President Healy*, did not fire. Carlos da Lisboa ordered his space station to fire two groups of missiles, aimed at the scout ship that had allowed itself to be detected. It took a few seconds longer for the single sun gun mounts on the scout to take out the missiles, but it was done with startlingly quick deadliness, making a deep impression on the Brazilians.

Dexter's face was back on the screens all over the world. The ships had become invisible to detection again. "I think that reasonable people are convinced that we cannot be shot out of the sky," Hamilton said. "Now we will show you one of our offensive weapons. Here are the target areas." His face was replaced on the screen by a map of Siberia. In red was outlined a one-square-mile area of frozen tundra. In Brazil the target was in the Amazon jungle; in the United States, a mesa that Hamilton himself had seen near the site where the two great spaceships had been built.

"We will give you four hours to be sure that no personnel are within the target areas," Hamilton said. "That will also give you plenty of time to have space monitors pointed to the proper spots. You may observe safely from the ground if you will stay at least a mile away from the target areas. Do not have aircraft flying directly over the areas." He smiled. "Good-bye, then."

Hamilton turned away from the cameras and toward

Rodrick, who was standing nearby. "I suspect we'll see some action in the next four hours," Hamilton said.

Rodrick nodded. Jennie moved forward to put her hand on Dexter's shoulder.

"We're ready," Rodrick said. "But I can't believe that they'll launch missiles. We've already shown them that we can destroy missiles."

"Duncan, never underestimate the stupidity of a politician," Hamilton advised wearily. "They're all in a stew down there. They're not used to four-hour ultimata. They like to call in all their advisers and talk things over for a few days. In the United States they like to leak information and get feedback through the media. They don't know what's going to happen. They're going to be afraid of losing their power, and based on my years of experience, I'll bet that at least one person is going to be crazy enough to say that it's a trick perpetrated by their enemies. I can't see Richard Phillips ordering an all-out first strike, and Theresita thinks that Mikhail Simonov is a solid-minded man."

"That leaves Carlos da Lisboa," Rodrick pointed out.

"The largely unknown factor," Hamilton agreed.

When it came, it came with a suddenness that caused the pulses of men and women in all the Omegan ships to pound, and it sent Paul Warden into an intense flurry of frenzied action. The scouts' sun guns jerked in two directions, toward both sides of the Atlantic Ocean, where submarine missiles, one after the other, popped up from the water to engage their rocket engines and begin a relatively short ballistic curve toward the major cities of both the United States and Russia. Carlos da Lisboa's Operation Victory had been launched.

The *Spirit of America*'s multiple, computer-operated sun guns aimed and moved faster than any human mind could direct. They took their toll of the medium-range submarine missiles even as they continued their upward climb toward the top of their trajectories. Hamilton's eyes were riveted to a screen that showed the separate launches begin to separate into hundreds as the surviving missiles reached apogee and the real warheads and decoys separated. He prayed that he had been right in placing his trust in the work of Harry and Max in implementing the plan, for if even one of those warheads got through, he himself, the man who had averted the near certainty of nuclear holocaust when Yuri Kolchak was alive, would be responsible for that which he had fought so desperately to avoid.

Sun guns flared from the ports of the huge starship. Scouts joined in the fire, and by ones and twos and then in groups of six or more the warheads flared and the decoys gave off lesser flares as they were destroyed. It was over in minutes. Not one blip was left on the screens.

But in war rooms in Russia and the United States, the orders had been given. Each nation had foreseen its own destruction in the strike from da Lisboa's Operation Victory and had alerted its ground and space forces to prepare for a massive retaliatory strike. Fortunately the orders to abort were given when the warheads were destroyed and before the defensive missiles and lasers could be sent out from the various space stations. But one Russian missile-base commander did not succeed in stopping the automatic processes. With a thunderous roar heard many miles away, a squadron of titanic intercontinental missiles, each carrying multiple warheads, lit the skies near the Ural Mountains.

President Richard Phillips was in the Hole, below the White House. "Who fired the sub missiles?" he was yelling. "Did we fire?"

"No, sir. We did not," said his chief military adviser. "Most of our subs have checked in. Some of them had reported enemy activity off the east coast. Brazilian subs. But none of our subs fired—I guarantee that."

"The Brazilians? Firing at us *and* the Soviets?" Phillips demanded.

"Looks that way. It would appear that they want us

and the Russians to let loose with everything we've got at each other."

"Get Mikhail Simonov on the hot line," Phillips ordered, furious.

"Oh, God, no," a man moaned in the background as the word came from Defense Command. "Mr. President, the Russians have fired an entire squadron of big ones, from the Karneski Missile Base near the Urals."

"We have no choice, Mr. President," said the chief military adviser. "You have only minutes to give the order. We must tell our space stations to fire."

"Hamilton's up there," Phillips said, his face going white. "He stopped the submarine missiles. He might be able to intercept these too."

"Mr. President, the Brazilians have launched from the Mato Grosso complexes."

"You *must* give the order, Mr. President. *Now*, sir, before it's too late!"

Near Moscow, in the underground complex that housed approximately the same equipment that was keeping Richard Phillips abreast of events, Mikhail Simonov was also being urged to order a full launch.

"What idiot fired from Karneski?" Simonov demanded.

"It doesn't matter. We must launch everything we have or be destroyed."

"Get Phillips on the hot line," Simonov ordered. "Now!"

Paul Warden, aboard the *Spirit of America*, whistled as his detectors counted off the numbers of missiles being launched from both Russia and Brazil. He nodded with satisfaction as the scouts in orbit over the Southern Hemisphere began to knock the Brazilian warbirds out of the sky. He concentrated on the Russian squadron and knocked them out before they cleared the atmosphere. There'd be some radioactive junk scattered over parts of Russia, but that was one helluva lot better than the alternative.

Carlos da Lisboa was purple with rage as he was

told that the Mato Grosso squadrons of ICBMs had been destroyed. "Launch all!" he screamed, and the order was given.

Renaldo Cruz and Evangeline had been keeping up with the action by radio. They were low, not in orbit, waiting for the time to come for them to use their sun gun to show its destructive power. Almost by accident, Renaldo noticed a seemingly innocent army base in Brazil alter form as the caps were blown from a hundred huge missile silos.

In Renaldo's opinion, things had gone far enough. For a hundred years the damned fools had been building thousands of atomic warheads, and with one hundred of the big Brazilian rockets in the air—with their hundreds of multiple warheads and thousands of decoys—one of them might get through. He acted on his own, without radioing for orders, for, down below, the rush of exhaust gases was billowing up from the silos. He positioned *Apache Two* and aimed the sun gun, its beam on wide play.

Evangeline, unprepared for the fiery explosion that covered such a wide area directly below, cried out in surprise. One missile cleared the fire, rolled slowly onto its side, and sank back.

"*Spirit,*" Renaldo sent, "I've been forced to give my demonstration a little prematurely. Tell da Lisboa that he should not try to launch any other missiles."

Meanwhile, connections had been made between the other two superpowers. "Premier Simonov," President Richard Phillips said, "please note that we have not launched any missiles."

"One squadron was launched before orders could be countermanded," Simonov replied. "This was after the submarine missiles were fired. There will be no others."

"Have you had the word that one of da Lisboa's missile fields was destroyed?" Phillips asked.

"Just before I picked up the telephone," Simonov replied.

"Mikhail," Phillips said, "I think it would be best if you and I did some talking with Dexter Hamilton."

"I have come to the same conclusion," Simonov said.

They had to wait a while to talk with Hamilton, but he did broadcast soon, before scheduled time for the sun gun demonstrations.

"Well, gentlemen," Dexter Hamilton said, his voice calm, his smile genuine, "we don't need to wait for the demonstration we promised you, since we were forced to stop the launch of approximately one hundred Brazilian ICBMs. I presume that you have had time to study pictures from your satellites. The weapon used against the Brazilian missile field will be used to destroy all offensive capacity in all three of your countries—methodically, mercilessly, and thoroughly if that becomes necessary. Now I know you're all in a stew and that things are happening suddenly, but we've got to move on to the next step. First, you will begin immediately to dismantle and destroy all nuclear warheads and all strategic missiles. Our ships will supervise your space stations, one by one and in an order we will give you, as they fire all nuclear-armed missiles toward the sun. On the ground, you will explode the missiles. I figure this will take a few days. In the meantime I want to see the three of you—Premier Simonov, President Phillips, and Carlos da Lisboa—aboard my ship. Scout ships will land to pick you up."

"Dexter," Jennie said, wiping a tear from her eye, "you sound like a warlord from a space opera."

Hamilton laughed. "Jen, I feel so damned good I can't stand it. Maybe I was getting carried away with power there, giving orders to the top dogs of the three most powerful countries in the world. But it's not my power, it's *our* power—Omegan power. And we're going to use it. We're going to bring peace to that tired old planet down there for the first time since it cooled down enough for life to form. *Pax Omega*. And through the power of arms. I'd rather have seen it done by good sense and diplomacy, but I guess we've never developed enough of that. So we've used whatever it took. And now we'll start building starships and get some of those folks down there out of misery and out to the stars."

THIRTY-EIGHT

Renaldo Cruz held the *Apache Two* at five thousand feet over Brazil's capital. Down below there was a spirited little war going on. The presidential palace was under siege from a surrounding ring of gun emplacements. The guns—laser and projectile—lit the night.

"*Apache Two*," came a call from the *Spirit*, "we are in contact with a General Cardon, who claims that he is now in command of victorious liberation forces."

"He's not in command of the palace," Renaldo sent back. "He may well be soon, though, because it looks as if there's been a breakthrough."

"Keep in touch," the *Spirit* sent.

Carlos da Lisboa had put on his battle fatigues. They were well used and bore the same insignia he had worn when he himself had led his coup d'état's final attack on the presidential palace. He had joined his elite palace guard, officered by men who had been with him in the jungles, back when he was a lowly colonel bent on taking the government of Brazil out of the hands of Leftists and bringing the country to its full potential.

"Mr. President," said one of his loyal officers, "the situation has deteriorated. The traitors are within the perimeters to the east."

"Then why do we waste time here?" da Lisboa screamed. "Gather your men, and let us meet the traitors and exterminate them."

The officers gave commands. Men looked to their weapons, squared their helmets, and glanced nervously at each other and then at the lancing, roaring firefight that was coming closer with each passing minute.

A Brazilian army tank burst into view, smashing through a decorative fence in the east gardens, spraying death from its laser cannon. "Get those men over here with the antitank missiles," da Lisboa yelled, waving frantically. A few yards away two young troopers with antitank missile tubes across their shoulders fell to the ground as an explosive round detonated not twenty yards away.

"Cowards!" shrieked da Lisboa. He ran to the men who were trying to dig themselves holes in the garden lawn and kicked one in the face, then bent quickly to seize the antitank missile.

The oncoming tank looked huge and evil. All around da Lisboa men were falling back as heavy infantry swarmed from behind the tank and began to devastate the vegetation of the garden with beams and shot. Da Lisboa stood with his eye squinted into the aiming device and was set to loose the killer missile when the man whom he had kicked in the face lunged forward, plunging his bayonet into the small of da Lisboa's back and severing the spinal column. The dictator started falling backward, as if pulled by the bayonet, as the antitank missile soared in a long arc to explode outside the walls. The trooper jerked his bayonet out of da Lisboa's back and screamed, "Da Lisboa is dead! Long live free Brazil!" Around him men began to lay down their weapons and raise their hands. The tank ceased firing its lasers.

It took a while for the word to spread, but gradually the guns fell silent. Fires smoldered here and there. Cardon made his way to a communications station and began to broadcast on the frequency on which da Lisboa had first been contacted. Renaldo answered. A half hour later the scout ship was landing to pick up General Cardon. Aboard the *Spirit of America* Renaldo told Rodrick, "I'm not sure he can speak for the country, but he apparently has the backing of the army."

Richard Phillips and Mikhail Simonov were already in the captain's mess, sitting across from Dexter, Oscar, and Max. All rose when Cardon was escorted into the room by Rodrick. Simonov looked questioningly at Dexter.

"It seems that Carlos da Lisboa is dead," Dexter said. "Brazil is now in the hands of the army, under this man, General Cardon."

"I don't like this," Simonov protested. "How can he speak for Brazil?"

"Well, Mr. Premier," the ex-President said, "he's all we've got."

"The dictator is dead," Cardon said. "My troops hold the palace and, more importantly, the bases of all armed services. I am Brazil."

Hamilton himself served coffee. He was relaxed, but he could feel the tension in his guests, especially in the Russian and Richard Phillips, who had been accompanied only by his secret service chief, Tom Watts. When Dexter Hamilton sat, he sipped his coffee for a few moments before speaking.

"I regret the violence, gentlemen. We didn't want it."

"In all bad there is some good," Cardon remarked. "Because of you we are rid of the dictator."

"Gentlemen, as you know," Hamilton said, "in the year 2040 three great starships went out from the Earth. You now are in one of them, the *Spirit of America*. I regret to inform you, Marshal Simonov, that the *Karl Marx* died in space, with only one known survivor, Marshal Theresita Pulaski. We know nothing, General Cardon, of the *Estrêla do Brasil*."

Simonov was sitting straight, his face cold. Once again his country had suffered shame at the hands of the Americans. He felt that, for the sake of Russian pride, Hamilton could at least have withheld the news about the *Karl Marx* from the Brazilian.

"In this ship," Hamilton said, "is enough weaponry to destroy the war-making capacity of any or all three of your countries."

"Is the United States not your country?" Richard Phillips asked.

"Yes and no," Hamilton said. "Of course, I love the United States and wish her well. It was the underlying strength of the United States and the genius of her scientists that put humans into space and sent them to the stars. But although I am still a citizen of the United States, I now live on Omega; that's the name of our new planet. We are not, Richard, a colony of the United States. We've declared independence. We have the means, the people, and the resources to go it alone, but that is not necessarily our preference. Oddly enough, I don't even hold an office, gentlemen. I'm just an Omegan, and a spokesman for a small but united people. And in the name of the Omegan people, I tell you now that we will not participate in your politics or your wars. We are of Earth, and we owe our country much, but we left all the petty rivalries behind."

"With such idealistic words, Lenin founded the USSR," Simonov declared.

"Aside from weapons, we have in the *Spirit of America* the means to feed all of Earth's people," Hamilton continued. "We have the means to make desert areas green again. We have treasures of great value. But most importantly, we have the greatest gift we can offer—the stars and the fruitful, empty, hospitable planets of the stars. Working together, we can relieve Earth's population and food problems."

"Dexter," Richard Phillips said, "how can you relieve Earth's population problem through migration to the stars, when we'd be hard-pressed to fuel more than five or six flights of this starship?"

"Well," Hamilton said, "that's one secret we won't

share with you. We have to hang onto a few trump cards. And it's going to take time. We need some time to find a couple of life-zone planets, because the one we're living on now has a few problems, including a couple of indigenous races with some peculiar ideas. We'll have to take first things first. We have a man on board who's aching to begin distributing some food plants that will grow on nothing much more than spit and love. He tells me that he can have crops ready for harvest in the arid areas within a few months. Marshal, the area in which he's most interested is in *your* sphere of influence. He's an African. He'll need Red Army protection and some labor. Can I tell him you'll supply that?"

"It seems to me," Simonov said, "that we put the cart before the horse. Why ask for my permission now?"

"Oh, I'm going to get around to clarifying some things for you," Hamilton said. "But remember, you have little choice. We're not out to rule the Earth. But we believe that unless the Earth changes, it's a hopeless place headed for destruction. Either you cooperate, or we destroy all offensive weapons systems, leave you with only your laser rifles and infantry, and go on back to Omega."

"Let's discuss what cooperation will be necessary," Phillips said.

"Fine, Richard. First, destruction of all nuclear weapons. Oh, I know that any half-assed country can build a bomb in a few months, but we've got to start somewhere. Next, the formation of international-co-operation organizations, to assure the success of our man's new agricultural revolution. Third, the coopera-tion of the three big powers in stamping out small wars. You all know where you have nukes and arms in your satellite nations. Clean them up. We won't worry about governmental reforms at the moment; we'll just concen-trate on cutting across national boundaries with agricul-ture. I think the governmental problems will take care

of themselves when we build some starships and start
sending people by the millions out to new worlds. I'm
hoping for some common sense from you gentlemen,
because Omegans are too few to keep a supervising
force here. We won't hold your hand or force you to
join us in the stars, but we'll blast you out of space if
you try to bring your wars out to us."

There was, of course, much more. Scout ships
went back and forth between the Earth and the *Spirit*
to shuttle various governmental figures, experts, and
military personnel from all nations. And a worldwide
broadcast was arranged on holo, in all languages. On
that broadcast the people of the world saw what its
leaders had already seen aboard the *Spirit of America*.
After a brief introduction by Dexter Hamilton, the pre-
sentation started with the pictures taken by Clay and
Gage Fergus aboard the Bese ship on Spreen.

There was reason behind opening the program in
that manner, for Dexter knew full well the unifying
value of displaying an outside threat to all. He explained carefully, with gruesome closeups of the bones
of dead Bese, the methods of making a living being a
part of a mechanical system. And the scenes of inde-
scribable torture from the Bese artworks made the tor-
tures of man, from the savage societies of old to the
Spanish Inquisition and the KGB's torture chambers,
look humane. The cameras lingered for a long time on
the beautiful, still, quite lifelike form of Sage Bryson as
she had been in the Museum of Life, and then panned
slowly over the other figures there.

"So this, then, is the enemy we may encounter,"
Hamilton narrated. "The Bese value life no more than a
child walking over an anthill values the life of the ants
he crushes. They are out there among the stars that are
the destiny of the human race, and I fear that it will
take the combined strength of all of us to assure that if
and when we meet this enemy, we will triumph."

The pictures of the mutilated dead, killed by Whorsk

during Rocky Miller's defection, were also shown, and the message of brutal enemies among the stars reinforced. Billions of people exclaimed at the beauty of the Eeperan cities and became hushed when Eeperan thinking was explained.

And the live cameras lingered over the glowing beauty of the Spreen fire diamonds and the fruitful garden of Amando Kwait, with seedlings and plants ready to start growing in ancient areas of famine.

The world stirred, looked up for the first time in a long time, and in every country of the globe men and women wondered how they could become a part of the drive to colonize the distant planets of the stars.

Even while the extended conferences continued with Dexter and Jennie going planetside for convenience, Amando Kwait and his pretty fiancée, Dena, began to ferry his precious cargo to Earth, using both Russian and American shuttles.

Dena, the Eurasian beauty who had come to love Amando, had not encountered the reluctance of a peasant population to change. Amando himself had forgotten how difficult it had been, even before the communist wars ravaged Africa, to teach new methods of agriculture to a population that had been practicing slash and burn, stick, and wooden-plow methods for thousands and thousands of years. Fortunately, his Omegan grains and fruits were so hardy that they could survive by themselves—if they were not eaten by goats or sheep. There was an overabundance of Red Army personnel to prevent that and, while the politicians were still talking, the Omegan plants were growing as if they were intended for the Earth, finding that the composition of even marginal soils was better suited than the best lands on Omega, where trace minerals had to come from using the waste of the underground beasts, the miners.

At the Utah construction site, three small, well-armed starships, built to a design worked out by Grace and Max, began to take shape quickly. Duncan Rodrick

picked crews for the ships from the space service, finding that some of the good officers with whom he'd
worked before leaving Earth were more than eager to
volunteer. He chose very carefully and wished for a
hundred like Clay Girard, whose loyalty would never
be in doubt.

In Angola the Red Army moved in to destroy that
nation's small stock of nuclear weapons. But Angola's
president, whose hatred for the South Africans was
greater than his desire to live, launched eleven medium-
range missiles with four warheads each. A scout from
the *Spirit of America* destroyed the last deployed warheads and decoys at a height of only fifty thousand feet
over the South African cities.

Machine tools and metal ingots began to be ferried
up to the *Spirit of America*. A few of the crew at a time
were given surface leave. Grace Monroe visited the
facilities of Transworld Robotics and spent some time
with Brand Roebling, telling him all about his son,
Derek—who, it seemed, would soon marry Dr. Mandy
Miller—and of his daughter, Jean, whose love of beauty
had served Omega well.

Jennie Hamilton was in charge of recruiting talented humans for the *Spirit*'s return trip. There was no
lack of applicants, but because of the ship's heavy cargo
of tools and materials, the number had to be severely
limited. She chose only married couples with children
under six years of age, and she was well pleased when
she had them all aboard. Harry, doing some spot interviews among the new passengers, was impressed by the
advances in thinking and technology that had taken
place in the relatively short time since he had left
Earth.

"We've got to keep in close touch with Earth's
scientific community," he advised. "We've done nothing but adapt some Eeperan technology, but here they're
coming up with a new and interesting theory about
twice a week. We can't become isolated."

It seemed to Jennie that the changes were taking
place too slowly. True, Amando's miracle plants would

soon make a great impact, if some local war didn't destroy his fields before he could introduce the plants into widespread areas. People were people, harboring the same ancient antagonisms. The nations of Eastern Europe, long under Soviet rule, were defying the Kremlin, setting up free and independent governments. Hamilton had to assure Premier Simonov and some doubting members of the Soviet government that any aggressive actions by the former satellites would be dealt with sternly. Hamilton visited Warsaw, Prague, Berlin, and Paris and told people drunk on new freedom, "War will not be allowed to be an instrument of policy ever again."

But in the privacy of his stateroom aboard the ship, he told Jennie, "They'll fight. It'll be Germans against Poles, or Poles and Czechs against the Russians. There'll be a renewal of tribal wars in Africa. The countries that had been annexed by Brazil will fight for their freedom."

"How can we prevent them from bringing their wars into space?" Jennie asked.

"We've got to keep our superior weapons secret from them for as long as possible," Hamilton said. "We've got to make Omega so strong that even when someone gets the red licked off his candy and sells the secret of the sun gun or the disrupter beams or the force fields to an Earth government, they won't dare attack us."

"The arms race all over again?" she asked grimly.

"I guess it's a lot like a motto I saw once in an old folks' home," Hamilton said. "It said, 'We'll kill anyone who advocates euthanasia for the aged, because we're prolife.' I guess we'll have to blast those who would bring war to the stars."

"When we have more planets opened, when the ships are bringing back huge cargoes of food and beautiful things like the jewels, maybe they'll see," Jennie said.

"Possibly. Let us hope so. We're entering a very exciting era, Jennie."

"Living with you has always been exciting," she said, laughing. "Sometimes too much so."

"Have you looked over past the space stations lately?" he asked. She nodded yes. "There are three of them under construction there, three ships built on the plan of the *Free Enterprise*. There's probably enough rhenium on Earth to power them, and it won't be too long before one of these bright young Earth boys discovers that we haven't told them all there is to know about the Shaw Drive, and then they'll have enough fuel to go anywhere they want. Meanwhile, South Africa is building a smaller ship. When it goes, it'll carry only white South Africans, and if I know them, they won't settle on any previously discovered planet. They'll establish a world of their own, and gradually they'll leave Africa to the black Africans. I think that as time goes on, we'll have planetary ghettos—a planet for Africans, a planet for Chinese, a planet for every race or national group that can muster the resources to build or charter a ship. We can't change human nature overnight. Maybe that's why the Lord made the Bese, to make us stick together just a little bit."

"It's going to be exciting," Jennie said.

"More than exciting," Hamilton agreed, looking at her with a light in his eyes that she could not fail to recognize. She'd seen that look many times, when he first decided to go into politics, when he decided to run for the Senate and then for the presidency, and when he started building the *Spirit of America*.

She knew then that it was going to be a long, long time before she was going to be able to settle down on Omega and watch her flowers grow. But she didn't mind. There'd be time for that, one day.

V

NEW BRAZIL

THIRTY-NINE

Judit Alvarez was awakened from sleep by the blood-chilling roar of an animal, followed by the agonized shriek of a woman. Bento, who had been sleeping beside her, was only a split second behind her as she leaped to her feet. He crouched and, still groggy from sleep, aimed his laser at the darkness. Now others were screaming. Judit drew her laser and ran toward the sounds.

The fires had been allowed to burn low, so that only beds of embers scattered along the bank of the river could be seen, and they cast no light. Only the rich and strange field of stars in the night sky tempered the darkness. People were still yelling when Judit was halted in her tracks by the approach of something quite large. It stood shoulder high to her and was moving leisurely toward her. Judit caught a rank odor, like rotting meat, and saw in the dim light the bare, dangling legs of its victim, a woman. She called a warning to Bento, who was coming behind her, and crouched into a firing stance, holding her laser pistol in both hands, unable to aim carefully due to the darkness. She hesitated, because of the woman, and that hesitation almost cost her her life.

With a muffled growl that was half-thunder and half-screech, the beast moved with blazing speed, and she fired, missing as she fell away from the swing of a massive paw. She felt the blow pass over her head, brushing her hair. And then the animal had accelerated and had disappeared into the night. Judit could see the woman's arms and legs dangling, flopping.

It took a long time to calm the panic. Fires were built up. No one had gotten a good look at the animal. A hysterical man was saying again and again, "We were sleeping, there, and it just appeared and seized her in its mouth."

Four hundred twenty-three people had survived the crash of the *Estrêla do Brasil*. Thirteen had died of injuries during the first two days. A small girl had drowned in the river. Others were ill, and the medical people feared that they were victims of some native infectious agent. There was good water, and apparently it was safe, unless the water contained the infectious agent that was making people burn with fever. Food was a problem, although the tropical trees along the river and on the hillsides provided clusters of small, delicious, hard-husked nuts and two varieties of ripe fruit.

Bento, the ranking surviving officer, had not pushed his authority. He had decided that there was food enough and water enough to allow the survivors to rest, to recover from their shock at being marooned on a planet many parsecs from Brazil.

Until the huge animal had raided the camp in darkness, the planet had seemed benign, even quite hospitable. There was no more sleep for anyone that night. The fires burned high and bright, and people huddled around them, eyes constantly searching the darkness.

At dawn Bento gathered the service personnel, fewer than thirty of them, including Judit. "I have made a mistake in allowing idleness for two days," he said. "We should have begun construction of shelters immediately. Today we will begin."

He told his troops to allow the people time to eat a breakfast of fruit and nuts and wash in the river, and then to assemble them. When they were all together he stood in the center of the crowd and said, "We know

now that we have natural enemies here. Our first task will be to construct a protective wall. As you see, there are rocks in plenty in the riverbed and along the seashore. Everyone who is able will work. We will build our wall here, in this glade, near the river. I want a construction engineer to be in charge. Are there any volunteers?"

A stoutly built man stepped forward. "Building a wall of uncut stone without mortar is not exactly a skilled undertaking, but I know the techniques."

"Your name?" Bento asked.

"I am Jesus Cunha. I am an architect and a builder."

"Good," Bento said. "Stand by, Jesus, and your labor force will be everyone who is left after I assign some specialists to other tasks. Six of our people have attended the military's school of survival in the Amazon jungles. Lieutenant Alvarez"—he pointed to Judit— "will be in charge of them. She will assign some to gather food from the known sources and to explore for other possible food sources. Others will begin to teach the weaker or injured among us the methods of making thatch for roofing. Now, I need someone who knows the skill of working metals."

Four men came forward. "Select a few others, not more than five or six, and set them to searching the crash site for any scraps of metal, anything that can be salvaged. We will need to rework the metal into tools. Can that be done?"

"I am José Luz," a dignified older man said. "I am a metallurgist. I had never thought to see myself in need of reverting to primitive methods of forging tools, but I know the methods. It is simply a matter of adapting ourselves to the old methods and experimenting until we have it right. It would perhaps be better and easier to start from nothing, find native iron ores, for it will be difficult to work the sophisticated alloys of the scraps of metal from the ship."

"Do what you can," Bento allowed. "First, we need axes and knives. Once we have cutting tools, we can begin the construction of permanent shelters for safety and privacy."

Luz quickly picked his contingent and led them away from the river toward the crash site. Bento detailed one of his service personnel, armed with a laser, to accompany them.

"We have very few laser weapons," he said. "These weapons will at all times be in the hands of those trained to use them, and all work parties will have at least one armed guard. We will lose no more people to the animals."

Judit assigned two of the men who had had survival training to a group that, for various reasons, was not strong enough to aid in building the wall. The fronds of one particular tree were palmlike and lent themselves well to being thatched together. It was not known at that time how long the leaves would last before decaying, but it gave the weaker survivors something to do, a purpose.

She and three men, with one laser among them—on Judit's belt—explored toward the north, climbing out of the valley to stand on a hill. They looked down on a scene of such beauty that Judit felt very optimistic. That feeling of well-being was brought under attack when one of the men spotted the tracks of a large animal. The paw marks were a full foot across and showed the deep imprints of seven claws.

"It came from below," the man said, pointing back toward the valley. "It could be the one that killed the woman and carried her off last night."

They had no difficulty following the tracks through the soft soil. Ahead of them was a low, rocky ridge topped by odd, sticklike trees with tiny leaves that clung to its branches without stems.

"We are not out here to hunt animals," Judit said.

"If this is the one who raided the camp, it would make people feel better if we killed it," Pedro Ramos said. He was a Brazilian army sergeant, just past twenty-five years old, small, wiry, with a broad, mestizo face.

"Give me the weapon, Lieutenant, and let me see if the beast is among the rocks."

"Perhaps it would be good for morale," Judit conceded. "But we'll go together."

"With respect, Lieutenant," Ramos said, "I have been Brazilian army champion in field competition with the laser pistol."

"Good credentials," Judit said, handing the sergeant the weapon.

It was odd country, Judit thought. The valley was tropical, rich and lush. The heights around it, both at the crash site and here, to the north, became open, with sparse, sticklike trees. Visibility was good, at least until Ramos led the group down among the boulders along the lower slope. Huge masses of stone towered over them. In one place the passage between two huge boulders with vertical sides was so narrow that they had to proceed in single file. All of them froze when they heard a rattling growl that seemed to come from all directions.

Ramos, weapon at the ready, circled around a boulder, halted, and listened as the growl came again. "There," he whispered, pointing toward a shadowy recess. "The rest of you stay back."

Ramos had taken only a few cautious steps toward the recess when something huge and fearsome erupted into the sunlight, a beast the size of a fighting bull, with long, yellowed teeth in a maw that seemed to be as large as a bathtub. The sergeant was startled by the loud roar of the beast, so the laser beam only lanced along the beast's side, burning fur. And then the animal was on Ramos, having moved with awesome speed. Judit screamed as the beast's terrible mouth seemed to make Ramos disappear, and blood spurted as the teeth penetrated. But as the mouth closed, the laser flashed at close range, burning into the beast's chest even as Ramos died, so that man and animal fell together.

The beast's death throes included the grinding of teeth. There was so much blood that Judit felt weak and had to swallow to keep from vomiting as she approached cautiously.

Ramos's body had been almost severed at the chest. The two men got sticks and managed to pry open the beast's mouth to pull Ramos out.

"There is no reason for the others to see him," Judit decided. "We will bury him here." She sighed, checked the charge on the laser weapon, and put it into her holster. "The soil is soft. I think we can scratch a shallow grave with sticks and our hands, and then cover it with stones."

She had her back to the shadowy recess. The men were pale, silent. They had faced death before, but always in honorable battle with weapons in their hands. This thing, this beast that had the power of a bull and the teeth of a monster from a nightmare, had shaken them—so much so, that when the second beast, slightly smaller but no less fearsome, burst silently from the shadowy cave, the man whose eyes had caught the movement could manage only a croak. It was the man's widened eyes that caused Judit to whirl, her hand going to her weapon. The animal was only yards away, its short, clawed feet moving silently and swiftly. She jerked the laser out and brought it up, and the beast was so close she could smell it, and then the laser beam flashed out and Judit danced aside as the dying animal staggered over the spot on which she had stood to pitch forward with a moaning growl. Judit wasted a charge, aiming the laser at the back of the beast's head to burn a neat hole through a thick skull into brain matter.

Her hands were shaking. She moved a few steps closer to the shadows and saw that the cave was shallow, not extending back into the ridge. There was the smell of carrion. She held the laser at the ready, moved into the shadows, and let her eyes adjust. Near the rock wall she saw scattered bones, bloody, with flesh still hanging in places. The skull had been crushed and broken, the inside of it licked clean. She turned away and vented her fright and her anger with one extended phrase of well-chosen Brazilian army profanity.

The job of gathering the woman's shattered, marrow-sucked bones was gruesome. They buried her bones with Ramos's body and, silent, alert, fearful that they would encounter other animals, climbed the ridge to see, to the north, a wide plain scattered here and there with animals, apparently grass eaters. Far away there was a range of mountains, low and blue on the horizon.

"If the flesh of the animals of this planet is edible," Judit said, "this is where we will come to hunt."

She led the party back to the river. Before the end of the day Bento and others had walked to the ridge to examine the bodies of the two animals.

"Let us hope that there are not many of these things," Bento said.

There had not been much progress on building the wall that first day, so the survivors enjoyed no added protection. Bento set a schedule for guards, and detailed civilians to stand watch over the fires and keep them going. During the night they heard the nearby growling of one of the bull-sized animals, but the fires kept it away.

"So," Judit said, "we have suddenly reverted to the conditions of our early ancestors. When the last laser charges are fired, we will face an animal as large as a saber-toothed tiger without weapons. We will have only fire. At the moment, since we still have cigarette lighters, we have no problem starting fires. But eventually the lighters will be empty too. It will rain here and the rains will put out our fires."

"We have metal," Bento reminded her. "Detail a few to look for flint. That will be better than using the dry-stick-and-friction method." He laughed. "I never did get that to work for me."

"It took me hours even to make the turning stick smoke during my survival training," Judit confessed. "But we were working in conditions of dampness and high humidity. I think the best thing to do is appoint a group whose main duty will be to keep a fire going under all conditions. We can build a platform of stone and shelter it so that we can keep embers going even in the hardest rains."

Jesus Cunha had his work forces carrying stones. The wall began to rise. José Luz had begun construction of a crude stone furnace. For decades Luz had done his work in an air-conditioned office at a desk, dealing in mathematical processes rather than in hands-on work with metals. He was almost sixty years old, still a relatively young man, and he looked upon his task of providing tools as a challenge. He was perhaps the only happy man on the planet. Losing his wife shortly before the *Estrêla* had left Earth led him to apply for a berth on the ship. He had done much of the groundwork in metallurgy for the Brazilian space program and had been recognized as the man who knew more about metals than anyone in Brazil. He found it interesting to re-create the achievements of ancient man, processes that had been spread over centuries, with knowledge being built fact by fact.

"Major," he told Bento, "we would need electric furnaces to create the heat necessary to melt and re-work the metals from the ship. The best I can do is to take shards of metal, sharpen the edges, and mount them on handles. What we need is a surface deposit of red paint rock, from which we can extract iron ore. I can make tools of steel then."

Bento assigned Judit to escort Luz in his search for the red paint rock that was rich in iron. Luck was with them: A surface outcropping was discovered along the ridge not two miles from where the two large animals had been killed. While others worked at the rock, chipping away with crude tools made from scraps of ship's metal, Luz finished his furnace and began to prepare charcoal. By the time a sizable pile of ore had been accumulated, he was ready. He had improvised a bellows from laboriously shaped wood and pieces of a leather jacket appropriated from a survivor and had a large audience when he first began to heat ore.

"So, my friends," he said dramatically as his helpers fanned the fire with his improvised bellows, "we revert to the science of four thousand years ago. Let us hope that we can make weapons and tools more durable than those used by the Celts when they invaded Italy in the third century after Christ. Their blades were so soft that they had to be straightened after each blow."

Bento and Judit exchanged a smile. Luz was enjoying himself.

"Why the Celts were so backward, I do not know," Luz continued. "Certainly others, long before them, made good steel. The Hittite king, Hattusilis the Third, had good steel—so good that a single dagger was deemed a fit gift for a king. And Homer's Greeks knew how to harden steel by plunging it into cold water."

In the bed of charcoal the iron ore was beginning to glow. Soon it became an incandescent sponge of metal and impurities.

"Fortunately, we have a bit of a head start on the men who first discovered that by building a fire in front of an exposed ledge of paint rock they could cause iron to form," Luz said. "We know the techniques. We have all the accumulated knowledge of thousands of years. And still we will have to work the iron as those first men did, except that we won't first have to make an anvil."

His anvil was a piece of the ship's hull, an alloy harder than steel. It had been mounted on a flat rock, then tied in place.

"We will have to make a hammer," Luz said, "and that will take time."

He had searched long and hard for just the proper-sized stone—a hard, smooth stone shaped by friction with other stones in the riverbed. With pieces of jagged metal, he had cut a handle of wood and mounted the stone with leather thongs. In the days ahead, José Luz taught the others a valuable lesson about attitude. As he laboriously heated iron ore and pounded out slag with the stone hammer, he would not even frown when the thongs broke, or the handle broke, or the stone fractured. He was ever patient. He was at his work bright and early. And in a few days he had a hammer, and then he began to shape an ax, pounding hard, resting when the thongs binding the piece of metal used as an anvil broke or were burned in two by the hot metal. He took time to forge four iron pins, turned at right angles on one end, and then with his first ax men cut down a large tree, flattened the stump, and Luz mounted his anvil with the iron pins driven into the green wood of the stump. When there were knives and axes, the work began on building permanent shelters inside the growing stone wall.

With knives available it was possible to shape spear shafts. Luz forged spearheads, and young men stalked an antelopelike animal on the northern plains, killed a young calf, and everyone gathered around a fire on which meat roasted on a spit, smelling utterly delicious. The biological experts and medical people had examined the flesh of the animal, saying that it seemed to be much like the red meat of earth animals, but there was some suspense when a volunteer ate a small piece of the meat that had been cooked quickly over glowing coals. When, hours later, the volunteer had not sickened, and the small carcass of the little animal was spitting and spilling its own juices down into the fire, the meat was distributed and eaten with great enjoyment. Next morning no one was sick or dead. The hunters went out again.

A deposit of clay was found along the riverbank, and soon crude, hand-molded vessels to hold water and food were being baked in the open fires. A kiln was under construction. Animal hides were being cured in the sun. Luz had his furnace going every day, and he had taught others how to work the ore. He was feeling great, the work having revitalized long-idle muscles. Log huts were being raised, and people were busy thatching roofs. Luz fashioned a few crude fishhooks, and children were set to fishing in the river, experimenting with a variety of insects as bait. The first fish caught was an odd, bullet-headed thing with rudimentary legs behind its fins, but the flesh was sweet and delicious when it was seasoned with salt taken from the evaporation pans that had been built along the shore.

When the rains came, there were huts for all. The wall was now eight feet high, and people who had never worked with their backs and hands were proud of calluses and feeling fit, their clothing too large on many who had lost soft, civilized fat and replaced it with muscle. An edible, oatlike grain had been found growing naturally in the plains. It made a tasty bread when cooked with a bit of animal fat and seabird eggs.

One could have set his watch by the rains. They came every afternoon about two hours after the sun had reached the zenith. It became routine to retire to the huts and remain there until the showers had passed and the sun began to dry the dripping foliage. On such an afternoon Judit lay beside Bento and looked at his face, eyes half-closed, a little smile on her face.

"You find something odd in my face today?" he asked.

"I was just wondering if our child will look like you," she said.

He sat up quickly, his mouth open.

"Well," she said, "what did you expect? I didn't have time to bring my medication from the ship, you know."

He smiled broadly, then sobered.

"You are not pleased?" she asked.

"I am," he said earnestly. "To think of a child, with you, is a happy thought. But to think of him—"

"Or her," she said.

"—having to live like a savage . . ."

Judit toyed with Bento's beard, which was sparse and scraggly. "Someday another ship will come," she said.

"Will it? When? When the survivors of nuclear war on Earth have rebuilt the factories, all the things that are necessary to make even one razor blade? Not even to consider the millions of components that went into a ship like the *Estrêla*. We are as near to going back into space as the survivors of a nuclear war would be."

"We don't know that they used the bombs," she said.

"True." He kissed her. "We can hope. But we will not live on hope. We will have to continue, assuming that we ourselves must take all the millions of small steps necessary before we lose the knowledge to make a razor blade, make a gun using gunpowder, and make a toothbrush. We won't see those things in our lifetime, and perhaps our child won't, but we must lay the foundation."

"Speaking of children," Judit said, "one of the teachers has organized them. They are making clay tablets, and they are asking each person to record the most basic elements of his speciality on the unbaked clay. Then they bake the tablets and store them."

"Yes," Bento said. "How do you make a sheet of paper and then something to write with?"

"We'll do that, Bento," she assured him. "We'll do all that is necessary. And if we never get to read a book by electric light, then our children or our grandchildren will." She threw herself atop him. "But I think a ship will come eventually."

"To find what?" he asked. "A bunch of savages in animal skins, carrying spears and bows and arrows?"

FORTY

Duncan Rodrick lifted his glass and saw that it held only ice. He was too content to get up and mix another drink of good Omegan gin, and tonic water brought back from Earth. He sucked on an ice cube and watched with no little appreciation as Jackie made a turn at the end of the swimming pool and stroked strongly. The sun was warm in the Omegan autumn. The water in the pool was sparkling, blue with the reflection of light off the painted bottom. A nagging moment of guilt came as he thought about all the things that needed to be done, all the problems still unsolved, but he said to hell with them. The *Spirit of America* had landed in Eden only yesterday, and he wasn't tired of looking at his wife, especially when she completed the workout and heaved herself out of the pool and ran, dripping, to sit in the chaise longue beside him; so beautiful in her brief swimsuit, her skin so uniform and smooth, that his teeth ached with appreciation.

He had come home. He didn't have any desire to leave home again, not in the near future. Jackie had met him as he came down a ramp from the ship and had saluted, but with a sparkle in her green eyes that held until they were finally alone, and then there was no saluting, only a very enthusiastic flinging of mature woman into his arms.

Hell, yes, there were problems. There'd always be problems. But he would worry about them later.

There had been changes on Omega during the months it had taken to complete the mission on Earth.

357

Some changes were either for the good or simply the result of time passing. Children had been born. People had made their selections and been married. He had congratulated Mandy and Derek Roebling on their marriage, and there hadn't been one hint of hypocrisy in his wishes for happiness for them.

"You know," he said lazily, "I've decided that a space jock should never marry anyone other than another space jock."

"Gee, thanks," Jackie said.

"Well, it takes one to know one," he said. "You're just as much service as I am. I guess that's why we get along so well. A good junior officer recognizes authority in a higher-ranking officer."

"Much more talk like that, and you'll have a mutiny on your hands from this junior officer," she teased, but she rolled off her chaise longue and squeezed in beside him, her wet swimsuit cool, her flesh soft and heated against him.

"Maybe a disciplinary session in the bedroom is in order," Rodrick said.

"What horrors can happen there?" Jackie whispered, doing naughty things with her hands.

"You are being careless with a loaded weapon, lady."

"Threats. Nothing but threats."

Later she decided to show him her surprise. It was one of those changes in Omegan life that was, he decided—after making the acquaintance of a tail-wagging, tongue-lolling pup with splayed feet and awkward, young enthusiasm—for the better.

"No reprimand, Senior Officer?" she asked as he watched the puppy, who looked very much like Jumper, chase his tail and then attack the captain's ankle with playful ferocity.

"No. I guess it's time. Lots of demand, I'd think."

"Lots," she confirmed. "I was besieged with complaints, with requests, and with demands. I told the medical labs to start growing the embryos of four or five breeds. Sorry if I jumped the gun."

"Cats too?"

"Oddly enough, no one seemed to be interested in cats. I guess we Omegans are all dog people."

"Well, give me a man, or a woman, who likes dogs every time," he said.

He helped her to prepare a light meal of fruits and cheese. They ate on the terrace, looking down on a bevy of sails on Stanton Bay. "I wish it never had to change," she said. "I wish it could stay just like this, without hordes of people."

"Be nice," he agreed. "Maybe a few thousand more; a total population of no more than, oh, say a few million. But this is an artificial society, you know. It's more communal than even Marx's ideal communism. Talented scientists working in the rocket-fuel factory, with no medium of exchange. To each according to needs, from each according to his or her abilities. Do you know that we have had not one instance of someone not being willing to pull his or her load? I think that's what I'm going to miss most as the population grows—that feeling of being in the same boat, of pulling together, knowing that if we went down, we'd all go down together without a trace."

They could hear the building machines working. Hamilton City was growing again, to house the newcomers who had been aboard the *Spirit of America*. A sophisticated shop would be going up shortly to hold the tools being unloaded from the ship. Machinery broke down, no matter how well it was designed and constructed, and the shop would give Omega the capacity to fabricate its own spare parts.

"We need people, all kinds of people, workers. We gave the politicians of Earth a bitter pill to take, and they didn't like it, no matter how calmly they swallowed it. Right now we're too dependent on them. We produce our own food, of course, and we make damned fine liquor." He sipped from a drink that Jackie had mixed for him after lunch. "We make our own rocket fuel, and we have the facilities to refine some metals. But we can't make one single cloud-chamber memory cell for a computer, or the million and one things we're accustomed to without even giving them any thought: watches and eyeglasses, paper and pens, china, eating utensils, refrigerators, hydrogen engines, or treads for the crawlers, not to mention a crawler or a scout ship or a starship . . ."

Jackie mused silently, letting him think. "We do a lot with plastics, and just about every month or so the plastics people come up with some terrific plastic substitutes for items that are a part of our life, but we don't have metals. Maybe we're being arrogant, thinking we have the right to dictate terms to governments on Earth, just because we've got Shaw's modifications of the Eeperan weapons."

"Stoner still thinks we should move the entire colony to a planet with metals," she said, "perhaps the Spreen planet."

"I'd hate to leave here," he replied, indicating with his hand the huge, odd world of Omega.

"Mandy thinks we should give it back to the Whorsk and the Eepera," Jackie said.

"Or wipe out all of them," Rodrick said grimly.

"I can understand how she feels," Jackie replied sympathetically.

"In a way," Rodrick said, "Mandy is typical of the entire race, humankind. She's a healer. She can be as tender as a new mother with someone who's sick or hurt. She's cultured, civilized, and likable. But she holds a grudge like an ancient Scot in a blood feud. Her answer to the problems with the other races on the planet is violence, just as violence has been the first resort in all periods of time. I'm not sure we handled the Eepera correctly. Maybe if Dexter had been here, we wouldn't have had to fight them."

"Ha!" Jackie said. "Whose plan was it to hold a smoking gun to the temple of the leaders on Earth? The diplomats and the statesmen, after all, were the ones who allowed wars to happen—called for them, in fact, when their own diplomacy failed. We're imperfect creatures in an imperfect universe. I don't think you made a mistake; I think you showed great restraint. We could have destroyed their cities. We could have used neutron bombs on them, leaving their buildings and pyramids standing while killing them all without lasting pollution of the planet."

Rodrick was silent. He got up from the table and fixed himself another drink. He could not remember when he'd had so many drinks in one day. When he sat down, Jackie had decided that it was time to drop discussion of serious things. "Tell me about Earth," she encouraged.

Rodrick raised an eyebrow. They had not slept until the sun was coming in the windows in order to talk, she bringing him up to date on things Omegan, he telling her in detail all the events on Earth.

"I mean the *important* things," she said, smiling. "Not the doings of visiting spacemen and the politicians. What are the women wearing? Who has been promoted in the service? Who has gotten married or divorced?"

Rodrick laughed. "The women are wearing clothes, and I didn't have time to listen to gossip."

"Men," Jackie said in disgust.

"Well, I do have one tasty tidbit. . . ."

"So tell me."

"Oscar Kost and Leslie Young."

She waited; then, after a while, "Well?"

"I married them on the way back home."

"You're kidding!" she said, with a laugh. "How wonderful."

"Wonderful? It'll be like trying to broil a steak over a pilot light."

"Oh, I don't know. I hear that older men make great lovers."

"Stick around a few years, and we'll find out if that's right."

It was good. No pressures for the moment, because he'd put them aside. He was keeping them submerged with good Omegan gin. He was thinking that maybe later, a lot later, he'd make love again to this slim, beautiful redhead whom he'd almost let get away. When his communicator buzzed an emergency signal, overriding the off switch that he'd pushed when he walked into the house the night before, he jumped, startled.

"This had better be good," he said. "Rodrick," he snapped into the communicator.

"Dunc? *Apache One*. We're at the pyramid of Suses. I think it would be a good idea for you to hop over here."

"Jacob, I'm not in the mood to hop anywhere." He closed the send switch, leered, and said, "Except onto my wife's bones."

"Well, I think you'll want to come over," Jacob said.

"Jacob," Rodrick sent, "do you want to tell me why?"

"You know how the Indian used to be called the vanishing American?" Jacob asked. "We've got a new wrinkle: the vanishing Eepera."

"Okay, Jacob. On the way." He rose and teetered a little bit. "Too good to last," he muttered. "Let's go."

"I'll drive," Jackie offered as he teetered again getting to the crawler. "And I'll fly."

"You talked me into it, you silver-tongued rascal," Duncan said, playing with her knee as she started the crawler.

Apache One was sitting in a square near the Great Misty River. The city was as beautiful as ever; the river broad and blue. Jackie put the scout down next to *Apache One*. Jacob and Theresita were seated on a marble bench. They came to meet Jackie and Rodrick.

"Quiet, isn't it?" Jacob asked.

"Seems to be," Rodrick said, looking around at empty streets.

"That's because there's not an Eeperan, at least not that we can find, in the whole city," Jacob said. "Theresita wanted to see Lyndon, so we popped over. The school is empty. All the homes and other buildings are empty."

"How about Whorsk?" Jackie asked.

"There's cooking smoke coming from some of their huts," Theresita said. "And the workers are in the fields, but we've seen none of the servant types in the city."

Rodrick looked at his wife. "I left you in command while I was gone. Would you care to venture any explanations for their sudden disappearance?"

Jackie frowned. "You know we pulled all our troops out before you left for Earth. We ran a check by scout now and then while you were gone."

"I'm listening," Rodrick said.

"We found a cultivated patch of the Eeperan drug on the other side of the Dinah River about two weeks after you left. We ran another drug test and found the drug in the bloodstream of a young marine. He confessed that he'd brought living plants back from Suses. He said he was just experimenting. He was studying chemistry and wanted to document the cellular changes brought on by the drug."

"Why didn't you tell me this last night?" Rodrick demanded, irritated.

"I don't know. Too many pleasant things to talk about, I guess. And I wanted you to myself for a while." She was looking him in the eyes. "We had a conference and decided that it was time to do something about the drug problem once and for all."

"We?" Rodrick asked.

"Stoner, Mandy, the Howards, Derek and Jean, Dr. Allano—everyone who interested themselves in the running of things . . . even a few who had, until the drug was found growing in Eden, been more than content to concentrate on their own work. It was decided to clean the drug out of the city."

"And how did you go about that?"

"It was simple, really. They offered no resistance at all. The Eepera themselves turned in huge quantities. The Whorsk burned the cultivated fields upriver. A house-to-house search turned up only small quantities of the drug. The new high priest decided that it was time his people stopped using the drug, and they don't have withdrawal symptoms, you know."

"When was this?"

"Four months ago," Jackie said.

"You didn't just walk away and leave them four months ago."

"No. We've sent regular patrols. We've had flyovers. The last flyover was four days ago. The city looked normal then. There were people here."

"Let's go to the fields and see what the Whorsk know," Rodrick said.

It was a pleasant walk along the riverfront. The walkways were marble, the riverfront architecture spectacular. But there was an uncomfortable feeling of loneliness in the air. The entire city had the atmosphere of an old farmhouse, long abandoned. When they reached the fields, Whorsk were harvesting grain, filling the air with dust and grain husks. Theresita, who could speak a bit of the language, asked the questions.

"He says, if I got it right," Theresita said, "that they were told five suns ago that it would no longer be necessary to deliver food into the city. He says he doesn't know where the Eepera went, but most probably downriver."

"We'd better take a look," Rodrick decided.

The two scouts lifted together. Rodrick, fully sobered, was at the controls. *Apache One* fell into the wing slot as he pointed the scout downriver.

The fog bank began twenty miles below Suses and towered into the sky. Rodrick lifted over it, added speed, and checked the river all the way to its mouth.

The cities below Suses had reactivated their force fields and were, once again, hidden below the mists.

"Jacob," Rodrick said, "I'm going in."

"I'll be right on your tail," Jacob said.

"Okay, here we go," Rodrick said, driving down. For minutes—he was traveling at low speed—it seemed as if he were flying through milk, and then the scout broke through into sunlight. The river was below, and he could see a city much like that of Suses in the near distance.

"If they open fire, we'll just go up and out," Rodrick radioed.

"I'll roger that," Jacob said.

Rodrick kept his eye on the pyramid sitting on the bluffs overlooking the river, just as the pyramid of Suses was situated, ready to give the scout all she had if he saw the telltale blink of a sun gun or if the new systems Max had installed on all scouts gave him a second's warning of the advance of the disrupter beam. He slowed and hovered when he was about two miles from the pyramid and activated his radio on the frequency used by the Eepera.

"This is Captain Duncan Rodrick. I would like to speak with Sistank, chairman of the Council of Twenty Cities."

An Eeperan voice came. "It will take some time to summon Sistank."

"I'll wait," Rodrick said.

There was always too much to do and too little time. The Americans knew precious little about the Eeperan cities below Suses. Rodrick had not wanted more war and could not afford to lose more personnel. The cities had cooperated by turning off their field generators and offering no hostilities, so he'd left them alone, with only occasional communication.

The radio came to life. "Captain Rodrick, I see your ships to the north of our city. I am Sistank."

"We want no hostilities," Rodrick said. "We just

want to know what has happened to the people of Suses."

"Then you may return to your city satisfied," Sistank said, "for the people of Suses are here, and in other of our cities. They are content and well."

"Thank you," Rodrick said. "May I ask why they have deserted the city?"

There was a long pause, and a different voice. Theresita, listening aboard *Apache One*, stiffened, recognizing the voice of Yanee.

"Captain," Yanee said, "contrary to what you might think, we did not leave our city because of the arrogance and the demands of your people. We are here for what little safety the protective force field gives us."

"We have noted that you have reactivated the fields in defiance of our agreement with you," Rodrick said. "From what do you seek protection?"

"My fellow members of the Council of Twenty Cities did not want to tell you," Yanee said, "but it will make no difference if you know. If you decide to flee while there is still time, that, too, will make no difference. They are coming, you see."

"The Bese are coming?" Rodrick asked.

"Where did you hear that name?" Yanee asked, his voice taking on a new tone.

"Is it the Bese who are coming?"

"They are coming," Yanee declared.

"How do you know they're coming, and when are they coming?"

"We cannot say when, we know only, by all the omens, that they will come, and soon."

"By the omens?" Rodrick asked. "You have not been contacted?"

"The coming has been foretold," Yanee explained. "That is all I can tell you. You did not tell me where you heard the name Bese."

"From the natives of a friendly planet some distance from here," Rodrick said.

"Captain Rodrick, were the natives of that planet small, furry, and skilled in working with light?"

"Yes," Rodrick said.

"Captain, would you please land? The large square directly below the pyramid would be a good place. I am quite near it. It will be to our mutual advantage to discuss this information you have given me. It just might be the key to saving all of us."

Rodrick thought for a moment.

"Let's come back with an armed force," Jackie suggested.

"No, if they were going to have a go at us, they'd have already fired," Rodrick said. "Jacob, stay aloft. If there's trouble, use your weapons as you get out fast."

Yanee, in a gleaming white tunic, came toward the scout as it landed. Rodrick and Jackie opened the ship and joined the prince, standing in the shadow of the scout.

"All right, Yanee, let's have it," Rodrick said, his eyes darting around the square, his hand on the hilt of his laser. He had no fondness for Yanee, since Yanee had helped seize Grace to deliver her into the hands of the high priest to drain information from her brain.

"You know the location of the planet of the Spreen?" Yanee asked.

"We do."

"Did you see the fire diamonds?"

"Yes," Rodrick said. "How did you know about the Spreen?"

"We, the Eeperan race, have traded with the Spreen since their planet was accidentally discovered during our earliest years in space. The secret of the location of the Spreen planet has been the property of the Bese, the Masters, the supreme rulers, forever. He who holds the secret and controls the traffic in fire diamonds has the greatest of powers, for our people valued those jewels above all else. You have in your hands the key to avoiding war with the Bese. You merely have to return to Spreen, take all Spreen into your power, and move them here. When the Masters come, you can tell them that you now control all production of fire diamonds, and they will not destroy you or this planet."

Rodrick knew several things that Yanee apparently did not. He saw no reason to share his knowledge. "I appreciate your suggestion. It will be taken under advisement."

"Act swiftly. Time is short."

"Tell me why you think the Bese are coming?"

"It is foretold. It is a complicated formula, laid down long ago by our wise men. It has to do with the cycle of our sun, with the repeated flood patterns of our river."

"And that's all?" Rodrick asked.

Yanee was quite impressive when he was standing on his dignity. "I know you have little regard for our gods and our priests, but in matters of importance they are never wrong."

"Well, Yanee, I thank you. I take it you and the council would like to keep the field in place?"

"Yes."

"I see no reason why not. But I warn you—and you will tell the others—that we will not suffer the loss of a single human life passively. We are on this planet to stay, and it would be preferable to us to live in peace with you. You seemed not too upset when you were ordered to destroy the drug crop. If you can cooperate in that matter, why not in others?"

"Why should we dispute the loss of one drug crop, when we have only to search the desert and the river-banks for it? Cooperation? I *have* offered it to you. I have given you the secret of surviving the Bese. But you seem little concerned."

"Yanee, I will say only that we have the situation under control," Rodrick said.

Yanee laughed. "So be it," he replied. "If we are lucky, we will not die with you." He turned and started to walk away.

Rodrick's communicator buzzed, and Theresita's voice said, "Ask him about Lyndon."

Yanee had heard. He stopped and turned. "Ah, the beautiful mother of my son. Tell her that the boy is here in this city, with his faithful Whorsk attendants. Tell her that he is very well and shows all signs of being a great Eeperan prince."

The two scouts lifted through the mist into the sun once again. "Race you home, Jacob," Rodrick challenged, burning rockets and going ballistic even as he spoke. The *Apache* was right behind.

"Jacob," Rodrick said, "I'm going home. I'm turning off my radio. I don't care if the Bese come during the night. I don't want to know about it until morning."

FORTY-ONE

The first captain's breakfast after the *Spirit*'s return from Earth was more social than business, although the first few minutes were taken up by Rodrick's account of his meeting with Yanee and Yanee's warning that the priests predicted an imminent coming of the Bese. When the food was served, the talk became casual. Mandy Miller-Roebling, with a smile, demanded to be put on the list for one of the puppies from Jumper and Cleo's next litter, Cleo being a feisty little Lhasa apso, the first dog bred from a frozen embryo on Omega. Clay said she'd be first on the list.

Juke, who had taken up food service simply because it gave him a chance to be near people, was serving strawberries topped with real whipped cream and sweet wine sauce. "If you're afraid the wine will give you a hangover," he told Grace, "I have aspirin-flavored sherry."

"Juke," Grace said, "back on Earth, Alcoholics Anonymous is working on self-closing beer cans."

Juke froze in midserve. "Grace," he wailed.

Grace snickered into her strawberries and blew whipped cream onto Max's uniform.

"Cruel, Grace," Juke said mournfully.

"I brought you seven new joke books," Grace said. "The latest by all the new comedians."

"You are forgiven," Juke said. "Would you have more whipped cream, Max?"

"Well," Rodrick said, "I guess we'd better talk a little business so we can call this meal tax deductible."

"Everybody wants to be a comedian," Juke complained.

"Paul, Evangeline," Rodrick said, grinning as he looked at them, chairs pulled as closely together as possible, unaware of anyone outside their own little intimate world. "Mr. and Mrs. Warden," he said.

Evangeline tore her eyes away from Paul's. "*Hmmm?*"

Rodrick rolled his eyes. Evangeline disengaged her hands from Paul's, punched him in the side, and nodded toward Rodrick. "*Hmmmm?*" Warden said, then grinned sheepishly and sat up straight, giving his attention to the captain.

"As you know, Harry stayed on Earth," Rodrick said. "He's looking after our first major purchase."

"A shipment of fur coats for all the ladies?" Mandy asked.

"Now why didn't I think of that?" Rodrick replied.

Juke rolled his eyes and retreated.

"We put the financial screws on tight on both the Russians and the Americans," Rodrick said. "The Americans wanted the fire jewels. We charged the Russians for Amando's plants and seeds. We had enough to pay for what we brought home and one more little item."

"All right," Stoner said, "we give up."

"She's about four times the size of a scout," Rodrick

said, "with a full life-support system that will keep a crew of six in space almost indefinitely."

"Hey!" Clay said, eyes lighting.

"Harry is going to bring her out here as soon as she's ready. We'll equip her with sun guns and the disrupter beam, and she'll already be carrying a good array of standard armament and missiles. With Max's and Grace's modifications, her Shaw Drive will be able to circumnavigate the galaxy on a fraction of the rhenium one of the big ships would use."

"Does she have a name yet?" Clay asked.

"Not yet. Any suggestions?" Rodrick asked.

"That's a matter for considerable thought," Betsy McRae said.

"Is she to be used as an explorer?" Clay asked, a gleam in his eye.

"Oscar?" Rodrick asked, for it had been Kost who had suggested the first missions for the new ship.

Oscar had to tear his attention away from Leslie, who sat at his side. "We keep hearing about these big, bad Bese guys. Now, while they did serve a purpose, being held over the heads of the Earth politicians as the outside threat of all time, I, for one, am getting a little tired of hearing how bad they are." He winked at Leslie. "And there's more than that. There's a possibility that they are very, very bad, and if they are, the idea is to find them and learn something about them before they find us. This new ship is small, fast, and we can equip her with the invisibility fields. We can cover a lot of ground and kill several birds with one stone. While we're looking for the Bese, we'll be scouting for new habitable planets."

"Right now, on Earth," Dexter Hamilton said, "they're pounding out treaties defining rights for the discoveries of life-zone planets. They'll end up, I'm sure, making it quite worthwhile for the ship, the personnel, or the country that makes a discovery. Land grants, cash—I don't know what, but it'll be good."

"There'll be another purpose for the first trip,"

Oscar said. "The Brazilian *Estrêla do Brasil* has not returned. The Brazilians told us where she was heading, which stars she was going to investigate first. We'll have a quick look for her while we're out there."

"Oscar, you say 'we,' " Jean Roebling said. "Does that mean you're going?"

"Not on your life," Oscar said quickly. "That's purely an editorial 'we.' I have everything I want right here on Omega." He gave Leslie's hand a squeeze under the table.

Clay took Cindy's hand and stood up, pulling her with him. "Here are your first two volunteers."

"You're a bit premature, Clay, but I'll remember that you were the first," Rodrick promised. "Now, we're sending both the *Spirit* and the *Free Enterprise* on another Earth run, loaded with fruits and more Spreen jewels. They'll bring back two thousand colonists to Omega. We'll take in a thousand here and start another settlement to the south, in the subtropical zones, where they'll be within easy reach of the fruit sources."

Mandy felt a moment of sadness. Rocky had wanted to move the settlement to the south. And now it was going there.

"Our agreement with the major Earth governments will prevent our being swarmed under with newcomers," Dexter said. "Each shipload comes with self-sustaining equipment. Each immigrant will have to become a citizen of Omega. We're going to have to burn the midnight oil to get ready. We've got a pretty darned good Constitution, and now we have to start setting up the governmental apparatus to implement it."

Stoner scowled. "If there is a government, I'm against it."

"That means elections," Hamilton said. "Ruling bodies."

"We all vote for Dexter Hamilton for President and everything else," Stoner said. "Dunc, I'll go with the new ship. It's going to get too damned crowded here."

"I know what you mean," Rodrick said. "Our two governmental experts, President Hamilton and Professor Kost, will be in charge of establishing the Republic of Omega. We need officers for the next Earth trips. Ito and Emi can handle the *Spirit,* with the help of a chief engineer." He looked meaningfully at Max. Max looked pained. He'd already discussed that possibility with Grace, and she'd told him that she couldn't possibly go. She had brought back several tons of material from Transworld Robotics and had already started the manufacture of labor robots. There was much work for them to do on Omega: The factories had to be run, the fields tended.

"Max, one more trip. Take along a young engineer and train him for these milk runs to Earth," Rodrick said.

Max groaned.

"Gage Fergus is chief on the *Free Enterprise.* We need a navigator and skipper."

"Us?" Cindy gulped, as Rodrick looked directly at her and Clay.

"Listen, you young guys have got to start pulling your load sometime," Rodrick said, grinning.

"Great!" Clay said. "Wow. What will they say when they find out a ship like the *Free Enterprise* is being run by a couple of people not quite twenty?"

"They might run around like Chicken Little," Betsy teased, "crying that the sky is falling."

"Captain, we still want to be on the list for the new ship," Clay said.

"I'd like your input on one more item," Rodrick said. "The Eepera."

"I say we leave them alone," Jacob West said. He and Theresita had been sitting at the far end of the table, still acting like honeymooners. "Let 'em hide under the fog bank. They don't have the metal or the smarts to build anything in secret that would threaten us."

"Well, I don't like it," Mandy protested. "We should know what they're doing."

"I agree with both of you," Grace said. "Watch them *and* leave them alone."

"Grace, don't I remember that you once advocated trying to save the Eepera from themselves?" Mandy asked sweetly.

"Now, ladies . . ." Hamilton said.

"Are they basing their predictions of the Masters' arrival on nothing more than the omens of their priests?" Jean asked.

"I believe so," Rodrick said. "Although—and I'll guess Mandy would agree—that Yanee is a good liar."

"Nothing can get within a million miles of this planet," Paul Warden assured them.

"Unless they, too, have modified the field," Max growled.

"You, sir," Grace said, "are a paragon of sweetness and light."

"It's this fatal attraction I have for beautiful women," Max said.

"Whoops," Jackie said, standing up to reveal that she'd been holding the pup in her lap all during the meal. And there was a great, dark circle on her skirt. "Meeting adjourned," she said, "at least for me."

"And so," Dexter Hamilton whispered to his Jennie, "do great decisions go aglimmering in the face of daily necessity."